Praise for the Green Mountain Romance series

"*All You Need is Love* is the quintessential romance and, boy, does it deliver!" —*RT Book Reviews* (4 stars)

"If you're looking for a heartwarming, feel-good story to lose yourself in for a few hours, then this is one book you should look into! —*Night Owl Reviews* (Top Pick)

Praise for the *New York Times* bestselling McCarthys of Gansett Island series

"With the McCarthys of Gansett Island, Marie Force makes you believe in the power of true love and happily ever after. Over and over again."
—Carly Phillips, *New York Times* bestselling author

"This is one sexy story . . . Hang out with Evan and Grace and you'll want to stay on Gansett Island, too!"
—*USA Today*

"This is another beautifully written love story. It draws you in and stays with you after you are done reading."
—*Guilty Pleasures Book Reviews*

"[Force] is quickly becoming one of my favorite romance series writers." —*Lisa's Reads*

"As always, Force's writing is wonderfully entertaining . . . Force hits a home run with *Season for Love* and her entire Gansett Island series." —*Ravishing Romances*

"Ms. Force has the ability to make you fall in love with her Island and all of the quirky and sweet characters that reside there . . . [A] fantastic series!" —*Joyfully Reviewed*

I Want to Hold Your Hand

Marie Force

BERKLEY SENSATION, NEW YORK

THE BERKLEY PUBLISHING GROUP
Published by the Penguin Group
Penguin Group (USA) LLC
375 Hudson Street, New York, New York 10014

USA • Canada • UK • Ireland • Australia • New Zealand • India • South Africa • China

penguin.com

A Penguin Random House Company

I WANT TO HOLD YOUR HAND

A Berkley Sensation Book / published by arrangement with HTJB, Inc.

Copyright © 2014 by HTJB, Inc.
A Hard Day's Night by Marie Force copyright © 2014 by HTJB, Inc.
Excerpt from *I Saw Her Standing There* by Marie Force copyright © 2014 by HTJB, Inc.

Berkley Sensation Books are published by The Berkley Publishing Group.
BERKLEY SENSATION® is a registered trademark of Penguin Group (USA) LLC.
The "B" design is a trademark of Penguin Group (USA) LLC.

For information, address: The Berkley Publishing Group,
a division of Penguin Group (USA) LLC,
375 Hudson Street, New York, New York 10014.

ISBN: 978-0-425-27931-1

PUBLISHING HISTORY
Berkley Sensation mass-market edition / June 2014
Read Pink edition / October 2014

PRINTED IN THE UNITED STATES OF AMERICA

10 9 8 7 6 5 4 3 2 1

Cover photos by Shutterstock.
Cover design by George Long.
Interior text design by Kelly Lipovich.

To all the men and women in uniform serving our country around the world—and all the people at home who love and miss them.

And for John Gomes, the "Nolan" of my hometown, who was much loved and is dearly missed.

CHAPTER 1

—◆—

A new boy moved to town over the summer. His name is Caleb Guthrie. Hunter and Will like him, but I haven't decided yet.

—From the diary of Hannah Abbott, age twelve

Hannah Abbott Guthrie looked forward to the second Thursday of every month, when she met her high school friends in St. Johnsbury for lunch and an afternoon at their favorite spa. The tradition began after Hannah lost her husband, Caleb, in Iraq almost seven years ago. She'd continued to meet the girls every week long after the first awful wave of grief passed into the new reality of life without Caleb.

Like her family, her friends had been there for her one thousand percent, and Hannah loved her "escape from it all" days passionately. This time, she was even considering the possibility of taking her friend Becky up on the standing invite to spend the night in St. Johnsbury so she wouldn't have to drive home after the relaxing afternoon.

Her brother Hunter had volunteered to come by when he got back to town to check on Caleb's old dog, Homer, so he wouldn't have to spend the whole day and night alone. Even with Homer covered, she was playing the invitation by ear. Since Caleb died, she had a lot of trouble sleeping, and if she was going to be up at all hours, she preferred to rattle around in the privacy of her own home.

Hannah picked up the overnight bag she'd packed just in case she decided to stay, gave Homer a snuggle and let him know Uncle Hunter would be by to see him later. She locked the door to the huge Victorian she'd inherited from Caleb. The house was far too big for one person, but Caleb had loved the house that had come from his grandmother, and Hannah would never sell it.

She unlocked her aging SUV and put her bag into the back before sliding into the driver's seat. The day was chilly but sunny, an early spring day in northern Vermont, where winter hung around far longer than it did just a few hours south. In deference to the lingering winter, Hannah had chosen to wear a heavy coat rather than the new spring jacket she was ready to break out any day now.

With the key in the ignition, she turned it and got a clicking sound that didn't bode well for going anywhere. "Come on," she whispered. "Not today. Do this tomorrow when I've got nowhere to be." She turned the key again and got the same *click, click, click* noise that she recognized as a dead battery. "You've got to be kidding me!"

She leaned her head on the steering wheel as she tried to remember where everyone was today. Her dad and Hunter had gone to a business conference in Montpelier. Will was in New York helping his girlfriend, Cameron, pack up her apartment for her move to Vermont. Colton was up on the mountain at the family sugaring facility, Wade knew as much about cars as she did, Lucas and Landon were working a twenty-four-hour shift at the volunteer fire department and Max was at school in Burlington.

Her sisters, Ella and Charley, were as useful in this situation as Hannah and Wade. Her mom had taken Hannah's grandfather for his annual physical this morning. That left one person she could call and, as luck would have it, he was the last person she wanted to call.

"If I call Nolan he's going to get all hopeful, and I can't do that to him," she said, reasoning with herself and the cold air. It had been enough that recently she'd danced with him at the

Grange and then let him drive her home. That was more than she'd done with any man in all the years since Caleb died.

But Nolan wasn't just any man. He'd been less than circumspect about his feelings for her, never missing a chance to inquire about her to one of her family members—all of whom *loved* relaying Nolan's thoughtful sentiments to her at every possible opportunity.

"You're being foolish. You can either call Nolan and continue with your plans or miss the day with the girls. Those are your choices." The one thing she didn't feel foolish about, after living alone for close to seven years, was talking to herself. If anyone knew how often she had full conversations with herself, they'd probably have her committed.

She reached for the cell phone she kept in the car for emergencies and made the call, holding her breath while she waited for him to answer the phone at the station he ran in town.

"Nolan's."

At the sound of his deep voice a flutter of nerves filled her belly.

"Hello?"

"Oh sorry. Hey, Nolan, it's Hannah."

"Hannah." With the single word came hope, surprise and hesitation. That he managed to convey so much by only saying her name was one of the many reasons she'd kept her distance from him. His feelings for her were a badly kept secret, and being around him made her nervous. She'd known him all her life, so the nerves were stupid, really, but she had them every time she laid eyes on the man. "What's going on?"

"Well, my car won't start, and I've got somewhere to be for once."

"What's it doing?"

"Clicking."

"Sounds like the battery. I'll be right there."

"Oh um, do you have time?"

"Of course I do," he said as if that was the stupidest question he'd ever heard. "That's my job. I'll be there in a few."

"Thanks, Nolan." She put the phone in her purse and waited, feeling anxious and unsettled. He had that effect on her, and he wasn't even there yet. In the last six weeks, she'd tried not to think about the night she'd danced with him and then let him drive her home. She'd tried not to think about how she'd let him kiss her good night, or how much she'd really, *really* liked kissing him.

Her fingers found their way to her lips as she relived the moment on her front porch. He'd insisted on walking her to the door. "I had a good time tonight," he'd said. "Thanks for dancing with me."

"It was a terrible chore." She hoped her wittiness hid the nerves that were rampaging through her.

"I'm sure it was," he said with a good-natured laugh. "I'm known for my two left feet."

"You're a smooth dancer."

"Am I?" he asked, sounding surprised.

"Very."

"Huh. I always thought I kind of sucked at it."

"You don't."

The words had hung in the air between them, which had gone heavy with expectation.

"Hannah . . ." His fingers on her face were soft despite the hard work he did with his hands every day.

She'd been rendered breathless and speechless by the yearning she'd seen on his handsome face, which had been illuminated by the porch light. And then his lips were on hers, gentle and undemanding but no less earth-shattering than a much more passionate kiss would've been. Hannah had ruined it by pulling back from him when she didn't even want to. Why she'd done that was a question she still couldn't answer six weeks later.

He'd called her the next day, but coward that she was, she'd let the call go to voicemail and hadn't seen or spoken to him again—until today. Although, she'd listened to his sweet message over and over again until she knew the words by heart.

Oh hey, Hannah, it's me, Nolan. Um, I, ah, wanted to say I had a nice time last night. There's a new Mexican place in Stowe that I've been wanting to check out. I remember you love Mexican food, so if you'd like to go sometime, you have my number. Call me, okay?

She hadn't returned the call or told anyone about the kiss. Not her mother, her sisters or especially her nosy brothers and father, who would've made way too much out of what had been a rather simple kiss. Except it hadn't been simple at all. It was the first kiss she'd received since being widowed, and she couldn't escape the feeling that she'd somehow betrayed Caleb's memory.

Of course she knew that was ridiculous. Caleb would be furious at her for moldering away in the home they had loved, still alone after all these years. Her husband was a get-things-done kind of guy who hadn't stood around waiting for life to find him. He'd gone after his dreams with gusto and passion, including his desire to serve his country.

If he came back to life for one day and found her stuck in the same place she'd been for almost seven years, he'd kick her ass from one end of Vermont to the other. Hannah knew she had to own the guilt she felt over kissing Nolan and not pass it off as a betrayal of Caleb's memory. She knew without any shadow of a doubt that her husband had loved her as much as it was possible for a man to love a woman, and he'd want nothing but the very best for her.

No, the guilt belonged to her alone, and the least she could do was own it. Kissing Nolan had absolutely nothing to do with Caleb. Heck, he would wholeheartedly approve of her seeing Nolan, a man he had respected and considered a close friend. At least she hoped he would. She had no way to know for sure.

So what was the hang-up? Hannah wished she knew, but she kept coming back to the same excuse time and time again. She wasn't ready to move on with another man, and she didn't see any point to leading Nolan on when she wasn't ready for the things he wanted from her.

A knock on the window startled Hannah so badly she jumped. With trembling hands, she opened the door.

"Sorry to scare you. Thought you heard the truck."

Hannah couldn't believe she'd been so lost in thought about all the reasons why she couldn't have a relationship with this perfectly nice—and totally sexy—man that she hadn't heard a thing. How had she failed to miss the arrival of the huge tow truck that was now parked at her curb? She got out of the car. "I was . . . um . . ."

"A million miles away?" he asked with an adorable grin that showcased the deep dimple on the left side of his face.

His dark hair was infused with streaks of silver that made him look a bit older than his thirty-five years. But it was his intense brown eyes and the way they seemed to take a full inventory of her features every time she was in close proximity to him that undid her like they always did.

She felt stripped naked of all her defenses when he looked at her the way he was right now. Hannah cleared her throat. "I guess I was."

"A lot on your mind?"

Desperate for something to do with her hands, she jammed them into her coat pockets. "No more than usual."

He stared at her for a long moment, and just as she was about to remind him that he was here to work on her car and not set her on fire with the raw and needy desire she saw in his eyes, he said, "I tried to call you."

"I know."

"I'm sorry if I was out of line that night. I've gone over it and over it, and I can't believe I took such advantage of the first opportunity you've given me—"

"Nolan! Stop. Don't say that. You didn't take advantage of me. I can't stand that you think you did." Even though the last thing she wanted was to have this awkward conversation, she couldn't let him think he'd done something wrong when he hadn't. "You didn't."

He shook his head, dismissing her words. "I did take advantage. I've waited so long for you, Hannah. You have no idea how long. And the first chance I get, I couldn't leave well enough alone."

Shocked and further unsettled by how disgusted with himself he sounded, she had no idea what to say. How long had he waited? More than seven years? If so, that was news to her. Drawn to him despite her huge desire not to be, she laid a hand on his arm.

He looked down at her hand and then up at her eyes.

"You didn't do anything wrong. It was me. I shouldn't have pulled away from you the way I did because I didn't want to stop kissing you. I don't know why I pulled away when that was the last thing I wanted to do."

Nolan stood up a little straighter. "Hannah . . ."

"I'm very confused."

"Over what?"

"How can I want to kiss you one minute but still feel like I'm not ready for any of this in the next minute? I'm not sure what that means."

He took a deep breath, as if he was trying to maintain control. "Maybe we could figure that out together."

She ventured a look up at him, and her heart did a funny tap dance in her chest that left her breathless. This was not good. This was not at all what she had planned for today. "How do you mean?"

"Spend some time with me. We can do anything you want. No pressure, no kissing, no nothing unless you want it. I'd be completely happy if I got to hold your hand, Hannah."

Unnerved by his urgently spoken words and the kindness behind them, she licked her lips and tried not to notice the way he zeroed in on the movement of her tongue. "Why me?"

"Hell if I know," he said with a gruff laugh, "but I can't remember a time when it wasn't you."

"Wait, so you're saying—"

"Forget I said that. The past doesn't matter. All we have is right now, and I want to be with you, even if we do nothing more than have a meal together every now and then. Would that be possible?"

"I . . . Um, my car. I have somewhere to be."

His lips flattened with displeasure that she regretted causing, but she wasn't able to answer his question. Not without some time to think about how she felt. She didn't have a spontaneous bone in her body. Not anymore. Not since Caleb died and took her youth and vitality and hopes and dreams with him.

"Pop the hood."

The brusque, businesslike tone was in sharp contrast to the pleading edge his voice had taken on when he asked her to spend time with him.

Hannah got back in the car and did as he asked, her fingers slipping off the hood latch before she was able to get it open. She left the driver's side door propped open so she could hear him if he needed her to do anything else.

Nolan lifted the hood, which gave her a moment's reprieve from his intense gaze to collect her thoughts. He wanted to spend time with her. He had no intention of pressuring her for things she wasn't ready for. He was sweet and handsome and kind and hardworking and all the things she liked and admired in a man—not to mention sexy as all hell. That last thought shocked her to the core. When was the last time she'd thought about anything having to do with sex?

"The battery is definitely dead, which is weird. It's relatively new. We just replaced it a year or so ago. Did you leave your headlights on last night?"

"No."

"Hmm."

"Can you fix it or should I cancel my plans?"

He popped out from under the raised hood. "How far are you going?"

"Just to St. Johnsbury."

"I can fix it, but I need to push the car to the end of the driveway so I can use my truck to jump it. Can you shift it into neutral?"

"Sure. Do you want me to help you?"

"Nope. Sit tight and hold the wheel steady and then hit the brakes when I tell you to, okay?"

"Okay."

He dropped the hood but didn't latch it, took off his coat and tossed it on the lawn, which was finally devoid of snow. He wore a gray work shirt with a red name patch sewn above the chest pocket. His biceps bulged from the effort to move the car, but it started to creep toward the street, picking up speed as it went.

"Okay, stop."

Hannah pressed down on the brake to slow the momentum.

In a matter of minutes he had her car attached to his truck with jumper cables. She watched him as he worked, noting the way his hair fell over his forehead and how the shirt stretched across his broad chest. Had she ever noticed how muscular he was until she danced with him at the Grange?

Truthfully, she'd never given herself permission to look too closely for fear of seeing something she couldn't handle. But she looked now, and she had to admit she liked what she saw—and she was sick and tired of her own company. That was something she'd confessed to herself during the long, cold, lonely winter she'd just endured.

With her parents, grandfather, nine siblings and a litany of aunts, uncles and cousins living nearby there was always something going on around her. But at the end of the day, Hannah was alone in the big house where she'd once been happily married. She was thirty-five years old and had been a widow for one-fifth of her life, longer than she'd been married as of this upcoming seventh anniversary of Caleb's death.

It was probably time to start living again.

"Try it now," he said.

Hannah turned the key and heard the welcome sound of her engine turning over. "Thank you so much."

"No problem." He removed the jumper cables and let her hood drop before bending down to grab his coat off the ground.

Hannah watched his every move, noting the way his navy blue work pants stretched across his taut backside as he bent over. The visual made her skin tingle with awareness—the kind of awareness she hadn't experienced in a very long time, the kind of awareness that still had the power to frighten her. She opened the window.

He paused outside her door on his way to the truck. "Drive safely and call me if you have any more trouble."

"I will. Send me the bill."

"Don't be silly. There's no bill, Hannah."

"Thank you for helping me."

He paused as if there was something else he wanted to say besides, "No problem."

He'd started to walk away when Hannah called out to him. "Nolan."

Turning back, he raised a brow. "Yeah?"

She forced herself to say the words. "I'd like to spend some time together. Like you said. If that's okay."

Judging by the flabbergasted look on his face, that was the last thing he'd expected her to say. "You would? Really?"

Hannah nodded. "I'll call you."

"I'll be waiting."

CHAPTER 2

—◆◇◆—

Okay, I've decided . . . Caleb Guthrie is a bully.
He pulls my braids on the playground every day
and then runs away. All the boys laugh when he
does it. I just want to punch him.

—From the diary of Hannah Abbott, age twelve

Nolan went on with his day as if the most momentous thing in the known universe—or at least his known universe—hadn't just transpired in Hannah Guthrie's driveway. *Thank God for dead batteries*, he thought as he returned to the garage and got busy dealing with the cars customers had dropped off for repairs that morning.

He went through the rote motions of changing oil, replacing a timing belt and fielding calls from customers while trying not to think about Hannah and the hope she'd given him earlier. Since the night they'd danced and kissed, he'd berated himself at least a thousand times for moving too quickly, and then to hear that she'd *liked* kissing him and hadn't wanted to stop . . .

Holy hell, how was he supposed to function knowing that? And how was he supposed to cope with the overwhelming guilt that came with his feelings for Hannah? He carried that guilt with him all the time.

Caleb Guthrie had been one of the best friends Nolan had

ever had, and the pain of his loss was something Caleb's unruly tribe of friends still carried with them all these years later. Caleb had been the sun around which the planets orbited. He'd been their fearless leader, and they were lost without him in so many ways.

After living the life of an army brat with his officer father, Caleb arrived in Vermont at the start of seventh grade when his father finally buckled to pressure from his family and retired as a full colonel. The kids from tiny Butler, Vermont, hadn't known what to make of Caleb, who had friends all over the world. They were his "Sultans," as Caleb called them. He'd named his group of friends after the Dire Straits song "Sultans of Swing," his dad's favorite song, and he collected Sultans everywhere he lived.

Becoming one of Caleb's Sultans was a high honor, one none of them took lightly. It involved a foolish initiation ritual made up entirely by Caleb, who picked and chose his Sultans carefully. Upon entering the inner circle, Nolan had found a friend unlike any he'd ever had—funny and brazen and playful and serious and daring, brilliant yet twisted in his humor and approach to life.

He'd lightened Nolan up, taught him there was more to life than work and had exposed him to people and ideas and adventures that ranged from skiing the Rocky Mountains to spring break in Mexico to years of Mardi Gras in New Orleans where the Sultans worshiped their Creole patron.

Life with Caleb was all about fun. Life without him was a huge, gaping void that no one else could ever fill. Nolan couldn't begin to speculate on the hole that Caleb's death had left in Hannah's life. The two of them had been amazing together, truly, deeply in love, and devoted to their friends and family as much as they were to each other. The Sultan parties every Labor Day weekend at their house were legendary, and despite the agony of Caleb's loss, Hannah and the Sultans continued the tradition without him, knowing he'd expect nothing less.

But goddamn it was tough. Young, vital men with their whole lives in front of them weren't supposed to die at twenty-eight. They weren't supposed to die without giving the people they left behind some idea of how they were supposed to carry on without them.

Nolan liked to think that Caleb would approve of his affection for Hannah. He chose to believe that because the possibility Caleb *wouldn't* approve was simply unbearable. Nolan had always loved Hannah as a friend and hadn't entertained anything other than friendly feelings toward her until about two years after Caleb died.

That's when everything changed for him. It'd been over a Labor Day weekend with the Sultans, watching her carry on like everything was fine as she kept the unruly guys in food and beer, when Nolan had realized he felt something more than friendship for her. *Why did it have to be her of all people?* He'd asked himself that question almost every day for five years. He couldn't say exactly, other than she touched him deeply, far more deeply than any other woman ever had.

He fixed things. That's what he did. He wanted to fix things for her. He wanted to make her smile again the way she used to when Caleb was alive, the way she used to before life pulled the rug out from under her and left her reeling. He wanted to put the pieces back together again for her, to make right that which could never be made right.

The Abbott family had tuned in to the fact that Nolan's feelings for Hannah went beyond that of a lifelong friend, but the other Sultans didn't know. Well, except for Hannah's brothers, Hunter and Will, who were fully initiated into Caleb's tribe. But Nolan didn't think they'd told the others. Why would they? It wasn't like anything had ever come of Nolan's feelings for her.

Until a recent Saturday night at the Grange. Until today when she said she wanted to spend some time with him. How long would she have to wait to hear from her? Would she panic on the drive to St. Johnsbury and decide she'd been impetuous?

Leaning into the hood of a Chevy sedan, Nolan released a deep breath and tried to figure out how long he'd been staring at the V-8 while thinking of nothing but Hannah Guthrie and how she'd looked that morning—lovely and flushed and embarrassed and undone by their conversation.

Waiting to hear from her might actually kill him. It was certainly killing his concentration, he thought, as he got busy changing the spark plugs and filters on the older-model car.

Every time the garage phone rang, his heart stopped for a moment, which was flat-out ridiculous. She said she'd call him. She hadn't said she'd call *today*. But why hadn't he asked her to call to let him know she'd arrived safely after the trouble with her battery?

He wiped the grease off his hands with a red oil rag and threw it aside in frustration. Was it possible for a person to drive himself nuts? If it was, he was well on his way. Since his productivity was positively shot, he decided to break early for lunch.

He was on his way out the door to grab something to eat at the diner when the phone rang. Under normal circumstances, he would've let voicemail pick up the call, but there was nothing normal about circumstances under which Hannah Guthrie might be calling. So he ran back in and grabbed the phone.

"Nolan's."

"Hey, it's me. Hannah."

Come on. No way. Had he gone straight around the bend into the land of the delusional? Had he wished so hard for her call that he'd made it happen out of sheer will?

"Nolan? Are you there?"

It was really her. "Oh yeah, sorry. I'm here. Is everything okay with the car?"

"That's why I called. I figured you'd be worried about whether or not I got here, and I did, so I wanted to tell you."

Was it his imagination or was she rambling? And did she sound nervous? The calm, cool Hannah he knew and loved never sounded nervous. She was always in perfect control of her emotions, something he admired greatly about her in light of what she'd been through. "That's good to know. I was hoping it wouldn't give you any more trouble."

"It didn't."

Nolan wasn't sure what he was supposed to say next. His brain spun with possibilities, each of them rejected.

"I also wanted to tell you . . ."

His heart pounded as anticipation beat through him in time with his heart. "What, Hannah? What did you want to tell me?"

"Ever since I saw you this morning, I can't stop thinking about enchiladas."

Since that had been about the last thing he'd expected her to say, he laughed. "Is that right?"

"I'm drooling, in fact. So I was thinking, maybe we could check out that place in Stowe later? If you're not busy. I know it's last minute—"

"I'm not busy." He was but he'd get out of it. The racing team could meet without him. "What time will you be back?"

"Around six thirty."

"How does seven sound?"

"Sounds good. I'll see you then?"

"I'll be there. I can't have you drooling all over the place. What will people say?"

Her laughter made him smile. "See you soon."

Nolan put down the phone and let out a very loud, "*Yes!*"

"See?" Becky said as Hannah hung up the phone. "Was that so hard?"

"It was excruciating. I sounded like a complete idiot."

"You did not! He's probably dancing for joy around the garage after hearing from you."

"Be quiet. He is not. I never should've told you any of this."

"Yes, you should have, and you told me because you wanted me to force you to do something about it."

"That isn't why I told you!"

"Yes, Hannah," Becky said gently, "it is. You needed permission to act on what you feel for Nolan. I'm glad I was the one you confided in and that I was the one who gave you the push you needed to make that call. It's high time, isn't it?"

"I suppose. It's just that I still feel . . . I don't know. It's ridiculous, but it feels disloyal to Caleb."

"Aw, honey, Caleb loved you so much. He'd want you to be happy. You know that."

"Of course I do, but it's hard to think about moving on with someone else. I never wanted to move on without him."

"You don't have any choice. You're a young, beautiful, vibrant woman with so much life left to live and so much love left to give. I can't even begin to understand what you've been through, and you've handled it all so gracefully and with such dignity."

"Not always," Hannah said with a laugh, looking to lighten

things up a bit. She didn't allow herself many trips to the maudlin side of town where nothing good ever happened, but once in a while . . .

"I'm sure you've had a lot of rough moments, and you may continue to have them for the rest of your life. But that doesn't mean you can't also have other things, too, such as a wonderful, sexy guy who looks at you like you're the cat's meow."

"He does not."

"Um, yes, he does. Ask anyone."

Every time someone said that to her, Hannah felt twitchy and off balance. She'd known Nolan forever—even longer than she'd known Caleb. He had been one of her husband's closest friends and had served as a groomsman at their wedding. "Do you ever think that maybe Nolan is too close?"

"How do you mean?"

"He and Caleb were the best of friends. I've known him my whole life. He's always been there, you know? How does that suddenly turn romantic?"

"The same way it did for you and Caleb, remember?"

As if she'd ever forget the night Caleb kissed her at the quarry and changed everything between them forever. She had to admit Becky made a good point.

"I want you to do something for me," Becky said.

"What's that?"

"I want you to have dinner with Nolan and not blow it up into a big freaking deal in your mind before it actually is. It's dinner. Nothing more, nothing less."

"If I'm to believe what you and everyone else says, it's already way more than that to him."

"So what? That's his deal, not yours. Don't take it on. Go to dinner. Eat a meal. Enjoy his company and relax. Can you do that?"

"I guess so. I can probably relax easier with him than I would with someone I just met."

"I know you can do it. Go have a wonderful time. You've so earned the right to some fun and happiness, Hannah."

Hannah hugged her longtime friend. "Thanks for the pep talk and for letting me off the hook on the sleepover."

"Once you told me about Nolan asking you out, I was prepared to kick you out of here if I had to."

Hannah smiled at Becky's emphatic words. Sometimes she felt like the people in her life needed her to move on more than she needed it for herself. Up until the last couple of months, she'd been perfectly fine to rattle around in her big old house alone and to spend more time living in the past than she did in the present.

At some point over the recent winter though, she'd begun to feel anxious and lonely and perhaps ready to step foot out of her self-imposed cocoon to take a peek at what had been going on in the world while she was holed up with her grief.

After two hours of laughter and pedicures she was on the road home, her mind spinning with thoughts about the evening she'd agreed to spend with Nolan. Would it be awkward or easy? Would he try to kiss her again or would he keep his distance? Which did she prefer? She couldn't say for certain.

By the time she pulled into the driveway twenty minutes before Nolan was due to arrive, her nerves were stretched thin. An accident on the main road into town had added half an hour to the ride. Inside the house, she used the phone in the hallway to leave a message for Hunter on his office voicemail to let him know she'd decided to come home and he was off Homer duty.

"Hey, Home Boy," she said, using the nickname Caleb had given his dog as a puppy after the multicolored mutt had decided he belonged with Caleb. No one was really certain of his breed, but speculation ran the gamut from German shepherd to Lab to beagle. "Where are you, buddy?" Hannah checked the sitting room, where she and Homer spent most of their time, as well as the studio, where she worked and he kept a bed on the floor, but saw no sign of Homer.

At sixteen, he didn't do the stairs on his own anymore, so he had to be somewhere on the first floor. She went into the kitchen and stopped short when she found him sprawled on the floor, his eyes open and trained on her, his distress apparent.

Hannah dropped to the floor next to him. "Hey, buddy. What're you doing in here?" She stroked his face and back and noted the choppy cadence of his breathing and his seeming inability to raise his head off the floor. He tried to stretch his paw out to her the way he always did, but couldn't muster the strength. Tears filled her eyes. "No, Homie. Not yet. Please not yet." She lay down on the floor next to him, petting him as she wept.

Hannah knew she should get up and call Myles Johansen, the local vet. He'd been making house calls to check on Homer for quite some time now and had told her to call any time she needed him. Somehow she knew if she got up, if she made the call, that this time would be different.

"Oh, Homie, I'm sorry I left you today. I know you haven't been feeling good for a long time, but you've stuck around because you don't want to leave me alone. I promise I'll be okay. Before I call anyone though . . . While it's just you and me . . . When you see Dad, make sure you tell him I love him, and I miss him, okay? You'll take good care of him, won't you? He'll be so happy to see you."

One more minute, she told herself, sobbing as she clung to Homer. One more minute and then she'd get up to call Myles.

"Hannah?" Nolan's voice echoed through the first floor. "Are you home?"

How long had she been lying there with Homer? She wiped her eyes with her sleeve, trying to fix the unfixable. "Back here."

"You didn't answer the door, so I hope it's okay I came in—" Nolan halted in the doorway to the kitchen when he saw her on the floor with Homer. "Oh God, Hannah, what is it? What's wrong?"

She shifted slightly to the right so he could see Homer stretched out on the floor, his breathing shallow and labored.

"Oh no. What can I do?"

"Would you mind calling Myles for me?"

"Of course. Anyone else?"

"Hunter. He'll tell my parents. And the Guthries. They should be here."

"Yes, yes, I'll call them. You stay with Homer."

Hannah breathed a sigh of relief at knowing she didn't have to be the one to make the calls, to say the words . . . "It's okay, buddy," she whispered to Homer. "Everything is okay. You can go if you're ready. I understand that you're tired and you've had to live a long time without your best friend. That's been so hard on you, but you took good care of me. Dad would've been so proud of you for taking such good care of me."

She tried to quiet her sobs so as not to upset Homer. This wasn't about her. It was about him, and she wanted to give him everything he needed.

Nolan returned to the kitchen and squatted next to Hannah. "Myles is on his way, and I left a message for Hunter. I also called your mom when I couldn't reach Hunter. Hope that's okay."

Hannah nodded, grateful to him for taking charge.

"What can I do for you?" he asked, resting a hand on her shoulder. His voice, she noticed, was thick with emotion. He'd loved Caleb, too, and that mattered right now.

"This helps. Thank you." Hannah leaned into him, resting her head on his chest as she continued to stroke Homer's silky ears and coat. The dog's eyes were closed now, his breathing even more shallow, if that was possible.

Nolan sat next to her, keeping his arm around her as she leaned against him, grateful for his presence and his strength.

CHAPTER 3

———◆———

I did it. I finally punched Caleb Guthrie right in the face. He was shocked, and he stared at me with blood rushing from his nose. The school called my mom to come get me, and I had to stay in my room all night. It was soooooo worth it.

—From the diary of Hannah Abbott, age thirteen

Myles arrived a short time later and let himself in through the front door. Nolan must've told him where to find them, because he appeared in the kitchen and kneeled on the floor next to Homer. "How long has he been like this?"

"I don't know." Hannah wiped new tears that formed when she heard the tension in Myles's tone. "He was fine this morning—or as fine as he ever is these days. Walking around and eating and everything. I came home after a few hours out and found him here."

Myles, who was blond and blue-eyed and handsome, had once asked Hannah to dinner, but she'd declined. Despite her rejection, he'd been a source of great comfort to her as Homer slipped into old age. With a stethoscope in his ears, Myles listened to Homer's chest. "His heart rate is extremely low." Myles looked at Hannah, sadness reflected in his gaze. "We can wait and see, or we can help him along. It's up to you."

"Is he suffering?"

"I don't think so."

"What should I do?" Hannah asked.

"I can't tell you that, Hannah," Myles said kindly.

"Could we make him more comfortable?" Nolan asked.

"That we can do."

With Hannah's approval, the two men worked together to gently move Homer to the sofa in the sitting room, the spot he'd claimed as his own the day he came to live with Caleb.

Stirred by the movement and activity, Homer woke briefly, sighing when he landed on the sofa before going back to sleep.

Hannah sat with his head on her leg, petting and stroking him so he'd know she was there. Tears ran freely down her face when she thought of how much Caleb had adored Homer, how in tune the two of them had been with each other, how Homer had followed Caleb around like a shadow whenever he was home and waited by the door for him to return when he was away. Caleb's deployments had been as hard on Homer as they'd been on her.

Nolan sat next to her on the sofa and took hold of her free hand.

Myles occupied the easy chair next to the fire that had burned down, leaving the room chilled.

"Would you mind lighting the fire, Nolan? I don't want Homer to get cold."

"I'd be happy to."

Nolan soon had the fire warming the room and casting a cozy glow over Homer.

"Should I help him along, Myles?" Hannah asked after a long period of quiet.

He got up to check Homer's heart again. "I don't think you'll need to."

That news started the tears flowing again.

Nolan put his arm around her and offered silent comfort as she focused on the slow rise and fall of Homer's chest.

So many memories came flooding back to her, of the years she and Caleb and Homer had spent moving around with the army as Caleb advanced through the officer corps and the leave time they'd spent at home in Vermont. Each time Caleb deployed, Hannah and Homer came home to be with her family. She and Homer had propped each other up and gotten each other through the long absences.

On the day they lost Caleb, they'd been here in Vermont passing an ordinary day at home until the army chaplain showed up with two other officers, all of them wearing the telltale class A uniforms, and shattered her world. Somehow Homer had known . . . He'd understood and had grieved right along with her.

The front door slammed open, startling Hannah from her memories. Hunter came into the sitting room, looking harried and a bit undone, which was wildly out of character for her calm, cool, collected twin. "I came as soon as I got Nolan's message. Is he . . ."

"No, but soon," Hannah said, resigned now despite the overwhelming sadness. Losing Homer truly marked the end of an era for her as well as Caleb's friends and family. "Come see him." She held out a hand to Hunter, who wrapped his hand around hers as he knelt on the floor next to Homer.

Tears filled Hunter's eyes as he bent to kiss Homer's sweet face. Then he reached for Hannah, hugging her tightly. "Are you okay?"

"I've been better, but we knew this was coming."

"Still . . ."

Her twin knew her better than just about anyone, so he understood how hard the loss of Homer would hit her. "Still," she said, forcing the hint of a smile to reassure Hunter. He worried about her endlessly.

Their parents came in a short time later, followed by Hannah's brother Will and his girlfriend, Cameron, who'd just returned from New York City.

"We came as soon as we heard." Will hugged and kissed Hannah, before bending to kiss and pet Homer. "How is he?"

"Not so good."

Her mom had brought food that she set out in the kitchen. The others wandered in there, but Hannah never left Homer, and Nolan never left Hannah.

"I'm sorry our plans got messed up tonight," Hannah said.

"This is more important."

Only because she was watching him so closely did she see Homer take one last deep breath before his chest stopped moving altogether. She bent to hug him, whispering in his ear, "I love you, Homer. Don't forget to give Dad my message. You guys have fun together. I'll see you both again someday."

Nolan's hand lay warm on her back, rubbing her shoulders as she sobbed for Homer and for Caleb and for all that she had lost. She hugged Homer until his fur was wet from her tears.

"Let Myles take him, Han," Hunter said through his own tears.

"He needs his blanket."

"Where is it?" Will asked.

"Upstairs in my room on the bed."

Will headed for the stairs. "I'll get it."

Her brother returned a minute later with the battered quilt Caleb's mother had made for Homer when he was a puppy. Thinking of a much younger Homer dragging his "blankie" around from room to room made Hannah cry again as they all worked together to wrap Homer in his beloved blanket.

A knock on the front door preceded Amelia and Bob Guthrie into the house.

"Oh no." Amelia's eyes shone with tears as they rushed into the room and saw Homer wrapped in the blanket. "We're too late."

"Just by a few minutes." Hannah stood to greet her in-laws with hugs. "Why don't you spend some time with him before Myles takes him."

"We'd appreciate that," Bob said gruffly.

Hannah felt Nolan's hand on her back as they joined her family in the kitchen. Everyone hugged her, and Hannah moved through each embrace on autopilot. She knew Homer was gone, but the pain couldn't seem to permeate the numbness. It was far too reminiscent of the day Caleb died, when she'd been surrounded by loved ones wanting to do something for her when there was nothing anyone could do. She remembered all too well what it felt like when the numbness wore off and the pain rushed in.

"I'm so sorry," Cameron whispered.

"Thank you. Glad to have you back."

Cameron's watery smile was reassuring. Hannah adored her, and having her here definitely lifted Hannah's spirits.

She hugged her parents next.

Unshed tears swam in his eyes as her dad kissed her

forehead. "I'm so sorry, baby," Lincoln said. "Homer was a good old boy."

"Yes, he was. Caleb will be happy to see him again."

Will slipped from the room, and Cameron went after him.

"Everyone wanted to come over," Hannah's mother, Molly, said, "but I told them you had a full house. They're all thinking of you."

"I know." Hannah had little doubt her other seven siblings were upset about losing Homer. "Thank you for running interference."

"What can we do for you?" Molly asked, smoothing a hand over Hannah's hair.

Hannah shook her head. "Nothing special. It helps to have you here."

"We should tell the Sultans," Hunter said, echoing a thought that had been on Hannah's mind since shortly after she arrived home to find Homer in such dire condition. "They'd want to know."

"Would you call them?" Hannah said. "I don't think I could do it."

"I'll take care of it." Hunter's eyes were rimmed with red, his jaw set in a way that reminded Hannah of the months after Caleb died when her twin had tried so hard to hold it together for her that he'd buried his own grief.

"You guys don't have to stay," Hannah said to her family. "I'm okay. I promise. And Nolan is here." She looked at him and was comforted by his nod as much as his quiet, steady presence over the last couple of hours. A flutter of nervous energy passed through her at the thought of leaning on him, at the thought of him wanting her to lean on him.

When the others eyed him speculatively, Hannah added, "We had plans tonight." Watching her family process that momentous news with far more decorum than she'd expected from them also helped to lift her spirits ever so slightly. She could tell they were nearly bursting with the need to ask a thousand questions that they wisely contained. She was in no mood to deal with an Abbott inquisition right now, and they knew it.

However, she also knew she was only postponing the inevitable. She'd be in for a grilling after she'd had sufficient time to mourn Homer.

Her family stayed while Myles gathered up Homer's body. They stayed while she spent some tearful time with Caleb's parents. And they stayed until they were certain Hannah was okay. Convincing them to go took some doing on her part, but she finally succeeded in assuring them she'd be fine.

When she was left alone with Nolan, she turned to him, unsure of what she should say. She appreciated that he waited for her to gather her thoughts and didn't feel the need to immediately fill the silence.

She forced a smile for his benefit. "Heck of a first date, huh?"

"One for the record books," he said as he took her hand once again. He couldn't seem to refrain from touching her, and Hannah couldn't deny that she liked being touched by him. "But I'm glad I was able to be here with you tonight."

"So am I. Can you sit for a minute?"

"For as long as you'd like." He released her hand only to add a log to the fire before he sat next to her and reached for her again.

"What're you thinking?" she asked after a long period of companionable silence.

"That this brings back a lot of painful memories for me, so I can only speculate as to how you must feel."

"I feel pretty awful, but it helps to imagine Homer crossing the bridge and finding Caleb waiting for him. I can picture Homer running for Caleb the way he used to, both of them young and strong and thrilled to be together again." She wiped away new tears. "They must be so happy to see each other."

"Yeah," Nolan said gruffly, brushing quickly at his face with his free hand. "I bet they're having one hell of a reunion."

"Thinking about that brings comfort, you know?"

He nodded.

"Remember how Caleb would pat his chest and Homer would jump into his arms?" Hannah asked.

"I remember. I also remember that Homer wouldn't do that for anyone but Caleb no matter how hard we all tried to get him to do it for us."

"That's because Caleb was the only one he trusted enough to catch him."

They sat in silence for a long time, watching the fire, lost in their own thoughts and memories. It was nice, she thought, to have him there with her, to share the grief with someone who'd loved Caleb and Homer and felt their loss almost as profoundly as she did.

"We need to do something for Homer," Nolan said.

"Like what?"

"We should do what Caleb would've done—a full-on funeral with all the bells and whistles he would've insisted on."

For the first time in hours, Hannah had reason to truly smile imagining the send-off Caleb would've given his beloved companion. "You're absolutely right. It needs to be huge and awesome and over the top."

"Totally and completely over the top."

"We need the Sultans."

"We couldn't do over the top without them."

Hannah turned so she faced him. "This is a really great idea, Nolan. And you're right. It's exactly what Caleb would've done."

"You would've thought of it. Eventually."

"When should we do it?"

"We'd need to give the guys some notice to get them here. Weekend after next?"

"That works for me. I love this. Thank you so much for honoring Homer and Caleb by suggesting it."

Nolan shrugged off her praise. "Do you want me to go so you can get some rest?"

"No." She dropped her head against his shoulder. "I know you have to work tomorrow and everything, but if you don't mind staying a while longer . . ."

Nolan put his arm around her and kissed the top of her head. "I don't mind."

Will never said a word on the ride from Hannah's house to his cabin on the outskirts of town. The cabin was now their place, Cameron recalled, the excitement of her move to Vermont dimmed by the news they'd been greeted with upon arriving back in Butler.

Cameron wished she could think of something to say that would make Will feel better, but she decided to wait until he was ready to talk about it. Recalling the tortured, grief-stricken look on his face when she'd found him in Hannah's mudroom, her heart broke for him.

The cabin was cold and dark when they arrived. And it was unusually quiet with his dogs spending one more night at his parents' house.

"Weird without the boys here," Cameron said, hoping to spark some conversation.

He squatted before the hearth to start the fire. "I know. I hate when they're not here. Sucks the life out of the place."

Cameron went into the bedroom and found the suitcase that contained her pajamas. She put on the flannel moose pajama pants Will had bought her along with one of his UVM sweatshirts and joined him in the living room.

He stared into the fire, lost in thought and miles away from the cozy room.

She couldn't bear to see him in pain so she went to him and curled her arms around him from behind. "What can I do for you?"

Will blew out a deep breath and covered the hand she'd placed on his chest with his. "Having you here makes everything better."

"I'm sorry about Homer."

"Thanks. Even though I knew he was getting old, I refused to believe he could ever die."

"I know."

"It brings it all back. With Caleb."

"I know that, too."

"When Hannah said Caleb must be happy to see Homer . . ." He shook his head. "That killed me."

"Come here," she said, urging him to turn into her embrace.

He did as she asked, his arms encircling her. "Sorry," he said, his voice muffled by her hair. "This wasn't how I expected to spend our first night of officially living together."

"Please don't apologize for being upset, Will. I only met Homer a couple of times and didn't know Caleb at all, but I'm heartbroken for Hannah. I can only imagine how you must feel."

He hugged her for a long time as Cameron stroked his hair and back, wishing there was something she could say or do to make him feel better.

"I'm so glad you're here to stay," he said, breaking the long silence.

"So am I."

He pulled back so he could see her face and kissed her softly.

As she caressed his cheek, she stared at the face she'd longed for during the weeks apart while she packed up her life for the move.

"What do you suppose it means that Hannah and Nolan had plans tonight?" he asked.

"I suppose it means that maybe things have progressed a bit since they danced at the Grange."

"God, that would be awesome. I couldn't believe it when she said they'd had plans for tonight."

"I was proud of you and the rest of your family for biting your tongues on that one."

"Wasn't easy," he said with the first hint of a smile.

"I bet Hannah knows she's in for it as soon as things settle down a bit."

"For sure." He leaned in to kiss her again, a bit more intently this time. "I don't know about you, but I'm totally wiped out. What do you say we hit the sack?"

As the thought of hitting any horizontal surface with Will Abbott made her heart leap for joy, Cameron said, "Fine by me."

They stood together in the bathroom to brush their teeth and then Cameron rushed into bed, pulling the down comforter up to her chin as her teeth chattered. She couldn't believe it when he emerged from the bathroom naked.

"Are you for real? I'm freezing, and you're *naked*?"

"I'm counting on you to warm me up."

"You're going to be very disappointed."

"Never." He curled up to her, big and strong and warm and solid. "I still can't believe you're here to stay and I get to sleep with you every night. I feel like the luckiest guy in the universe."

"I feel just as lucky."

"You're wearing way too many clothes though." His hand worked its way under the sweatshirt, making her startle when his cool hand touched her much warmer belly.

"There's no way you're getting me naked tonight, mister. I'm way too cold."

"I'll warm you up. I promise."

"No!" Cameron screamed when his other freezing hand landed on her back.

He laughed at her reaction and put his arms around her, hugging her close to him. By now she knew him well enough to expect him to cajole her out of her clothes, something he was exceptionally good at, but he didn't try. Rather, he held on tight.

"Are you okay?" she asked.

"I feel like I did when Caleb died, which is ridiculous because . . . Well, it feels ridiculous."

"It's not ridiculous."

"I hope this doesn't set Hannah way back, right when she seems to be stepping forward a bit."

"It's apt to give her a few difficult moments, but we'll all be there for her, and we'll get her through it."

"I think about him all the time," Will said. "Caleb . . . He was . . ." Will blew out a deep shaky breath. "He was unlike anyone else I've ever known."

Because he seemed to need to talk about the brother-in-law he'd loved, Cameron said, "How so?"

"It's hard to describe him to people who didn't know him and do him justice. But he was smart and strong and fearless and probably more than a bit crazy. He could be loud and obnoxious, and he loved to get drunk, and by drunk I mean *hammered*."

"What did Hannah think about that?"

"It was the only thing I ever heard them fight about. She used to say she wasn't having kids with him until he finished growing up."

Cameron could feel his lips curve into a smile against her neck.

"I wish you could've seen him play hockey. He was a madman on the ice and spent a lot of time in the penalty box."

Cameron chuckled at the picture he painted.

"He was also freaking brilliant. He graduated with a perfect 4.0 GPA. Who does that?"

"Not me, that's for sure. What did he major in?"

"American history. He probably could've played professional hockey, but he chose the army instead. I think a lot about what might've been different if he'd chosen hockey instead."

"Why do you think he chose the army?"

"His dad was an army officer, and it was all Caleb knew growing up until his dad retired and moved here when he was in middle school. Army life left a big impact on him. Colonel Guthrie has never been quite the same since Caleb died. He blames himself."

"That's so sad."

"The whole thing totally blows. It's weird how life goes on and time goes by and you don't think about it all day, every day anymore. Then Homer dies, and it's like it just happened."

"It's a reminder."

"Yeah."

"For what it's worth, I think Caleb must've been a truly amazing person to have so many people still passionately committed to his memory seven years after he died."

"All of us, everyone who loved him, we'll always be passionately committed to his memory. It's all we've got left of him, you know?"

Moved by his words and the emotion behind them, Cameron nodded, kissed his chest and breathed in his familiar scent, comforted by his presence and extremely grateful to be loved by a man who loved so deeply.

"I worry about whether Hannah can really move on with someone else or if maybe he was it for her."

"I hope that's not the case. She's so young and gorgeous and wonderful. I'd love to see her happy with Nolan or someone else if that doesn't work out."

"So would I." He shifted to gain access to her lips and kissed her. "I want her to be as happy as we are."

"I want that, too."

He nuzzled her neck. "Are you feeling warmer yet?"

"A little," she said, smiling.

"I bet I can make you warmer than this big bulky sweatshirt." As he spoke, he eased the sweatshirt up and over her head, and because she was dying to feel his skin next to hers, she let him.

The brush of his chest hair against her breasts never failed to stir and arouse her, and this time was no different. After hearing him speak so eloquently about the friend he'd lost, Cameron loved him even more than she had before. She looped her arms around his neck and curled her leg around his hip.

"I'd never get over losing you after what we've had," he whispered against her lips.

"I wouldn't either." The mere thought of losing him after waiting so long to find him struck fear in her heart, making her shiver, but not because she was cold.

"I love you so much."

"I love you, too. I love that we get to be together all the time now."

"Nothing has ever made me happier."

"Me either." He was usually all about the preliminaries, but tonight it seemed they both needed the immediate connection.

Cameron sighed with relief and completion when he entered her and made slow, sweet, sexy love to her, all the while gazing down at her with all the love he felt for her apparent in his golden brown eyes. He never looked away, and neither did she. It was the single most intimate moment she'd ever shared with anyone.

She arched into him. "*Will . . .*"

"Yes, honey, come for me." His breathing became faster, matching the movement of his hips.

Cameron clung to him as they hit the peak together.

His head dropped to her shoulder, and Cameron combed her fingers through his hair while they absorbed the rippling aftershocks. She held on tight to the most important person in her life, wanting to keep him close forever.

CHAPTER 4

*I'm not happy with Hunter and Will for inviting
Caleb to our house ALL the time. They know I
don't like him, but every time I turn around HE
is there. He gives me these weird looks. I try to
ignore him, but it isn't easy.*

—From the diary of Hannah Abbott, age fourteen

Nolan came awake slowly and had no idea where he was until he breathed in the scent he'd recognize anywhere as Hannah's. Her soft hair brushed against his chin, and her hand was warm upon his chest. They'd fallen asleep in her sitting room, reclined against a pile of throw pillows. The fire had long ago died out, leaving the room chilly and dark.

While he knew he should leave her to sleep in a real bed, he couldn't bring himself to disturb her after the difficult evening she'd endured. His heart broke for her at having to absorb yet another painful loss. He wanted to keep his arms around her and protect her from ever being hurt again.

Ever since that Labor Day weekend five years ago, his feelings for her seemed to grow stronger all the time. The need to be with her, to talk to her, to touch her, to protect her was nothing short of overwhelming.

She came awake with a gasp that had him instantly on alert and releasing his hold on her when she struggled.

"It's me, Hannah. Nolan. We fell asleep." He was almost afraid to touch her, but he caressed her hair, trying to offer comfort. "Are you okay?"

"Mmm. I was dreaming." Trembling, she rested her head against his chest, probably because it was handy.

Nolan wasn't sure what he should do. Stay? Go? Offer comfort? Say nothing? After a few minutes of intense internal debate, he settled on the most innocuous of his many questions. "Do you want to talk about it?"

She didn't say anything for a long while, but he noticed that she seemed to relax against him even as the trembling continued. "It wouldn't be fair to talk to you about my dream."

"Why not?"

"Because it was about Caleb."

"You can talk to me about Caleb, Hannah. You know that."

"I want to be fair to you. I know . . . I've known for some time now that you . . . You care about me."

Because he couldn't resist the need to touch her, he slid his hand up and down her arm, hoping to provide comfort more than anything else. "I do care about you, and I cared about Caleb."

"He cared about you, too."

"I miss him all the time."

She blew out a deep breath that shuddered through her body. "I dreamed about him seeing Homer again. Caleb was waiting for him, and Homer ran to him the way he always did."

"He jumped into Caleb's arms?"

She nodded. "Just like old times. Homer was making the sounds he used to make when Caleb got home from deployments. We called it his joyful noise. They were so happy to see each other."

As Nolan became aware of the warm seep of her tears though his shirt, she wiped her face. The huge lump that had settled in his throat made it difficult to speak, but he cleared his throat and made an effort for her. "I'm glad you got to see their reunion."

"I am, too, except . . ."

"Except what?"

"I . . . for the first time, I didn't feel like I belonged with them. I was on the outside looking in."

"You don't belong with them right now because you still have a lot left to do here." Where those words had come from, Nolan couldn't have said.

"You think so?"

"I know so. You've got so much life ahead of you, so many things you need to do before you join them."

"I'm sorry to dump all my crap on you."

"That's not what you're doing, Hannah."

"Sure, it is, and you're a very good sport to let me ruin our first date so spectacularly."

"You call this ruin? I got to sleep with you in my arms. I call that perfection."

"Nolan . . ."

"Too much? Sorry." He said he was sorry, but he really wasn't. He'd spoken the truth. "Do you want me to go?"

"No."

"My truck is out front for the whole neighborhood to see. I don't care who knows I'm here, but I'd hate for you to be the subject of gossip."

"Why don't you put it in the garage then?"

Thrilled that she wanted him to stay, he said, "Are you sure?"

"I'm sure." She got up to see to the logistics of opening the garage door for him and met him in the mudroom when he came back in. They returned to the sitting room where he stoked up the fire before joining her on the sofa.

"Let's lie down this time and do it right." She produced a wool blanket that she tossed over them.

With her pressed against his chest, Nolan had a hell of a time hiding what her close proximity was doing to him.

"This is nice," she said softly when they were settled.

"Very nice." His voice sounded tight and strangled, and he wondered if she heard it, too.

"Are you okay?"

"I'm great."

"You sound funny."

He released a nervous laugh. Did she really have no idea how badly he wanted her? Not just physically, although that was the overriding need at the moment, but every other possible way, too.

"What's so funny?"

"You are."

"Why am I funny? I'm just lying here minding my own business."

"Right. That's all you're doing."

"What else am I doing?" she asked, sounding genuinely baffled.

"You're filling my senses with the scent I'd know anywhere as yours. You're tickling my face with your silky soft hair. Your breath on my neck is giving me goose bumps, among other things."

Much to his dismay, she began to withdraw from his embrace.

"Wait, don't go. I never said any of those things were bad."

She stopped trying to get away, but she hung her head with dismay that broke his heart. "I'm being utterly unfair to you."

"How do you figure?"

"I'm a hot mess tonight, and you're just being nice to put up with me. I don't have any right—"

He laid his finger over her lips. "Stop. You have every right to do or say anything you want when you're with me. There's nothing you could do that would be wrong. Not with me anyway."

She rolled her bottom lip between her teeth in a move that made him even harder as she studied his face. "Nothing?"

"Not one thing." His heart slowed to a crawl as he waited to see what she would do. When her eyes shifted subtly to his mouth, he stopped breathing altogether. Then she leaned forward and laid her lips on his, just that, nothing more, but it packed a more powerful punch than full-on sex with any other woman ever had.

"Help me, Nolan," she said as new tears spilled from her eyes. "I don't remember how to do this."

With his hands on her face, he used his thumbs to brush away her tears. "You're doing just fine. Way better than fine." He guided her toward him, taking pains to move slowly when his inclination was to devour. Her lips gliding over his was the closest thing to heaven he'd ever known.

He kept his hands on her face, letting her know he wouldn't ask for anything more than whatever she was willing to give.

Without breaking the kiss, she relaxed against him, her mouth opening over his in blatant invitation. It took every bit of willpower he could muster to wait for her to make the next move. The last thing he wanted was to scare her off by taking more than she had to give. Right when he was certain she'd gone as far as she was going to, he felt her tongue slide over his bottom lip. He couldn't contain the groan that rumbled through him.

She pulled back and studied his face. "Was that okay?"

"Hannah . . . Christ, you have no idea what you do to me." His heart was beating so hard he wondered if it might implode inside his chest.

"What do I do to you?"

"What *don't* you do? You walk into the room, and I want you. You speak, and I want you. You cry and I want to cry, too, because you're hurting. I can't bear to see you cry."

"I'm sorry. I just—"

He stopped whatever she was going to say by kissing her again. "Don't ever apologize to me for the way you feel."

She did that thing with her bottom lip and her teeth again, and he wanted to beg for mercy. "Why me, Nolan?"

"I don't know," he said with a small laugh. "I've asked myself that over and over again. I've felt so guilty . . . Caleb was my friend, you know? One of the best friends I ever had, and to be thinking the way I do about his wife . . ."

"What do you think about his wife?"

"So many things I'd never dare to share for fear of you running away from me screaming."

She smiled at that, and the small movement of her lips lit up her entire face. "You underestimate me."

"I'd never be so foolish as to do that."

She focused on his mouth again. "I like kissing you."

"That works out well, because I *love* kissing you."

"Caleb wouldn't want you to feel guilty for caring about me."

"You don't think so? I have these visions of him gutting me with that big hunting knife of his."

"Stop it," she said, laughing.

Nolan much preferred her laughter to the tears.

"He loved you."

"He would've gutted me if I'd so much as looked at you."

"Maybe . . . But you didn't feel this way then." She ventured a glance at his eyes. "Did you?"

Nolan shook his head. "Not until a couple of years after."

"What changed?"

"I don't know exactly. I remember it was during one of the Sultans weekends here, and you were running around taking care of us the way you always do, and I thought how amazing you were to still put up with us."

"Those weekends make me feel connected to him, as odd as that might sound. It was comforting to do what we always did, even if it was difficult, too."

"It's always so strange to not see him in the middle of everything. When I think of him, and I do every day, I picture him as the sun and the rest of us his planets, circling around him and whatever adventure he'd dreamed up."

"That's a very apt—and very lovely—description."

Nolan knew he needed to ask, but he hesitated just the same. "Is this . . . You and me . . . Is it too weird in light of what we both felt for him?"

She took a moment to consider his question, during which he had to struggle to get air to his lungs. What if it was too weird for her? What if it was too close to the past to enable the future?

"I think it might be weirder to be with someone who didn't know Caleb. At least you understand. You were there. For all of it."

Nolan nodded, knowing what she meant.

She propped her chin on her hands, which were flat against his chest. "So . . ."

"So."

"We're going to do this?"

"Define *this*."

Hannah raised a brow. "Do I really have to?"

Nolan discovered he also adored her playful side. "Yep."

"Date. And stuff . . ."

"And stuff? What stuff?"

Her face turned bright red, which was absolutely adorable. "*Nolan.*"

"*Hannah.*"

"Don't make me say it."

"Okay, I won't." As he gazed into her warm brown eyes, he knew he needed to ask her one more thing, the one thing that made his heart pound and his mouth go dry. "Are you ready for this, Hannah? Because if you're not, that's okay. I'm not going anywhere."

"I think I might be ready." She looked down before bringing her gaze back to meet his. "Mostly because it's you who's asking."

Nolan closed his eyes against the rush of emotion her words invoked. Was this really happening or would he awake to discover he'd been dreaming, too? God, he hoped not because holding her was like having all his dreams come true at the same exact moment.

She licked her lips and focused again on his mouth. "Do you think it would be okay if we . . ."

"What, Hannah? Tell me what you want."

"I want to kiss you again."

Nolan released a shaky breath and framed her sweet face with his hands. "You don't ever have to ask first." Slowly, he eased her toward him, watching her intently. That's how he saw her eyes flutter shut and her lips part in anticipation.

As their lips met, her hand curled around his neck, almost as if she wanted to keep him there as long as she could. Again he had to remind himself to go slowly to not scare her off by showing her the full extent of his desire before she was ready to know.

Then her lips parted and her tongue dabbed at his bottom lip, setting off a wildfire that burned through his system in a flash. The instant her tongue connected with his, he forgot all about going slow and taking his time. His fingers slid into the silk of her hair as he tilted his head to delve deeper into the sweetness of her mouth.

She shifted, trying to get closer, and ended up with her belly pressed against his erection. Blinded by desire, he gasped but didn't break the kiss and decided to stop caring if she figured out how badly he wanted her. He drew her closer, wrapping his arm around her while keeping one hand anchored firmly in her hair.

She whimpered against his lips, and he was about to pull back, but she stopped him from moving with a firm grip on his hair. In the midst of the hottest kiss of his life, Nolan had the presence of mind to wonder if it was possible to expire on the spot from an overabundance of desire.

Hannah had forgotten how wonderful it was to be held and kissed by a sexy man who wanted her madly. And this was madness. There could be no other word for the way he made her feel. She'd gone from being tentative about kissing him to pressing against him shamelessly.

That thought had her pulling back, reining herself in even though that was the last thing she wanted to do.

"What's wrong?" he asked, studying her with eyes full of warmth and affection.

"Nothing."

"Something."

Her face flushed with heat. "I feel like I'm throwing myself at you."

His bark of laughter surprised her. "Please, by all means, throw yourself at me. Any time you'd like."

"And you won't think less of me if I do?"

"Hannah . . . Beautiful Hannah, I will never think you're anything other than gorgeous and sweet and strong and courageous. So damned courageous you take my breath away."

Hannah shook her head. "I'm nowhere near as courageous as you think I am."

"Yes, you are, and there's nothing you can do or say with me that would be wrong. I promise."

"You'll have to be patient with me. I'm very out of practice with all of this."

He ran his hands up her back to squeeze her shoulders. "You don't feel rusty to me at all."

Hannah laughed at the way he waggled his brows. "You're very smooth, you know that?"

"I'm not feeding you bullshit, Hannah. I mean every word."

"I know." She looked down at him, drinking in the sight of his kiss-swollen lips, the slash of color in his cheeks that hadn't been there earlier, the fall of his hair over his brow and the heat in his eyes, all directed at her. "You're going to be tired tomorrow."

"It'll be totally worth it."

In between heated kisses, they talked for a long time that night—about everything and nothing. She had no recollection of falling asleep in his arms, but the sound of his heart beating under her ear woke her the next morning. Before she had time to process the fact that she'd spent the night in Nolan's arms, her front door opened and her dad called out to her.

Hannah sat up abruptly, rousing Nolan from a sound sleep as she tried to do something with her unruly hair.

Her parents strolled into the sitting room and stopped short at the sight of her, Nolan and the blanket.

"Oh," her mom said. "So sorry." With her hand on Lincoln's chest, Molly steered her husband out of the room.

CHAPTER 5

———◆◇◆———

Caleb spent the summer with his grandparents in Missouri. He's different this year. Maybe he's FINALLY growing up! He's a lot taller, and he's got muscles all of a sudden. It's so weird! I still don't like him.

—From the diary of Hannah Abbott, age fifteen

"Shit," Nolan muttered, running fingers through his hair.

"At least we were dressed," Hannah said with a small smile.

"There is that."

"Feel free to sneak out. I'll let them know it was on the up and up. Not that I feel the need to explain myself to them, but I will just the same."

"I'm not sneaking out. We'll face them together."

That he was unwilling to take the easy way out of an embarrassing encounter with her parents made Hannah's insides flutter.

"Shall we face the music?" he asked with a wry smile that drew one from her, too.

"If we must."

Nolan's hand on the small of her back eased her nerves as Hannah walked into her kitchen to find her mom bustling about making coffee and her dad pretending to be absorbed in the newspaper he'd already read at home.

"Sorry to barge in on you," Molly said.

Was it Hannah's imagination or was her fearless mom having trouble looking at her or Nolan? Her entire family had been coming and going without so much as a knock at her house since Caleb died. They'd never had to worry about walking in on something because nothing had ever happened. Until last night . . .

"We just wanted to check on you," Lincoln added, seeming mortified by the entire thing. "After Homer and all . . ."

"It's fine, Dad. We were talking and fell asleep. Nothing scandalous."

"We . . . didn't see your truck outside, Nolan, or we never would've come in," Molly said, her face flushed with embarrassment that was so far out of character for her that Hannah could only stare.

"It's in the garage." Nolan's voice was calm despite the awkwardness of the situation. "We didn't want the whole town talking about us before we were ready to be talked about."

The press of his fingers against her back reassured her, as did his steady presence next to her. She'd forgotten what it was like to be half of a couple. Not that she'd go so far as to call them an official couple, but having him stand by her side in front of her parents went a long way toward lowering her defenses where he was concerned.

"Makes a lot of sense," Lincoln said gruffly, which brought back fond memories of how ridiculously overprotective he'd been when Hannah first began dating. He'd grilled all her dates as if they were planning to run away and marry her rather than take her to the movies. Only Caleb hadn't been intimidated, but he'd known her dad for years by the time he started dating Lincoln's daughter. "That coffee ready yet, Mol?"

"Coming right up."

Nolan took advantage of their preoccupation with the coffee to press a light kiss to her temple. "I've got to get to work. I'll call you later."

Hannah smiled up at him and nodded.

"See you later, Mr. and Mrs. Abbott."

"Bye, Nolan," they said in unison.

Hannah walked him through the mudroom and held the door to the garage open for him as he stepped into the boots he'd left there the night before. "Sorry again about my folks."

"They're fine," he said. "They're doing what any decent parents would do the day after their daughter suffered a painful loss."

Hannah experienced a pang of sadness at the thought of Homer. She was really and truly alone now. Well, except for her humongous family and loving friends, especially the one who was looking at her now with concern etched into his handsome face.

"You okay?"

"I will be. Your company helped a lot last night. I appreciate you staying."

"It was a terrible hardship, but somehow I survived."

Her smile stretched from ear to ear.

"That's a beautiful thing," he said softly, gazing down at her with unabashed affection. He tucked a strand of hair behind her ear and ran his finger over her cheek, making her nearly swoon from the sweetness of his gesture. Then he zeroed in on her lips, making her body heat from the memories of what had transpired between them during the night.

Hannah licked her lips, and his eyes burned with desire as he gazed at the slide of tongue over lips. "What's a beautiful thing?"

"That smile. I'd do anything to see it every day." He brushed a kiss so fleeting over her lips that Hannah barely had time to register that he was kissing her before it was over.

She wanted to plead for more, but this wasn't the time or the place for more.

"I'll see you soon."

Hannah nodded and pressed the button to the garage door opener, closing it after he'd backed his truck into the driveway. Before she returned to face her parents, Hannah took a series of deep breaths, hoping her face wasn't as red as it felt. She pressed cold hands to her face, but that did nothing to address the pounding of her heart or the dryness in her mouth.

When she walked back into the kitchen, her dad popped up from the table with comical speed. "I've got to get going to work." He kissed his wife, who patted his arm as she smiled at him. "George and Ringo are probably tearing up the Rover waiting for me." He kissed Hannah. "Let me know if I can do anything for you, honey. Anything at all."

Hannah leaned into him, breathing in the familiar and comforting scent of the aftershave he'd worn all her life. "Thanks, Dad." She had no doubt that he'd sell his soul to the devil to save her from one additional minute of pain in her lifetime, and she loved him for that. But she also knew he had no desire whatsoever to hear the details of her evening with Nolan.

Her mother on the other hand took a seat at the table with a steaming mug of coffee, settling in to talk it out.

Her dad left, and Hannah turned to face her mother.

Molly raised a brow in silent inquiry. "So."

"So." No one said Hannah had to make it easy on her.

"Not in the mood to chat?" Molly asked.

Hannah took her time pouring a much-needed cup of coffee. She moved deliberately to stir in cream and a bit of sugar. "Not particularly."

"Hannah . . ."

"*Mom . . .*"

Molly blew out a breath that gave away her exasperation. "You always were the toughest of my nuts to crack."

"In a pack of ten, a girl's gotta do what she can to stand out."

"I have to say that in spite of your decision to torture your poor old mom, I'm glad to see you smiling this morning. We were worried that Homer's death would be a setback for you."

"I'm trying not to let that happen." Hannah stared into her mug as the dream from the night before resurfaced with clarity that made her heart ache.

"What is it, honey?" Molly asked. "I hope you know I'm not looking to pry, but I want to help if I can."

"I know you do." Hannah debated for a full minute, trying to decide if she could really give voice to the torturous thoughts that had plagued her since she woke from the dream. "Last night," she began haltingly, still staring at her mug, "I dreamed about Caleb for the first time in a long time."

"Oh honey. That happened when Nolan was here?"

Hannah nodded. "He was great about it though."

"I'm glad you weren't alone."

"In the dream . . . Homer was running to Caleb." She finally glanced at her mother. "The way he used to."

Molly's eyes glistened as she smiled. "Leaping into his arms?"

"Yeah. They were so happy to see each other."

"Of course they were." Molly brushed at a tear as she forced a cheerful tone. "They were the very best of friends."

"Caleb looked so good. He was smiling and laughing and holding out his arms to Homer. His hair was long, like in college, and he just seemed so . . . alive and so . . ."

Molly's warm hand covered hers. "So what?"

"So beautiful," Hannah said with a sigh. "He was so beautiful. He hated when I said that. He said it made him feel like a pussy." Molly's ringing laugh made Hannah smile. "Sorry, I know you hate that word."

"Caleb loved a lot of words I hate."

"That he did." Her husband's colorful vocabulary was one of the things she missed most about him, even if his language had mortified her at times. There was nothing he wouldn't say, and the word *filter* wasn't in his dictionary.

Molly continued to chuckle and dab at her eyes. "I can so hear him saying that."

"He said it all the time because I told him frequently how beautiful he was."

"He never had a doubt that you loved him with your whole heart and soul, Hannah. Not one single doubt."

"I know. When I saw him in the dream, I wanted so badly to run to him, but I couldn't. Even though I was asleep, I knew I could only look but not touch. And then when I woke up with Nolan . . ." Hannah swallowed hard because this was the part that had torn her up. "I realized that if faced with the choice, I'd always choose Caleb, which is so unfair to Nolan. How do I start something with him knowing I'd always choose Caleb over him?"

"You'll never have to make that choice, honey. Life and fate and God or whatever you want to believe has already made it for you. Caleb was your past, and perhaps Nolan is your future, but you don't have to choose one of them over the other. You'll always love Caleb, and any man you end up with will have to understand that Caleb is as much a part of you as your lovely brown eyes or your art or your great big family."

"What if, in the next life, they're both standing there before me at the gates to heaven, and I go running to Caleb?"

"If you were to have thirty or forty years with Nolan, you might not run to Caleb. Did you consider that?"

It had never crossed her mind that she might one day come to love someone else more than she'd loved Caleb. How was that even possible? But if her mother was right, it was not only possible, it was probable that she might form a deeper bond over decades than the one she'd shared with Caleb in the twelve years they'd had together.

"What're you thinking?"

"That I probably have no business starting something with Nolan when I'm still so screwed up over Caleb."

"You're not screwed up, Hannah. You're the strongest, most courageous, resilient person I've ever known, and I couldn't be more proud of the way you've conducted yourself in the years since we lost Caleb."

Her mother's forcefully spoken words brought tears to Hannah's eyes.

"You've earned the right to be happy, and if Nolan makes you happy, spend time with him. Give yourself permission to start over."

"I want to. I really do, especially because it's him, and he loved Caleb so much. He gets it, you know?"

Molly nodded in agreement. "When he first took a shine to you, I couldn't decide if his friendship with Caleb would be a pro or a con. I can see how it would help you to move forward with someone who lived through it and understands what you've lost."

"Right. But . . . I often wonder if it would be easier and less risky to just be by myself."

"It'd be both those things and awfully lonely, too."

Hannah could attest to the loneliness. After years of contentment with her own company, she'd begun to chafe a bit lately at the boundaries she'd set for herself. As the long cold winter came to an end and spring began to bloom all around her, she wondered if it wasn't also time to step outside the cocoon and start over again.

The night she'd spent with Nolan, the heated kisses they'd shared, the desire he could barely hide made her want to reach for the brass ring that'd been out of her reach for so long now.

"Why are your cheeks suddenly bright red?"

Damn her mother's never-ending intuition. "No reason."

"That doesn't look like no reason to me. You know you want to tell someone . . . Why not me?"

Hannah laughed at her mother's shameless campaign for info. "Fine! I kissed him. A lot. There! Are you happy?"

"Are you? That's the more important question."

"I'm . . . intrigued."

"That's not happy—yet. But it's an excellent start."

After a quick stop at home to shower and change, Nolan arrived at the garage where six cars had already been delivered by their owners. His eyes were gritty from the lack of sleep, and he was chugging his second coffee of the morning as he started with the easiest job—an oil change and filter on a Dodge SUV.

An hour into what should've been a half-hour job, Nolan snapped out of a daze to discover he was staring at the engine as he relived the amazing night with Hannah. Thinking about how it had felt to hold her and kiss her and sleep with her in his arms ran through his mind like a movie he never wanted to stop watching.

For so long, he'd thought about what it might be like to spend that kind of time with her, but the reality was much better than the fantasy. And if he continued to think about her, he'd still be here at ten o'clock tonight when he certainly had better things to do.

He buckled down and finished the oil change, rotated tires and dug into a complex transmission issue, all before noon when his so-called assistant, Skeeter, came rambling in looking like something the cat had dragged home. That thought made Nolan chuckle under his breath as the always eclectic Skeeter was known throughout Butler for putting his dead cat in his mother's freezer and forgetting about it for ten years.

"Mornin'," Skeeter grumbled. His fine white hair stood straight up, giving him the appearance of having grappled with electricity and come out on the bad end of the encounter. At just barely five foot, eight inches, he had a wiry, compact frame and a face full of broken blood vessels thanks to his love of moonshine.

"Afternoon." Nolan knew it was pointless to remind Skeeter that he'd promised to show up early in the day to deal with two cars in need of body work. No one did bodies the way Skeeter did, which was one of many reasons Nolan tolerated his flakiness. When he decided to show up, that is.

"Had to help Dude with the puppies."

The best part of Skeeter's flakiness was the wide variety of excuses he always arrived with. "What puppies?"

"Her bitch Maisy had a litter couple weeks ago. Them pups are driving poor Dude crazy with their nonstop yippin' and crappin'."

"What breed is Maisy again?"

Skeeter snorted out a laugh. "Who the fuck knows?"

"Take me to see the puppies." The words were out of his mouth before he took the time to think about what he was saying.

"Right now?"

"Yeah. Now."

"As long as you ain't gonna blame me if the work don't get done."

"Now, Skeeter, when have I *ever* blamed you for not getting your work done?"

"*Shit*," Skeeter said with a low chuckle as he spat out a stream of chewing tobacco into the parking lot. "When don-cha blame me?"

Chuckling, Nolan wiped the grease off his hands, closed the main garage doors, switched the office phone over to the answering service and locked up. When he emerged into the parking lot, he wasn't at all surprised to see Skeeter sitting in the passenger seat of his truck. He was miserly when it came to gas, hoarding the free gas Nolan gave him once in a while.

Nolan drove through town, over the one-lane covered bridge and past the huge red barn on Hells Peak Road where Hannah and her siblings had grown up. The sight of the barn spurred the memory of her parents catching them sleeping together on the sofa that morning. *So embarrassing.* Nolan hoped Mr. and Mrs. Abbott didn't think less of him, because that would truly suck. He'd always loved them and their family had given him a respite in the storm of his childhood. He would hate to lose their respect.

"Whatcha want with puppies anyhow?" Skeeter asked as Nolan navigated the twists and turns on the way to the home of Gertrude "Dude" Danforth, Skeeter's so-called girlfriend.

"A friend of mine recently lost an older dog, and she might be in the market for a puppy at some point."

"A friend, huh? Would this so-called *friend* be related in any way to Hannah Guthrie?"

Damn if the question didn't make Nolan want to fidget. He resisted the urge and shrugged in reply to the question. "Maybe."

"Heard she lost old Homer yesterday."

"Yeah."

"He was Caleb's dog, right?"

"Uh-huh."

"That's gonna be tough on Hannah."

"Uh-huh."

"You're sweet on that girl, ain'tcha?"

Nolan released a gruff laugh. *Sweet on her.* That was putting it mildly. "Something like that."

Skeeter grunted in reply, but didn't pursue the matter any further. For that, Nolan was grateful as he pulled into the long dirt driveway that led to Dude's place. The rusty wagon wheel that held up her mailbox was the only indication that anyone lived in this remote corner of Butler, and Nolan drove slowly as one never knew what creatures they'd find patrolling Dude's property.

People in town called her Snow White because of her eclectic collection of "pets," which ranged from a bombastic rooster to a domesticated raccoon to coyotes that used to run wild until Dude took them in and made them part of the family. Some believed Dude was responsible for converting Fred the Moose from a wild animal to the somewhat civilized fellow he was now. The Snow White nickname was particularly amusing once you got a load of Dude, who stood well over six feet tall and at least two feet wide. Nolan had never seen her in anything other than denim overalls, flannel shirts, shitkicker boots and a huge straw hat. Since she was never without the hat, people speculated as to whether or not she slept in it.

Nolan would've asked Skeeter if that was true, except for the idea of Skeeter sleeping with Dude wasn't something he wanted to think about, so he kept his curiosity to himself. He brought the truck to a stop next to the chicken coop where Dude was spreading feed, oblivious to her visitors.

Skeeter got out of the truck and barked out a greeting to her.

She spun around and met him at the waist-high chicken-wire fence with a warm, suggestive smile. "Back so soon, lover?"

Oh my God. Nolan's stomach turned, and his eyes darted around the cluttered yard, searching for anything to look at besides the kiss Dude was planting on Skeeter's willing lips. *Christ, have mercy.* She had to duck her head to even get to his lips. *Stop looking!*

"Nolan wants to see the pups," Skeeter explained when they came up for air.

She looked over Skeeter's shoulder at Nolan. "That right?"

Nolan nodded.

"For you?"

"For a friend."

"I need to know who before I'll consider giving one up."

"Hannah Guthrie."

"Oh," Dude said, her face softening again. "Of course. Come have a look." She stepped out of the chicken coop and led them across the yard to a barn that had a sagging roof and rusty old farm implements discarded outside. To the far left was a tractor that had seen much better days.

Maisy and her pups were inside a stall lined with wool blankets. The new mother was lying on her side as her babies climbed all over her, some of them attached to her extended teats to feed while others wrestled with their siblings. Maisy raised her head to check out the visitors, caught sight of Dude, and relaxed again.

Nolan smiled with delight at the tiny, energetic puppies. They had patches of brown, black and white, their breed impossible to determine on sight. "Any thoughts on their lineage?" Nolan asked.

"Nope," Dude replied. "Maisy is very private about her love life, so I have no idea who the daddy is. And God only knows what she is. My guess is part beagle, part shepherd, part Doberman, but I honestly haven't the first clue. She's a sweet girl though. Wonderful disposition. She's a lover, too. Very snuggly."

Mesmerized by the frenetic activity in the stall, Nolan noticed one of the puppies stood off to the side of the fray, taking it all in as his or her siblings carried on. "What's up with that guy?"

"He's a bit aloof, that one. Likes to watch the others act like asshats while he remains above it all."

The description reminded Nolan of the way Hannah was with her siblings. She was quieter than the other nine Abbotts, reserved, more likely to observe rather than seek the center of attention. "Is he spoken for?"

"Not yet."

Nolan watched the puppy as one of the others approached him, wanting to play. He nuzzled the intruder and sent him on his way with a gentle nudge that made Nolan smile. "I think Hannah would adore him." He hoped he was right about that. In truth, he had no way to know whether or not she'd welcome the puppy so soon after losing Homer.

"I'll keep him for her," Dude said. "They need another week or so with mom before I start finding homes for them."

"You'll let me know when I can come pick him up?"

"I will." She rested her hand on Nolan's arm. "It's a sweet thing you're doing for her. Every time I've lost one of my precious fur babies, I always get another one right away. I like to think I'm honoring the memory of the one I lost by giving a good home to a new friend. Your Hannah will think so, too."

At hearing Hannah called "his" Hannah, Nolan's heart skipped a happy beat even as he wondered what she'd have to say about being called "his" anything. He'd wanted her for such a long time, and after last night, he wanted her more than ever. It wasn't even the physical part, which was amazing. It was her. Just her. Being around her calmed him and completed him in a way that nothing or no one else ever could. He'd accepted that fact of his life quite some time ago, when he began to understand it would be her or no one.

"We oughta get back to work," Skeeter said, jarring Nolan from his contemplation.

The idea of Skeeter being the one to suggest they get to work was as comical as the antics of the puppies flipping over each other in a scrum of paws and tails and sharp little teeth. "Thanks for this, Dude," Nolan said with one last glance at the little fellow in the corner.

"My pleasure. I think the world of Hannah, and I hope he brings her some much-deserved happiness."

Nolan hoped so, too, because her happiness was suddenly his top priority.

CHAPTER 6

—◄•►—

Something unbelievable happened tonight . . . A
bunch of us were at the quarry. We had a fire
going and some of the boys were drinking and
getting obnoxious. I took a walk down to the
water, and Caleb followed me. He kissed me.
I mean really kissed me. He said he's been in love
with me since we were twelve and that's why he
pulled my hair. I'm so confused! It was a good
kiss. A really good kiss . . . Not that I have
anything to compare it to.

—From the diary of Hannah Abbott, age sixteen

The ride back to town was quiet, and Nolan appreciated
the silence as he pondered whether Hannah would welcome his company again tonight. He'd never been so torn about
how best to proceed, but nothing had ever been more important
or more fraught with peril. She was hesitant about moving forward with someone else after what she'd been through in the
last seven years. As Caleb's close friend, he understood that
hesitance better than most men would.

But after the night they'd spent together, Nolan didn't
know how he'd cope if she pulled back from him. A taste of her

sweetness had him completely addicted and impatient for more. He had to curb that impatience until she was ready for more. That much he knew for sure.

"Looks like the father-in-law is waiting for you," Skeeter said.

"Huh?"

"Look."

Sure enough, Lincoln Abbott's Range Rover was parked outside the garage. "Shit."

"What'd you do?"

"Nothing."

"Yet?"

"Shut up, Skeeter, and get busy fixing Mrs. Morrison's dents, will you?"

Snickering to himself—because he was the only one who found this situation funny—Skeeter got out of the truck. "Sure thing, boss man. Good luck. Let me know if you need a wingman. I gotcha back."

"Shut *up*, and go away. Far away."

"I'm going, I'm going."

As Nolan crossed the parking lot, he began to understand the way someone marching out to face a firing squad might feel. Even though he'd been close friends with Lincoln Abbott's three oldest kids as well as his late son-in-law for decades, Nolan had never approached the man as someone who was romantically interested in his beloved eldest daughter.

"Mr. Abbott," Nolan said, attempting to keep the panic out of his voice.

"Mr. Roberts."

Oh Jesus. What was that about?

"Everything okay with the Rover?"

"Everything's just fine. That's not why I'm here, and you damned well know it. Get in."

"Sir?"

Lincoln rolled his eyes. "Get in the car."

"You're not planning to take me out somewhere and shoot me, are you?"

"Do I have reason to do that?"

Nolan swallowed hard. "No. Sir." *Not yet anyway . . .* Nolan wisely kept that thought to himself.

"Get in then. I won't kill you or anything. Not this time."

"Good to know." Nolan climbed into the SUV, which smelled of leather and expensive cologne. Hannah's dad was a fan of the finer things in life, an Anglophile of the highest order, and a die-hard Beatles fan. Nolan wasn't at all surprised to hear "Let It Be" playing on the stereo. He wished he had the nerve to encourage Mr. Abbott to take the song's advice to let it be, but he'd never say such a thing to Hannah's father, especially not in his current mood.

Lincoln hit the gas, sending gravel flying on the way out of the garage parking lot.

Nolan caught Skeeter's surprised gape as they passed the open door to the bay where he was working. Hopefully, Skeeter would hold down the fort at the garage, where it seemed like nothing productive was going to happen today—or send ransom if need be. "What do I smell?" Nolan asked of a scent making his mouth water, reminding him he'd skipped breakfast in his haste to get to work—for all the good that had done him.

"Lunch."

"Oh." He had other questions, but decided it was in his best interest to keep his mouth shut. He'd begun to actively sweat by the time Lincoln pulled up to the home of his father-in-law, Elmer Stillman.

"Elmer's still on crutches, so I've got lunch duty today. Come on in."

Hannah's grandfather had sprained his ankle on a recent camping trip with Lincoln and Hannah's brothers, and Nolan had been meaning to stop by to see how Elmer was getting along. But he hadn't planned the visit to unfold quite this way. Did her grandfather know that Nolan had slept with her on the sofa last night? He hoped not, but he'd been around the Abbotts long enough to know there were few secrets in that family.

The firing squad feeling returned as he followed Lincoln into Elmer's cluttered house.

Sans crutches, Elmer hobbled into the kitchen to meet them and didn't seem one bit surprised to see Nolan. *Great . . .*

"I see you were able to convince Nolan to join us for lunch," Elmer said to his son-in-law.

"*Convince* isn't quite the word," Nolan said. "I believe *premeditated abduction* might be a better way to describe it."

Elmer's delighted guffaw made his blue eyes sparkle with mirth. He was absolutely full of the devil, and Nolan had always loved him. That is until he'd teamed up with Lincoln on this abduction—and Nolan had no doubt the two of them were in on this together. Exhibit A: Elmer had clearly been expecting both of them.

"*Abduction* is such a strong word," Elmer said. "It conjures images of criminals rather than a concerned father and grandfather."

"Fair enough," Nolan conceded as he took a seat at Elmer's round kitchen table. His mouth watered at the sight of hot pastrami as Lincoln doled out three sandwiches, which Nolan recorded as Exhibit B of their premeditation. He eyed Hannah's grandfather warily. "What do you know?"

"I was informed of where you slept last night," Elmer said, pointing his crooked index finger at Nolan.

"Of course you were."

"You, of all people, know how this family works," Lincoln said, gesturing with a handful of pastrami.

"Yes, I do, which is why I shouldn't be surprised that you two kidnapped me in the middle of a workday to put me under the hot lightbulb."

The other two men exchanged slightly guilty glances.

"We're sorry about interrupting your workday," Elmer said.

"No, you're not," Nolan said, laughing as he reached for the soda Lincoln had put in front of him.

"He's a tough one," Elmer said.

"I take it you two have pulled this crap before?"

"We may have had a conversation or two about how we might . . . assist one of the kids in a romantic sense," Lincoln said haltingly.

"You're a couple of buttinskies," Nolan concluded as another thought occurred to him. "You wouldn't have had anything to do with Hannah's nearly brand-new battery crapping out on a day when most of the family was conveniently out of town, would you?"

They took an immediate and intense interest in their sandwiches.

"You look like a couple of guilty little boys," Nolan said, charmed by their machinations on his and Hannah's behalf.

"We had to do *something* to help you out," Lincoln said. "She danced with you at the Grange and then . . . *nada*."

"How do you know that?"

"Wait, so are you saying that something *did* happen?" Elmer asked, leaning in to ensure he didn't miss anything.

"I'm certainly not telling you guys. I wouldn't want to encourage your bad behavior."

"How is it bad behavior to help things along when it's clear to everyone who knows you that you're crazy about my little girl?" Lincoln asked.

"You do know your 'little girl' is thirty-five years old, right?"

"What the heck does that have to do with anything?"

Realizing they were talking in circles, Nolan decided it was time to cut the two matchmakers a break. "Listen, boys, you know me. You've known me all my life."

"Why do you think you're here?" Elmer asked. "Why do you think we messed with her battery rather than letting Myles know that Homer wasn't doing all that great and could do with an extra house call or two?"

"What's Myles got to do with anything?" Nolan asked, utterly confused.

"Ah," Lincoln said smugly, "our young friend here has no earthly idea that he's had some competition for Hannah's affections."

"Hannah and *Myles*?" The thought of the good-looking vet being interested in Hannah struck a note of fear in Nolan's heart. "Since when?"

"Since he asked her out," Lincoln said.

"She didn't actually go out with him though." If Hannah had gone out with Myles, Nolan would've heard about it—and the news would've killed him.

"She hasn't gone out with him *yet*," Elmer said. "I wouldn't count him out. He's tall, blond, buff . . . The ladies seem to like him."

While he tried to wrap his head around Elmer's use of the word *buff*, Nolan wished he had the nerve to tell them that

Hannah never would've kissed him the way she had the night before if she were interested in someone else. However, he couldn't play that card and protect their privacy, too, so he decided to meet smug with smug. "I'm not worried about Myles."

"A wise man doesn't underestimate his rivals," Elmer said.

"Duly noted, but I don't see him as a rival. If Hannah wanted to go out with him, she would have." He glanced at Lincoln and was surprised to find steel in his normally amiable eyes. "What?"

"It sounds to me like you might have reason to be a bit *overconfident* where my daughter is concerned. Is that possible?"

"Now wait just a minute—"

"Hey, Gramps? Where are you?" Hannah's melodic voice drifted through the house, and the three men froze.

The expressions on the faces of Hannah's father and grandfather gave all-new meaning to the term *deer in headlights* and Nolan held back the overpowering urge to laugh at their discomfort.

Hannah came into the kitchen and stopped short, her sharp gaze taking in the scene at the table, and her mouth tightening with displeasure that seemed directed primarily at him. Great. That was just what he needed right as they were moving forward toward . . . something . . .

"What's going on?" Hannah asked suspiciously.

"Nothing, honey." Lincoln jumped up to kiss his daughter. "We're just having lunch."

"The three of you randomly decided to get together for lunch for the first time ever? And it just happens to be today?"

"It was the funniest thing," Elmer said. "We ran into Nolan and happened to have an extra sandwich . . ."

Her gaze landed on Nolan, seeking an explanation. It wouldn't do him any good to toss Lincoln and Elmer under the bus, but the vague sense of hurt and confusion coming from her made him want to spill the entire story to her. He would when he could, he decided. "They invited me. Can you join us?" Nolan held out a hand to her and tried not to panic when she gave his hand a long look, ignored it and slid into the fourth chair at the table.

"Have my other half," Elmer said. "I'll never be able to eat all this." He pushed the sandwich across the table to her.

"Nolan, get Hannah a 7-Up from the fridge. She knows I've always got a cold one for her."

"Thanks, Gramps," Hannah said with a warm smile for her grandfather. Apparently he'd been granted immunity.

Nolan got the soda, opened it and put it on the table in front of her.

"Thanks," she said without looking at him.

This was definitely not good. Everything in him clamored to tell her how he'd ended up at Elmer Stillman's table in the middle of the day, but the heat of her father's glare had him biting his tongue—literally.

"I'm so sorry about Homer, honey," Elmer said, covering Hannah's hand with his much bigger one. "He was a good boy, and he lived a nice long life."

"Yes, he did."

"How're you holding up?"

"I've had better days, but it helps to think of him reuniting with Caleb."

"I'm sure they're having one hell of a game of fetch up there in heaven."

"I hope so." She took a delicate bite of the oversized sandwich and a sip of her soda. "I've decided to have a funeral for Homer the way Caleb would've done."

"That's a fine idea," Elmer said.

"I spoke with Myles this morning."

Lincoln and Elmer both looked at Nolan meaningfully. He trained his face to show no emotion even though the mention of Myles's name struck a note of fear around the area of his chest that housed his heart.

"He can keep Homer until we're ready to bury him," Hannah continued, speaking primarily to her grandfather. "I wondered if you might be able to make me a box or something to bury him in."

"I'd be honored, honey. Truly."

"Thank you."

Nolan's throat closed around the lump that settled there as her quiet strength got to him the way it always did.

She chatted with her father and grandfather about the plans for Homer's funeral as she finished the sandwich and soda.

Nolan told himself it didn't matter that she never looked his way, but it did matter. It mattered greatly. By the time she stood to leave, he was in full-on panic mode. The idea that the progress they'd made the night before might be undone by her overly involved father and grandfather was unfathomable to him. "Could I hitch a ride back to town with you, Hannah? I've got to get back to work."

She still didn't look at him. "Um, sure. I guess."

Wow, this was worse than he'd thought. She was actually blaming *him* for the family powwow, as if he would've sought out the company of her father and grandfather on the same day her parents caught them sleeping together? Was she crazy? How could he fix this with her without digging a ditch for himself with Lincoln?

"Thanks for lunch," he said to Lincoln and Elmer as he got up from the table. "I think."

Lincoln gave him a pointed look that conveyed a world of expectations. "Our pleasure."

His mind racing with thoughts about what he should say to her and what he *could* say to her, Nolan followed Hannah from the house and got into the passenger seat of her SUV. "How's the car running?" he asked when they were buckled in and on their way.

"Fine."

"Hannah, listen . . . I have no idea what you're thinking right now, but I didn't initiate that lunch. You have to know that after your parents caught us together this morning, my goal today would've been to stay as far away from the men in your family as I possibly could." Was it his imagination or did her shoulders lose some of their tension?

"How did you end up there?"

"Um, well, you probably ought to ask your dad about that."

She shot him an annoyed look. "I'm asking *you*."

"Don't make me tell you."

"Man up, Nolan. You're either loyal to me or you're loyal to him. You can't have it both ways."

Nolan let out an unmanly whimper. "I can't? Really?"

"*Nolan . . .*"

"Fine! He came to the garage and basically told me to get in the car. It wasn't like I felt I had a choice or anything. He's your dad, and I didn't want to do anything to screw things up with your family when things between us are . . . you know . . ."

"What? How are things between us?"

Apparently, Hannah came by her torture skills naturally. "New and moving in the right direction, or so I thought."

She killed him with her silence. What was she thinking? Did she disagree with what he'd said? What if she did? Where did that leave them? He'd long ago accepted his feelings for her were going to either make his life complete or be the death of him. At the moment, he couldn't say which outcome was more likely.

Hannah pulled into the station and kept the car running as she stared straight ahead.

Nolan cleared his throat and tried to think of something he could say—anything to break the uneasy silence. "I owe you dinner at the Mexican place in Stowe. Want to go tonight?"

"I'll have to let you know. I'm supposed to see Cameron at some point today about a project we're working on. I don't know yet when she's available."

He wanted to ask about the project. He wanted to know everything about her. But he decided to quit while he was ahead. "I'll call you when I'm done here. It might be a bit late since I've had a few distractions today."

"Okay."

"Hannah?"

"Yes?"

"Will you look at me?"

She took her own sweet time complying with his request. The uncertainty he saw in her gaze was like a spike to his heart.

He couldn't resist the need to touch her. His hand cupped her cheek, and he was filled with relief when she tipped her head toward his hand, her eyes closing on a sigh.

She licked her lips. "Nolan . . ."

"Hmm?" The slide of her tongue over her bottom lip made him hard.

Her eyes opened slowly and locked on his. "I'm a very private person."

"I know that."

"I wouldn't appreciate you talking about what happens between us with anyone else."

"I never would. Do you believe me?"

She nodded, and her gaze dropped to his mouth.

Goddamn, she was annihilating him with her eyes and lips as the desire to kiss her overtook him. "Hannah . . ."

"Not here."

"Come inside. Just for a minute. Please?"

She held his gaze for the longest moment of his entire life before she raised her hand to the key and turned the engine off.

CHAPTER 7

God, I'm so in love with Caleb Guthrie. How did this happen? We've waited a long time to you know . . . do IT. This weekend, we're going to tour some colleges, and we're going to stay in a hotel together. (Our parents think we're staying with friends. We told a lot of lies to pull this off . . .) I'm so scared, but SO ready. We're both interested in UVM, but we're checking out Maine and New Hampshire, too, because they're farther away and require an overnight stay.☺

—From the diary of Hannah Abbott, age seventeen

Nolan was out of the SUV so fast he almost tripped over his own feet in his haste to open her door.

"Hey, boss," Skeeter called from the bay on the far left side of the garage where he did his bodywork.

"Not now."

"But—"

"*Not now!*"

"Well, alrighty then."

Hannah laughed softly as he took her hand and half dragged her into the main reception area on the far right side of the building. He led her around the counter and into his office, closing the door behind them. Spinning around to face her, he found her looking up at him expectantly.

Nolan wished he'd brought her somewhere classier than his dirty garage, but desperate times called for dirty garages. He backed her up to the closed door, and her hands landed on his chest. All he could see were her sweet, pink lips, and he had to remind himself to take it slow.

Then her hand curled around his nape to drag him down to her, taking the lead in what quickly became the hottest, most sensual kiss he'd ever experienced. When her tongue darted into his mouth, he forgot all about going slow. He cupped her bottom and lifted her right off her feet, groaning when she wrapped her legs around his waist and pressed her heated core against his throbbing erection.

The phone rang, and he ignored it. Skeeter called for him, and he ignored him. A huge crash sounded from the garage, and he ignored it. His world had been reduced to the sweet taste of Hannah's lips, the erotic tangle of her tongue with his, the heat between her legs and the tug of her fingers in his hair.

He could drop dead right now, and he'd go happy. Except he'd never do that to her after what she'd already endured. Nolan planned to live a good long time so he could kiss her this way every single day of what was left of both their lives.

The rumble of voices right outside the door had him reluctantly ending the kiss. He leaned his forehead against hers, both of them breathing hard.

"He's in there," Skeeter said. "I don't know what he's doing, but I wouldn't bother him right now if I was you."

"I'd like to see him," a familiar voice said. "I'll wait."

Nolan let out a moan when he realized Hannah's twin brother was out there. "This day gets better and better."

"Is my sister in there with him?" Hunter asked.

"Um, I don't know nothin'," Skeeter said. "I'm just the hired help."

Nolan was going to kill him the second he got the chance.

Hannah began to giggle uncontrollably, and Nolan decided right then and there that whatever abuse the Abbott family intended to toss his way was worth it if it made her laugh harder than he'd seen her laugh in more than seven years.

"I'm glad you're enjoying this," he muttered, taking another kiss while he could.

"I'm sorry. They're totally out of control."

"You said it, not me." He held her hips until she was standing. When she reached for the door, he stopped her. "Not yet."

"Why not? You know Hunter. He's not going anywhere until he gets what he came for."

"And what's that? A piece of my hide?"

"Perhaps," she said with a coy grin that got his motor racing all over again.

"Are you enjoying this?"

"It is kinda funny. You have to admit it."

"No, I don't."

"Can I open the door?"

"Not yet."

"You never said why."

"Do I really have to spell it out for you?"

Her eyes traveled over him, stopping abruptly when they landed on the bulge in the front of his pants. "Oh. *Oh*."

"Don't do that. You're not helping anything."

"What am I doing?"

"You're looking at it."

She rolled her lip between her teeth as if she was trying not to laugh again.

He furrowed his brows in annoyance. "Don't you dare laugh."

"I wouldn't dream of it." She moved toward him, and Nolan took a step back out of self-preservation.

He bumped up against his desk, which was covered with discarded coffee cups and paperwork he hoped to get to before the next millennium. "Hannah, knock it off. Your brother is on the other side of that door, and if I know him, he's got his ear pressed against it listening to everything we're saying."

"Before I go, I just wanted to say . . . thanks."

The incredibly sweet way she looked at him as she said that didn't help his "condition." He cleared his throat. "For what?"

"For being a good sport, for putting up with my family and for that kiss against the door, which was amazing."

"It was pretty good, wasn't it?"

She smiled as she nodded, and then she surprised the living

shit out of him when she leaned in and pressed her lips softly and chastely against his. "I'll see you later."

His head was still spinning when she casually walked through the door, as if she hadn't just rocked his world. And then he came out of the fog to realize Hunter was still out there, talking to his sister at the moment and no doubt here to add to the Abbott family day of torture. Nolan scrambled around the desk and sat, grateful for the barrier between his raging erection and his old friend, who also happened to be Hannah's insanely over-protective twin.

He picked up a pen and pretended to be interested in the invoice from the company that provided gas to the station, which he really needed to pay one of these days, and was still staring blankly at it when Hunter strolled in and shut the door. As usual, he looked like he'd just stepped out of an issue of *GQ* magazine. He was on the receiving end of an endless amount of abuse from their group of friends for his snappy style sense, but Hunter took it all in stride and ignored the bullshit. Nolan had always admired that about him and considered Hunter and Will Abbott among his closest friends.

But one look at his old pal told him today's visit was anything but a social call.

"What can I do for you, Hunter?"

Hunter eyed the visitor chair in Nolan's office and wisely refrained from sitting. Some substances even the best of dry cleaners couldn't remove from twill trousers. "I'd like to know what's going on between you and my sister."

"Don't mince words."

"Why bother when we both know why I'm here."

"I'm trying to figure out why you feel it's any of your business."

As expected, Hunter's dark eyes narrowed with anger. "Are you seriously asking me that?"

"Yeah, I am. You know me, Hunter. Do you think I'd ever do anything to hurt her? In a million years, do you think I'm capable of that?"

Hunter blew out a deep breath. "I don't think you'd hurt her intentionally."

Nolan held his steady gaze, refusing to back down.

"Does she know about the racing?"

The question caught him off guard. It was about the last thing Nolan expected him to say. "I don't know. We haven't talked about it, but that doesn't mean she hasn't heard about it."

"She hasn't."

"How do you know that?"

"Because if she knew, she wouldn't have been making out with you in your office just now."

"We weren't making out."

Hunter rolled his eyes. "Get real. No one knows her better than I do, and all I had to do was take one look at bright eyes, swollen lips and pink cheeks to put three and three together to get making out."

Nolan absolutely refused to blink. He wouldn't give Hunter the satisfaction.

"Nothing to say to that, huh?"

Nolan shrugged. "I wouldn't dare pretend to know her better than you do."

"You have to tell her about the racing."

"Why is that so important to you?"

"Because she needs all the facts before she gets too far down the road with you. She needs to know about your so-called hobby."

"It's more than a hobby, Hunter. You know that." Their stock car team raced in a recreational league and had attracted the attention of a few sponsors. They had the potential to reach the next level but only if everyone on the team was committed. Nolan was as committed to the team as he was to anything in his life, but Hunter's concerns had given him pause.

"I do, and that's exactly why you need to tell her. She's had enough loss in her life. If she's going to date a guy who gets off on driving in two-hundred-mile-an-hour circles just for fun, she needs to know about the risk she's taking."

"It's not a risk. You know how safety conscious my whole team is. I've been at this for years, and I know what I'm doing."

"You haven't been *driving* for years. I'm well aware of how good you are, but she knows nothing about it. She couldn't be more removed from such things if she tried, so you have to tell her."

"Not yet."

"Soon. Before this goes too much further."

"You won't say anything before I do, will you?"

"Not if you do it soon."

"I don't appreciate being bullied into telling her something I'm not ready to tell her."

"I'm not bullying you, Nolan. I'm looking out for my sister who's already suffered through a lifetime's worth of grief. That's all I'm doing."

"Fair enough."

"For what it's worth, I like you two together. You'd be great for her, but you've got to come clean about the racing. She deserves to know what she's getting herself into."

"I understand, but I need some time."

"A week. You've got a week to tell her, or I will."

Even though the ultimatum made him angry, he couldn't argue with the rationale behind it. Hunter loved his sister and didn't want to see her hurt. Nolan felt the same way about Hannah, and what Hunter said made sense even if it scared the living shit out of him. He couldn't see Hannah sticking around for long after she found out what he did for fun when he wasn't working.

Satisfied that he'd made his point, Hunter turned to leave.

"Hunter."

He turned back to face Nolan.

"We both want the same thing, you know. We want to see her happy again."

Hunter nodded and stepped out of the office, closing the door behind him.

For a long time after he left, Nolan stared at the classic Mustang calendar from two years ago that was pinned on the wall. He knew Hunter was right, but he couldn't picture himself telling Hannah the truth about his racing obsession. Not yet anyway.

Hunter left the garage feeling oddly out of sorts. Earlier in the day, his dad had told him what'd happened at Hannah's that morning. For once, his father wasn't being gossipy. He was concerned about Hannah and wanted Hunter's take on her and Nolan.

It didn't bother Hunter that she'd spent the night with Nolan. He loved Nolan. They all did. There wasn't a more stand-up guy to be found anywhere. He was a good friend, fun to be with, loyal to the end and as trustworthy as all hell, even if he'd always been a bit secretive and closed-mouthed about his dysfunctional family. All that said, Hannah was his sister, his twin, his closest confidant, and Hunter would do harm to anyone who caused her a moment of pain—friend or not.

After his conversation with Nolan, Hunter had intended to go back to work but found himself heading toward the diner instead. He was nothing if not a glutton for punishment. As he pushed open the door, he immediately sought her out, his gaze homing in on her as she poured coffee at one of the booths and then turned to face him.

The impact of that face, those eyes, the high cheekbones, the bow-shaped pink lips, the long ponytail of dark blonde hair, the full breasts hit him like a punch to the gut every damned time.

"Oh Hunter," she said. "I was hoping you'd stop in today. I need to talk to you."

It took a second for his tongue to untie itself so he could reply to her. She wanted to talk to *him*? And why oh why did his foolish heart have to stand up and do a happy dance all because Megan Kane was happy to see *him* for once? Right in that moment, Hunter actively hated himself and his pathetic dancing heart, but he took a seat in the booth Megan gestured to and waited for her to pour him a cup of coffee.

"I'm taking a break," she called to her sister, Nina, who owned the place with her husband, Brett.

"Sure, no problem," Nina replied, waving to Hunter.

Megan slid into the booth across from Hunter.

He got busy stirring cream into his coffee—anything to keep from staring at the creamy complexion and big blue eyes that haunted his dreams night after night after night. While he was feeling hateful, he added his subconscious to the list of things he hated about himself.

"I have to know if it's true," Megan said, her tone full of urgency that immediately put Hunter on alert.

"If what's true?"

"That woman, the one from New York . . ."

"Cameron?" he asked, suddenly not liking where this was heading. "What about her?"

"Tell me she's not really moving in with him."

The utter devastation on Megan's face stunned him. If this whole thing weren't so ridiculous, it would be funny. Here he was crazy about a woman who was crazy about his brother who was crazy about someone else altogether. Funny, right? Yeah, not so much . . .

"Megan . . ." As much as he wanted her for himself, he didn't have it in him to break her heart. "What am I supposed to say?"

"So she *is* moving in with him."

"Yes."

Her sharp gasp and the immediate flood of tears made him feel helpless. "Thank you for telling me the truth." She attempted a stoic expression that failed miserably. "I just don't get what he sees in her. They have absolutely nothing in common."

Hunter had no clue how to reply. Did he dare attempt to spell out what Will saw in Cameron, or was he better off saying nothing? Before he could decide, she continued.

"I mean, I guess she's not ugly or anything."

Hunter choked on his coffee. Cameron was gorgeous and funny and warm and loving and fascinated by the Abbott clan as well as their business. He'd never seen his younger brother so happy or more in love.

"I want to understand, but I can't. She swoops into town and next thing we know he's totally *gone* on her? What do we even know about her other than the fact that her dad is totally loaded? Is that what he wants in a woman?"

Hunter could no longer hold his silence. "That has nothing at all to do with it, Megan. She doesn't live off her father's money, not that it's any of your business or even mine. Why does anyone love anyone?"

Her eyes nearly bugged out of her head. "He *loves* her? Like he's *told* you that?"

Hunter wanted to shoot himself for throwing that grenade into the conversation. "Not in so many words, but it's pretty obvious to all of us that he's . . . you know . . ."

"What?" she asked in barely more than a whisper.

"In love. Deeply in love."

Moaning, she dropped her head into her hands. "Why *her*? Why not me? What did I do wrong?"

He was stuck in the middle of a nightmare of his own making with no escape plan. "You didn't do anything wrong. Sometimes things just happen, and there's no explaining why."

She glanced up at him with a tear-stained face that killed him. As far as he knew, other than a random encounter years ago when they were right out of high school, Will had never encouraged her affections nor had he ever led her on. His brother's lack of interest hadn't deterred Megan from carrying the proverbial torch all these years. "Thank you for being honest with me. I appreciate it."

"I'm sorry it wasn't what you wanted to hear."

She shrugged. "I suppose I'll have to get used to it if she's actually moving here and he's in love with her."

The idea struck him out of nowhere and was pouring from his mouth before he could question the wisdom. "You know what might make you feel better? If you went out with someone else." To his knowledge, she hadn't dated anyone else in all the years she'd held out hope that Will might one day change his mind about her.

"How would that help?"

"It might get your mind off Will and give you something fun to do."

"I don't know. Maybe. I'll think about it."

He swallowed hard and went for it before he could talk himself out of it. "I'd be happy to take you to dinner sometime. Any time. You tell me when." Oh my God! Could he sound any more pathetic?

"That's really nice of you, Hunter, but I don't want your pity. I'm not that desperate. Not yet anyway."

Staring at her, his mouth agape, he tried to get his spinning brain to form the words. "I don't pity you," he said, sputtering. "That's not it at all."

She shook her head. "I appreciate the offer, but I can't see how it would be a good idea for me to go out with Will's brother to get my mind off him. You understand I'm sure."

He understood a little too well. She'd never go out with him because of who he was to Will. Awesome. "Sure." Hunter tossed a five-dollar bill on the table. "I understand perfectly, but con-sider it a standing offer if you should change your mind."

As he got up, she pushed the five across the table to him. "The coffee is on me."

While she was still focused on the money, he said, "I don't pity you, Megan. Not even a little bit." Filled with despair, he left the bill on the table, walked out of the diner and crossed the street to return to his office above the store, all the while thinking it might be time to take his own advice and go out with someone else.

Except the only one he seemed to want wanted his brother.

Sometimes life was truly a bitch.

CHAPTER 8

———◄•►———

*How did I spend so much time hating Caleb
when he was capable of that?!? Oh my God, it was
AMAZING! My friends told me it would be
awful and it would hurt and all this other
dreadful stuff, but I must've picked the right guy
because it was none of those things. If we both live
to be 102, I'll never forget our first time together.
I'm buying a new, bigger lock for the box where
I keep my diary. If any of my annoying brothers
ever found this, my life would be over.*

—From the diary of Hannah Abbott, age seventeen

Hannah's lips tingled for thirty minutes after she left Nolan and the garage. That was how long it took to drive to Caleb's parents' home on the other side of Butler Mountain. Her emotions were taking her on a wild ride today—the excitement of her new relationship with Nolan, her despair over Homer's loss, the lingering pain brought on by her dream about Caleb, the tinge of shame at being caught sleeping on the sofa with Nolan.

It didn't matter that she was thirty-five years old or that she'd been married and widowed before she was thirty. All that mattered was that her parents had discovered them together long before they were ready for people to know there was something to be discovered.

With hindsight it was clear that she should've known better than to let him stay, even with his truck tucked in her garage, away from Butler's prying eyes. But it had felt so damned good to be held and kissed by him, to be comforted at her time of loss by someone who'd loved her husband almost as much as she had.

There was also some guilt mixed into the emotional mess. Yes, she felt guilty for the way she'd kissed Nolan, not only last night but just now, too. She'd practically jumped all over him like a bitch in heat, rather than the respectable widow people in town knew her to be.

Respectable widow. Were there any two words that conjured a more boring image of a woman in her mid-thirties who was just figuring out that she was, in fact, still very much alive, despite her unbearable loss? What if she no longer wished to be a respectable widow? She'd grown to despise the word *widow* and all it conveyed.

Kissing Nolan was the most exciting thing to happen to her in years, and she couldn't wait to do it again, even if it made her feel guilty to move on from the husband she'd planned to love forever.

As she arrived at the Guthries' tidy Cape Cod–style home, she told herself this wasn't the time to be thinking about moving on or other men. While she might have that option, Caleb's parents and brother would never get to move on with someone else, because they couldn't replace him.

A horrible thought occurred to her as she parked the SUV and turned off the engine. Was that what she was doing? Was she *replacing* him? The thought brought tears to her eyes for there was no replacing Caleb Guthrie. He'd been one of a kind, a bright light in all their lives who'd been taken from them far too soon. But as much as she might wish otherwise, he was gone and he wasn't coming back. Spending time with Nolan wasn't wrong if it made her feel happy again. Caleb would've wanted that for her, or at least she hoped so.

They'd never discussed what she should do if he didn't come back from the war, because he'd absolutely refused to acknowledge the possibility that something could happen to him, which was fine with her. That kind of reality was one she had absolutely no interest in until it was thrust upon her suddenly and violently on a soft, sweet May day almost seven years ago.

This time of year always brought back the pain of that day. Every time the forsythia bloomed, she was forced to remember something she'd much rather forget. But just as she couldn't bring him back, she also couldn't forget the grief or the agony she'd endured for years. Maintaining that level of grief was exhausting.

She'd always been a happy person, content with the little things in life. Joy had come easily to her until Caleb's death snuffed out the joy and everything else that made her feel young and alive. Being with Nolan made her feel joyful again. He made her feel hopeful, which was another emotion she'd done without for far too long.

A knock on her window startled her.

Her brother-in-law, Gavin, grinned at her. Since he lost the big brother he'd worshiped, his grin didn't light up his eyes the way it used to.

Happy to see him, Hannah opened the door and let Gavin hold it for her while she gathered her bag and the item she'd brought for her in-laws.

"Caught you woolgathering," Gavin said, kissing her cheek. Like his brother, he was tall and muscular and wore his dark curly hair much longer than their army officer father preferred. His jaw was covered in scruff, and as always, his startling resemblance to Caleb filled her with yearning.

"Good to see you, Gav." She hugged him and held on a bit longer than she probably should have. They'd been to hell and back together and had struggled to maintain their close friendship after Caleb died. Whenever they were together, they were reminded of who was missing. "It's been a while."

"I know. I'm sorry. Things have been hectic."

"Don't be sorry. I know all about hectic."

"I feel so awful about Homer. That news hit me like a ton of bricks when my parents called last night."

"I'm sure it did. It was a tough night." She glanced up at the handsome face so similar to her husband's that she'd had trouble looking at him for a long time after she lost Caleb. "I dreamed about him reuniting with Caleb."

Gavin crossed his arms and looked down, but Hannah saw the muscle pulsing in his cheek that gave away his raw emotions. "I bet that was some reunion."

"Nolan suggested we do what Caleb would've done and have a big over-the-top Sultans funeral for Homer."

He looked up, the smile stretching across his face so much like his brother's that Hannah had to look away. "I love it. That's exactly what we need to do."

"We're hoping to do it next weekend. You can come, right?"

"I wouldn't miss it."

"Good." She hesitated before she said, "Do you think, maybe, you could say a few words about Homer and what he meant to Caleb and to the rest of us?"

"I'd be honored. Thanks for asking me." Gavin hugged her again. "I came over to check on my folks in light of everything . . . But I gotta get back to work." He owned a logging company that had been very successful in recent years. Caleb would be so proud of the brother who was only eleven months younger than him—his "Irish twin" as their mother had liked to say. The two of them had been as close as any two brothers could possibly be, and his grief had been difficult to bear.

"How are they?" Hannah asked, eyeing the well-kept two-story brick house with trepidation.

"Hanging in. Just like the rest of us. What else can we do?"

What else could they do indeed? "I'll see you next weekend, Gav."

He kissed her cheek. "I'll be there."

Hannah waved to him as he backed his big pickup out of the driveway and drove off. She took a deep breath of the cool early-spring air and headed for the mudroom door at the house where she'd been treated like a member of the family since the day she started dating Caleb. "Hello," she called out, trying for a cheerful tone even though walking into that house was like a punch to the gut every single time.

"In here, honey," Amelia called from the family room. On most days, Amelia could be found in her comfortable recliner, needlepoint or knitting needles in hand. Today, however, she gazed out the window that overlooked the mountain in the distance. "This is a nice surprise." She raised her plump cheek to Hannah's kiss. "You and Gav in the same afternoon."

The walls of the family room were covered with pictures of Caleb and Gavin. A shadowbox containing Caleb's medals was the focal point of a wall devoted to his military career. The picture of him in uniform, a fierce expression on his lean face, never failed to stir Hannah's emotions.

"We're both on the same wavelength." Hannah tore her gaze from the picture she didn't have at home. It was a painful reminder of how and why she'd lost him.

"Today hasn't been the best day I ever had," Amelia said.

"I had a feeling that might be the case." She thought about the item she had in her purse that she'd intended to give Caleb's parents, but now she wasn't so sure.

Perceptive as always, Amelia said, "What's on your mind, hon?"

"I've come from seeing Myles Johansen, and he gave me Homer's collar. I thought you might like to have it." She retrieved the worn brown leather collar from her purse.

Amelia's eyes filled with tears as she took the collar from Hannah. "That's very sweet of you. Are you sure you want to part with it?"

"I'm not really parting with it as long as you have it."

Amelia ran her fingers over leather that had gone smooth with age. "That's true. We'll keep it safe and treasure it."

Hannah shared a smile with the woman who'd been like a second mother to her. "We've decided to throw a big old Sultans funeral for Homer."

"What a wonderful idea! Caleb would love that."

"I thought so, too. We're doing it next weekend. I hope you and Bob can come."

"Of course we will. It'll be so great to see everyone."

It was always great to see everyone when the Sultans came together, but there was always someone missing, too, and that made the boisterous gatherings particularly difficult for Hannah. But she kept up the tradition because his friends had been so very important to Caleb, and she couldn't imagine not doing it.

"Are you okay, honey? You know how Bob and I worry about you."

"I'm sad about Homer, but it's comforting to think of him with Caleb, wrestling and chasing balls and doing all the stuff they loved to do together."

Amelia's lips formed a small smile. "I've been thinking about that all day. How happy Caleb must've been to see his buddy."

"I should get going and at least try to get some work done today," Hannah said as she rose.

"Bob will be sorry he missed you and Gavin. He ran to the store to get something for dinner."

"Tell him I said hello, and I'll see you both soon."

Amelia stood to hug Hannah, both of them holding on longer than they normally did. When Amelia pulled back from the embrace, her eyes were full of tears. "I'm so sorry, Hannah. I'm a mess today. I keep thinking it'll get easier, but it never really does." She swiped at the tears as if they irritated her. "I don't have to tell you. You're one of the few people who truly understands what it's been like to lose him."

"Losing Homer is bound to set us back a bit." Hannah wished she could find a way to adequately comfort Caleb's mom.

"No matter how much time goes by, it never gets any better. Even when I'm enjoying myself I feel guilty because Caleb is still gone. If he can't enjoy himself anymore what right do I have to enjoy anything?"

Hannah was hit with a pang of fear over what might become of her close, warm bond with Caleb's parents and brother when they learned she was seeing Nolan.

Would they approve? Would they be disappointed? Would they think less of her for moving on from their son? As if she'd ever truly move on . . .

"Don't mind me." Amelia forced a smile. "You don't need to be weighted down by my woes. You've got enough of your own."

"You can always talk to me. You know that."

"I do, and you're a dear. Bob and I say all the time that we never would've survived without you and Gavin. We couldn't love a daughter of our own any more than we love you."

Hannah hugged Amelia again. "I love you, too."

The gnawing fear stayed with Hannah all the way home, growing and multiplying into full-fledged panic and regret over what she'd done with Nolan. She had no right to be with him if it could potentially hurt people she loved so dearly—people who'd certainly had enough pain and suffering for one lifetime.

She could love again, even marry again if she chose to, but they could never replace the son and brother they had lost. The loss had united the four of them over the last seven years, and they'd drawn strength from each other as they coped with their overwhelming grief. At times, Hannah had turned to them rather than her own family to get her through a tough time, and the thought of losing their respect was unimaginable.

Acutely aware of Homer's absence in the big, lonely house, Hannah lit the fire and curled up on the sofa in the sitting room. All thoughts of work were abandoned as her brain spun out of control with worries and fears and doubts. When Cameron called, Hannah let it go to voicemail. As much as she wanted to see Cameron and dig into their project, she didn't have it in her tonight to be cheerful or upbeat.

And when Nolan knocked on the door and called out to her, knowing she was home because her car was in the driveway, tears rolled down her cheeks as she forced herself to stay on the sofa. It was the right thing to do.

She wasn't ready after all. Not even close.

Nolan stood outside Hannah's door for a long time, trying to figure out what he should do. He knew she was in there, and all he could think about was how she'd left the garage in high spirits earlier after kissing him with abandon. What had happened in the hours since then? Was she upset about Homer? If so, he wanted to be there for her and help her through her grief.

Or had she changed her mind about them?

Last night, he'd opened the door and called for her when she didn't answer, but they'd had solid plans then. Tonight, they didn't, so he didn't feel right going in to look for her, especially if she'd decided she wanted to be alone.

He sat on the porch, his feet on the stair below, and ran his hand over his freshly shaved face, feeling like a fool now for the way he'd rushed home to shower and shave before he came to her. And he'd blown off yet another meeting with his racing team to see her tonight.

After several minutes of contemplation, he got up from the porch and went to his truck, where he kept a cell phone for emergencies when out on road calls. Sometimes it had service, but most of the time it didn't. He hoped for a miracle as he powered up the phone and searched for Hannah's number in his contacts. The phone rang and rang before her voicemail picked up.

"Hey, Hannah, it's me Nolan." Could he sound any stupider? He cleared his throat. "I'm outside, and I'm worried about you. Anyway, well, I'll try you again later."

Shaking his head at the lame message, he found Hunter's work number in the contacts. Even though Hunter was about the last person Nolan wanted to speak to after their confrontation earlier in the day, he was the one Hannah would most want if something had happened to upset her.

"This is Hunter." He sounded brusque and busy and maybe a bit frazzled.

"It's Nolan."

"Oh hey. I didn't recognize the number."

"I never use this phone. I'm at Hannah's. Her car is in the driveway, but she's not answering."

"Did it occur to you that she's not answering because she doesn't want to see you?"

Nolan held back the flash of anger that ripped through him. "Yeah, it occurred to me, except the last time I was with her, she very much wanted to see me, if you catch my drift."

"I'd rather not catch your drift, if it's just the same to you."

"Hunter, I'm worried about her. I don't know what to do. She's been in a better place lately, or so it seemed, and now with Homer and everything . . . I'm worried."

"I'll be right there."

"Thanks." Nolan returned the phone to the glove box and was leaning against the truck when Hunter pulled up a few minutes later in the tricked out silver Lincoln Navigator SUV that was so *him*. Hunter Abbott was a classy dude, right down to the soles of his Italian leather loafers. He'd always been a little too good for their Podunk town, not that he put on airs or anything like that. He was just a cut above the rest of them.

Nolan pushed off his truck and went over to meet Hunter. "I'll take off now that you're here."

"Don't go yet."

"Why not?"

Hunter jammed his hands in the pockets of his coat and eyed the big gray and blue Victorian with an air of trepidation. "Whatever's going on, it might help to have you here."

"Why?" Nolan wasn't intentionally trying to irritate Hunter. He honestly had no idea where Hunter was going with this line of reasoning.

Hunter continued to stare at Hannah's big dark house. "When she came out of your office today, she was smiling in a way I haven't seen in a very long time." He pulled his gaze off the house and looked at Nolan. "I liked seeing her that way."

"What way?"

"Happy. Lighthearted. Young. We're still young, you know? She's been through so damn much. I want her to be happy again, and if you make her happy . . . Just stay, would you?"

As if he'd ever leave after hearing that. "Yeah."

Hunter nodded and went up the walkway to the stairs. Unlike Nolan, he didn't knock. Rather he went right in and closed the door behind him.

Nolan returned to his perch against his truck, resigned to wait for as long as it took. He wasn't going anywhere.

CHAPTER 9

—◄●►—

*Hunter, Caleb and I are going to share an
apartment at the University of Vermont. I feel
sort of sorry for Hunter. He's calling himself our
"chaperone." Caleb and I want to be in bed
together all the time. Hunter is never going to
speak to us again.*

—From the diary of Hannah Abbott, age eighteen

The dark house was a somber reminder of a time Hunter
would much rather forget. Hannah had kept the house
dark for weeks after she got the news about Caleb, as if letting
in the light would be too painful.

He stepped into the sitting room, where the fire's glow was
the only light to be found in the house. "Hannah?" She was
curled up on the sofa asleep, her face streaked with tears that
made him ache. What had happened since she emerged from
Nolan's office with high color in her cheeks and a shine to her
eyes? He sat next to her on the sofa and rested his hand on her
shoulder. "Hannah?"

Her eyes opened slowly, taking him in. "Hey. What're you
doing here?"

"Nolan called. He was worried when you didn't answer
the door."

"Oh." Her mouth tightened, and her eyes closed as if she were remembering something painful.

"What's wrong, Han?"

"Nothing."

"You know there's no point in lying to me."

"I don't want to talk about it. I'm tired."

Hunter kicked off his shoes and moved to the other end of the sofa, propping his feet on the coffee table.

"What're you doing?"

"Getting comfortable."

"You must have better things to do than watch me sleep."

"I gotta few things to do, but I'm not leaving you here alone when you're clearly upset about something that's keeping you from spending time with the guy outside who's crazy about you."

Her eyes widened and brightened at that news. "He's still here?"

"He's still here."

"But . . ." She sagged into the sofa. "You should tell him to go."

"Why, Hannah?" he asked gently.

Staring into the fire, she ran her hand over the chenille throw that covered her legs. "Because this . . . With him . . . It can't happen."

"Why not?"

"Because."

"I saw you today after you were with him in the office. You were as happy as I've seen you in a really long time. What happened since then?"

She stared into the fire, her eyes shiny with unshed tears.

"Talk to me, Han. Get it off your chest. Whatever it is, we'll figure it out like we always do."

Turning to face him, she smiled faintly. "What would I do without you?"

"You'll never have to find out."

"Don't make promises you can't keep."

"Hannah . . ."

She rolled her bottom lip between her teeth and released it along with a shuddering sigh. "I saw Gavin and Amelia this afternoon."

"Oh."

"Yeah."

"Did they say something that upset you?"

"No, nothing like that. You know how wonderful they are to me. I was just . . . I got to thinking . . ."

"About?"

Hannah focused on her fingers, which were clutched together in her lap. "There's no replacing Caleb."

"Is that what you think you'd be doing with Nolan?" he asked as gently as he possibly could. His heart raced and a lump lodged in his throat as he got a better idea of what was on her mind.

She shook her head. "No. But it's just now occurring to me that I could fall in love again. With Nolan, perhaps, or someone else . . . At some point. But Caleb's parents and Gavin . . . They can't go out and get themselves another son or brother."

"They'd never begrudge your happiness with someone else. They love you. They want you to be happy."

"Intellectually, I know that. But emotionally . . . The four of us share an unfortunate bond, and that bond has been a source of enormous comfort to me over the years, and to them, too, I suppose. It would kill me if I did anything to hurt them or cause them more pain than they've already had."

Hunter dropped his feet to the floor and reached for his sister. "Come here."

She curled into his side, her head resting on his chest.

He put his arms around her and held her tight. "You're my hero, you know that?" When she shook her head and began to protest, he said, "Shut up, and listen to me."

Her muffled laugh was followed shortly by a sniffle.

"You've been so amazingly strong through this whole thing."

"Not always."

"For the most part. We all admire you so much. You have no idea how much, and there's nothing any one of us—Caleb's family included—want more than to see you happy and smiling again. It's what Caleb would want, too. I knew him as well as I know anyone, and I can say without a single hesitation that your happiness was the most important thing in his life."

"I miss him so much," she whispered. "All the time."

"I know, honey. We all do."

"I'm afraid I'm going to hurt Nolan."

"He's a big boy, and he knows what he's getting into—better than most guys would. He was there. He loved Caleb, too, and he's painfully aware of what you've lost." Hunter paused before he added, "I think you'll hurt him more if you never give him a chance."

She blew out a shaky deep breath. "What will people say if I'm with him?"

"Who the fuck cares what they say?"

Even though his vehemence made her laugh, she said, "I do."

"They'll say how lucky Hannah Guthrie is to have such a nice guy interested in her. People think the world of him in this town. Your family thinks the world of him. Caleb's family thinks the world of him. You know what people say about him?"

"I've heard a few things."

"Then you know he has a reputation for being super honest in his dealings with customers. If you bring your car in for brakes and it doesn't need brakes, he doesn't do it just because he could make an easy buck. He calls you and says, 'This car doesn't need brakes. You've got another year or so before you need to worry about that.'"

"Sounds like him."

"That's who he is, and it's one of many reasons I've decided he may be good enough for my sister."

Hannah laughed as he'd hoped she would. "*May* be good enough?"

"He'll still have to prove himself worthy of you, which is up to you to decide, but I'll be keeping a close eye on him as will all the other men in your life."

"I wouldn't have it any other way."

"Do you feel any better?"

"Yes, but I'm still scared."

"Of what?"

"Of hurting him, of falling for him, of really letting go of Caleb. I worry I'll lower my defenses and something will happen to him like it did to Caleb. I don't know if I could go through that again. I was lucky to survive it the first time."

Thinking of the "hobby" Nolan hadn't yet shared with Hannah, Hunter tightened his grip on her shoulder. "I never said there wasn't any risk involved, but I suppose you have to decide if the risk is worth the potential payoff. Judging from what I saw earlier today, it seems like it might be worth the risk."

She was quiet for a long time, and he wondered what she was thinking about but didn't ask.

"He's really waiting outside?"

"He really is. He's worried about you."

Hannah raised her head off his chest and leaned in to kiss his cheek. "Thank you—for this and a million other things."

He forced a smile even as the sight of her tear-stained face broke his heart. She didn't give in to tears very often, and he'd give everything he had to spare her another minute of pain or sorrow. "That's what older and wiser twin brothers are for."

Rolling her eyes, she snorted with laughter. "You never forget those three minutes you've got on me, do you?"

"Nope, and I never will."

"Love you best of all," she whispered the way they had as children when their siblings would drive them crazy and they'd take refuge with each other. They hadn't said the words in ages.

He blinked rapidly to keep from bawling his head off. "Love you best of all, too, Hannah Banana. How about I go let poor Nolan in from the cold?"

Smiling at his childhood nickname for her, she nodded.

"I'll call you tomorrow." He kissed her cheek and pushed his feet into his shoes.

"Hunter?"

"Yeah?"

"You really ought to take some of your own advice one of these days."

As the image of Megan's shattered face danced through his mind, he shrugged off the comment with a cavalier grin. "I'd much rather give it than take it." Her smile stayed with him as he walked out the front door and found Nolan right where he'd left him—leaning against his truck.

"Everything okay?" Nolan asked, straightening as Hunter approached.

"It will be. With time and patience."

"I've got plenty of both I'm happy to share with her."

"You have to tell her about the racing. Not tonight, but soon."

"I know."

Hunter nodded, satisfied his sister was in good hands.

"I'll take good care of her."

"If I didn't already know that, we wouldn't be having this conversation, and I certainly wouldn't be sending you in there to her."

Nolan stood up a little straighter. "Oh. So . . . It's okay if I . . . You know . . ."

Hunter laughed. "Yes, you stammering fool. It's okay. She's waiting for you."

Nolan wiped suddenly sweaty palms on his jeans and headed up the sidewalk, mindful of Hunter watching him. He knocked lightly on the door and opened it. "Hannah?"

"In here."

His heart thudded and his mouth went dry as he followed her voice to the cozy sitting room. It would've been easier, he knew, to fall for someone whose life was less complicated, who hadn't been to hell and back, who hadn't loved another man with her whole heart and soul. It would've been easier, but there was no one else quite like Hannah, and if being with her meant navigating an emotional minefield, he was fully prepared to suit up and do battle.

Ugh, he thought, *bad analogy. Horrible analogy.* Caleb had been killed when he stepped on a landmine in an area that had been deemed safe by sweepers. He'd been playing soccer with some Iraqi kids when he chased after the ball into a field adjacent to the base.

Nolan often thought how like Caleb it was to befriend the local kids, to strike up a game with them, to be the one to chase after the ball. The random circumstances of his death had made it that much harder to cope in the aftermath. It would've been easier, for all of them, if it had happened in the heat of battle rather than during a rare moment of leisure in an area no longer in the active war zone. They'd thought he was safe there.

"Nolan? Are you okay?"

Hannah's voice brought him back to the present, where he realized he was standing in the doorway to the sitting room, staring at her on the sofa. "I'm sorry. I was thinking . . ."

"What about?"

"I was actually thinking about Caleb."

She patted the sofa cushion next to her, inviting him to join her.

He took off his coat and laid it over the back of an antique easy chair before sitting next to her.

"What about Caleb?"

"I'd rather not say because it's something you won't want to talk about."

"Ah . . . the bad stuff."

He nodded.

"I'm sorry."

The unexpected apology caught him off guard. "For what?"

"For not answering the door or the phone earlier. For worrying you."

"Don't be sorry. Don't ever be sorry for doing whatever you need to. I get it, Hannah. Believe me. I get it."

She reached for his hand and curled her fingers around his. "I know you do, and that helps. It helps a lot."

"Are you hungry?"

"A little bit I suppose."

"Want to get a pizza?"

"That sounds really good."

"I'll call it in. What do you like on it?"

"Anything."

"Coming right up." He got up to use the phone in the kitchen and returned with a glass of wine for her and a beer for him. "I helped myself. Hope that's okay."

"I got the beer for you," she said with a shy smile that touched him.

"I'm honored."

"So am I. I'm honored that you want to spend time with

me, that you're willing to put up with all my issues, that you seem to care—"

"I only *seem* to care?" he asked, pretending to be insulted. "Let me set the record straight. I care greatly. Tremendously. Incredibly." He curled the end of a long strand of her silky dark hair around his finger. "Enormously. Hugely. Vastly. Extremely." By now she was giggling softly, which he adored.

"Are you done?"

"Not quite. You got a thesaurus handy?"

"There might be one upstairs." She zeroed in on his lips in the second before she leaned in to kiss him.

Whispering against her lips, he said, "Exceedingly. Exceptionally."

"I never knew you were so good with words."

"Neither did I. Apparently, all I needed was the right inspiration." He put his beer on the table and curled an arm around her, wanting to keep her close. "I'm usually told I'm good with my hands."

She raised a brow in a saucy expression that made his blood hum with desire. "Is that right?"

"Uh-huh. I can take apart a carburetor and reassemble it with lightning speed. I could show you sometime." He waggled his brows. "And you ought to see me rotate tires."

She shook with silent laughter. "That's not at all what I thought you were going to say."

"Hannah! I'm shocked to discover a dirty mind under that angelic face."

Her shoulder bumped against his chest. "You set me up."

"Are you gonna tell me what happened to upset you earlier?"

As her smile faded, he wanted to shoot himself for tossing a serious question into the midst of their playful banter.

"You don't have to tell me if you'd rather not."

"It's not that I don't want to. It's more that I'd rather relax and enjoy our evening without bringing sad stuff into it."

"That's fine." Pausing, he added, "As long as you know I'm on board for the sad stuff, too."

She laid her hand flat upon his chest. "I know, and I appreciate that. More than you can ever know."

He wondered if she could feel the crazy way his heart beat

when she touched him and hoped she knew it was all because of her.

"What happened earlier in your office . . ."

"What about it?" he asked, his heart now slowing to a crawl while he waited to hear what she would say.

Looking up at him shyly, she said, "I liked it."

"Jesus, Hannah." He blew out a ragged deep breath. "You have no idea what you do to me when you look at me that way or say things like that."

"What do I do to you?"

"You know full well," he said, chuckling at the innocent expression on her sweet face.

"Tell me anyway."

"How about I show you. Would that be okay?"

She seemed to summon the courage to nod.

He took her hand and pressed it against the fly of his jeans where his desire for her was fully apparent.

Her eyes widened, and her lips parted, which only made him harder.

He removed their joined hands from his lap. "Any questions?"

"Just one."

"What's that?"

"Will you kiss me again like you did earlier?"

"How did I kiss you earlier?"

"Like I was just Hannah rather than Hannah the widow who needs to be treated with kid gloves."

"You are just Hannah to me, but I'd never want to push you too far too soon or force you outside your comfort zone before you're ready—"

She stopped him with the firm press of her lips against his, and Nolan forgot all about anything that didn't involve the glide of her lips over his, the delicate tease of her tongue, the sweet flavor of her mouth, the tug of her hands in his hair and the press of her soft curves against his body. Kissing Hannah was quickly becoming his favorite thing to do.

They ended up reclined on the sofa, locked in an endless kiss that had him wanting so much more. And then her hand found its way under his shirt, and the heat of her palm against his lower belly made his muscles quiver. He'd been with other women, but nothing in his past could compare to the all-encompassing desire Hannah aroused in him. He wanted to comfort and protect her, but he also wanted to strip her naked and kiss every inch of her pale, soft skin.

Banishing those thoughts as way beyond the parameters of what was going to happen tonight, Nolan concentrated on the increasingly erotic kiss. By the time the doorbell rang announcing the arrival of the pizza, he'd nearly forgotten all about his so-called parameters.

"You'd better get that," he said as he reluctantly released her and reached for his wallet to hand her a twenty. "I'm in no condition . . ."

Hannah's soft laughter didn't do a thing to ease the ache between his legs. "Seems to be happening a lot lately."

"It's all your fault."

"If you say so." She took the bill from him, got up and headed for the front door, straightening her hair and shirt as she went.

Nolan fixated on the gentle sway of her sexy ass, which made him envious of worn denim for the first time in his life. Releasing a tortured groan, he fell back against the sofa cushions and ran his fingers through his hair, trying to cool himself off before she returned.

He expected her to take the pizza into the kitchen and call him in there to eat with her. But she came into the sitting room, put the pizza on the coffee table and once again surprised the living shit out of him when she stretched out on top of him. Hovering less than an inch above his face, she said, "Where were we?"

CHAPTER 10

———◦‹›◦———

*Will is coming to UVM this year, too! I think
Hunter is relieved he won't have to put up with
me and Caleb by himself anymore. He's been a
good sport about how much time Caleb and I
spend alone. It'll be good to have Will living with
us, too. Hunter will have someone to hang out
with when we're "busy."*

—From the diary of Hannah Abbott, age nineteen

Hannah wasn't sure what possessed her to come down on top of Nolan that way, and for a mortifying second she thought he was too surprised to react. But then he sprang into action, one arm encircling her waist while the other threaded into her hair, drawing her into another incendiary kiss.

All her senses went on high alert as his tongue tangled with hers and his fingers tugged lightly on her hair, making her scalp tingle. The faint scent of soap, aftershave and laundry detergent made her want to burrow closer and breathe him in. She'd forgotten what it was like to be lost to desire, to be surrounded by a sexy, aroused man, to be absolutely certain he wanted her as much as she wanted him.

He released his tight hold on her hair, and his hands met at the waistband of her jeans.

Hannah could barely breathe as she waited to see what he would do next. When his hands slid down to cup her ass through her jeans, she broke the kiss and sucked in a greedy deep breath.

"Is this okay?" he asked, squeezing lightly as his lips and tongue went to work on her neck.

Because she couldn't find the words just then, she nodded, and he squeezed again, harder this time. She needed more but couldn't seem to get close enough until he abruptly sat up, arranging her so she straddled his lap with the hard column of his erection pressed against the part of her that pulsed with desire.

She was on fire. That was the only possible explanation for the heat that threatened to consume her on the spot. Reaching for the hem of her sweater, she drew it up and over her head, revealing a skimpy white tank top that doubled as a bra.

His eyes widening with surprise and what looked to be pleasure, Nolan released the tight grip he had on her backside and shifted his hands to her ribs, spreading his fingers until they came to right below her breasts.

Hannah leaned her forehead against his. "This is crazy," she whispered, staring into his eyes, which had taken on the color of dark chocolate.

"You make me crazy."

"Do I?"

"Yeah," he said with a gruff laugh. "Although *crazy* might not be the right word. *Insane* is more like it."

She combed her fingers through his hair, straightening it as she went. "I was really upset earlier, but I feel better now. I feel better when I'm with you."

"Hannah . . . God . . ." His strong arms banded around her, crushing her to his muscular chest. "I've wanted you for so long, but I never thought . . ."

"What? What didn't you think?"

He released his tight hold on her, and with his hands on her face, forcing her to look directly into his eyes, he said, "I didn't dare to hope I'd ever get to hold you and kiss you and touch you or that you might want me, too. I never thought I'd get so lucky."

"I do want you, too. I want you more all the time. I feel foolish for pretending for so long that I didn't know you had feelings for me or that I didn't have them for you."

His hands moved up and down her back, further enticing her through the thin cotton of her top. "You weren't ready to acknowledge it yet." With a charming grin, he added, "Good thing I'm a patient sort of guy."

"Good thing," she said, kissing him. "I would've hated to miss out on this, whatever it turns out to be."

"No matter what happens between us, I'd never want to lose my friend Hannah. That'd be . . ." He shook his head, as if the thought of it was too much to fathom.

"Unbearable."

"Totally unbearable."

Only when the eye contact became too intense to maintain did she look away. "You must be hungry."

He nibbled on her neck, making her shudder from the sensation that shot through her entire body. "Famished, but not for pizza."

"*Nolan*," she said on a moan.

His hands moved slowly upward until they cupped her small but incredibly sensitive breasts. "Tell me to stop."

The word was on the tip of her tongue, but she didn't say it. Rather she wrapped her arm around his neck and held on tight as he caressed her breasts, ignoring her tight nipples for so long she was on the verge of pleading when he finally rolled them between his fingers.

As a gasp escaped through her tightly clenched jaw, Hannah tilted her hips, needing to get closer to him.

He groaned and moved against her, letting her know with every tilt of his hips what he wanted from her. "Do you trust me?"

"Yes, you know I do. Of course I do." She fisted his hair and held on as he managed to stimulate her through two layers of denim and another layer of silk.

"Turn around."

"What?"

"You heard me."

Filled with uncertainty and overwhelming curiosity, she did as he asked, her movements awkward and hesitant.

He arranged her so she was still on his lap but facing away from him. The hard column of his erection was wedged against her bottom, making her twist to get closer.

"Easy, honey," he said, chuckling softly against her ear, which made it difficult to remain still. "Relax against me. I've got you."

Muscle by muscle, she made an effort to release the tension and fear and guilt and grief and every emotion that didn't involve the incredible pleasure he made her feel.

His hands moved over the front of her in a relaxing caress that missed all the most important areas that yearned for his touch. "Still trust me?"

Hannah bit her lip and nodded, gasping when he tugged at the button to her jeans and slid the zipper down. She held her breath, waiting to see what he would do next as desire pounded through her in a steady drumbeat that she hadn't experienced in a very long time.

Moving slowly, he slid his hand inside her jeans and down to cup her over skimpy silk panties. "How about now?"

She wanted to move against his hand, but his other arm was banded around her waist, making it impossible for her to move as his cock throbbed against her bottom.

"Hannah?"

"Yes, yes. It's okay." She wanted to beg him to move his fingers, to do something to ease the growing ache, but for what seemed like forever he didn't do anything other than drive her wild with the heat of his hand against the silk of her panties. And then he pressed harder, his fingers slipping between her folds, using the silk to create friction where she needed it most.

Somehow her legs ended up outside of his, which slid apart to give him better access. The arm that had been tight around her middle shifted and his hand found her breast through the thin tank, rolling and tweaking her nipple.

"Let it happen, honey," he whispered against her ear, making her shudder. "You're so sexy, so beautiful and I want you so bad. I want to feel your soft skin against mine as I sink into your heat. I want to feel you come when I'm deep inside you. I want to touch you everywhere and kiss you and lick you."

His words and hands worked together in perfect tandem to

tip her over the edge into pleasure so sharp and so intense, she ended up trembling uncontrollably and sobbing, wrecked by the total abandon he'd drawn from her.

Removing his hand from her pants, he turned her effortlessly into his warm embrace. "Shh, honey, it's okay. Please don't cry."

As she burrowed her face into his chest, she wanted to tell him she was sorry for falling apart on him, but she couldn't speak as her body continued to tingle and shudder from the pleasure that moved through her in waves that radiated from her core.

"Talk to me, Hannah. Tell me what happened."

"I don't know."

He wiped the tears off her face. "Did I scare you or push you too far with what I said?"

She shook her head. That was the last thing she wanted him to think. "It was so amazing. I loved what you said—and what you did. I'd forgotten. I just . . . I'd forgotten." The moment the words were out of her mouth she regretted them. "I shouldn't say that. It's not fair—"

He kissed her softly, with only the sweet press of his lips against hers. "I want to know everything you're thinking and feeling, even if it's something you think will make me uncomfortable. I still want to know."

"I can't believe you really want to take on me and all my crap."

"It's not crap. It's life. It's your life, and I want to be a part of it. I told you once before I'd be perfectly satisfied if I only got to hold your hand, and I meant that."

Hoping to lighten things up after her emotional firestorm, she shifted ever so subtly on his lap, pressing against his erection. "It seems only one of us was perfectly satisfied."

"I was perfectly satisfied the second Hunter told me you wanted to see me. That's all I needed tonight, Hannah."

"You said before that you feel lucky to be with me. I feel lucky, too."

He drew her head onto his shoulder and held her that way for a long time, until her trembling had stopped and her tears had dried.

"Ready for some pizza?" she asked many minutes later.

"Yeah, I'm ready."

They ate the pizza and snuggled on the couch to watch a movie on TV. It was after midnight when Nolan sat up and stretched, unable to sit so close to her and keep his hands to himself any longer. "I should go," he said, although leaving her was the absolute last thing he wanted to do. "I have a meeting right after work tomorrow—or I guess it's today now—and then I'll be over to get you."

"What if I'm busy?" she asked with a coy grin that made him smile back at her.

"Get un-busy."

"It's very bossy of you to make such demands."

"Are you complaining?"

"I didn't say that. When you get me, what are you going to do with me?"

He leaned in to kiss her, lingering when the sweet softness of her lips captivated him. "You'll have to wait and see."

"What should I wear?"

With his hand flat against her thigh, he said, "I love these jeans."

Her eyes sparkled with laughter that was a much more welcome sight than the tears had been. "That's good to know." She reached up to straighten his hair, and his heart thudded when her eyes met his.

"I really have to go or I'll be tempted to stay, and if I'm tempted to stay, I might be tempted to do all those things I told you I want to do with you."

She zeroed in on his mouth, licking her lips in an innocent move that set his blood on fire all over again.

"Going now."

"Okay."

Nolan forced himself to his feet, forced himself to put on his coat and forced himself not to touch her again.

Hannah wrapped a blanket around her shoulders and followed him to the front door.

He turned to her and despite the alarm sounding in his

brain to keep his hands to himself, he wrapped her up in a tight hug.

Her hands found his hips under his coat.

"I don't want to go," he said as he breathed in the scent he'd become addicted to. He wanted to throw off his coat and carry her upstairs, but she wasn't ready for that yet.

"I don't want you to go."

With his forehead propped against hers, he released a ragged breath. "Soon, sweet Hannah. Soon enough." He kissed her forehead and opened the door to the frigid air that slapped some sense into him as he jogged to his truck at the curb.

All the way home, he thought about her responsiveness, her sweet, sexy kisses, the way she arched into him trying to get closer, the way she'd come apart under his hand . . . Christ, he was only human, and she appealed to him on every possible level. She was the perfect combination of shy and sultry, demure and yet brazen at the same time. He'd expected the former, but the latter had come as a huge and not unwelcome surprise.

He gripped the wheel tighter as he navigated twisting roads on his way through Butler, which was dark and deserted at this hour. As he drove across the one-lane covered bridge and past Hannah's parents' house, he wondered what they really thought of their daughter taking up with the town mechanic. Lincoln and Molly Abbott had been a source of stability and sanity during his tumultuous childhood, and Nolan admired them more than just about anyone. He could only hope they considered him worthy of their gorgeous daughter.

Driving down the long dirt road that led to his house, the headlights cast a wide swath of light over the yard, highlighting the man sitting on Nolan's stoop.

"Son of a bitch," he muttered. In no mood to deal with this after the excellent night with Hannah, Nolan thought about turning around and leaving. He could always sleep at the garage if he had to. It wouldn't be the first time. But running away wouldn't solve the problem. He'd learned that lesson the hard way.

Slamming the truck into park, he shut it off and got out.

"Keeping some late hours these days, son." As always, Vernon Roberts's words were slurred.

"What do you want?"

"Oh you know. The usual."

Money. That was all he ever wanted from his only child. Nolan thought of the plans for the post-and-beam house he'd had drawn up years ago to replace the ramshackle cabin where his grandfather had raised him after his parents discarded him. He would've built the new house years ago if not for his leech of a father who showed up every couple of months in need of another transfusion of cash.

Every time, Nolan said never again, but saying it and doing it were two very different things. "I don't have any money."

"Don't screw with me." Vernon could sound amazingly sober when it suited his agenda. "I know how much that garage of yours brings in every month."

Anxious as always to get rid of his father as fast as he could, Nolan reached for his wallet and pulled out six twenties and two tens and held the cash out to the older man. "That's all I've got. Take it or leave it."

Vernon staggered over to the truck and pulled the bills from Nolan's hand with shocking dexterity. The money disappeared into the pocket of his shabby-looking coat. "Heard you've been messing around with that Abbott girl. Smart move. Those people are loaded. Although screwing a widow is risky—"

Without thinking, Nolan reacted, taking his father by the lapels and slamming him against the truck. "Don't you say another fucking word about her or her family, or I swear to God, I'll kill you. You understand me?"

The stench of booze on Vernon's breath nearly made Nolan gag, but he didn't release the tight hold. "Hit a nerve, huh?" Vernon asked with a mean sneer.

Nolan bashed him against the truck again. "I said, *do you understand me?*"

"Yeah, yeah, I won't say nothing about your precious girlfriend, but I'm sure other people will have plenty to say about a classy gal like her taking up with a good-for-nothing grease monkey like you."

Sick to death of his father and the misery that surrounded him, Nolan let go of his coat. Vernon slithered to the ground in a heap, and Nolan resisted the urge to kick the shit out of him. He'd love nothing more, but all that would do was draw attention to the nightmare he'd lived with all his life—a nightmare not even his closest friends knew about. Nolan had gone out of his way to keep his shameful family a secret. Most of his friends knew his grandfather had raised him, and that was all they knew because he never, ever talked about his parents.

"Get out of here before I forget I'm not legally allowed to kill you."

His father grunted with laughter and pain as he pulled himself up. "You'd like that wouldn't you?"

He had no idea.

"Good to see you as always, son."

"*Go.*" Nolan had no idea where his father would go or how he would get there. He'd stopped caring about such things years ago, right around the time his father had started hitting him up for money. He used to pray to a God he no longer believed in to do him a huge favor and rid the world of Vernon Roberts. However, God saw fit to take Caleb Guthrie instead, and Nolan had lost all faith in the Almighty after that.

Waiting until Vernon staggered toward the driveway and walked out of sight, Nolan went into the house, slamming the door behind him. Seeing his father always set him off, filling him with anger and resentment and despair. When his grandfather had been alive, he'd encouraged Nolan to rise above the anger, not to let his father get to him and not to take on his father's problems when Vernon had made it very clear that he wanted money and only money from his family. All other offers of help had been rebuffed often enough that they'd stopped trying a long time ago.

Even with his grandfather's voice in his head preaching self-preservation, Nolan felt like a monster for leaving his father out in the cold. He stoked up the fire in his wood stove and sat on a footstool to remove his boots. Wasn't that the ultimate irony? The guy had never done a single thing other than make Nolan's life miserable, and he still felt bad for not offering him shelter for the night.

He shook his head with disgust at himself, at his father, at the family he'd had the poor fortune to be born into, for all the years he'd wished for something normal as he cobbled together a family made up of friends such as Skeeter, who was one of the few who knew the truth about Nolan's parents. Their oddly dysfunctional relationship filled a void in Nolan's life—a void left by a drunken father who'd never given a shit about his son.

Tired of dwelling on things that couldn't be changed, Nolan's thoughts shifted to Hannah and the evening he'd spent wrapped up in her. His despair resurfaced when it dawned on him that if she spent time with him, eventually she'd be subjected to Vernon. A bolt of fear shot through him, making him sit up straighter as he tried to picture beautiful, kind, sweet Hannah in the company of a dirtbag like Vernon Roberts.

Nolan dropped his head into his hands, wishing he had the strength to stay away from her so that scenario would never unfold. He could wish for that kind of strength, but he was powerless to stay away, and he'd do everything he could to make sure her path and Vernon's never crossed.

No matter what it took.

CHAPTER 11

———◆———

*Caleb had a hat trick in last night's game and
sent UVM to the playoffs. I'm so proud of him.
We heard scouts from the Bruins and a couple
other NHL teams will be at the playoffs. His
coach said he could easily go pro, but he's not sure
if that's what he wants. I love to watch him play
hockey. He's amazing! He talks about going into
the army and loves the ROTC program, but I
want him to pursue hockey. As rough as it can be
(and he's the roughest one on the ice), it's still
"safer" than the military. The thought of him in
the army scares me, which he says is silly. We've
had a few fights over this decision, which will
have to be made in the next year or so.*

—From the diary of Hannah Abbott, age twenty

After a restful night of dreamless sleep, Hannah enjoyed
her first cup of coffee in the kitchen, which boasted a
spectacular view of Butler Mountain. She missed Homer and
their morning routine, but every time the sorrow threatened
to intrude, she tried to think of him with Caleb, which always
made her feel better.

Her thoughts returned again and again to Nolan and the time they'd spent together and the surprisingly sensual man who lived beneath his equally sexy exterior. Though she'd known him most of her life, he was still an enigma to her in many ways because he didn't talk endlessly the way Caleb had, sharing every thought that popped into his always busy mind.

Nolan was much more reserved, self-contained in a way that kept him somewhat removed from the rest of them even when he was right in the middle of the fray with their group of friends. There was so much she didn't know about him, so much she had yet to learn about him, and she couldn't wait to see him again.

The phone rang on the counter, jarring her out of her daydreams about Nolan. Her brows knitted when she saw the veterinary clinic's phone number on the caller ID as she took the call.

"Hi, Hannah. It's Myles."

"Hi, Myles."

"I hope I'm not calling too early."

"Not at all. I've been up for a while."

"I was thinking of you, because of Homer and everything . . ."

"That's very nice of you. I miss him, but it's nice to think of him being reunited with Caleb. They were such buddies."

"Yes," Myles said, his tone hushed. "They certainly were. So, um, the other reason I called is I wanted to ask if maybe you might like to have dinner sometime."

Hannah winced and closed her eyes. "It's so nice of you to ask, Myles."

"I hear a *but* in there."

"I'm seeing someone." Hannah cringed as she held the phone tighter. If she had her druthers, her personal life would remain just that—but that was almost impossible in a small town like Butler, where everyone knew her and Nolan and where everyone would be interested in them as a couple.

"Is it Nolan?"

"Yes."

"I thought I might've seen more than friendship between you two the other night, but I wasn't sure. I'm so sorry. I didn't mean to make things awkward between us."

"You haven't. I appreciate you calling and everything you did for me when Homer died."

"I was happy to help out. Give me a call when you're ready to bury him, and I'll take care of everything for you."

She'd already invited him to the funeral in appreciation of his special care of Homer as he aged. "Thank you so much, Myles. I'll call you next week."

"Sounds good."

Hannah put down the cordless phone as the doorbell rang. Was it going to be that kind of day? She went to the front door and opened it to find her sisters, Ella and Charley, holding cups of coffee and a bag from the bakery. "Why are you ringing the bell?"

"We were told we're no longer allowed to walk right in," Charley said with her typical bluntness. She shared her lighter coloring with their brothers Will and Wade, while Ella had dark hair and eyes like Hannah and Hunter. "And of course we had to come over to find out why."

"Of course you did," Hannah said, amused as she stepped aside to admit her younger sisters.

When they were settled around the kitchen table, Charley broke out warm cinnamon buns and put them on the plates Hannah provided.

The cinnamon scent made Hannah's mouth water as her sisters watched her warily.

"Are you going to make us drag it out of you?" Charley asked.

"Stop being such a bull in a china shop," Ella said. "She'll tell us when she's ready to."

"Um, hello, this is *Hannah*," Charley reminded Ella. "She's never going to be ready to tell us, so we have to pull it out of her. Just like always. Remember how long she'd been sucking face with Caleb before she admitted he was her boyfriend?" Charley looked at Hannah, stricken by what she'd said. "I'm sorry. Bad example."

"It's okay to talk about him, Charley. I'd hate for you or anyone to think you can't mention his name around me. You know that."

"You don't have to tell us anything you don't want to," Ella said, kind as always. Hannah had never, ever heard her say a bad word about anyone. Ever. "We mostly wanted to see how you're coping after Homer died."

"I'm okay. He's with Caleb, and that makes me happy."

Ella's eyes shone with unshed tears as she got busy with her breakfast.

"*She* might not want to know why we have to knock now, but I still want to know," Charley said over a mouthful of sweet confection. "Just for the record."

"It astounds me at times that you two came from the same parents," Hannah said.

"It astounds me on a daily basis," Ella said dryly, making the three of them laugh.

"You guys love me," Charley said. "You know you do."

"Someone has to," Hannah said.

"Insult me all you want. I still need to know what you've been up to, big sister."

"A little of this, and a little of that," Hannah said, gratified when both of them stared at her.

"With *who*?" Charley asked.

"It's actually *whom*," Ella said.

"Shut up!" Charley said, tossing a napkin at her. "We're just getting to the good stuff."

Hannah shot them a withering look. "*Whom* do you think?"

"Nolan?" Ella asked hopefully.

Hannah nodded and then covered her ears when they started shrieking.

"Hail freaking Mary," Charley said. "Finally! Was it good?"

"Charley!" Ella said. "Don't you dare ask her that!" Even as she said the words though, Ella stared at Hannah seeming to hope she might share the dirty details.

Charley scowled at her. "Why not? If anyone deserves a good lube and filter job from the hottest mechanic in Vermont, it's Hannah."

Hannah was too busy laughing to reply to that audacious statement. A lube and filter job? Where did Charley come up with this stuff?

"He is pretty hot," Ella agreed. "He's all dark and broody and mysterious."

"And built like a brick shithouse," Charley added. "Don't forget that."

"True," Ella said. "And I love the hint of silver in his hair. You can tell he's going to be a hot older guy, too. You know how some guys get handsomer as they get older?"

Charley nodded in agreement.

"Nolan will be like that. Don't you think so, Hannah?"

"Oh you two remembered I was here?"

"Stop being all secretive and spill the beans," Charley said.

"What did you hear?" Hannah asked, stirring cream into her coffee.

"Mom said we have to ring the bell at your house from now on," Ella said. "That's all she said."

Hannah was thankful for her parents' discretion, but unfortunately they'd told her sisters just enough to whet their appetites. "The night Homer died, Nolan had come over to go to dinner and he ended up staying with me. They came in the next morning, and he was still here—on the sofa and fully clothed." Did they look disappointed or was that her imagination?

"And nothing happened?" Charley asked.

"I never said that."

Charley smacked her palm on the table, making the other two startle. "I knew it! Do tell!"

"You don't have to, Hannah," Ella said, eyeing Charley warily.

"Yes, she does," Charley said. "We've waited years for her to start dating again. I want every detail."

"You're not getting every detail," Hannah said. "All I'll say is I like him, I like being with him and I like kissing him. That's it."

"That's so awesome," Ella said dreamily, a wistful expression occupying her face.

"So you haven't . . . you know . . . done *it* yet?" Charley asked.

"Not that it's any of your business, but no," Hannah said.

"Are you scared to do that with someone else?" Ella asked.

Her question went straight to the heart of Hannah's deepest anxiety about getting involved with someone new. If last night's emotional meltdown was any indication of what might happen during the actual act, she had good reason to be worried. "A little."

Ella's hand covered Hannah's on the table. "You should take your time and go really slow."

"No way," Charley said. "Just do it and get it over with. Until you do, it'll be all you think about—and worry about."

They both made good points, and Hannah had certainly considered both scenarios. "We're taking it slow." The memory of his hand inside the front of her jeans chose that moment to pop into her brain, launching a bolt of heat that settled between her legs. "For the most part."

"Oh my God!" Charley said. "You just turned bright red! What were you thinking about?"

Hannah shook her head. Some things were far too personal to share, even with her sisters. "I've said all I'm going to say."

"You're no fun," Charley said.

"For once, I have to agree with her," Ella added.

"Gee, thanks a lot," Hannah said. "You know I count on you to be the voice of reason with her."

Ella shrugged. "I can't help being curious and also happy for you. He's a really nice guy."

"Yes, he is," Hannah said, smiling over her coffee mug.

"So I have a bit of gossip about one of our brothers," Charley said with a mysterious grin.

"Which one?" Ella said, pouncing.

"Colton."

He was the last one Hannah would've guessed. "Colton Abbott, man of the mountain, has done something *gossip-worthy*?"

Charley leaned in and kept her voice down, as if someone other than her sisters might hear her. "According to Mom, he shaved off his beard and cut his hair, and Mrs. Andersen told me she saw him shopping at the mall in St. Johnsbury—for clothes."

Ella and Hannah stared at Charley, their mouths hanging open.

"He's got a girlfriend!" Ella said.

"I know, right?" Charley said. "One more thing . . . He asked

Mom and Dad to take his dogs this weekend because he was going to be 'away.'"

"Away where?" Hannah asked, truly astounded by this information.

"He didn't say, and they didn't ask."

"We need to have a talk with Mom about her prying skills, which are definitely not what they used to be," Hannah said.

Charley nodded in agreement. "No kidding. I already told her I was very disappointed in her. She said he's a grown man, and he has a right to his privacy."

"Since when does anyone with the last name of Abbott have a right to *privacy*?" Hannah asked.

"What she said," Ella replied gravely.

"Exactly!" Charley seemed pleased that her sisters finally agreed with her on something. "We've got to do some serious snooping to get to the bottom of this."

"I can't believe he left the mountain for a whole weekend," Ella said. "He never does that. He only comes down on Sundays for dinner and to do his laundry."

"Apparently, he's coming down for something else these days," Charley said with a dirty grin.

"Wow," Hannah said, sitting back in her chair. "This is truly stunning. And no one has any idea who she is?"

"Nope," Charley said. "Or if they do, they aren't saying."

"Very interesting," Hannah said. "At least I'm not the only one you all are talking about."

"We're talking mostly about you," Ella said.

"Fantastic," Hannah said.

Her sisters left a short time later to get to the store before Hunter got pissed at them for being late. He was big on family members setting the right example for the rest of their employees. Hannah agreed with him, but she didn't share that opinion with Charley or Ella.

Hannah had just settled into her studio to attempt some work for the first time in days when her brother Wade came in. Apparently, he hadn't gotten the memo about the new knocking rules. "Hey," Hannah said, pleased to see the most elusive of the Abbott siblings. His long dark blond hair was secured with a leather tie, and even though it was just barely spring, he wore a hoodie over a thermal shirt along with cargo shorts and sandals. While he most closely resembled Will, his face was more angular but no less handsome. "What brings you by?"

He bent to kiss her upturned cheek. "I was away the other night when Homer died. I just heard when I got back to town, so I came right over. Are you doing okay?"

"I miss him, but he was ready to see Caleb again."

Wade's lips tightened as he nodded, keeping his focus on the beads on her worktable. The emotional wallop of Caleb's death still caught all of them off guard from time to time, and Wade was no different. He'd adored Caleb in his own quiet way and had been as devastated by his loss as the rest of their family.

"So you said you were away. Somewhere fun I hope."

"Just down in Rutland for a few days."

"What's down there?"

"Some friends."

"Female friends?" Hannah asked in a teasing tone.

Wade shrugged and continued to stare at the beads. He was always quiet and intense, but it didn't require much insight to see that something was troubling him.

"What's wrong, Wade?"

"Nothing. You've got enough going on. You don't need to be taking on other people's crap, too."

"If you're upset about something, that's not crap. I'd be happy to listen if you need to talk."

He wanted to. As she abandoned her stool, and took him by the hand, she could see that he wanted to very badly. She led him to the small sofa she kept in her studio and sat next to him.

Wade leaned forward, his chin propped on his hands.

Watching him, Hannah became more concerned with every minute that passed in silence.

"There's a woman," he finally said. "A very special woman."

"How did you meet her?"

"At a yoga retreat."

Despite the razzing from his brothers, Wade had been into yoga for years as part of his health-conscious lifestyle. "What's her name?"

"Mia." He seemed a million miles away. "We have a lot in

common. She's vegan like me, into fitness and yoga and rock climbing. All the things I love."

"Sounds like she's perfect for you."

"Yeah."

"So what's the problem?"

"She's married."

Hannah gasped in shock. "Oh, Wade! And you're seeing her anyway?"

"Not like that. Just as friends." He swallowed hard and seemed to be grappling with his emotions. "I think he's abusing her, but I can't prove it, and she won't talk about it."

Hannah's mind raced as she tried to process what he'd said. "What makes you think that?"

"Little hints, clues here and there, stuff she says about him that make him sound like a controlling asshole. Bruises on her arms." He released his hair from the leather strap that held it and buried his fingers in its depths. "You can't tell anyone, Hannah. This can't be fuel for the family gossip machine."

"You have my word I won't tell anyone."

"Remember John Junior?" Wade asked, referring to the dog their father had found along the side of the road and brought home to join the family. True to their father's obsession, the dog had been named after one of the Beatles.

Surprised by the shift in topic, Hannah said, "What about him?"

"You know how we had him for all those years, treated him well and still, every time we went to pet him, he shied away like we were going to hit him?"

"It used to make me sad that he had so little faith in us even after all that time."

"He was trained to be afraid of people at an early age. Mia is like that, too. She can't bear to be touched, shies away from hugs, flinches at the slightest noise. All the signs are there, but she won't admit anything is wrong, and it makes me crazy that I can't do a damned thing to help her when I know she's in trouble."

"When you spend time with her," Hannah asked, treading lightly out of fear that her always-reticent brother might stop talking, "how does that go? Where does her husband think she is?"

"At yoga. We meet at a restaurant twenty miles from her house so there's no chance of running into anyone she knows."

"And these meetings . . ."

"All we do is talk. I swear to God, that's all we've ever done."

"Do you talk to her between meetings?"

"By e-mail. She can't take a chance on calling me, but she has my numbers at home and at work and my address and every possible way to get in touch with me. Just in case."

"In case of what?"

"In case she ever needs me."

"Wade—"

"Don't. Please don't tell me I'm playing with fire because I already know I am. But what am I supposed to do? Forget she exists and go on with my life like I never met her? You have no idea how much I wish I'd never met her, because she's all I think about." His voice broke ever so slightly. "And I can't have her."

Heartbroken for him, Hannah rested her hand on his shoulder. "Has she talked at all about leaving her husband?"

He shook his head. "We don't go there. I have a feeling she's afraid to even consider it."

"There has to be somewhere she can go to get help."

Turning to face her, he said, "You think I haven't tried that? But she won't even admit something is wrong, so how am I supposed to get her help? It's a fucking mess, and I'm smack in the middle of it even though I know I shouldn't be. I can't seem to help it though."

"There's nothing wrong with caring about someone or trying to help them."

"Yes, there is if it puts her—and maybe even me—in danger of some sort. I can't even think about what might happen to her if he ever discovers we're friends. The thought of that keeps me awake at night."

"How long has this been going on?"

"A year this month."

"Wade! Oh my God! A *year*?"

"Trust me, there's nothing you can say that I haven't already said to myself. But you really can't tell anyone, Hannah. I mean it. I only told you because I had to tell someone, and you're the only one who isn't all up in my grill all the time trying to get me to be like the rest of you."

Hannah tugged on his shoulder, encouraging him to let her hug him.

He sagged against her, seeming so defeated and exhausted that she ached for him.

"I'm here. No matter what happens, I'm here, and I'll do anything I can to help you—and Mia."

"Thanks, Han. And for listening, too."

"Any time."

"I'd better get to work. I've been off the last few days, and I'm sure the place didn't shut down while I was gone." Fittingly, he ran the health and wellness portion of the family's business.

"No such luck."

He kissed her cheek. "I'll let myself out."

"Keep me posted on what's going on?"

Nodding, he got up and left the room.

Watching him go, Hannah feared for Mia—and for him.

CHAPTER 12

❦

*Caleb is acting strange and secretive. I'd be
worried he had someone else if he wasn't with me
every minute of the day except for when he's in
class or at practice. Not sure what's going on.
Hunter and Will were no help at all when I tried
to get it out of them.*

—From the diary of Hannah Abbott, age twenty-one

When Cameron called later that afternoon, Hannah
took the call and apologized for not being available
the night before.

"It's totally fine," Cameron said. "I'm exhausted after the
big move, and a night at home was just what we needed."

"Things are going well then I take it?"

"Mmm," Cameron said. "Very well."

Hannah laughed at the satisfaction she heard in her new
friend's voice.

"Sorry. I don't mean to be so giddy."

"You should be giddy and enjoy every second of your
happiness."

"I had no idea what I was missing in life until I met your
wonderful brother."

"He is quite wonderful."

"Anyway, as much as I'd happily talk about Will all day, that's not why I called. I have a little time this afternoon and was hoping we could get together to talk about the retreat."

"I'd love to. How about I come to you? The diner at two?"

"Works for me. See you then."

"Thanks, Cameron."

Hannah managed a couple of hours of work in the studio and packaged several matching sets of earrings, bracelets and necklaces to take to Will at the store before she broke for lunch. All morning she'd thought about the idea Cameron had approached her with to make the home Caleb had left her into a retreat tailored to women who'd lost their spouses to war.

She loved the idea of bringing people together to share their losses and heal together. The house was far too big for one person to rattle around in alone, and giving it a purpose, especially one dedicated to Caleb's memory, had appealed to her from the first time Cameron suggested it.

Filled with ideas about how they might use the space, she wandered upstairs, opening doors and peering into unused rooms, imagining them full of women working as she was to put their lives back on track after their unimaginable loss. She pictured new friendships and lasting bonds among those who came to Guthrie House.

It would be known as Guthrie House, but the official name would be the Captain Caleb M. Guthrie Memorial Retreat. Hannah felt a charge of excitement as the project took shape and came to life, even if it was only in her imagination for now. Behind the third door on the right side of the second-floor hallway, Hannah encountered several boxes stacked together next to the wall. Her stomach dropped when she remembered they contained Caleb's personal effects, sent home from Iraq after his death.

In all the time he'd been gone, she'd never been able to bring herself to open the boxes, to touch his things, to deal with whatever she might find among his possessions. She knew it was ridiculous to still be frightened by a couple of boxes. But how could she really move forward the way she needed to as long as they were sitting untouched? There might even be things in there his parents would like to have, so it was selfish of her to continue to pretend they weren't there.

She checked her watch and saw that she had more than an hour before she had to meet Cameron. "No time like the present," she said with determination that couldn't quell the overwhelming dread that settled in her belly as she pulled the tape off the first box.

Inside, were faded T-shirts in a variety of brown, as well as tan and army green camouflage uniforms with the GUTHRIE patch sewed over the chest pocket. Hannah ran her fingers over the captain's bars on the collar, remembering how proud Caleb had been to receive that first significant promotion. He'd joked about the day he'd pin his first star and officially outrank his colonel father. Had he lived, Hannah had no doubt he would've gotten there.

The second box revealed Caleb's tattered leather-bound copy of *The Road Not Taken: A Selection of Robert Frost's Poems*, with a bookmark before "Stopping by Woods on a Snowy Evening," Caleb's all-time favorite poem. She used to tease him about how many times he could read the same poems over and over again, but he'd say they moved him the same way every time. A dog-eared copy of Thoreau's *Walden and Civil Disobedience* and several of the military thrillers he'd loved were stacked next to the Frost book.

Beneath the books she found a pile of worn denim and T-shirts with snowboarding logos, all of which she pulled out and set aside to give to Gavin. At the bottom of the box were several spiral notebooks that she withdrew for a closer look. On the cover of each, a range of dates had been written. She flipped open the one with the earliest date and found a variety of journal entries and drawings and observations Caleb had written about life in the war zone, about missing his wife and family, about his misgivings about the war itself and his disillusionment with the decisions coming from Washington.

Taken in by Caleb's familiar scrawl, Hannah greedily read the first notebook and was reaching for the second when she glanced at the clock on the bedside table and realized she had ten minutes before she was due to meet Cameron. She took the notebooks to her own room to devour later when she had the time to truly immerse herself. What insights would she find within the journals and how would she feel about them?

It was not for nothing she'd avoided those boxes all this time, she thought as she brushed her hair and teeth in preparation to leave the house. Somehow she'd known another emotional journey awaited her, and it had taken until now, until she was on the cusp of moving forward with someone else, to be able to confront those memories.

On the way out of the bedroom, she glanced longingly at the journals, wondering if she'd find some last words to her from Caleb within their pages. She'd heard talk of "just in case" letters left behind by soldiers going to war, but Caleb had told her there was no need for such a thing because he had no intention of getting himself killed, and in typical Caleb style, he'd refused to even discuss the possibility.

In the car, she took a moment to calm herself, hoping her hands would quit trembling before she got to the diner. She drove slowly, all the while thinking about the journals. Would she be better off at this juncture in her life to leave the past where it belonged and not open old wounds by reading them? Would she ever know a minute's peace if she didn't read them?

"Why did I have to open those boxes? Why, why, *why*?" Because, she supposed, she'd always suspected she would find some closure there, and until now she hadn't really wanted closure. She hated that word. *Closure.* As if there could ever be such a thing when you lose your vibrant twenty-eight-year-old husband so suddenly and tragically.

But she also conceded that if she had any prayer of a relationship with Nolan, she had to make peace with the past. The retreat was a good step in the right direction. It honored Caleb's memory and provided a meaningful service to other women who'd lost spouses to war.

That, coupled with the road race the Guthries sponsored every year around the anniversary of Caleb's death, would ensure that no one forgot the name of the young man who'd given up potential fame and fortune as a professional hockey player and instead made the ultimate sacrifice in service to his country.

Hannah found a parking space a block from the diner and

walked in a few minutes later to find Cameron already waiting for her in a booth.

"Thank God you're here," Cameron said under her breath.

Megan approached the table with two mugs of coffee that she all but dropped in front of them before turning and storming off.

"I see things are going better between you and Megan," Hannah said.

Cameron's laughter drew a foul look from Megan, directed at Cameron's back. "Is she looking at me?"

"Um, maybe."

"I've never had anyone hate me so much—at least not that I know of."

"She needs to grow up and get a clue."

"She needs to grow up and realize she's focused on the wrong Abbott brother."

"What does that mean?" Hannah asked.

"You don't know? About Hunter?"

"What about him?"

"He likes Megan."

Hannah tipped her head as she studied Will's gorgeous blonde girlfriend. "You wanna run that by me one more time?"

Cameron leaned in close to Hannah. "Hunter. Likes. Megan. A lot."

Astounded, Hannah said, "How do you know this?"

"I pay attention. What can I say? I'm obsessed with all things Abbott, so I probably notice stuff the rest of you miss."

Had she been so self-absorbed that she'd failed to notice her twin's interest in Megan? Or had he done a very good job of hiding it? Probably some of both.

"I didn't say this to upset you."

"I'm not upset. I'm shocked. Here you think you know someone as well as you know yourself, and he's keeping this huge secret."

"He's keeping it secret because he likes her, but she likes Will, but he likes me. From Hunter's perspective, there's no point in pursuing her when she's crazy about his brother."

"But Will isn't interested in her," Hannah said. "He never has been."

"That doesn't seem to matter to her, does it?"

Hannah took a sip from her mug as she processed this intriguing new information. "Tell me this, oh wise one . . . Who is Colton getting busy with?"

"Colton is getting busy? That's news to me!"

Hannah shared what she'd learned from Ella and Charley earlier in the day.

"He really shaved off his beard?"

"And cut his hair."

"Will said he's had the beard since high school." Cameron's blue eyes widened with dismay. "Wait! The beard picture is all over the syrup bottles! It's part of the corporate identity!"

"How could he do this to us?" Hannah asked, amused.

"I know, right? He's not thinking about me or the website. That's for sure. I'm not taking all new pictures of him just because he decided to change his look for a woman."

"More importantly, who is this mystery woman?"

"I'll keep my eyes and ears open."

"You're going to be an excellent addition to the Abbott family, Cameron."

"Oh don't jinx me. We just moved in together. If Will hears I'm making plans to change my name, he might kick me out."

"No, he wouldn't. He's crazy about you, and you have to know it's only a matter of time before he proposes."

Cameron frowned as she looked down at her coffee.

"You don't want to marry him?"

"It's not that. I love him so much. You know that."

"Then what is it?" Hannah asked, trying not to panic on Will's behalf. She'd never seen her brother as happy as he'd been since he met Cam.

"I'm not a big fan of marriage in general. From everything I've seen, it just messes up a perfectly good thing."

"That's not always true. My parents are going strong at thirty-six years. My grandparents were happily married for fifty-four years before my grandmother died. And . . ." Hannah took a breath as her heart slowed to a crawl when she thought of the journals waiting for her at home. "The six years I was married to Caleb were the happiest of my life."

Cameron blew out a deep breath. "I'm so sorry, Hannah. It was thoughtless of me to crack on marriage to you of all people."

"Don't say that. I hate when people feel like they have to watch what they say around me, especially people I'm close to, and I hope you and I are going to be close."

"I hope so, too," Cameron said softly. "And you make a compelling case for marriage. I've just never pictured myself married. I don't know why, but I don't see it for me."

"That was before you met Will Abbott and fell head over heels for a traditional kind of guy who's going to want the wife and two-point-five kids."

"What am I supposed to do with half a kid?" she asked with a smile.

"You guys will figure it out."

"Anyway, enough about me. We're supposed to be talking about you and your retreat and all my incredibly awesome ideas for promoting it." Cameron opened a binder and pulled out several papers that she laid flat in front of Hannah. In the center of each page was a proposed logo.

Hannah's eyes gravitated to the one that included a picture of Caleb in uniform over the simple words *Capt. Caleb M. Guthrie Memorial Retreat*. She ran her fingers over the picture of his chiseled face, looking like the fierce and focused warrior he became after he joined the army.

"This isn't how I remember him," Hannah said, staring at his familiar face. "For most of the time we were together, he had long curly hair down to his shoulders and a goatee he grew every winter and shaved off in the spring. I'll never forget the first time I saw him after the big army haircut. I barely recognized him without all the hair."

She glanced at the other logos, one of which included a photograph of her big Victorian and another that featured Butler Mountain, but her gaze kept returning to the photo of Caleb. "This is the one," she said, running her finger over his face. "I want him present in this entire project."

"That's my favorite one, too. I hope you don't mind that Will shared the photo with me."

"Of course not. I really appreciate all you're doing to help me with this. I could never do it without you."

"Sure, you could. I'm just making it easier." They went over some rough plans for a website that included a registration function that would be totally automated as well as a Facebook page that Cameron was prepared to launch as soon as Hannah chose the logo. "The next big question is how soon do you want to roll it out?"

"To be honest, I thought it would take a lot longer to put all the pieces together. I can't believe how much you got done when you were getting ready to move."

"I had a lot of sleepless nights where I could either work or freak out about how I was totally upending my life for a man. I chose to work."

Hannah smiled even as a thousand emotions churned through her all at once.

"We don't know each other all that well, Hannah, but even I can tell you're not yourself today. Is everything okay?"

God, she wanted to tell someone about the journals she'd found and who better than the one person in her life who hadn't known him? Who hadn't known her with him. "Things have been a bit strange lately," she said hesitantly.

"Because of Homer?"

"For one thing." Hannah appreciated that Cameron gave her a moment of silence to collect her thoughts. "This past winter was a tough one for some reason. I was very out of sorts for much of it."

"Any particular reason?"

"None that I can think of other than all of a sudden I'm tired of being a grief-stricken widow. It's like the load of grief has become too heavy to tote around or something. Naturally, I feel guilty for even thinking that way. Who am I to say there's a time limit on grief, and I've reached it?"

"I was nine when someone told me my mother died giving birth to me."

Startled by the confession, Hannah met Cameron's gaze across the table, waiting to see what she would say next.

"A nanny told me, of all people. She thought I knew, and felt terrible when she realized I didn't. My father was so furious. I've never seen him that mad before or since. He fired her on the spot, which made me feel awful for her. It wasn't her fault that no one had told me. I was a disaster for years after that.

The thought that my mother had *lost her life* because of me . . ." Cameron shook her head as if it was still too big to understand all this time later. "I went totally off the deep end emotionally. It took years of therapy before I accepted it wasn't my fault, and the worst thing I could do was sacrifice the life she'd given up so much for. I know all about how heavy that load becomes when you haul it around long enough."

"Thank you for sharing that with me. It helps to know someone understands how difficult it is to be stuck on Pause for so long. Things are changing all around me, and even though I'm not entirely sure I'm ready to press Play and go for broke, at least I'm not on Pause anymore."

"Leaving Pause means leaving the comfort zone that's kept you safe for all this time, too."

Nodding in agreement, Hannah fiddled with her spoon. "This morning I went through the boxes they sent home from Iraq after Caleb died. They've sat in one of the spare bedrooms for years. On the way over here, I was asking myself why now. Why after all this time did I decide to open them?"

"Why do you think?"

"Because I'm ready now, or I thought I was until I found his journals from Iraq."

"Oh God, Hannah. Did you read them?"

"Not yet. I looked at one of them, but I didn't really have time to dive in."

"Are you going to?"

"I don't know. I've only just started seeing Nolan—"

"Wait! You're actually *seeing* Nolan now?"

"I figured you would've heard that already, as well connected as you are in my family."

"I hadn't heard a word! I took it as a good sign that he was there with you the night Homer died, but I hadn't heard there was more to it than that. I'm so happy for you. He seems like a really great guy."

"He is . . ."

"But?"

Sighing, she said, "I worry I'm going to hurt him if it turns out I'm really not ready for a new relationship."

"Take it slow. Baby steps."

"That was the plan."

"Was?"

Megan stopped at their table. "Do you want anything else?"

Startled by her sudden appearance, the two women shook their heads.

She slapped the check on the table and started to walk away, but didn't get far before she whirled around to zero in on Cameron. "I don't know what makes you so special, but there are a lot of people in this town who care about him, and we won't appreciate it if you hurt him by leaving whenever you get tired of slumming in Vermont."

Aghast, Cameron stared at Megan. "You don't need to worry about him." She spoke in a low, calm tone, but the flush that appeared on her cheeks indicated she wasn't as calm as she appeared. "I'll take good care of him. And I'm sorry you feel that Vermont equates to *slumming*, but I think it's quite beautiful, and I plan to be very, *very* happy here for a very long time."

Clearly infuriated by Cameron's gentle dressing down, Megan turned and stormed off.

"That was freaking amazing," Hannah said, awestruck. "How did you come up with that so fast? I would've thought of that two hours from now and been pissed with myself for not thinking of it in the moment."

"I've given some consideration to what I might say to her when she finally confronted me. I was ready for her."

"I'd say so! I'm impressed. I can't believe Hunter actually *likes* her. What's wrong with him?"

"He must see something in her the rest of us don't."

"I need to have a conversation with him."

"I want to go back to the conversation we were having before we were rudely interrupted by what's her name. You said taking it slow *was* the plan. What did that mean?"

"He kissed me, and I kissed him back. And I liked it. A lot."

Cameron's smile stretched widely across her face. "What's wrong with that?"

"I said I was ready to press Play. I didn't say I was ready for Fast Forward."

"Want to know what I think?"

The slightly calculating look on Cameron's face made Hannah nervous. "Um, I guess so . . ."

Laughing, Cameron said, "You pressed Play a while ago. Probably during the tough winter, and once you take that first step forward, it's tough to hit Rewind and go back."

"Isn't that what I'd be doing by reading Caleb's journals? Especially now?"

"Maybe for a short time, but the train has left the station, Hannah. You're moving forward whether you consciously want to or not. Life has this unbelievably maddening habit of going on even when we think it absolutely shouldn't."

"That's very true. For a long time after Caleb died, I wondered how it was possible that people around me were able to laugh or sing or listen to music or fall in love or enjoy *anything* that required emotions I no longer possessed."

"They were still there. They were just put away for a while until you were ready to feel them again."

Hannah had to admit that what Cameron said made a lot of sense.

"How do you feel about Nolan?"

"I feel good about Nolan," she said with a smile. "I feel extremely good about Nolan."

"That's the best news I've heard in a long time."

"How can you say that with all the good stuff that's going on in your life recently?"

"Because no one deserves to feel good about something or someone more than you do. From all accounts, your courage has been amazing."

"These accounts you speak of are overblown."

"Whatever you say. I believe them, not you."

Hannah saw Will come into the diner and press a finger to his lips, asking her not to tell Cameron he was coming.

He swooped in and kissed Cameron's neck, drawing a squeal of surprise from her.

Hannah had never seen her brother so playful or animated around a woman.

"Where did you come from?" Cameron asked.

He bumped into her to get her to move over and let him in. The second he was seated, he put his arm around her. "Across the street at the office where you now supposedly work."

"I'm on a break. Hunter never said anything about punching a time clock."

"Very funny, but did you forget our plans to go shopping for a car to replace that toy of yours with something more Vermont-appropriate?"

Cameron withdrew her cell phone and powered it up to check the time. "Wow, I had no idea it was so late. Hannah and I were very busy."

"Sure, you were." He dropped his gaze to the page with Caleb's photo. "Oh wow. Look at that."

"You haven't seen it?" Hannah asked her brother.

He shook his head as he continued to study the logo.

"I wanted you to see it first in case it wasn't what you wanted," Cameron said to Hannah.

"What do you think of it, Will?" Hannah asked.

"I love it, although that picture isn't really him to me."

Hannah smiled at him. "I said the same thing."

"The military photo sets the right tone for the retreat," Will said. "That's for sure."

"I haven't spoken to Caleb's family about this yet," Hannah said. "What do you think they'll say about it?"

"If I had to guess, I'd say they'll be honored on his behalf and proud of you for keeping his memory alive in such a meaningful way."

Will's gruffly spoken words brought tears to the eyes of both women.

Cameron fanned her face to keep the tears at bay. "Beautifully said." She leaned her head on his shoulder as he pulled her in closer.

Hannah nodded, unable to find the words to convey to her brother how much it meant to her to receive such a heartfelt endorsement.

Will picked up their check. "Let me get this for two of my best girls." He kissed Cameron's forehead before he got up to walk over to where Megan waited with a big, welcoming smile for him.

"Ugh." Cameron twisted around in her seat. "Look at her. Pouring on the charm."

"You need to tell him what she said to you."

Cameron shrugged off the suggestion. "What does it matter? She's no threat to me. If he were interested in her, he would've been with her years ago, right?"

"True."

Cameron reached across the table for Hannah's hand. "If you need a friend with you when you read Caleb's journals, call me. I'll come running."

Hannah squeezed Cameron's hand. "Thank you for everything. I can totally see why my brother is crazy in love with you. I think I might be, too."

"She's all mine, Hannah," Will said. "Back off."

"Now, children, don't fight," Cameron said as they gathered their belongings and left the diner. "There's plenty of me to go around."

CHAPTER 13

*We're engaged! I'm so excited I can't even breathe!
That's why he's been acting so strange. He was
nervous about the proposal. He asked me when
we were on the porch swing at his grandmother's
house. It was perfect because he knows I love that
house as much as he does! We're going to get
married right after graduation. Our life is going
to be the most incredible adventure. I can't wait!*

—From the diary of Hannah Abbott, age twenty-two

As she followed Will and Cameron, Hannah saw Megan
glare at the hand sitting possessively on Cameron's
lower back as Will guided her through the door. If it was true
that Hunter had feelings for Megan, he faced an uphill battle
in getting her to redirect her affections.

Outside, Will and Cameron had stopped short at the sight
of Fred, the town moose, ambling toward Cameron's bright
red Mini Cooper, which was parked in front of the diner.

"I swear to God, if he so much as looks at my car, I'm
going to have him made into a very large purse," Cameron
muttered under her breath.

"Don't speak that way about Fred," Will said in mock horror.

"I thought it was bulls who had a thing for the color red," Cameron said.

"Apparently moose do, too," Hannah said, trying desperately not to laugh as Fred came closer and closer to Cameron's tiny car.

"Do you think he's still mad about me crashing into him?" Cameron asked, sounding nervous now.

"He's never been known to be particularly vindictive," Will said, "but you did hit him awfully hard."

Cameron took a step back, and Will's hands on her shoulders kept her from tripping over his size-thirteen boot. "Make him stop!"

"Right," Will said, laughing. "As if anyone tells Fred what to do."

"My insurance company will never cover a second mooseastrophy," Cameron said. "I was lucky they covered the first one."

Hannah stepped forward. "Hi, Fred."

The moose's large milk-chocolate eyes shifted from Cameron's car to the hand Hannah held out to him.

"You don't want to hurt Cameron's car, now do you? She didn't mean to hit you." As she spoke to the huge animal, she noticed a crowd had formed on the sidewalk in front of the diner and across the street on the porch at the store. "Why don't you head on home now? Okay?"

Fred seemed to think it over for a minute before he let out a big moo that launched Cameron right off her feet into Will's arms. Fred pawed the ground with a giant hoof and then started slowly down Elm Street on his way out of town.

"Oh my God," Cameron said. "You're a moose whisperer!"

"Seriously, Han," Will said. "That was awesome. I had no idea you and Fred were so close."

"Neither did I," Hannah said as her heart rate slowed to a more normal beat after the rush of adrenaline that came with facing off with Fred.

Will nudged Cameron toward her car. "Let's get your car to the dealer for a trade-in before Fred changes his mind and comes back."

"I'm getting a different color this time." Cameron handed him the keys. "You'd better drive. My hands are still shaking."

Hannah watched them drive off, waving as they went by.

"That was totally hot," a deep male voice said against her ear.

She spun around and found Nolan standing behind her. "Where'd you come from?"

After a nearly sleepless night following the confrontation with his father, Nolan had arrived at the garage feeling out of sorts and cranky. Because he'd fallen behind yesterday, he got right to work on two oil changes, a tire rotation and a brake job. It was all routine stuff, so he could do it without thinking. Unfortunately, that gave him far too much time to obsess about how the sweet pleasure of his evening with Hannah had given way to ugliness with his father.

Skeeter came stumbling in around ten, looking as sleep deprived as Nolan felt and holding two large cups of coffee. He handed one of them to Nolan who accepted it with a grateful nod.

Through bloodshot eyes, Skeeter took a closer look at Nolan. "What's a matter with you?"

"Nothing. What's a matter with you?"

"Not a darned thing," Skeeter said with a cat-that-swallowed-the-canary smile full of pure male satisfaction.

Nolan couldn't bear to think about what had him so satisfied. Ever since Skeeter had started seeing Dude, or whatever it was you'd call what the two of them were doing together, he'd walked around with a sleepy, dopey look on his face and had the need to share details that made Nolan want to find the highest cliff to jump from.

"Heard Vernon was poking around town yesterday."

Nolan's shoulders stiffened at the mention of his father's name.

"You see any sign of him?"

He took a drink of coffee and said a silent prayer of thanks to the god of caffeine, who was going to get him through what promised to be an endless day. "Maybe."

"Aw, fuck, Nolan. What'd he want?"

"What does he always want?"

"Did you give it to him?"

"I gave him what I had on me, which wasn't much."

"One of these times, you need to say no."

"I don't want to talk about it."

"I know, boy," Skeeter said with a deep sigh. "You never want to talk about it."

Because he couldn't deny that, he did what he always did when things became too much for him—he worked like a demon. He worked straight through lunch and into the afternoon before lightheadedness set in, reminding him he needed to eat.

"I'm going to hit the diner," Nolan said to Skeeter after he'd thoroughly washed his hands. "You want anything?"

"Wouldn't say no to a BLT on wheat."

"Okay."

Nolan had emerged from the garage to find Hannah staring down Fred, and his heart had literally stopped at the sight of her relatively tiny body standing before the huge animal. It took everything he had not to run over and get between her and Fred, but Fred had saved him the trouble by strolling off as if he had not a care in the world.

Once the panic subsided, Nolan walked directly to Hannah, drawn to her in a way he'd never been to anyone else.

When she asked him where he'd come from, he gestured to the garage. "Forgot to eat."

Her gaze coasted over his face. "You look exhausted. Is everything okay?"

"It is now."

She smiled, and he felt a thousand times better. That was all it took. Christ, he had it bad for her, and it seemed to be getting worse all the time. And then he remembered the things he was keeping from her—including his passion for fast and risky driving as well as his deadbeat father—and the agonizing fear that he wasn't good enough for her sucked the wind from his lungs.

"Nolan? Are you okay? You really need to eat." She took him by the arm and pulled him toward the diner. "Come on."

As he followed her up the stairs, her hand still on his arm, it occurred to him that she was making a rather public declaration by dragging him into the diner. He discovered he quite liked her public declaration, even if his stomach ached with more than just hunger. After spending even a little time with her, after holding her and kissing her and touching her soft skin, he couldn't imagine going back to the empty life he'd been leading before her.

But the second he told her about his high-stakes passion or let her into the nightmare that was his family, he'd lose her. He had almost no doubt about that, and the thought depressed him more than anything had in a long time.

"What's troubling you?" she asked when they were seated in a booth.

He wanted to reach for her hands, but wasn't sure she was ready to go *that* public, so he resisted. "Nothing now."

"How about before?"

"Could we maybe talk about it later? I've had a bitchy day until about five minutes ago, and all I want to do is sit here and look at you. Is that okay?"

She blushed as she nodded, and under the table, her hand curled around his. "Does this help?"

"Yeah," he said gruffly. Her touch affected him so profoundly that all he could do was gaze at her, drinking in every detail of her face, focusing primarily on the rosy pink lips that were still a bit swollen from their passionate kisses the night before. Longing zipped through him and had him shifting in his seat to accommodate the sudden pressure against his fly. He released a shaky breath as Megan approached the table to take their order.

Nolan asked for a cheeseburger and fries as well as Skeeter's BLT to go.

"Just a Diet Coke for me," Hannah said.

"You don't want anything to eat?" Nolan asked.

She shook her head. "I'll steal a few of your fries."

He held her hand between both of his as he continued to stare greedily at her. "We're kind of going public here," he whispered, aware of the attention they were generating from other patrons.

"That's okay," she said with a hint of hesitation that he tuned right in to.

"Are you sure?"

"I . . . Sometimes I wonder . . . What people will think of me if I start to date again."

"How do you mean?"

"Everyone has been so kind to me since Caleb died, and I know it's weird, but I worry about letting them down or something." She glanced up at him, slaying him with her expressive eyes. "That's stupid, right?"

"It's not stupid. You want them to respect you, and you want them to know you still respect Caleb and his memory."

"Yes," she said, sounding relieved. "That's it exactly. Speaking of his memory . . ." Hannah told him about the retreat she planned to open at the house and showed him the logo Cameron had left with her.

He studied the picture for a long moment. "Won't this tell the world that he's still very much on your mind?"

"I suppose it will."

"People know you haven't forgotten him, Hannah. How could you? How could any of us ever forget him?"

On the other side of the diner, Percy Flanders and Cletus Wagner, best friends of Hannah's grandfather, watched them closely. At one point, Cletus leaned over to catch a glimpse of what was going on under the table. Upon righting himself, he raised a nosy white eyebrow in Nolan's direction.

"Do you want me to let go?" he asked, aware that she'd noticed the attention from the old men.

"No."

"I wish I had the balls to lean across this table and kiss you."

Her nervous laughter further inflamed him. He wanted her so fiercely. "It might be best to save that for a more private setting."

He groaned at her suggestive words and was forced to release her hand when his lunch landed with a clatter on the table. "What's her problem?" he asked after Megan stormed off.

"She's mad at me."

He doused the burger and fries with ketchup. "At *you*? Why?"

"Because I'm friends with Cameron."

"Still not getting it."

"Megan is madly in love with Will, or at least she has herself convinced she is."

Nolan paused with a fry halfway to his mouth. "Megan is in love with *Will*? Since when?"

"Um, pretty much forever."

"Seriously? Wow, I totally missed that one. So she hates Cameron."

"Naturally. And she hates me because I love Cameron."

"Yikes. That's a whole lot of hate going around."

"I know! It's so silly—and get this. I heard this morning that Hunter actually has a thing for Megan."

"Hunter as in your twin brother Hunter?"

Exasperated, she said, "Yes, my twin brother. What other Hunter do you know?"

"I figured it had to be some other Hunter, because I so don't see him with her."

"Me either, especially when she's so *flagrant* about her feelings for Will. Poor Hunter. And in other Abbott news, apparently Colton has a girlfriend." She leaned in closer to whisper. "He shaved off his beard *and* cut his hair."

"All of this just since I last saw you?"

"It's been a busy day."

"I'd say so."

She dipped one of his fries into ketchup and popped it into her mouth. "So what's your meeting tonight about?" All at once, she seemed uncertain. "I'm sorry. It's none of my business. I didn't mean to pry."

"You're not prying. You're interested. There's a difference. And I want to tell you about my meeting, but that's a whole separate conversation we need to have very soon."

"Is it an AA meeting?" She quickly added, "If it is, that's okay."

Laughing, he said, "No, nothing like that. It's an addiction of another kind."

"I confess to being intrigued."

She wouldn't be intrigued once she heard how he liked to spend his free time. She'd most likely be horrified and never want to see him again.

Her hand covered his—on top of the table this time. "Whatever it is, I want to hear about it. I want to know you, Nolan."

"And what if you don't like what you learn about me?"

"I suppose we'll have to cross that bridge when we get to it. So far, I like everything I know about you."

"*Everything?*"

She nodded as she gazed intently at him. "Uh-huh."

He quickly finished his lunch and signaled for the check, which he paid with haste, and picked up the bag with Skeeter's takeout. "You left something important in my office yesterday. You should come and get it."

Hannah's brows came together in an adorably confused expression. "What did I leave?"

"I'll show you when we get there. Come on."

Excited, confused, intrigued and aroused by his obvious desire to be alone with her, Hannah walked quickly to keep up with him. He kept a tight hold on her hand as they moved briskly on the sidewalk, attracting the attention of several passers-by, who nodded in greeting to her.

At the garage, Nolan dropped the white bag containing the BLT on top of a tall red tool chest. "There's your sandwich," he called to Skeeter.

"Hey, boss, Mrs. Andersen called while you were gone—"

"Take a message."

"I did. That's what I'm trying to tell you."

"Tell me later." Nolan slammed the office door in Skeeter's bemused face.

"That wasn't very nice," Hannah said.

Like the day before, he pinned her to the door with the weight of his big body pressed against her. "I'll apologize later." He tipped his head and dropped a series of kisses along the column of her neck. "I'm addicted to the way you smell, the way you taste." He dragged his tongue lightly over her neck, making her shudder.

With her fingers curled into his belt loops, she held on for dear life as she felt the sharp bite of his teeth. She gasped and arched against him, desperate for more.

"His truck is here," a familiar voice said from the outer office. "I know he's here somewhere."

"Um, I wouldn't go in there," Skeeter said. "He's . . . um . . . busy."

"Goddamn it," Nolan whispered.

"Is that Mrs. Andersen?" Hannah whispered back.

"The one and only. She's an auto-hypochondriac. Always thinks something is wrong with her car and nothing ever is."

"She's got a crush on you."

He drew back from her. "What?"

"That's why she makes up problems with her car—so she can see you."

"That is so not true."

Smiling, Hannah tugged him by the hair, urging him to kiss her while he still could.

As his lips slid over hers, a loud pounding sounded on the door. "Nolan! It's Mrs. Andersen. I need to speak with you about Sadie."

"The car has a name?" Hannah whispered.

He rolled his eyes.

Hannah snuggled tighter against the erection that pulsed against her stomach, drawing a tortured gasp from him.

"Maybe I can help you," Skeeter said.

"I don't want *you*," Mrs. Anderson said disdainfully. "I want *him*."

"Told you," Hannah whispered.

Groaning in frustration, Nolan stepped back from her and ran his fingers repeatedly through his hair, as if trying to regain his sanity. "We're still on for tonight, right?"

"Absolutely. I'll see you after your meeting."

He sat back against the desk, gazing at her.

"So what did I leave here yesterday?"

"Me."

Smiling, she crossed the small space to him, stepped between his outstretched legs and put her arms around his neck. "You were right. That was something important."

"Is it later yet?" he asked with a sigh.

"Not yet, but it'll be here before you know it, and I'll be ready."

He nuzzled a sensitive spot by her ear, setting off a series of tremors that had her nipples tightening. "Don't forget the jeans."

"They're in the dryer as we speak."

After a groan filled with anticipation and one last tight squeeze, Nolan let her go. "See you soon."

"Yes, you will."

"Poor Mrs. Anderson. She'll be crushed when she sees you come out of here."

Hannah patted his face. "Let her down easy, and tell her you're taken."

He surprised her when he took hold of her hand and touched his lips to her palm. Looking up at her, he said, "Am I?"

"What?" she asked, breathless after the shockingly erotic brush of his tongue against her sensitive palm.

"Taken?"

"Yes, you are."

With his hands now on her face he kissed her softly. "You have no idea how happy it makes me to be taken by you."

A shudder of desire rippled through her entire body.

"You'd better go before I forget where we are," he said gruffly.

"Right." Hannah picked up her purse and hooked it over her shoulder, her hands trembling slightly. She forced herself to meet his gaze, which was still intensely focused on her. "I'm happy to be taken by you, too."

Somehow her legs responded to her order to move. Somehow she managed to walk out of his office, where she said a quick hello to her neighbor, Mrs. Andersen, but kept moving so the older woman wouldn't have a chance to grill her about why she'd been holed up in Nolan's office.

Somehow she managed to walk across the street to the store to drop off the jewelry she'd forgotten to give Will when she saw him earlier. The upstairs offices were oddly deserted, so she left her parcel on Will's desk and went downstairs to the store. She had a cider donut as she caught up with Dottie, who ran the donut counter, and smiled at the gaggle of women who'd gathered in front of her father's legendary display of Beatles memorabilia.

"Busy day?" she asked Dottie.

"Exceptionally busy. Just the way we like it."

Hannah looked around the Green Mountain Country Store, where every inch of space was as familiar to her as anything in her life. The sights, the scents, the products, the barrels of peanuts and pickles, and the wooden beams that held the place together were hardwired into her DNA. The store was as much her "home" as the red barn where she'd been raised and the Victorian where she'd lived so happily with Caleb.

His name passing through her mind triggered a reminder

about the journals that waited for her at home and snapped her out of the fog she'd been in since she left Nolan.

"So . . . a little birdie told me you might be dating again?" Dottie asked with a hopeful smile on her kind face.

"Maybe."

"If the rumors are true, you've chosen a very fine young man."

Since she didn't want to talk about her relationship with Nolan and was unsettled by the prospect of others talking about it, she offered Dottie a small smile and a nod of agreement before she said her good-byes.

Hannah walked to her car, got in and took a moment to collect her thoughts. Watching people she'd known all her life walk past on the sidewalk, it became clear to her that she needed to speak to Caleb's parents about Nolan—before someone else did.

CHAPTER 14

After many late nights, endless lists of pros and cons and many arguments, Caleb has chosen the army over hockey. It was a tough decision for him, especially with three NHL teams showing interest and me pushing him in that direction. I try to tell myself that as long as we're together, I'll be happy, but I've never gotten over my fears of him going into the military. I want him to be at peace with what was a difficult decision, so I'm trying to embrace my future as an army wife. It's not easy, but I'm making the effort for him.

—From the diary of Hannah Abbott, age twenty-two

The instant Hannah cleared the doorway, Nolan exhaled the deep breath he'd been holding. He'd spent more time trying to control his emotions in the last few days than he had in the whole rest of his life combined, or so it seemed. Being around Hannah, being free to express himself to her—finally— had him clinging to the razor's edge of sanity and desire.

He was once again throbbing with need and had hours of work ahead of him before he could be with her again. Pushing himself off the desk, he went around to sit in the chair, figuring he could take a few minutes to pay some bills and hopefully cool off, too.

Mrs. Andersen filled the doorway with her considerable figure, clearing her throat to get his attention.

"Hi there, Mrs. Andersen. How are you today?"

"I'm just fine, Nolan. How are you?"

"Great."

"Do you mind if I come in for a minute?"

"Um, sure," he said, gesturing to the visitor chair that had seen much better days. When she was seated, she took a good long look at him that nearly had him withering under her glare. "Something on your mind?"

"I know it's none of my business . . ."

Oh jeez, Nolan thought. *Don't go there.*

"But I've noticed your truck outside Hannah's house a few times recently. Late at night, too."

He wanted to tell her that she was right. It was none of her business. But his grandfather had raised him better than that, so he didn't say a word. Rather, he let her dig her own ditch.

"You know we're all so protective of Hannah, and she's been through such an awful thing . . ."

Nolan refused to make this easy for her, so he held his silence.

Mrs. Andersen cleared her throat as a faint blush tinged her full cheeks with color. "I just hope you're being . . . careful with her."

That was it. He'd heard enough, and since she'd managed to totally kill the erection Hannah had left him with, he stood abruptly. "Thanks for coming in and for your concern, but I've got to get back to work. We checked your car, and there's nothing wrong with the brake lines. They're as good as new. Let me get your keys."

"Nolan, wait. I apologize if I was out of line. I care for Hannah. Everyone does."

"So do I. You have nothing to worry about."

"That's good to know."

Nolan got her keys and sent her on her way, knowing she'd be back again in a week or so with another manufactured problem with her car. She was a nice enough lady, and he didn't mind indulging her—most of the time. However, he had no desire to speak to her about his relationship with Hannah. It was bad enough the entire Abbott family was involved. The rest of the town could butt out.

He threw himself into work for the remainder of the day, forcing every other thought out of his head until later when he could be with Hannah again. That was the only time lately his life seemed to make sense, and he needed much more of her. Soon.

For the second time in as many days, Hannah arrived at the Guthries' home and pulled into the driveway behind Amelia's car. On the way, Hannah had thought about what she needed to tell them and how they might take the news. She had no doubt they'd be thrilled about the retreat. But the part about her and Nolan . . . She couldn't say for sure how that would go, which scared the hell out of her.

She took a deep breath for courage and got out of the car to go inside.

Bob met her at the mudroom door and opened it for her. "Hi, Hannah." Tall and imposing with steel-blue eyes, he'd intimidated Hannah for a long time before she discovered a softie lived under all his military bearing and bluster. She returned her father-in-law's embrace. "Good to see you. Sorry I missed you yesterday."

"I was, too," she said.

"Thanks for bringing Homer's collar to us. That was really nice of you. Come in. Amelia's in the kitchen making something that drew me out of my office to investigate."

"How's the book coming?" He was working on a memoir about army life that would end with the loss of his son to war.

"Slow but steady."

"I can't wait to read it."

"Oh hi, Hannah," Amelia said, wiping her hands before she came over to kiss and hug her. "Twice in two days. How lucky are we?"

Hannah was relieved to see that her mother-in-law looked more like herself today, less shattered than she'd been the day before. "I have some news I wanted to share with you, so I'm glad you're both here."

"Have a seat," Bob said, holding one of the kitchen chairs for her.

Hannah slid into the chair and a glass of iced tea appeared before her as they joined her at the table.

"What's going on, honey?" Amelia asked kindly.

"Well, you know I love the house as much as Caleb did. As much as all of you do."

"Of course we know that," Bob said. "You've taken immaculate care of the place. My mother would be so pleased."

"That's nice of you to say. I've been thinking lately though that it's a bit big for one person, and it's a shame to see all that great space not being used. I told you about Will's new girlfriend, Cameron, right?"

"The one from New York?" Amelia asked.

"Yes, that's her. She came up with the great idea to use the house as a retreat of sorts for other women who've lost their husbands to war."

Her in-laws exchanged glances, but nothing in their expressions gave away their feelings on the matter, so Hannah pressed on.

"We thought it could be a place where other widows could make friends, share their common grief and hopefully heal together. What do you think?"

"It sounds like a wonderful idea to me," Amelia said.

Bob nodded in agreement.

Hannah withdrew the paper containing the logo for the retreat and put it on the table in front of them. "Cameron came up with this, and I wanted to see what you think of it before we go any further."

"Oh," Amelia said, her hand over her heart. "You'd name it for Caleb?"

"Yes," Hannah said. "I want him and his face and his name to be very present in this entire effort, but only if you're comfortable with it."

Bob smoothed his hand repeatedly over the paper bearing his son's image. His grief was palpable as he stared at his son in the uniform he'd proudly worn for twenty-two years. "I think it's a brilliant idea and an amazing way to honor his memory," Bob said gruffly after long moments of silence.

Relief flooded through Hannah. She'd worried about what

they might think of how she planned to use the home that had been in their family for two generations. After Caleb died, she'd offered the house to them, but they'd insisted it had belonged to him and was now rightfully hers.

"I agree," Amelia said. "I'd love to be involved in some way. Perhaps I could be your official cook or something."

"I'd love that," Hannah said, sincerely. "That'd be wonderful."

"I could be your maintenance guy," Bob offered with a shy grin that reminded her of Caleb when he'd done something he knew she wouldn't like, which was often.

"Thank you both so much," Hannah said, fighting tears. "I can't tell you how much it means to me to have your support and your involvement."

"You know how important it is to us that people don't forget him," Bob said.

Hannah laid a hand over his. "None of us will ever forget him. He was simply unforgettable."

"That he was," Bob said with a small smile that didn't reach his eyes. "Thank you for this and for all you've done over the years to honor him. He was a very lucky man to have such a lovely and devoted wife."

"We were both lucky."

Amelia dabbed at her eyes with a napkin.

"You might want to consider a board of directors to help you run the place," Bob said. "I could assist with that, too, if you're interested."

"I'll take all the help I can get. I have no idea what I'm doing, so whatever you're willing to do is fine with me."

"I'll ask around and drum up some board members to help you out."

"I was going to ask Mrs. Hendricks for her advice about the practicalities of running an inn," Hannah said of the woman who ran the Admiral Frances Butler Inn, the only bed-and-breakfast in Butler.

"Oh I'm sure she'd love to help," Amelia said. "I'll talk to her at our bridge night this week and let you know."

Surrounded by their love and support, Hannah was paralyzed with fear over how they'd respond to the other thing she needed to tell them. If she had her druthers, they'd never know she was seeing another man. But in their small town, such things didn't remain private for long, and too many people already knew. She couldn't take the chance of them finding out from someone else.

Clearing her throat, she dug deep for the courage she would need to say the words. "So there's one other thing I wanted to talk to you about."

"What's that, honey?" Amelia asked. "Are you all right? You're suddenly pale."

"Um, it's just that it's hard for me to talk to you about this . . ."

"Whatever it is, you know we love you and want only the best for you, right?" Amelia asked.

Touched by their endless support, Hannah nodded. "That means so much to me." She took another deep breath. "I wanted to tell you I've begun to date." She paused, gauging their reaction, which was impossible to read. "I think of Caleb all the time. Every day. All day. But . . . I . . ."

"Please, Hannah," Bob said gently. "You don't have to explain yourself to us. Ever."

She couldn't contain the tears that spilled down her cheeks in a flood that left her feeling raw and exposed.

Amelia handed her a napkin and then dealt with her own tears. "Is it Nolan?"

Shocked, Hannah stared at her. "How do you know that?" she asked in barely more than a whisper.

"He came to see us," Amelia said. "A while ago."

"He . . . he came here."

"He comes quite often to check on us," Bob said.

The thought of Nolan remaining faithful to his late friend's parents triggered a storm of emotion inside her. "I didn't know that."

"Will and Hunter do, too," Amelia said. "The other Sultans call and send e-mails frequently. We're very blessed to have all of you in our lives. Caleb knew how to pick his friends. That's for sure."

Hannah was still trying to get her head around the fact that Nolan had spoken to the Guthries about her. About them. She wasn't sure how she felt about that. "Yes, he certainly did."

"Don't be angry with Nolan," Amelia said. "He was very

sweet telling us that he had asked you to go out with him, and it was very important to him that we were okay with it. Because if we weren't, he wouldn't pursue anything further with you."

"How long ago was this?" Hannah asked.

"Oh weeks ago, wasn't it, Bob?"

"More than a month," her husband agreed.

So after they'd danced at the Grange and after he'd kissed her the first time, but before the recent developments.

"You don't seem pleased, honey," Amelia said. "He was very nice and very respectful, and we appreciated the gesture. We love him like one of our own. You know that. The poor guy doesn't have much family to speak of, so he's been an honorary Guthrie for longer than I can remember. Don't be angry with him. We'd hate to be the cause of that."

"I'm not angry. I'm just surprised he did that when nothing had really happened yet."

"He said as much and that he was hoping it would turn into something special, but not if it caused us any additional grief," Bob said. "We assured him he had our blessing to date our beautiful daughter-in-law and that we couldn't think of anyone more deserving of her than him."

Hannah pinched her lips together, hoping to stem the tide of emotion that threatened to break her again.

"It was an incredibly sweet gesture," Amelia added, almost as if she was trying to convince Hannah to forgive him when there was really nothing to forgive. It was a sweet gesture.

"I don't want you to think I'm getting over Caleb or anything like that. I'll never completely get over losing him."

"We know, Hannah," Bob said. "But you're a young, beautiful woman with decades of life in front of you. We don't expect you to spend all that time alone mourning the past. Caleb wouldn't have wanted that either."

Hannah didn't mention the journals she'd found among his things to his parents because she wanted a chance to read them before she shared them with anyone. She wanted one last moment between her and the husband she'd adored and would bring them to his parents the next time she came to visit.

"It means a lot to me to have your support. And I hope you

know that no matter what happens in the future, you'll always be part of my family and my life."

"We wouldn't have it any other way," Bob said. "Don't worry about our approval, Hannah. You have it. No matter what you decide to do. We approve and we support you. Always."

"That's a priceless gift and one I'll cherish forever," Hannah said through her tears as she got up to hug him and then Amelia. "Thank you so much."

"Thank you, honey," Amelia said as she embraced Hannah. "You made our son very happy, and it gives us peace to know he was so deeply loved."

"He was," Hannah whispered.

"We know." Amelia got up and left the room, returning a minute later with a white envelope and tears in her eyes. "I have something for you from Caleb. I was under strict instructions to give it to you when I thought you were ready, and it seems like you might be ready now."

Hannah's heart leapt into her throat as she stared at the envelope. "What is it?"

Amelia handed it to her. On the front, in Caleb's familiar handwriting, were the words "For Hannah. Worst Case."

"Oh my God," Hannah whispered when she realized what it was. "You've had it all this time?"

Amelia wiped the tears from her cheeks. "He was very clear about when I was to give it to you. Not until it seemed like you were doing better and ready to hear what he had to say."

"Do you know what it says?"

Amelia shook her head. "That's between the two of you."

"I . . . I should go."

"Are you okay to drive, Hannah?" Bob asked, looking at her with concern.

"I'm fine."

"Please tell me you're not angry with me," Amelia said. "He was very adamant about how and when he wanted you to have that letter."

"Of course I'm not angry," Hannah said, hugging her mother-in-law. "You think I don't know how he could be?"

"You knew better than anyone," Amelia said with a tearful laugh.

She left them and drove home thinking about the letter Caleb had left for her and trying to process the fact that Nolan had gone to them, seeking their approval. The Guthries were important to him, too, and he'd been protecting his relationship with them as much as hers. But it touched her deeply to realize how respectful he'd been toward them and how much easier he'd made it for her to share the news with them than it would've been otherwise.

At home, she propped the letter on her bedside table to read later when she had worked up the fortitude to face it. To discover after all this time that Caleb had, in fact, considered his own mortality was shocking, to say the least. Finding out about the letter had thrown her for a loop, but she'd promised this night to Nolan, and she didn't have the heart to cancel. She also didn't want to cancel because she was eager to see him.

She rushed through a shower and dried her hair until it fell in long silky waves over her shoulders. She found a bottle of aromatherapy lotion that Charley had given her for Christmas last year and smoothed it over her skin before applying mascara and eyeliner as well as a hint of bronzer to her pale cheeks. Digging through her underwear drawer, she found a pretty pair of panties and a matching lace-trimmed bra that had also come from Charley. She pulled on the jeans he'd requested along with a pale green cashmere sweater with a cowl neck. Leather boots, earrings and a spritz of her favorite perfume completed the ensemble.

When she was ready, she sat on the bed and stared at the envelope on the bedside table. She picked it up, turned it over between her hands and brought it to her nose to see if it smelled like him, but it smelled only like paper and must from all the years it had waited to be read.

While she was extremely tempted to read it, fearing a setback, she returned it to the table and got up to go downstairs to wait for Nolan. Tonight, she wanted all her thoughts focused on him.

CHAPTER 15

—◄•►—

I haven't had time to write lately with graduation on Thursday, Caleb's commissioning ceremony on Friday and the wedding on Saturday. By Saturday night, I'll be Caleb's wife—and an army wife. We're so ready and so excited to start our life together. First stop is Ft. Benning, Georgia. Sometimes I think about how much I used to "hate" him. I think maybe I actually loved him all that time . . .

—From the diary of Hannah Abbott, age twenty-two

The meeting lasted for what felt like forever. Nolan had to force himself to pay attention when all he could think about was getting the hell out of there so he could go to Hannah.

Hannah . . . He'd thought about her nonstop all day, ever since she'd told him he was taken. *Taken.* What a great way to describe how he felt about her. He was taken with her, taken by her and completely and totally in love with her. It was such a relief to finally admit that to himself.

"Nolan." Skeeter nudged him in the ribs. "Pay attention."

Embarrassed to be caught zoning out, Nolan cleared his mind of everything but the conversation going on right in front of him.

"I reserved some practice time next weekend in New Hampshire," the crew chief, Dave Lassiter, was saying.

"I can't do it next weekend," Nolan said. "I've got a funeral to go to." He didn't mention the funeral was for a dog, since he doubted the other guys would appreciate how important it was that he be there for Hannah.

"Who died?" Skeeter asked, his brows knit skeptically.

"No one you know."

Dave's hands were on his hips, his mouth set with displeasure. "Nolan, I gotta ask . . . Is your head in the game this year? You've missed more meetings than you've made, and now you're 'unavailable' for hard-to-come-by practice time?"

"I've had some personal stuff going on," Nolan said, annoyed by the insinuation that he wasn't interested in the team anymore. "I'm committed. I'm just not available next weekend. Can we do it the week after?"

"I'll see what I can arrange."

Nolan had joined the team years ago as their chief mechanic and had been tapped to drive in an exhibition race last year after their driver's pregnant wife insisted he give up his thrill-seeking activities to ensure their unborn child had a father in its life. The team had asked Nolan to take the wheel that night, and he'd pulled off a stunning upset that had cemented his standing as the team's driver.

He couldn't deny he loved the rush, the adrenaline, the teamwork and the thrill of winning. Until recently, Nolan had been fully committed to the team and its goals. Now he was torn between the sport that had long been a passion of his and passion of a different sort.

He left the meeting the second it ended, went home to shower off the filth of a long workday, shaved and changed his clothes, and was back in his truck twenty minutes later wearing a black V-neck sweater and jeans. Filled with anticipation, he drove faster than he should have in his haste to get to her.

Arriving at her house a short time later, he parked on the street and headed up the sidewalk. He rang the bell and waited, hoping tonight she would open the door rather than leaving him to wonder what had happened since the last time he saw her.

And then there she was, looking gorgeous and sexy, stealing the air from his lungs with the way she looked at him, as if she had been waiting impatiently for him to get there.

"Hey," he said, his hands propped on the doorframe, which kept him from immediately reaching for her and hauling her into his arms. "You look beautiful."

She took a long perusing look at him that instantly fired him up. "You don't look too bad yourself."

"Get your coat."

"Where are we going?"

"Out."

"How come?"

"Because I've never officially taken you anywhere, and I don't want you to think that all I want from you is what we've been doing on your sofa every night."

"Oh it isn't?" she asked with a coy grin.

"Not hardly."

"I kind of like the sofa stuff."

"I like it, too, and we'll get to that. Later. Now about that coat?"

"Fine. If you insist."

"I do."

She turned and walked to the hall closet.

Only because he was watching her every move so closely did he catch the slight wiggle she included for his benefit that had him gripping the doorframe that much tighter.

She returned to the door wearing a coat and carrying her purse.

He stepped aside to let her go by, and bit back a groan when she brushed against him. Closing the inside door, he tested it to make sure it was locked before he followed her to his truck and held the passenger door for her. When she was settled, he went around the front of the truck and got in the driver's side. His heart was beating fast and his hands felt clammy—the same way they'd been on the first date of his life when he'd been a stupid, naïve teenager.

This was so much more important, thus the nerves.

"Where are we going?" Hannah asked as they pulled away from the curb.

"I promised you Mexican food in Stowe days ago." Though the last thing he needed was additional heat, he adjusted the temperature to make sure she didn't get chilled. "You're not cold, are you?"

"Nope. I'm good." She glanced over at him, and he could feel her watching him. "Why do you seem nervous?"

"Do I?"

"Uh-huh."

"I'm not nervous, but I couldn't wait to see you tonight. I barely heard a word that was said at my meeting, and when it was over, I flew out of there to go home and clean up."

Her hand landed on his arm, traveling down until she reached his hand. Their palms came together, fingers linked, and that was all it took to calm and settle him.

"Much better," he said.

Holding hands, they rode in companionable silence until they arrived in the village of Stowe. At the restaurant, he ushered her inside, where they were seated at a secluded corner table.

Hannah ordered a glass of white wine, and he asked for a beer.

"This is nice," she said of the relaxed atmosphere as they enjoyed a basket of chips and salsa.

"I would've taken you somewhere nicer, but I know how much you love Mexican."

"You don't have to try to impress me, Nolan. I don't need any of that."

"What if I want to spoil you?"

"Well, that's up to you. As long as you know I don't *need* it."

"Duly noted." Since he couldn't stand to be so close to her but unable to touch her, he slid his chair closer to hers and put his arm around her.

She leaned into him, her hair brushing against his face. "You smell good," she whispered.

"So do you."

He ordered a burrito, and she got the enchiladas she said she'd been thinking of for days.

"How was the rest of your day?" he asked while they waited for their food.

"Enlightening."

"How so?"

"I saw the Guthries."

"Oh yeah? How are they?"

"Sad about Homer, of course, but doing okay."

"That's good to hear. I need to get over there to see them."

"I heard you were there a month or so ago."

Every cell in Nolan's body froze as she said those words.

"They told me that you talked to them. About me."

"And?"

"And what?"

"Are you mad I did that?"

"No."

He could finally breathe again when she said that single word.

"At first, I was surprised more than anything because nothing had really happened yet when you talked to them."

"Yes, it had. I'd danced with you—in public. I'd kissed you. I wanted to kiss you again. I wanted to be with you, and I couldn't do that if it wasn't okay with them. I just couldn't. I hope you understand."

"I do understand. I went there today for the same reason. I didn't want them to hear about us from someone else."

"What did they say?"

"That they love us both and support whatever decisions I make. They also said they couldn't think of any man more worthy of me than you."

Pleased and touched, Nolan said, "They did? Really?"

"Uh-huh."

"That's nice of them."

"It's true. And it was very sweet of you to think of them and how they might feel about Caleb's close friend dating his wife."

"I wouldn't be able to stand it if I did something that hurt them."

Placing her hand on his face, she turned him toward her and kissed him. "Thank you for thinking of them. It means a lot to me that you did that."

"I was sort of hoping you'd never find out," he said with a

sheepish grin. "I was afraid it would make you mad if you heard about it, but I couldn't not do it, you know?"

"I do, and it was the right thing to do, even if it did surprise me a little."

"I should've told you myself."

"It's okay that you didn't."

He took a drink of his beer and thought about the other thing he needed to tell her. "There's something else you should know before this goes any further. Something I wouldn't want you to hear through the grapevine."

"What's that?" Her tone was relaxed, but he felt the tension creep into her shoulders.

"About six years ago I was asked to be the chief mechanic on a stock car racing team."

"That sounds like fun."

"It is. I love it."

"Are you like one of those pit crew guys on TV who can change a tire in ten seconds?"

"I used to be, but now I play a bigger role on the team." He took another sip of beer because his mouth was suddenly dry.

"What kind of role?"

"As of a year ago, I'm the driver."

"Wait, so you . . . You're the driver."

"I'm the driver."

"Isn't that dangerous?"

"It can be if you don't know what you're doing. But I know what I'm doing. I've been driving and messing with cars since I was twelve."

"Still . . . You can't always trust that everyone on the track with you is as good at it as you are."

In typical Hannah fashion, she'd zeroed right in on the absolute truth of the matter. "I suppose so, but you don't need to worry, Hannah. I take every precaution, and I've never even come close to a wreck in more than thirty races and hundreds of hours of practice."

"Are you good at it?"

"I've won five times, which has earned us a few sponsors and a bit of recognition on the circuit."

Before she could reply, their meals arrived, and the waiter asked if he could get them anything else.

"I think we're good," Nolan said with a glance at Hannah, who nodded.

It killed him not to ask her what was going through her mind, and he had to force his dinner past the lump of fear in his throat. What if she asked him to give it up? Could he? Would he? He honestly didn't know how he could give it up without letting down a lot of other people who'd worked really hard to get where they were. Those people were his friends, and letting them down wasn't high on his list of priorities.

But she was at the very top of his list, and if she asked him to, he'd probably stop racing. He hoped she didn't ask.

"Could I maybe come see you race sometime?"

"I'd love to have you there. Any time you want."

"I'm not going to lie to you. It makes me very nervous to think about you endangering yourself for fun."

"I swear I'm as careful as I can possibly be. I have no desire to maim or kill myself. I've got far too much to live for. Especially lately."

The postscript drew a faint smile from her. "Why do you do it?"

He thought about that for a second. "It's hard to explain the thrill of flying around the track, jockeying for position, outmaneuvering the opposition, working with a team to achieve results. It's an incredible high."

"You really love it."

"I really do."

She focused on her meal, so he did the same, trying to quell his anxiety. He'd told the truth about his "hobby," and she hadn't freaked out or demanded he stop racing or stop seeing her. That had been his greatest fear, that she'd make it an either-or thing. He should've known she was built of better stuff than that, but still. He was relieved she hadn't issued any ultimatums. Yet anyway . . . After she saw him race, that might be a different story.

"In two weeks, the team will be going to New Hampshire for a weekend to practice before our season begins later this spring. If you'd like to come along, I'd love to take you with me."

"That sounds like fun."

He wiped his mouth with the cloth napkin in his lap,

reached for her hand and held it between both of his. "Will you do something for me?"

"Sure."

"Will you be honest with me about how you really feel about the racing? Good? Bad? Ugly? Whatever it is, will you tell me the truth?"

She nodded.

"Thank you," he said, leaning in to kiss her.

"I can't eat another bite. It was so good."

He signaled for the check. "I'm glad you enjoyed it."

They were on the way out of the restaurant when an older woman stood and waved to them. "Hannah! I thought that was you!"

Oh jeez, Nolan thought, *Mr. and Mrs. Guthrie's next-door neighbors*. Thank God the Guthries knew he and Hannah were seeing each other.

"Hi, Mr. and Mrs. Davis. How are you?"

Mrs. Davis cast a shrewd eye on Nolan before she returned her attention to Hannah. "Doing quite well, and you?"

"I'm fine. You know Nolan Roberts, right?"

"Sure, we do," Mr. Davis said. "Good to see you Nolan."

"You, too."

"Well," Hannah said. "We were just leaving. Enjoy your dinner."

Mrs. Davis smiled sweetly and waggled her fingers. "Nice to see you two."

Nolan kept his hand on Hannah's lower back as they left the restaurant and stepped into the chilly air.

"Thank goodness Bob and Amelia already know or they'd be finding out right about now," Hannah said.

"I was thinking the same exact thing."

"Myrna Davis is the biggest gossip in Butler. I bet she thinks she's stumbled upon one hell of a scoop."

"You think she's already on the phone with Amelia?" Nolan asked.

"I know she is! She wouldn't be able to resist."

"I'm sure Amelia is bursting her bubble by telling her she already knows. Poor Myrna," Nolan said, making Hannah laugh.

"Poor Myrna needs to mind her own business."

"What fun would that be?" He held the passenger door to the truck for her. "Incidentally, I got a talking to from Mrs. Andersen about how special you are and how I need to treat you well or face the wrath of the entire town."

Hannah's mouth fell open as she turned to face him. "Are you *serious*? She actually said that?"

"Words to that effect."

"People are certifiably insane in that town."

"No argument from me, but it's nice they're protective of you."

"Like it's not enough that my whole family feels like they have a right to know everything I do, now the rest of the town wants in on the action?"

"They feel invested in you, Hannah. They watched Caleb grow up, and they lost him, too. I suppose it's only natural they'd be protective of his wife."

"Technically, I'm not his wife anymore."

"Yes, you are. You'll always be his wife. Someday you might be someone else's wife, but you'll always be his, too."

Hannah rested her hands on his shoulders. "It means so much to me when you say things like that. But it means just as much to me that you don't think of me first and foremost as his widow."

He moved in closer to her, stepping between her legs to put his arms around her. "That's not how I think of you at all, even though it's definitely part of the overall picture. It's not the focus though."

"What is the focus?" she asked, sounding a bit breathless.

"So many things." Pushing her hair back, he exposed the elegant length of her neck. He trailed kisses from her ear to her throat. "Your sweetness, your incredible kindness to everyone, the patient way you put up with your siblings even when they're making you crazy." As he spoke, he continued the gentle, sensual assault on her neck. "The love and care you've shown to Caleb's family, the incredible way you've honored his memory, the amazing generosity you've shown to his friends by opening your home to us any time we get the urge to be together. And then there's your artistic talents, your dazzling smile, your expressive eyes that never miss a thing—"

"*Nolan*," she said on a shudder.

He wasn't sure if it was the words, the kisses or the cold

that was making her tremble. "I wasn't finished." Her unsteady laughter made him smile. "In fact, I was just getting started." He drew back to look into her eyes. "The word *widow* is not the first thing I think of when you come to mind. It hasn't been for a very long time."

With her hand curled around his nape, she drew him into a kiss that went from zero to holy shit in about three seconds. Her tongue curled around his as she tugged on his hair almost to the point of pain, but it was the best kind of pain.

Nolan lost all track of time as he fell deeper into her and the sweet, sexy sounds she made as he kissed her. He gripped her hips and pulled her in closer to him, pressing against her in an increasingly urgent rhythm.

And then he remembered where they were and that people they knew were inside the restaurant. Reluctantly, he drew back from her, gazing into eyes that had gone sleepy with desire. "How about we take this somewhere more comfortable and less public?"

"Yes, please."

"You're a sexy siren one minute and politely demure the next," he said as he reached around her to fasten her seatbelt. "It's quite a potent combination."

"I like to keep you guessing."

"That's not all you're doing to me." He kissed her again, chastely this time, before closing her door and moving painfully around the truck. He was like a walking, talking hard-on these days, and the constant state of arousal was making him a bit edgy.

As soon as he'd backed out of the lot, he reached for Hannah's hand and held it all the way home.

After a long period of silence, she said, "Nolan?"

"Yeah?"

Hesitantly, she said, "When we, you know, go to bed together . . . It can't be at my house."

Nolan nearly swallowed his tongue at the casual way in which she said such life-changing words. "Okay." She didn't need to spell out the reasons why she didn't want to make love to him for the first time in the home she'd shared with Caleb. But the fact that she was thinking about that and making plans for what seemed inevitable now did absolutely nothing to help the throbbing ache in his lap.

"Was it okay to say that?" she asked in a small voice that tugged at his heart.

He squeezed her hand. "I told you there's nothing you could say to me that wouldn't be okay. If something is on your mind, I want to know. No matter what it is. All right?"

"Yes. Thank you."

"God, Hannah, don't thank me. I should be thanking you. I feel like I'm dreaming or something because I get to be with you this way."

"You make me feel very special."

"You are very special."

They arrived at her house a short time later, and he went to help her out of the truck.

He kept an arm around her on the way up the walk to her porch. She unlocked the front door and reached for his arm, pulling him inside with her.

Nolan smiled at her obvious desire to spend more time with him and willingly followed her, shedding his coat as he went.

"Would you mind lighting the fire?" she asked. "I'll be right back."

"No problem."

He went into the sitting room as she went upstairs, piquing his curiosity about where she might be going and why. The firewood had already been laid in the hearth, so he struck a match and lit the kindling, blowing on the flame until it took. He was still kneeling in front of the fireplace when she rejoined him, wrapping her arms around him from behind.

Her soft curves pressed against his back and the heat of the fire against his face made for a potent combination.

He covered her hands with his, holding them flat against his chest where his heart beat fast and hard for her.

She shifted slightly to the right and kissed the sensitive spot just below his ear.

Nolan turned and drew her into his arms, looking down at her looking up at him as the fire crackled and sizzled. "I don't know if it's you or the fire, but I'm overheating. Can I take this sweater off?"

Nodding, she reached for the hem and helped him to raise it over his chest.

He pulled it from behind and tossed it aside.

Hannah's gaze skirted over his chest, taking a long perusing look that made him hard as stone.

And then she touched him, and he wanted to beg for mercy.

CHAPTER 16

❖

The wedding was amazing! We had it in the backyard at home on a perfect spring day. Gavin was Caleb's best man, and Hunter, Will, Nolan and Turk were his groomsmen. I told him he couldn't have ALL the Sultans or the wedding party would be bigger than the guest list. Since I refused to pick between Ella and Charley, Becky was my maid of honor, and my sisters and cousins were my bridesmaids. For as long as I live, I'll never forget the day I married the love of my life.

—From the diary of Hannah Abbott Guthrie,
age twenty-two

Hannah drank in her first look at Nolan's bare chest, which was as finely built as it seemed through his clothes. He had muscles everywhere, and suddenly the view of the top half wasn't enough. With her hands on his shoulders, she urged him to lie back on the rug in front of the hearth.

"Hannah . . ." He sounded tense and almost hesitant.

"Please? I want to look at you."

Blowing out a deep breath, he stretched out and watched her warily as she looked to her heart's content at dark chest hair, well-defined muscles in his shoulders, chest and belly as well as the enticing V-cut over his hip bones that dropped off into his jeans.

"Do you think less of me for wanting to kiss and lick those incredible abs?"

His nervous laughter made her smile. "Um no, definitely not." He combed his fingers through her hair. "Do anything you want, Hannah. I'm all yours."

She began with her hands flat against his pectorals, smoothing her palms over his chest and ribs to his belly, watching in stunned amazement as his erection lengthened under well-worn denim. She wanted to touch him there, too, but she didn't dare. Not yet anyway.

His heart beat hard under her hands as he watched her every move with sexy, half-closed eyes.

Hannah bent over him and left a path of kisses along his collarbone before moving down to run her tongue over his nipple, which drew a sharp gasp from him as his hands fisted her hair. "Does it feel good or bad?"

"Good," he said through gritted teeth. "So damned good."

Pleased with his reaction, she did it again before moving to the other side. He sucked in a sharp breath, which created a gap in his jeans and exposed the crown of his penis. She couldn't take her eyes off the sight of his straining, weeping cock, which got bigger before her eyes.

"Hannah," he groaned. "Touch me. Please touch me."

He didn't have to ask her twice. She tugged on the button to his jeans and carefully and slowly unzipped him. When she hesitated, he took her hand and placed it over his erection, pressing down from above.

"Yes," he whispered harshly as he moved his hand over hers, setting the pace and showing her what he liked. With his free hand, he brought her down to him, sucking her tongue into his mouth with a frenzied level of need he'd never shown her before.

She loved it. She loved the way his hips rose and fell against her hand, the way his hand gripped the back of her head to keep her anchored to him. She loved the all-consuming way he seemed to want her.

All at once, he slowed the pace of their hands over his cock. "Stop or I'm going to come."

She wanted nothing more than to give him some of the same pleasure he'd given her, so she brushed his hand aside, dipped her fingers under the waistband of his black boxer briefs and curled her hand around his thick erection.

His groan of pleasure thrilled her and fired her own desire as she stroked him gently but rapidly.

"Hannah . . . Oh God, *Hannah* . . ." He came hard, his eyes closed and his head thrown back in complete abandon.

She loved seeing him like that and knowing she'd given him such exquisite pleasure.

His breathing was harsh and uneven as he opened his eyes and met her gaze. "Wow."

Hannah smiled at him as she reached for a box of tissues on the coffee table and wiped his belly. When she was done, she tossed the tissues into the fire and curled up to him.

His arms came around her, his hand slipping under the hem of her sweater to rest against her back.

"I'm feeling kind of warm, too," she said, hoping he'd get the hint that she wasn't ready to call it a night just yet.

"Are you?" He lifted her sweater from behind, and Hannah sat up a bit to help him raise it over her head, leaving her in only the barely-there bra she'd worn with him in mind.

His hungry gaze traveled over her torso before focusing on the swell of her breasts above the bra. He shifted so she was lying on her back and he was hovering above her, looking down at her as if trying to decide where he wanted to touch her first.

She helped him along by tugging him into another heated kiss.

As his tongue rubbed against hers, his hand moved from her belly to the front clasp of the bra, which he released and pushed aside, baring her breasts and making her tremble with anticipation and desire.

"Is this okay?" he asked as he cupped her right breast and ran his thumb over the nipple.

"Yes," she said, arching her back to get closer to him.

"I want to feel your skin against mine," he whispered, arranging her so she was on her side facing him, her breasts snug against his chest. "God, that's amazing. You feel so good." With his hand on her ass, he aligned their bodies and let her know he was already hard again.

Hannah couldn't get close enough to him. The friction of his chest hair against her tight nipples felt so incredible, but she wanted more. She needed relief from the torturous ache between her legs. And then he was kissing her neck and throat, making his way down her body as he eased her onto her back and kissed the upper part of her breasts.

On his knees now, he cupped her breasts and bent his head to worship her breasts with his mouth, driving her slowly out of her mind even before he sucked her nipple into the heat of his mouth.

She cried out from the sharp pleasure of his lips and tongue on her nipple while holding his head tight against her chest so he couldn't get away. *More, more, more* . . . The drumbeat of desire beat loud in her chest and between her legs where the throb became ever more insistent.

He switched to the other side, but pinched the first nipple between his fingers as he sucked on the other one. At that moment, she would've given him anything he asked of her, regardless of where they were or what had come before. She would've given anything to ease the ache.

"Hannah," he whispered as he kissed his way to her belly. "We have to stop or we won't be able to."

The thought of stopping made her moan. "Not yet."

He rested his forehead on her belly and took a couple of deep breaths. Then he released the button on her jeans and unzipped her, tugging the jeans down over her hips. Waiting to see what he would do next, her thighs quivered and the throb intensified. His hand covered her sex over the silk panties that matched the bra. Lying before him all but naked, Hannah expected to feel self-conscious or shy, but the overwhelming desire left no room for any other emotion.

He kept his hand still as he bent to lave at her nipple again, sucking harder this time as he let the heat of his hand permeate the thin scrap of fabric covering her.

She grasped his hips, working her hands inside his jeans to push them down.

Sliding his hand inside her panties, he worked one finger into her as he continued to punish her nipple with his lips and teeth.

Hannah teetered on the verge of explosive release, which detonated the second he touched her throbbing clit. And then he was kissing her again, ravenously, deeply, as his fingers coaxed a series of trembling aftershocks from her heated core.

"I want you," she whispered. "I don't want to wait."

"Hannah . . . You need to be sure."

"I am sure. We could go to your place . . ."

He released a shaky breath as he came down on top of her, settling into the V of her legs with only two pairs of underwear between them and what Hannah wanted more than the next breath. "No, not there. Tomorrow night we'll go somewhere for the weekend. Somewhere far away from here."

She ran her hands over his back. "People will talk if we run away together."

"They're already talking."

"Don't you have to work?" She knew the garage was open six days a week.

"Yeah, but I haven't taken a full weekend off in years. Skeeter will cover for me. I hope."

"Are we really going to do this?"

He raised his head to meet her gaze. "That's up to you. I'd wait forever if that's what it took to make sure you're comfortable and ready."

She smoothed the hair back from his face. "I'm as ready as I'm ever going to be, and as long as it's you, I know I'll be comfortable. Well, I'll probably be pretty *un*comfortable before I'm comfortable, but that's kind of the idea, right?"

Nolan laughed and shook his head. "You're out to kill me, aren't you?"

"Most definitely not."

"I'm sorry. I shouldn't have said that."

"You were teasing, and I knew it."

He kissed her again, softly and sweetly, his eyes locked on

hers. "I should go before we forget all about our plans for tomorrow."

She put her arms and legs around him, anchoring him in place on top of her. "Don't go yet."

Nolan finally left at three, but not before they'd aroused each other to the point of climax once again. Left feeling needy and hungry for more, Hannah was awake for hours, over-thinking everything, especially the decision they had made to go away for the weekend.

She was ready. She'd meant it when she told him that, but that didn't mean she wasn't nervous, too. Sex was a big step in any relationship, but particularly so in the first significant relationship after losing a spouse. Even though she and Nolan had only been a couple for a short time, they'd been friends for most of their lives and the closeness they had shared over the years had created a deeper bond than she would've had with someone else so soon.

Something Charley said kept running through her mind: *Get the first time over with so you can stop obsessing about it.* While she didn't always agree with Charley's approach to things, she couldn't disagree with her logic in this case.

Another thing nagged at her as she made her first cup of coffee in the morning, and that was Nolan's outright dismissal of her suggestion that they go to his place. Why had he been so quick to say no to that? When she thought about it, she realized she'd never been to his home, even when they were kids. Their entire friendship had transpired between school, the garage, her parents' home, the Guthries' home and the house she'd shared with Caleb.

Because he didn't talk about his family—ever—no one really knew much about him beyond the fact that he'd been raised by his grandfather, Nolan Roberts Sr., who'd owned the garage and passed it down to Nolan when he retired. Beyond that, Hannah knew nothing about where he'd come from or what had become of his parents. She wondered if he would maybe share that with her someday.

She read some more of Caleb's journals, taking the time to savor his words about the war and the men he served with.

Then she spent the rest of the morning in her studio, working on some new designs and other busy work intended to keep her mind occupied. Luckily, the rest of the Abbotts must've been busy, too, because her usual stream of visitors didn't materialize that day, which was just as well. She wasn't in the mood for lighthearted sibling banter when she had a weekend away to plan for.

With that in mind, she broke at lunch to take a hot bath and shave her legs and other critical areas. She washed and dried her hair and packed a bag for two nights away, tossing in a silk nightgown and robe Charley had given her for Christmas two years ago. Hannah had long ago gotten rid of the lingerie she'd owned when Caleb was alive as it was too painful to confront those memories every time she opened her dresser drawers.

She'd also moved out of the master bedroom and into one of the smaller bedrooms that she had redecorated to match her own style rather than that of his late grandmother. Sleeping every night in the bed she'd shared with him was another thing that was too difficult after he was gone. It had quickly become clear to her that if she was going to keep the house they'd both loved, she had to make some changes to protect her sanity. Switching bedrooms had helped.

With her bag packed, she sat on the bed and reached for the phone to call her mother. It wouldn't occur to her to leave town for a couple of days and not tell her parents she was leaving. They worried enough about her without her giving them extra reason.

"Hi, honey," Molly said when she answered. "I was just thinking about you."

"What about me?"

"Oh this and that. Wondering mostly how you're doing without Homer."

"It's quiet without him, but I'm doing okay."

"You should think about getting another dog. You've always loved having pets."

"I will. In a while."

"When you're ready."

Speaking of ready . . . "So I wanted to let you know I'll be away for a few days."

"Where you going?" her mother asked, more out of interest than any nosiness. Molly Abbott liked to know what was going on with her children, but she also knew when to give them their space.

"Away with Nolan for the weekend."

A long pause was the only indication her mother gave that she was at all surprised. "That sounds like fun. Where you headed?"

"We're not sure yet." They'd decided to get in the truck and drive until they found a place they wanted to stop. "Will you let Hunter know where I'll be? I don't feel like talking it to death right now, and he'd want to do that."

"I'll tell him. Do you want to talk about it at all, Han?"

"Sort of but not really," she said with a nervous laugh that made her mom laugh, too.

"It's nice to hear you laugh again."

"It's nice to have a reason to laugh."

"Things with Nolan have moved somewhat quickly, no?"

"Sort of, but we've known each other so long. It's not like starting from scratch with someone new. There's a lot of history there."

"That's true. He's a wonderful young man. You know we've always loved him."

"Yes," she said softly. Her mother's endorsement meant everything to her.

"You're okay about everything that might happen this weekend?"

"I guess we'll see, won't we?"

"I'm only a phone call away if you need me."

"I know. Thank you for that and a million other things. I don't know how I would've gotten through everything without you and Dad."

"Oh Hannah. You got *us* through it, and you don't even realize that, do you? That same strength is going to see you through whatever comes next, too."

Hannah closed her eyes against the burn of tears. "I'll call you when I get home."

"I'll look forward to that. I want you to relax and enjoy yourself and not worry about anything. You've earned the right to be happy."

"Thanks, Mom. Love you."

"Love you, too, honey."

Hannah clicked off the phone and returned it to the cradle. Curling up on her bed, she stared at the letter from Caleb on the table. It suddenly became clear to her that before she took this monumental step with Nolan, she had to make peace with the past and leaving that letter unread would mean leaving unfinished business behind. She wanted a clean slate before she left with Nolan, and there was only one way to get that.

Frightened of a setback and anxious as all hell, she sat up and reached for the envelope, holding it tight against her chest. "Please, Caleb . . . Please help me to let go. Please give me the strength to move forward without you, to love again, to take chances. Please help me . . ."

Breaking the seal on the envelope, her hands trembled, and she was moved by the fact that he'd once touched the paper she now held in her hands. Through a sea of tears, she began to read . . .

My darling Hannah,

If you're reading this letter, then the worst possible thing has happened, and I have to admit I was wrong about something. You know how I hate to be wrong.

Hannah laughed through her tears at the true statement. Caleb Guthrie had never been wrong about anything. Ever.

When I came here, I honestly believed it would be only a matter of time before I was back with you, where I belong. It never occurred to me that anything would actually happen to me, so I fear I have failed to adequately prepare you for the worst thing. I'm sorry for that, my love. One of my friends asked me if I'd written to my wife, just in case, and when I told him I hadn't, he encouraged me to do it. To not do it, he said, would be terribly unfair to you. Since he made a good point, here I am trying to write a letter that you'll only see if I'm dead. Kind of weird, to say the least!

After all these damnable deployments, one thing is very clear to me: Nothing is right in my world unless you're sleeping next to me. I have this sneaking suspicion you feel the same about me. So it pains me greatly to imagine a time when I will have broken the amazing bond we shared and forced you to move forward without me. I'm sorry for that, too.

On many a day, I wish I'd chosen Door Number 2 and gone the hockey route so I wouldn't have to be away from you for such long periods of time. It's so much harder than I ever thought it would be to spend even one day without hearing your voice, touching your soft skin or having your gorgeous brown eyes look at me with everything from true love to utter vexation. I yearn for you, Hannah, almost every second of every day. I long to make love with you. I dream about you and how it feels to lose myself in you.

Hannah took a pause to mop up her tears and to absorb the shock of realizing he'd had regrets about joining the army, that he'd ached for her the exact same way she'd ached for him—and continued to ache for him to this day.

So much of our life has been focused on my goals— when I was playing hockey and since I've been in the army. It wasn't lost on me that sometimes your goals got overlooked in the shuffle as you supported me with your special brand of unwavering strength.

Now it's your turn, and I want you to do one more very big thing for me. I want you to love again. I want you to share that wonderful, amazing, generous heart with someone else. Being the arrogant jackass that I am, I also want you to always remember the incredible life we had together. But I'd never want those memories to imprison you. So I'm setting you free. I'm begging you to go have the magical life you deserve, full of love and happiness and joy. Please don't let my death steal those things from you. That would be the ultimate tragedy.

Keep in mind that I'm alive and well as I write these words, so the idea of you with another guy makes me

*want to commit murder. But the thought of you spending
the rest of your life alone while you mourn for me would
be so much worse. Please don't do that . . .*

*I also don't want you to be saddled with that big old
house if you don't want it anymore. If my parents and
Gavin aren't interested, do whatever you want with it.
Sell it if that is best for you. I would totally understand if
it's too much for you to manage on your own. And if you
wouldn't mind, take particularly good care of Homie for
me for as long as he's got left. Other than you, he was
my very best friend, and I know you'll love him enough
for both of us.*

*In case you had any doubt whatsoever, YOU are the
love of my life. And you were right—as always. We
should've talked about this shit at some point. I'm sorry
I had to leave you, Hannah, but I'll never be far from
you. I love you always, and I'll see you again someday.*

Caleb

*PS: Please don't be mad at my mom for holding on to
this until she felt it was time for you to have it. I told her
to wait as long as it took, years if necessary, and to only
give it to you when it seemed you were ready. I hoped by
then you might be more able to do what I've asked of
you. Love you so much, babe. More than you'll ever possibly know.*

Hannah wiped the flood of tears from her face and clutched
the letter to her chest, careful not to let tears smear precious
ink. He'd given her exactly what she needed along with the
uniquely Caleb humor and arrogance she'd missed so much.

Reading the letter was like spending time with him again,
and if she'd come upon it years ago, the "sound of his voice"
in the letter would've been too painful to bear. One of the
things people had said to her repeatedly in the weeks after he
died was that time would heal her broken heart. Back then,
she'd thought that was the stupidest thing she'd ever heard.
How could *time* make losing her young husband *better*? And
what if she didn't want her heart to heal?

But those seemingly insensitive people had been exactly right. Time had dulled the ache and softened the initial blow. Against all odds, her heart had healed. It might never be entirely whole again, but it was no longer shattered beyond all repair. The time she'd spent with Nolan had shown her she was capable of loving again, but it had taken years to get there.

While she'd long ago accepted that the grief would always be with her, it wasn't the only emotion she was capable of feeling anymore. She'd come to understand that allowing in other, more productive emotions wasn't a betrayal of Caleb or the life they'd had together. It was about survival. It was about life marching forward when you thought it couldn't possibly go on without the one person you'd loved the most.

After reading the letter again, slowly this time to fully absorb every word, she cried for all they had lost, for the life they wouldn't get to share, for the children they'd never get to have, for the days, weeks, months and years that Caleb had been robbed of, for the glorious winter days he should've been skiing on Butler Mountain, for the crisp autumn nights he would've spent by the fire pit with his beloved Sultans, for the bright summer sunsets he'd never see again, for all the spring awakenings to come without him and for the sweet, precious time they should've had together.

She cried until no tears were left, until her eyes ached and the pillow under her was soaked. And at some point during the firestorm, she finally said good-bye to Caleb in a way she hadn't before. His words had accomplished what he'd hoped they would. She would love and miss him forever, but he'd set her free to make room in her heart for a new love.

Hannah returned the pages to the envelope and tucked it into the bag she'd packed for the weekend, intending to share the letter with Nolan because she knew it would mean everything to him to have Caleb's blessing of their relationship. Then she went into the bathroom to dry her eyes and wash her face.

Nolan would be here soon, and she was excited about their time away together, even more so now that she knew for certain she was doing exactly what Caleb had wanted her to do.

He had indeed given her a precious gift with that letter, and she would treasure it always.

CHAPTER 17

—◄●►—

On the day our country was attacked, all I can think about is how different the world is now from a few short months ago when we were making life decisions. Having a husband in the army is a much scarier proposition now, especially since he's an infantry officer. Part of me wishes I could rewind the clock and convince him to choose hockey. But if I know Caleb, he would've dropped his stick and skates on the ice and run for the nearest recruiter after 9/11.

—From the diary of Hannah Abbott Guthrie, age
twenty-two

Leaving the garage in Skeeter's unreliable hands for the next two and a half days, Nolan went home at noon to change and pack a bag before he picked up Hannah. Normally, he'd be stressing out about leaving the garage for even a day, let alone more than two days, but he had other things on his mind besides whether Skeeter could actually run his business into the ground in that short amount of time. Left to his own devices, Skeeter was capable of just about anything, but Nolan decided to have faith.

He had much better things to think about as he searched through piles of clean clothes he'd never gotten around to putting away for something decent to wear, settling on a red plaid flannel shirt and yet another pair of faded jeans. What if she expected him to wear something nicer?

That thought sent him rummaging through his closet, where he found a dress shirt and a pair of black jeans he'd forgotten about. Hopefully, that would be good enough if they went out to dinner or something. He had to see about getting some better clothes. A classy woman like Hannah wouldn't want to be with a guy whose entire wardrobe was made up of denim and flannel.

Jeez, will you listen to yourself? She doesn't care what you're wearing. She's not like that, so quit thinking that way. He dropped his shaving kit and a box of condoms into the bag and then wondered if maybe that was being too presumptuous.

Nolan sat on the edge of his bed, hoping to calm his rampaging nerves. After what happened last night, it wasn't presumptuous to include condoms when they'd made plans to be alone together. Still, he couldn't ignore a lingering sense of intruding where he didn't belong. Even after all this time and everything he'd shared with her, in many ways, Hannah was still Caleb's girl and thus off limits to him.

He knew it was ridiculous to think such things, especially when she'd been practically naked in his arms last night, but he couldn't help it. The troubling thoughts weren't going to keep him from her, but they nagged at him just the same.

By the time he arrived at her house twenty minutes later, he had almost talked himself out of this entire thing. He was crazy to think that a low-key under-the-radar guy like him could ever make a woman happy after she'd been loved by over-the-top, outrageously obnoxious and incredibly brilliant Caleb Guthrie. Who was he trying to fool by thinking he'd ever be enough for her?

She came to the door looking beautiful as she always did—so beautiful she took his breath away. He took a closer look and what he saw slammed him like a fist to the gut.

"You've been crying."

She didn't deny it. Rather she stepped aside to welcome him into the house.

He stepped into the front hall. "Listen, Hannah, we don't have to do this—"

She silenced him with two fingers to his mouth and humbled him when she removed her fingers and replaced them with her lips. Her arms curled around his neck as he sank into the sweet heaven of her kiss.

He held her close, so close he felt her tremble when she withdrew from the kiss and rested her forehead on his shoulder.

"What's wrong, honey?" Surrounded by her alluring scent and the soft silk of her hair, Nolan desperately wanted to know what had upset her.

"I'll tell you about it while we're away, but for now, could we just do this for another minute?"

Relieved that she still wanted to go away with him, he said, "For as long as you want."

They stood wrapped up in each other in her front hall for a long time. Nolan had no idea how long it was before her trembling subsided and she raised her head off his shoulder to meet his gaze.

"Thank you."

"You don't have to thank me for holding you, Hannah. It's become my favorite thing to do."

"I'm thanking you for much more than that." She flattened her hands on his chest as she looked up at him. "I'm thanking you for your patience while you waited for me to be ready for this. I'm thanking you for years of friendship with me and with Caleb. I'm thanking you for being willing to navigate the treacherous waters that come with being the first relationship after . . . Well, you've been amazing, and I appreciate everything. I wanted you to know that."

Because he couldn't resist touching her, he framed her face with his hands. "You're the amazing one, Hannah. You amaze all of us with your good humor and your unwavering grace. Please don't thank me for feeling like the luckiest guy in the world because I get to hold your hand whenever I want."

He leaned his forehead against hers, more in love with her than he'd ever imagined possible. In that moment, it didn't matter that he was no match for Caleb Guthrie. It only mattered that he was apparently a perfect match for her. She was the other half of him. He'd long suspected that to be the case. Now he was certain.

"Are you sure you still want to go?" he asked after a long period of contented quiet.

"I very much want to go."

"Let's get to it then." He held her coat for her, picked up her bag and ushered her out the door, stopping to make sure the house was locked before he followed her down the sidewalk.

"Where should we go?" she asked when they were in the truck. Her hands folded and unfolded in her lap, which was the only indication of nerves he could detect in her.

"I did a little looking around online last night, and I found the perfect place."

"Where is it?"

"Up north a bit, half an hour or so from here in Lower Waterford."

"Oh I've heard about a great B and B up there called the Candlewick Inn, and I've wanted to check it out to get some tips for the retreat."

"That's where we're going."

"Great," she said with a warm smile for him that filled him with the confidence he'd lacked earlier. "I can't wait to see it." She reached across the seat for his hand. "Thank you for this, too. It's exactly what I needed right now."

"I hope you'll always tell me what you need so I can try to get it for you."

"My needs are usually pretty simple."

"I still can't wait to hear about every one of them."

She bit her lip and gave him a sultry look that fired him up, and they weren't even out of Butler yet.

"Does your family know where you're going?"

"My mother does. I told her to tell Hunter so he doesn't send out the search-and-rescue team, but they won't tell anyone else."

"Not even your dad?"

"Well, my mom might tell him."

"Which means everyone else will know, too," Nolan said with a low laugh.

"Does that bother you?"

"Hell no. I don't care. I've been around you Abbotts long enough by now to know how things work. I just hope . . ." He didn't know how to say it without sounding like an insecure nitwit.

"What do you hope?"

"A couple of things, actually. For one, I hope no one in your life thinks I felt this way about you when Caleb was alive."

"God, Nolan," she said softly. "No one would ever think such a thing."

"Sure they would. People can be mean and spiteful and say awful things that hurt innocent people like you. I'd never want to be the cause of that kind of pain for you. I knew you long before he did. What's to stop someone from saying I was jealous of him and happy to have him out of the picture?"

"You were one of his closest friends. How could anyone think that?"

Nolan shrugged, hating that she sounded so undone by the possibility. "It's something I've worried about." After a protracted stretch of silence, he glanced over at her. "What're you thinking?"

"That I've spent an awful lot of time considering how difficult it is for me to start dating again, but I haven't given nearly as much thought to what it's like to be you in this situation. I'm sorry you've worried about that. If anyone dares to breathe even a hint of that in your direction, they'll see a very ugly side of me."

"Is that right?" he said with a chuckle. "Easy, tiger."

"I'm serious! That anyone would dare to say such an awful thing after everything we've both been through since Caleb died . . . The thought of it makes me furious."

"You're very cute when you're pissed."

"This is no time for jokes."

"I'm not joking. You're seriously sexy when you're pissed. And when you're not pissed, too. You're sexy pretty much all the time."

"Nolan!"

"What? I only speak the truth."

"I want you to promise me if anyone ever says anything even remotely like that you'll tell me. Do you promise?"

"I'd be a little afraid to tell you. I wouldn't want to have to bail you out of jail."

"I mean it. I'd want to know so I could set the person straight."

"I'm the sort of guy who prefers to fight his own battles."

"I'd want to know. Do you promise?"

"Fine. I promise. Jeez, I never knew you had this pushy aggressive side to you," he said in a teasing tone. "It turns me on."

"Shut up," she said, laughing.

He brought their joined hands to his lap and placed her palm over his erection. "You think I'm joking?"

"Nolan . . ."

"Hmm?" He was having trouble keeping the truck on the road with the heat of her hand burning through his clothes.

"How much longer until we get there?"

"Not long."

She sighed and dropped her head back against the seat but kept her hand right where he'd put it. "You said that was one thing. What are some of the other things you worry about?"

"I'm afraid to tell you after the way you reacted to that one."

"Tell me anyway."

Nolan stared out at the stretch of road that was marked by trees in full bloom and grass just beginning to turn green. "I worry sometimes that after him I'll seem kind of boring to you."

"What? That's nuts. Why in the world would you think that?"

"He was so . . . multifaceted, I guess you would say. Complicated, complex, larger than life. I'm none of those things. I'm a pretty simple what-you-see-is-what-you-get kind of guy. How do I begin to compete with the memory of a guy who was all those things and so much more?"

"You don't have to compete with him, Nolan. I'd never want you to feel that way. He was what he was, and we all loved him, but he was far from perfect. At times I used to plead with him to sit down, shut up and just *be*. He usually lasted about five minutes, and then he was onto something else. He exhausted me. There were plenty of things about him I couldn't stand at times."

"Like what?" Nolan asked, truly amazed by the unprecedented view of the other side of what had seemed to him like a perfect marriage.

"The drinking was an issue. I hated how he couldn't have just a few beers socially. It was always about getting plowed. When he was drunk he could be loud and obnoxious, which was often embarrassing to me. His language was awful, and it drove me crazy that he forgot sometimes to apply the filter when my parents and grandparents were around. We used to have big ugly fights about those things."

"I had no idea you guys ever fought."

"Oh my God! Are you kidding? We fought like tomcats."

"You sure made it look good to the rest of us."

"Most of the time, it was good. But it was far from perfect."

"I'm truly stunned to hear that. It appeared blissful."

"A lot of times it was, but no one knows what really goes on inside a marriage except the two people who are in it."

"That's true."

"I loved him with everything I had, but I wasn't blind to his faults, and he wasn't blind to mine."

"What faults do you possibly have?"

"You'll just have to stick around to find out, won't you?"

As much as it pained him to lose her touch down below, he raised their joined hands to his lips. "I'll look forward to discovering every awful, terrible, sinister thing about you."

Her laughter pleased and relaxed him. It felt good to be able to air out the bad stuff along with the good. He'd never been with anyone who was as easy to talk to as she was. He let their hands fall back to his lap, but rested them on his thigh because he couldn't take any more of the sweet torture of her hand on his cock.

"Any other worries?" she asked, looking at him with genuine interest and concern reflected in her gaze.

"One more. It's kind of a big one."

"Okay. I can take it. Bring it on."

"I can't remember where I heard this, only that it stayed with me because of how it might apply to me—and you—if I ever got the chance to be with you. It might've been on TV or something, but the person said that most of the time after someone is divorced or widowed that the first relationship doesn't work out. And I really want this to work out."

"So do I, Nolan. I'm not with you or going away with you this weekend to check a post-widow box on my way to something better. You are something better. In the back of my mind, I always knew when I was ready, you were waiting and that was comforting. It's not like no one asked me out in all this time. People did."

"People. People like Myles Johansen?"

"How do you know about that?"

"I have my sources."

"Did my dad tell you that? I'll kill him. He's such a gossip!"

"He only pointed out that a wise man is aware of any potential competition when he's trying to win the heart of a certain woman. Since I was unaware of any potential competition, I believe he took some pleasure in illuminating me as to Myles's interest."

"I am going to kill him."

"No, you're not. He was looking out for you, and shockingly, I think he might've even been looking out for me, too. Which leads me to a confession . . ."

"What confession?"

"Apparently, he and your grandfather might've had something to do with the dead battery that brought me to your door that day."

Her eyes went wide with surprise and fury. "Are you *kidding* me? They're totally out of control!"

"It worked, didn't it?"

"They actually *messed with the battery* in my car to get me to call you?"

"I believe it was much more calculated than that. They messed with your battery on a day when they knew you had somewhere to be and on a day when most of your family was elsewhere, thus I was the only choice."

"That's nothing short of diabolical."

"I'll repeat—it worked, didn't it? Here you are. Here I am. Thanks to a little nudge from a couple of well-meaning old dudes."

"Well-meaning," she said with a snort. "If that's what you want to call it."

"I hate to side with the enemy, and I'd never disclose this to them under the threat of torture, but I do appreciate their . . . assistance, I guess we'll call it. They gave us the nudge we needed, and they put me out of the misery I'd been in since the dance at the Grange."

"Why were you in misery?"

"Because I'd kissed you and called you and you didn't call me back, so I figured I'd already blown any chance I'd ever had with you. If that's not misery, I don't know what is."

"I'm sorry I put you through that. I wanted to call you. I wanted to so badly."

"Then they did us a favor giving you a reason to call me, and for that you should probably cut them a break."

"I'll take that under consideration."

"Personally, I'd like to send them a thank-you note. Wish I'd thought of messing with your car sooner."

"You never would've done that!"

"Desperate times call for desperate measures, and after one taste of you, I was feeling pretty damned desperate."

"Just so you know, I spent an inordinate amount of time reliving that kiss and trying to figure out why I'd pulled away from you when that was the last thing I wanted to do."

"Why do you think you did that?"

"Because it was the first time since . . . everything. I'm sort of hoping that doesn't happen again." He heard her swallow hard. "This weekend."

"If it does, it does. You're under no pressure here, Hannah. None at all. Let's just relax and enjoy being together. Anything else is a bonus, all right?"

"Thank you for understanding that I'm a little nervous."

"Please don't be."

They arrived at the rustic country inn a short time later and pulled into the parking lot. Situated on twenty acres of rolling farmland in the foothills of the Green Mountains, the Candlewick Inn had come highly recommended by various websites as a premium romantic spot in Northern Vermont. Hearing that she was nervous, Nolan was glad he'd thought of the first item on their agenda.

Upon check-in, the innkeeper herself showed them to a spacious room with a country theme. Blond wood floors and navy blue accents took some of the focus off the king-sized bed that occupied the far corner of the room. It included a fireplace and a Jacuzzi tub. He'd requested both.

"I hope this meets with your satisfaction, Mr. Roberts," the friendly innkeeper said.

"It's perfect. Thank you."

She handed him a slip of paper. "Confirmation of your spa appointment in thirty minutes."

"Great, thanks."

"Enjoy your stay, and please feel free to let us know if we can do anything to make you more comfortable."

When they were alone, Hannah turned to him. "We have a *spa* appointment?"

"Yes, we do."

"*You* are going to a spa?"

"Apparently so."

"And what are you having done? I'm picturing you strapped to the waxing table, screaming your head off."

"As appealing as that sounds—and as intrigued as I am by how you might know what it's like to be strapped to a waxing table—that's not what we're doing."

"What are we doing?"

"A couple's massage."

Her eyes lit up with unmistakable pleasure. "Really? We are?"

He loved seeing her so happy, especially when she hadn't yet told him why she'd been crying before he picked her up. "Yes, we are."

"Have you ever had a massage before?"

"I can't say that I have."

Her delicate laughter made him smile. "This ought to be interesting."

"I remembered how much you enjoy your spa days with the girls, so I figured I couldn't miss with some spa time."

She shed her coat, tossed it over a chair and came to him, sliding her hands up his chest to rest on his shoulders. "Thank you for arranging this, Nolan. It's such a relief to be away from everything and everyone. Except for you, of course."

"You've had a tough week," he said, noticing when her smile dimmed and desperately wanting to know why. "Some R and R is just what you need." He hugged her and breathed in the fragrant scent of her hair. "We should get to the spa."

"You sound almost enthusiastic."

"I do? That wasn't intentional."

She smiled and let her hand slide down his arm to take his hand. "Don't knock it until you try it."

He wouldn't knock it, and he would try anything that made her smile so brightly.

CHAPTER 18

———◦◦◦———

Home in Vermont for the funeral of Caleb's grandmother. We were shocked to learn that she left her big, beautiful house to Caleb because he was the only one who ever loved it as much as she did. We're so sad to lose her but thrilled with her gift. The house has always been special to both of us, and we're looking forward to "someday" when we'll live there after Caleb retires. Since he's determined to be a general, someday is a long time from now! But it's nice to know we have a place to call home amid all the moving around.

—From the diary of Hannah Abbott Guthrie,
age twenty-five

Hannah couldn't believe Nolan was actually going to have a massage because he thought she would enjoy it. She had to suppress the urge to giggle madly when he came out of the men's locker room wearing a thick white robe that only emphasized his broad shoulders and muscular build.

"They told me I had to get totally naked under here," he whispered urgently. "No one told me it was a naked massage."

The laughter burst through Hannah's tightly clasped lips.

"Oh great. Go ahead and laugh."

"I heard you're getting a guy."

His face went totally flat. "No way."

Doubled up with laughter, Hannah was dabbing her eyes with the sleeve of her robe when a knock on the door preceded two very attractive women into the room, where two beds had been prepared next to each other.

"You'll pay for that," Nolan muttered as the technicians greeted them and then left the room while they got settled under the warm blankets.

Hannah hesitated for a second, feeling self-conscious as she removed her robe and scurried under her blankets while Nolan did the same.

"I just want to say again that I object to total nudity."

Turned toward him, Hannah rested her head on her folded arms. "Do you want me to tell them that?"

"So you all can have a good laugh at my expense? I don't think so."

"You're cute when you're indignant."

He glowered at her, which made her laugh again.

"He's a virgin," Hannah said when the technicians rejoined them. "So go easy on him."

His huff of annoyance made her shake with laughter as soft music and aromatherapy scents filled the air.

"Just relax and enjoy," Nolan's technician said. If possible, the muscles in his back got tighter when she first touched him.

Hannah wasn't sure which part she enjoyed more, watching him endure the massage or the incredibly soothing combination of scented oil and strong hands kneading the stress from her back.

She laid her hand over his. "Close your eyes and relax," she whispered.

"Hush, you're bothering me."

When the technicians told them to turn over, Nolan froze, and Hannah lost it all over again. "Stop being such a baby and do what you're told."

He did it, but she could tell by his rigid pose that he didn't want to.

Hannah kept hold of his hand, hoping he would relax before their hour ended. She closed her eyes and gave herself over to the incredibly indulgent massage. As she hadn't had a massage in a while, it was a lovely treat.

She realized she'd dozed off when the brush of Nolan's lips over hers woke her. Her eyes opened slowly to find him posed above her, his chest and shoulders glowing from the oil and the soft lights. He had never looked sexier, she thought, as she took a good long look.

"Can we please get the hell out of here?"

"It wasn't that bad, was it?"

"Excruciating."

His comment had her smiling all over again as she released his hand and tugged on her robe while resisting the urge to take a peek at him as he covered up. *Soon enough*, she thought, as a flurry of nerves overtook her. She only hoped the nerves didn't derail their plans for the evening.

"Don't get changed," he said gruffly when they met at the door.

"Excuse me?"

"They said we can wear the robes back to our room. Grab your stuff and meet me in the hallway."

"Okay." Hannah swallowed the fear and tried to clear her mind of all worries so she could focus on enjoying whatever he had planned next.

Carrying their clothes and shoes, they made their way upstairs to their room where the fire had been lit and an ice bucket containing a bottle of champagne had been arranged in the sitting area. Candles had been strategically placed around the room, giving it a cozy romantic glow.

Hannah put down her things and took a slow look around.

"Too much?" he asked, sounding uncertain.

"Not at all. It's lovely."

"Come sit by the fire." He ushered her to the love seat and sat next to her to uncork the champagne. "Do you like champagne?"

She accepted the glass from him. "I love it."

"I don't have to ask if you love this," he said, taking the cover off a dish that contained a wide variety of gourmet chocolates.

"Oh my goodness!" She leaned over the table to take a closer look at the selection. "I don't know which one I want."

"Have one of each."

"You're the devil. Champagne, chocolate and massages in the afternoon? You're spoiling me."

"That's the whole idea."

"I can't believe you arranged all this so quickly."

"A man with an Internet connection can be dangerous."

"This is really nice," she said, biting into a cream-centered chocolate that melted on her tongue. "God, that's good. Have one." She picked up another of the same one she'd tried and held it out to him.

He leaned in to take the bite from her. "That is good." Rather than sit back again, he tugged on her ponytail and brought her in for a chocolate kiss. "That's even better. Chocolate-flavored Hannah."

"I should grab a shower."

"Not yet."

She eyed him, trying to gauge his intentions. "Why not?"

"Because I'm not done getting you dirty yet." Smiling, he nudged her ponytail aside and kissed her neck and jaw, working his way to her ear. "Is that okay?"

"Yes," she said, feeling breathless and undone, and he'd barely touched her.

"Tell me what you want, Hannah." His voice was a raspy whisper that gave her goose bumps and made her nipples tingle. "I'll give you anything you want."

"You. I want you."

He drew back to gaze into her eyes. "Are you sure?"

"No," she said, laughing nervously. "I have no idea what'll happen if we try this, but I'm willing to try."

"Whatever happens is fine. Even if nothing happens. Okay?"

She nodded.

He caressed her face, his fingers moving lightly over her sensitive skin. "I thought about how best to approach this situation," he said with a spark of humor in his serious gaze. Replacing his fingers with his lips, he placed soft kisses on her face while studiously avoiding her mouth. "I figured if we waited until later, you'd have too much time to think about it, and too much thinking in this case is a bad thing."

Hannah focused on drawing air into her lungs, riveted by

his kisses and his words and the fact that he'd obviously given this some significant consideration, which she appreciated. Not that she could tell him that, because that would require words that she didn't have.

"Will you come to bed with me, Hannah?"

Before she could answer, he finally took her mouth in a deep searching kiss that had her clinging to him, trying to get closer. He kissed her for what felt like forever before he drew back, keeping his lips on hers and watching her with those intense eyes.

"Yes," she whispered.

He lifted her into his arms and continued the kiss as he walked to the bed and put her down next to it. "What the hell do we need with two hundred pillows?" he asked, chucking them aside with barely contained impatience.

Hannah laid two fingers over her lips.

"Are you laughing at me again?"

She shook her head. "I wouldn't dream of it."

He peeled back the covers, revealing smooth white sheets with eyelet trim. A hint of lavender filled the air when he unveiled the bed. Turning to her, he fixed his gaze on the deep V of her robe, and reached for the knot at her waist. "Still okay?"

Hannah nodded, holding her breath as the knot gave way and the robe fell open.

Nolan's gaze heated as he ran a finger from the base of her throat straight down the front of her, sliding between her breasts to her belly, the massage oil smoothing the way.

She appreciated when he pulled on the tie to his own robe, letting it fall open to her gaze. Hannah drank in the sight of his chest and abs as his hands came to her shoulders, easing the robe down over her arms. Closing her eyes, she focused on breathing as he unveiled her.

"Still okay?"

"Yes."

"Look at me, honey."

She forced her eyes open and looked up at him to find concern and affection and love in his gaze. "Are you sure?"

Nodding, she said, "We're going to mess up those lovely white sheets with the massage oil."

"I'm sure we're not the first ones to mess up their lovely white sheets."

The comment made her laugh and eased her tension.

With his hands on her hips, Nolan turned her to sit on the bed. "Do we need birth control?"

"I've been on the pill since I was fifteen." At his raised brow, she added, "Crazy periods."

"I haven't done this in a long time, but I'll understand if you want me to use a condom."

"I trust you, Nolan, or I wouldn't be here with you." She released the elastic that held her hair and reached for the lapels of his robe to bring him in closer to her. When he was within reach, she slipped her hands inside, covering his belly and sliding up to his chest while trying not to stare at the impressively large erection that hung heavily before her.

She licked lips gone dry and tugged on his robe. "Take it off," she said, summoning the courage she'd need to see this through. Caleb's words echoed through her mind, bringing tears to her eyes. *I want you to love again. I want you to share that wonderful, amazing, generous heart with someone else.*

Nolan shed the robe and stood before her gloriously naked, gloriously male, and Hannah wanted to touch him everywhere. He stood patiently while she ran her hands over him reverently, from chest to belly to hips to thighs. As he sucked in a sharp deep breath, his erection lengthened. Hoping to bring him some relief, she wrapped her hand around the base and stroked him.

His fingers sank into her hair as his head fell back in surrender. "Hannah . . ."

She leaned forward and slid her tongue over the wide tip.

"*Christ*," he muttered.

Encouraged by his response, she did it again, running her tongue down the length of him and back up before taking him into her mouth. His moan of pleasure filled her with enthusiasm until she felt him tug gently on her hair.

"This is supposed to be about you," he said through gritted teeth. "How did I lose control so quickly?"

She reached for him and lay back on the bed, bringing him with her. "It's supposed to be about *us*."

He came down on top of her, holding himself up on bent elbows.

Hannah smoothed her hands over his back as the heat of his body warmed her.

"That's my idea of a relaxing massage," he said. "Apparently it's all about getting the right masseuse."

She kneaded the tension from his neck, drawing a groan from him as he kissed her softly at first and with growing passion as she responded to the deep thrusts of his tongue. His kisses set her on fire and cleared her mind of everything except the sublime pleasure that came with holding him and kissing him, despite the hard, insistent press of his erection against her belly that reminded her of where this was leading.

Breaking away from her mouth, he kissed his way to her breasts, cupping and shaping them for his lips. He worshiped each breast, drawing and sucking on her nipples until they were hard and tight. "Still okay?"

"Mmm." She combed her fingers through his hair, letting him sweep her away on a wave of desire that required her full attention and left no room for memories or regrets or guilt.

Propped on arms that bulged with muscles, he moved down to kiss her belly and below. And then he was kneeling on the floor and sliding his hands over her inner thighs, opening her to his mouth and lips.

The shock of his tongue against her most sensitive flesh shot through her like lightning, quickening her breathing along with the already rapid beat of her heart. He slid his fingers into her at the same second he sucked hard on her clit, detonating a release she felt from the tingling in her scalp to the burn at the bottom of her feet.

She had barely recovered when he was above her again, looking down at her with fire in his eyes as he kissed her lips and entered her, slowly and carefully, but insistently, too, as if he knew if he gave her too much time to think about what she was doing she might not be able to do it.

Consumed by the stretching burn of his entry, Hannah wrapped her arms around his neck and held on tight to him.

"God, Hannah," he whispered against her ear, setting off a firestorm of goose bumps and tingles. "You feel so good." His fingers dug into her hips as he held her still until he'd worked his way all the way inside her, stopping then to kiss her. "Please don't cry, honey. You're breaking my heart."

She hadn't realized she was crying until he said that. Drawing him down to her, she hugged him and breathed in his familiar scent.

"Do you want to stop?"

"No, don't stop. Please don't."

Pulsing and throbbing within her, he stayed still for a long time until her emotions settled and she began to wiggle under him, needing more.

He seemed happy to give it to her, raising himself up on his arms to rock into her repeatedly, touching the spot deep inside that triggered wave after wave of sensation. Then he bent his head and captured her nipple between his teeth and pressed two fingers to her clit, tripping her over the edge into another heart-stopping release.

Her orgasm triggered something in him that had him gripping her shoulders as he surged into her, letting go with a moan of fulfillment uttered against her neck when he came down on top of her.

Hannah wrapped her arms around him as he continued to throb inside her, still hard and thick and wedged tightly into her. The last thing in the world she wanted to think of at that moment was the last time she'd done this, but the memory crystallized in her mind, a vision of Caleb's face above her as he gripped her hands and came inside her for the last time before his deployment. They'd spent two full days in bed, wrapped up in each other, getting up only to eat and shower before going back for more.

She didn't want to think about that now, but she couldn't push the memory away. It refused to budge.

Nolan must've sensed her distress because he raised his head and looked down at her. "Hannah . . . Look at me, honey."

She forced her gaze up to meet his.

"I love you. Focus on me. Hold on to me."

As he said the words, he began to move again, slowly, less urgently, the gentle glide of his flesh against hers once again requiring her full attention. The memory became less focused as she stared up at Nolan, watching a range of emotions play out on his face—desire, concern, love.

He loved her. She'd known of course, but to hear him say the words when she most needed to hear them had gotten her through the crisis.

"Hold on to me, Hannah. I'll never let you go."

She gripped his shoulders, her fingers digging into his flesh as he picked up the pace, his hands holding her bottom tightly to keep her in place for his deep strokes. And then he was kissing her, the thrusts of his tongue mimicking the deep thrusts of his cock, and the combination took her right back to the brink of release.

She teetered until he pressed his fingers between her legs and sent her over, going with her on a wild ride that had them clinging to each other through the storm.

Nolan withdrew and rolled to the side, bringing her with him.

As she was using him for a pillow, she could hear his pounding heartbeat as his chest rose and fell quickly, the scent of the massage oil filling the air around them. He put his other arm around her, securing her to his side.

After a long silence, he said, "Talk to me, Hannah. Tell me everything you're thinking."

"Everything?"

"Everything."

She flattened her hand on his belly and felt his abs ripple beneath her palm. "I'm thinking that was amazing."

"On that we agree. What else?"

"I'm thinking that the smell of massage oil will always remind me of being here with you."

"What else?"

Her hand glided over his stomach, aided by the slight sheen of perspiration and the residual oil. "You said you love me."

"I do. I have for a long time."

"I know. I love you, too." She tipped her head so she could see his face. "You know that, don't you?"

"I know you love me as a good friend."

"I love you as so much more than that, Nolan, or I wouldn't be lying naked in your arms."

The hand cupping her shoulder tightened and his lips pressed against her forehead. "There's only one thing you could give me that would mean more to me than your love, Hannah."

"What's that?"

"Your trust."

"You have that. You know you do."

"Then tell me what else you were thinking about."

He saw her so clearly, which made her feel naked emotionally as well as physically. "The last time I was with Caleb," she said softly. "I didn't want to think about that, especially not now, but the memory popped into my head and wouldn't go away."

"I thought of him, too."

Surprised by his confession, Hannah said, "What about him?"

Nolan raised his arm and ran his fingers through his hair. "I hoped he'd forgive me for what I was about to do with you. I guess I'll find out when our paths cross in the afterlife."

"Would you mind grabbing my bag for me?"

"Now?"

She nodded. "Please."

"Sure."

They disentangled their limbs and he got up, striding confidently across the room like it was no big deal to walk around naked in front of her. Hannah took advantage of the opportunity to check out the chiseled muscles on his back and the round cheeks of his ass. She'd like to bite him there, she thought, immediately mortified by where her thoughts had gone.

"Why are you blushing?" he asked when he dropped her weekend bag on the far side of the bed.

"I'm not."

"Yes, you are. Now tell me why. You're trusting me, remember?"

"I was admiring your backside."

"Is that right?"

"Uh-huh. It was giving me all kinds of ideas."

"Such as?" As he stood by the bed looking down at her, his cock twitched and lengthened.

Hannah wanted to crawl under the pillow and hide from the challenging look he sent her way, but instead she looked him square in the eyes. "Let's just say there were teeth involved."

His breath escaped through his lips in a hiss of surprise that made his eyes go dark as his erection surged. He stretched out next to her, facedown on the bed, looking over his shoulder at her, the dare obvious in his eyes. "Do it."

In her family, backing down from a dare meant weeks of ridicule. Hannah released the tight hold she had on the bed-covers and let them fall to her waist, watching his gaze shift to her breasts. She leaned over his back, kissing a trail over rigid muscle to the dimpled indents at the base of his spine before continuing on to her target, tormenting him with open mouth kisses over both taut cheeks before finally taking a bite of the right one.

He gasped and fisted the sheets. "Do it again." His voice was gruff and raspy with desire.

She marked the other side with her teeth, and he groaned.

"Turn over."

"Hannah . . ."

"Turn over."

His muscles flexed as he complied with her order. When he was settled on his back, he watched her with hooded eyes, waiting to see what she would do.

Hannah knelt between his legs, running her hands over his thighs as she eyed the formidable erection lying on his belly.

"Come here," he said, holding out his arms to her.

She stretched out on top of him, and sighed with content-ment when he wrapped his arms tightly around her.

"You're full of surprises," he said.

"I have to keep you guessing."

His rumbling chuckle made her smile. "So far so good."

After a long period of quiet, she said, "What're you think-ing about?"

"You and how awesome it is to be with you this way. And I can't help thinking about Caleb and hoping he'd approve."

"I want to show you something."

"More tricks?"

"Not now. Maybe later."

"Oh something to look forward to. What do you want to show me?"

"A letter."

"Okay . . ."

"From Caleb."

"Oh."

Hannah lifted her head from his chest so she could see his face, which was unreadable at the moment. "Amelia gave it to me the other day. Apparently, he'd asked her to hold on to it until she felt I was ready for it."

"Oh God, Hannah. Why didn't you say something? I could've . . . I don't know . . . I would've been there when you read it. If you wanted me to."

"You're sweet to worry, but it was something I needed to do myself. I hope you understand."

"I do. Of course I do. You don't have to show it to me. That's between you and him."

"It is, but I want to share it with you because I think it'll help for you to know what he wanted for me."

"If you're sure."

"I am." She reached for the bag he'd put on the other side of the bed and unzipped the pocket where she'd stashed the letter. When she handed the pages to him, she settled next to him, curled into the crook of his arm so she could read it again with him.

He grunted out a laugh at Caleb's opening line about admitting he was wrong about something, but then Nolan's breathing slowed as his eyes flew over the first page and then the second. When he was done, his eyes closed and he released a deep, shuddering breath and then folded the pages and gave them back to her.

Hannah stashed the letter in her bag.

"I said this to you when it happened, but I feel like I need to say it again. I'm so sorry for your loss."

Touched by his words, Hannah kissed his cheek and then his lips. "And I'm sorry for yours."

"It was so *him*, you know? Sounded like him . . ."

"Yes."

"Reading that was a punch to the gut for me, so I can't imagine what it was like for you."

"It wasn't the easiest thing I ever did, but Amelia chose the right time to give it to me. I was ready for it now in a way I wouldn't have been before now, before I knew it was actually possible for me to love someone else."

"Is that why you'd been crying earlier?"

She nodded. "I didn't feel right leaving with you until I'd taken that last step with him, and it was hard."

His arms banded around her, crushing her to his chest.

"Thank you for sharing it with me and for letting me know that Caleb wanted this for you. I don't know if he would've wanted it for you with me . . ."

"Why not you? He loved you."

"I know he did, but he might've preferred you to fall for someone he hadn't known."

"He didn't specify, Nolan. He didn't set limits on who I was allowed to fall for. He trusted me to know what was best for me—and who was best for me."

"And that's me?"

"Who else could it ever be? We've been dancing around this for years. In the back of my mind, I knew all along that when I was ready, you'd be there for me."

"You might've mentioned that to me."

Hannah laughed at his indignant tone. "Did I put you through hell?"

"No, not really. The only hell was in wondering if you'd ever be ready. I couldn't believe it when you showed up at the Grange that night, and when you danced with me and let me drive you home and kiss you . . . Whoa, talk about hope."

"You can thank Cameron for that. She talked me into going."

"Remind me to thank her the next time I see her."

"In all the time you spent waiting for me . . . Was there anyone else?"

"Here and there. Nothing serious."

"Have you ever been in love?"

He turned on his side to face her. "Not like this."

The raw emotion in his words and on his face undid her. "I'm afraid I'll hurt you somehow. That I won't turn out to be what you waited so long to have or I'll freak out at some point and take a step back or—"

With his hand cupping the back of her head, he pulled her into a kiss that stole the words off her lips and scrambled her brain. "First of all," he said when they had no choice but to come up for air, "you are *everything* I waited so long to have and then some. If you need to freak out, freak out. I'm not going anywhere. If you feel the need to take a step back, tell me and we'll figure it out. But you should know that after waiting so long to be with you, I'm going to fight like hell to make this work."

Aroused by his words and the emotion she heard behind them, Hannah ran a finger down the center of his chest, over his belly and down to where he throbbed against her leg. Curling her hand around his erection, she stroked him gently.

"What are you up to?" he asked. His voice sounded strained.

"Nothing much."

"That doesn't feel like nothing much. That feels like you starting something."

"Maybe I am."

"I don't want you to be sore, honey. It's been a while."

"I'm okay." She gave him a little push to get him to turn onto his back. When she had him where she wanted him, she straddled him.

His fingers pressed into her hips. "I wish you could see how hot you look right now with your hair loose around your shoulders and your lips swollen from kissing me. How can you think you're not everything I could ever want?" He gripped her hands and held on tight as she took him in, wincing from the stretch and burn. "Are you sore?"

"A little, but it's a good kind of sore."

"Go slow." Releasing her hands, he cupped her breasts and ran his thumbs over her nipples. He shuddered when she took him deeper. "Christ, you're so tight, Hannah."

"Is that good?"

"So good. You have no idea . . ."

She rolled her hips and took him to the hilt, making both of them moan with the sheer pleasure.

Nolan cupped her bottom and sat up, positioning her arms and legs around him and bringing his chest in tight against hers. "Oh yeah," he whispered. "Like that. Just like that."

Hannah was swept away on a sea of desire that overtook all her senses. The initial soreness subsided into an ache of a different kind as he guided her with his hands squeezing her bottom as his chest hair abraded her nipples. She managed to hold on until he pressed his fingers to her core and sent her crashing over the edge of release.

He went with her, holding on tight through the storm.

Clinging to him in the aftermath, Hannah was filled with gratitude for the second chance she'd been given, for the man who'd waited until she was ready for him and for the gift Caleb's letter had given her, freeing her to love again.

CHAPTER 19

—◆—

We talk a lot about starting a family, but I'm not sure Caleb is ready. His drinking and partying is something we fight about. He wants to have a baby, but I want a husband who's a grown-up before I bring a child into our family. It never goes over well when I say that to him, but I'm going to spend enough time raising kids on my own while he's deployed. When he's home, I need him to be committed to fatherhood more than he is to having a good time. It's a source of tension between us that I wish we could resolve.

—From the diary of Hannah Abbott Guthrie, age twenty-six

They never left the room that night or the next day, living off room service and spending most of their time in bed or in the Jacuzzi or the steam shower or on the sofa in front of the fire.

"Are you ever going to allow me to get dressed again?" Hannah asked late on Saturday afternoon while they cuddled in bed watching a movie neither of them was paying much attention to.

He ran his hand slowly down her arm and back up again, giving her goose bumps. "Maybe when it's time to go home, but not before."

"I wish we could stay here forever."

"Why do you say that?"

"Because when it's just you and me, it's perfect."

"You don't think it'll be perfect at home?"

"I'm not sure what to expect when people figure out I'm dating again."

"Who cares what they say? It's been seven years, Hannah. It's not like you ran right out and got yourself a boyfriend after your husband died."

"True, but . . . With the anniversary and road race coming up and Homer's funeral and everything . . . It's just . . . It's a lot on top of everything else."

"I know, honey, but I'll be right there with you for all of it. You don't have to do it alone anymore—not that you're ever really alone with that family of yours underfoot."

"Why don't you ever talk about your family?"

Only because she was sprawled all over him did she feel his muscles go tense under her. "I don't have a lot of family. You know that. My grandfather raised me."

"Where are your parents?"

"I don't know."

Hannah couldn't fathom a world in which she didn't know where her parents were. "You don't see them?"

"No."

"Do you not want to talk about this?"

"Not really."

"I'm sorry. I don't mean to pry."

"You're not prying." He raised his hand to comb the hair back from his face. "But there's not much to say. They're not around. They've never been around."

Hannah sensed a much bigger story, but she didn't dare pursue it when the subject had clearly upset him.

"I should probably check in with Skeeter to make sure he hasn't run me out of business while we've been gone."

Hannah released him and watched him get up. After spending more than twenty-four hours naked with him, she couldn't help but notice the return of tension to his shoulders and regretted pushing him to talk about his family.

He pulled on a clean pair of boxer briefs, retrieved his cell phone from his bag and kept his back to her as he placed the call while standing before the window that looked out over mountains in the distance.

Chilled by his abrupt withdrawal, Hannah pulled the covers up over her shoulders and waited. She hoped they could recapture the closeness they'd shared before she'd ruined it by bringing up the wrong topic.

"Nolan's Garage, Skeeter speaking."

"Hey, it's me."

"What's up, boss man? Didn't expect to hear from you until Monday."

That was because Nolan had told him he wouldn't hear from him until Monday, but when Hannah asked him about his parents, he went immediately into the protective mode he'd relied on most of his life. He didn't talk about his parents— ever, even with Hannah.

"Just checking in to make sure you haven't burned the place down or anything."

"We had just a small fire, but I got it contained before it did too much damage."

"Very funny."

"I know, right? Dude says I'm hilarious."

Nolan rolled his eyes. "Anything else?"

"I'm not sure if I should tell you this or not, but Gavin Guthrie was here looking for you. Seemed upset. I told him you'd be back on Monday."

Feeling like he'd been electrocuted or something equally unpleasant, Nolan swallowed hard. "What'd he say?"

"Just that he wanted to talk to you, and he'd be back on Monday. Should I not have told you that?"

Honestly, Nolan could've done without that news, but he didn't say so to Skeeter. "It's fine. Thanks for covering for me."

"No problem."

Nolan ended the call and returned the phone to his bag, his

mind spinning with concern over Gavin, who was another of Nolan's good friends. He wasn't as close to Gavin as he'd been to Caleb, but he'd known him forever, and they'd run around in a giant mob since they were kids.

"What's wrong?" Hannah asked.

He turned to find her watching him with those amazingly expressive eyes that saw all the way through him. And wasn't that what had made him go into protective mode earlier? Should he tell her about Gavin's visit or wait to hear what Gavin wanted before he potentially upset her?

While he leaned toward the latter option, he didn't want to disappoint her by keeping things from her. He went to sit on the edge of the bed. "Gavin came by the garage. Skeeter said he seemed upset."

"Oh no . . . What should we do?" She sat up, clutching the covers to her breasts.

"I know it's difficult to consider how this—you and me—might affect other people, especially people like Gavin and his parents. But we haven't done anything wrong, Hannah. It would kill me if you thought we had."

"I don't, but I also can't bear the thought of him being upset over something I did."

"Something we both did." He watched her carefully, pained by the distress he saw in her eyes. "Do you want to go home?"

She thought about it long enough that he was convinced she would say yes. "No, not until tomorrow. Should I call him? What should I do?"

"What do you want to do?"

"I don't know . . ."

"Tell you what—let's go out to dinner and take some time to think about it, and you can see how you feel afterward."

"That sounds good."

"I'll call downstairs and see about a reservation in the restaurant. The food is supposed to be excellent. Is that okay?"

"Sure."

She went along with his plan, but he could tell she was undone by the news about Gavin. For the first time since they arrived, they showered separately and got dressed in silence. He wanted to assure her he'd take care of the situation with

Gavin, and he would, but he didn't think that would be enough to soothe her. Still, he wanted to offer her something . . .

"Whatever's up with Gavin, I'll handle it."

"I don't expect you to handle it. He's my brother-in-law. If anyone should handle it, it should be me."

"He came to see me," Nolan reminded her, "which means his beef is most likely with me—not you."

"So you're saying I'm not involved? It's got nothing to do with me?"

"I never said that." As his frustration mounted, he forced buttons through buttonholes on his shirt. "Why are we fighting about this?"

"We're not fighting. We're talking."

It felt like fighting to him, but he wasn't going to make things worse by saying so. Hannah emerged from the bathroom wearing sexy black pants with a ruffled red silk blouse. Black high-heeled sandals brought her to his shoulder.

"You look gorgeous," he said.

"Thank you."

They left the room in uneasy silence that stayed with them into the dining room, where they were seated at a corner table with a view of the fireplace. As Hannah studied the menu, he noticed her brows were knit with tension and dismay. He hated himself for telling her about Gavin's visit to the garage. That could've waited until they got back to Butler.

"Hannah."

She glanced at him over the top of the menu.

"Could we please call a truce until we get home tomorrow, when we'll figure out a plan to talk to Gavin together?"

Her shoulders seemed to lose some of their rigidity. "Yes." She rolled her bottom lip between her teeth before glancing up to meet his gaze. "As long as you understand I don't ever want to be treated like the helpless woman who can't fight her own battles or needs to be protected from unpleasant things. I'm not that woman."

"I know. There's nothing helpless about you, but can you blame me for wanting to protect you from any more hurt after what you've already endured?" He took her hand and cradled it between both of his. "When I told you I love you, I meant it. I'd do anything to spare you further grief."

"And I love you for that and many other things. But you can't protect me from the people I love, and Gavin is someone I love and care about. I'm so mad at myself for not telling him about us when I saw him the other day. I should've told him then. It should've come from me, not his parents. I was so caught up in everything . . ." She shook her head in disgust.

"You didn't do anything wrong, Hannah. You have a right to be happy without feeling like you have to explain it to everyone."

"I don't feel like I have to explain it to everyone, but I should've explained it to him."

"Maybe."

"For the first couple of months after Caleb died," she said haltingly, "I had trouble being around Gavin."

"Because he looks so much like Caleb."

She nodded. "He wanted to help me and needed to share his grief with me, but I . . . I couldn't bear to hear the voice that was so much like the one I'd never hear again. I turned away from him out of self-preservation, which was just another hurt on top of everything else for him. It took a very long time for us to get back on track after that."

"I didn't know. I'm sorry." Filled with regret, Nolan brought her hand to his mouth and brushed his lips over her knuckles. "No wonder it hit you so hard to hear that he'd been looking for me."

"It hit me harder to hear he's upset."

"I hate to see you beating yourself up over this. We haven't actually been seeing each other all that long, and it's perfectly fair to take a little time to ourselves before we tell the world."

"In most cases, I'd agree with you, but this is different."

"I know."

When they ordered dinner—steak for him and salmon for her—he asked for another bottle of champagne.

Hannah gave him a wary look. "More champagne? This weekend is going to cost a fortune."

"It's money very well spent. And we need more champagne to continue celebrating what we've found together. No matter what happens or what gets thrown our way, we'll figure it out, okay?"

Her eyes were bright with tears when she said, "Okay."

The waiter returned with the champagne and uncorked the bottle. Without losing a drop he filled two crystal flutes and then left the bottle in an ice bucket next to the table.

Nolan raised his glass to her. "Here's to you and me and figuring it out together."

Hannah touched her glass to his and held his gaze as she took the first sip.

"It's all going to be okay," he said. "I promise."

After dinner, they wandered into the lounge where a trio was playing jazz, and the dance floor was crowded with swaying couples.

"Let's dance," Nolan said, taking her hand and leading her to the front of the big room.

Hannah went along with him, even though she wasn't really in the mood to dance. But he was trying to salvage their weekend, and after he'd gone to so much trouble to provide a much-needed getaway, she wasn't about to spoil it.

Nolan's arms came around her, reminding her of the first time they'd danced together weeks ago at the Grange. She felt the same sense of "rightness" she'd experienced then. Their bodies fit together as if they'd been made for each other, which she'd discovered this weekend didn't just apply to dancing. He was a thoughtful, considerate, sensual lover, who reawakened a part of her she'd thought gone forever.

"What're you thinking about?"

"You really want to know?"

"I really want to know."

"I'm thinking about how well we fit together, and not just when we're dancing."

His groan rumbled through her chest and sent a flurry of sensation from her ear to her nipples, settling in a throb between her legs.

"You said you wanted to know."

His arms tightened around her, and his erection pressed into her belly, telling her what her words had done to him. One of his hands slid lower, and she felt the press of his fingers against the top curve of her bottom.

With her arms curled around his neck, she looked up at him expectantly.

He came through with a kiss that made her knees go weak. "Let's get out of here," he whispered in her ear.

"Yes, please."

Her hand encased in his tight grip, Hannah followed him from the lounge, her gaze dropping to the appealing way the black jeans molded to his muscular backside and legs. He seemed to be a man on a mission as he walked them swiftly back to the room where they'd already shared so many blissful hours.

They were barely inside the door when he had her pressed against it, his mouth devouring her in a series of deep, sweeping kisses. Hannah buried her hand in his hair to hold him in place. And then his hands were on her bottom, lifting her against his hardness.

A needy, urgent sound escaped from their joined lips, and she wasn't sure if it came from him or her. She went to work on his shirt buttons, pulling and tugging. One of them came popping off, making her gasp. "Whoops," she said against his lips. "I'll sew it back on for you."

"I don't care," he said gruffly, his hands slipping under the hem of her blouse to tug it up and over her head. His eyes went dark with desire when he saw the lacy black bra she wore under it. "You're so incredible, Hannah. Do you have any idea how much I want you?" His lips skimmed her neck. "And not just like this. In every way. All the time."

She trembled in his arms, overwhelmed by everything he made her feel. Things she hadn't felt in so long, she'd forgotten what it was like.

He released the clasp on her pants and let them fall around her ankles, leaving her only in the bra, a matching thong and the heels. Nolan took her hand and stood back to take a searching look at what he'd unveiled. "Breathtaking," he whispered, leading her across the room, where he turned her to face the bed.

Hannah continued to tremble as she waited to see what he would do. She heard him unbuckle his belt and unzip his jeans.

He cupped her bottom, squeezing and caressing.

Tipping forward, she braced her hands on the bed as he drew her panties down over her hips until they rested just below her cheeks. "Is this okay?" he asked in that rough, gruff voice that told her just how badly he wanted her.

"Yes . . ." She fisted the sheets. "Nolan . . . Please, hurry."

He moved quickly to align their bodies, pushing into her in one quick thrust that stole the breath from her lungs and made her scream from the sheer pleasure that shot through her. She pushed back against him, begging him with her body to move.

Wrapping one strong arm around her belly he held her in place for his fierce possession. His other hand cupped her mound, circling the tight bud of her desire with a calloused finger that detonated her release. She came hard, and he was right behind her, pressing into her one last time as his lips skimmed the sensitive skin on her back.

Hannah's limbs were made of rubber as they disentangled themselves. She pushed her panties the rest of the way off, crawled onto the bed and landed facedown on a pillow as every inch of her body throbbed with satisfaction.

Nolan molded himself to her and pulled the covers up and over them, cocooning them in warmth and bone-deep pleasure.

She summoned the last bit of energy she possessed and turned to face him, smoothing his hair and caressing the scruff on his jaw. His eyes were closed and his chest still heaved from exertion. Hannah traced the outline of his lips, startling and then laughing when he took a gentle bite of her fingertip.

"Thank you for this weekend, Nolan. It's been amazing."

"For me, too, honey. You have no idea how much I love being here with you or how much I love holding you this way. It's what I've wanted for a very long time."

"I'm sorry I made you wait so long."

"Don't be sorry. It was well worth the wait. You were well worth the wait."

"I hope you still think so when people start to find out about us and look at you differently because you're see-ing me."

"I don't care what anyone thinks. We both know how this happened—and when it happened. That's all that matters."

As Hannah drifted off to sleep in his arms, nagging worries filled her dreams.

CHAPTER 20

❖

"Captain" Caleb is leaving for Iraq tomorrow.
He brought Homer and me home to Vermont to
be with my family while he's away. He's
downplaying the whole thing like it's no big deal.
I appreciate what he's trying to do, but I'm
terrified. This isn't his first deployment, but I've
never been this anxious before. He assures me
he'll be fine, so I choose to believe him. It's good to
be home for a while so I can finally make his
grandmother's house more "ours" than it is now.
I've got plenty to do!

—From the diary of Hannah Abbott Guthrie, age
twenty-seven

As Nolan drove home to Butler the next afternoon with the windows down to let in the warm spring air, Hannah turned her face into the sun, welcoming the warmth after the endless winter. "I was thinking," she said.

"About?"

"Sunday dinner at my parents' house."

"You want me to drop you there?"

"I want you to come with me." Nolan had been a frequent

guest at Sunday dinner over the years, so no one would be surprised to see him there. Of course the context was different now, which was why he hesitated.

"Oh."

"Do you want to?"

"It's not about wanting to. It's about whether your family is ready to see us together. Does everyone know?"

"I assume by now everyone knows, and I'm sure they all know where we've been this weekend. Well, not where, but that we were away together."

"Right . . . That's sort of the part that worries me. People I've known all my life looking at me differently because I'm with you now."

"You're going to have to face them sooner or later. Unless," she added in a teasing tone, "you're sick of me after this weekend."

"I'm hardly sick of you," he said, squeezing her hand, which he had laid flat on his thigh. "As you well know."

"Then I guess there's no time like the present to face the Abbott family as my new . . . What shall I call you? Boy toy? Lover boy?"

"You're enjoying this, aren't you? I feel like I'm going to puke, and you're over there making fun of me."

"I'd never do that."

"Yes, you would."

"I'll protect you from the evil Abbotts. Don't worry."

"I'm very worried."

"How about I use your phone—if we can get a signal—to call my mom so she can do some prep work on our behalf?"

"That'd be good." He dug the phone out of his coat pocket and handed it to her.

Hannah punched in the familiar number and waited for the call to go through. After a few ominous-sounding clicks, the call finally connected and Molly answered.

"Hi, Mom, it's Hannah."

"I know that, silly. How was your time away?"

"Excellent. We're on our way back now and were thinking about crashing dinner if that's okay."

"Absolutely okay. We'd love to have you both."

"Um, the thing is . . . Nolan's not really up for the Abbott inquisition, so if you could run some interference for us, we'd both appreciate it."

"I'm on it. Don't worry."

"Great, thank you. We'll see you soon."

"See you then—and Hannah? I'm so glad to hear your time away was excellent. I've been thinking about you."

"Thanks, Mom," she said softly before she ended the call. "We're good to go," she said to Nolan.

"Can I wear this or should I go home and change first?" He was wearing faded jeans with a black thermal shirt.

"As much as I'd love to see where you live, you look fine. You should see what my brothers wear sometimes. Well, except Hunter who puts them all to shame."

"About going to my house . . . It's not that I don't want to take you there. You know that, right?"

"I guess."

He gripped the wheel so tightly his knuckles turned white from the strain. "It's just sometimes . . . Occasionally, there's drama. Family drama. I don't want you anywhere near that."

"Nolan, I have nine siblings. Do you think I don't know about family drama?"

"Not this kind you don't," he said with a bitter edge to his voice.

"I've shared a lot with you, things I haven't shared with anyone else. I wish you'd feel safe doing the same. It would hurt me if you didn't feel safe to share your troubles with me."

"God, Hannah . . . Don't put it like that. You know I'd never hurt you."

"Then don't. Share your worries with me. Tell me what puts that pained look on your face whenever we talk about your home or your family."

His jaw pulsed with tension as he stared at the road. "You wouldn't understand coming from what you come from. What with your Sunday dinners and your coat hooks in the front hall with your names on them and your parents who always do and say the right things. You wouldn't get it."

Stung by the sharpness of his words as much as the agony she heard behind them, Hannah held her silence for many miles, deciding to let it go for now. But she hoped that some-day he'd trust her enough to share his pain with her.

"After dinner, I'd like to go see Gavin."

Nolan visibly relaxed when he realized she'd changed the subject. "That's fine."

"Your lips are swollen," Charley whispered to Hannah as they helped to clean up after dinner.

"Shut up. They are not."

"Yes, they are," Ella said. "So how was it?"

"I'm not having this conversation."

"Yes, you are," Charley said. "We deserve to know."

"How do you figure?"

"We're your sisters," Charley insisted. "We get to know everything."

"Where is that written?"

"Come on! Don't be lame! Spill it."

"It was great, if you must know," Hannah said, glancing over their shoulders to make sure no one was listening, especially Nolan.

"Did you cry?" Ella asked with sweet compassion.

"A little."

Sniffling subtly, Ella hugged Hannah.

"Caleb left me a letter."

"What?" Charley asked breathlessly, her eyes gone wide with surprise.

"He gave it to his mom to hold on to until she felt I was ready. She gave it to me on Thursday after I told them I'm seeing Nolan."

"Oh my God," Ella whispered. "What did it say?"

"A lot of things, but mostly he wants me to be happy, he wants me to love again and to not let his death steal the joy from my life."

Ella swiped at the tears that now flowed freely down her cheeks.

Charley was suddenly very interested in her feet.

"What an incredible thing for him to do," Ella said.

"Were you mad she waited so long to give it to you?" Charley asked.

"No, because she did exactly what he told her to do by holding on to it until now."

"Holding on to what?" Hunter asked as he came into the kitchen carrying a stack of plates.

"Caleb left her a letter," Ella told their brother.

"Oh he did? And you just found it now?"

Hannah relayed the story of Amelia holding on to it for her.

"Wow." Hunter leaned against the counter, his arms crossed over his chest. "And here I've been kind of pissed all this time because he didn't do that, and I so wished he had for your sake." He took a closer look at his twin. "You seem really happy, Han. I take it the weekend away went well?"

"Uh-huh," she said, as Ella giggled softly.

"Oh God." Hunter groaned and rolled his eyes. "I'm so out of here."

Nolan came in with some of the serving bowls, which he placed in the sink before turning to face the three sisters. "Are you guys talking about me in here?"

"Not at all," Charley said with a disdainful snort. "Don't be so full of yourself."

"Right," he said. "How foolish of me to think someone with the last name of Abbott might be gossiping." He surprised Hannah when he put his arm around her and kissed her square on the lips. "You'd better not be kissing and telling."

"I wouldn't dream of it."

"*Right*," he said again, releasing her and shaking his head on the way out of the kitchen.

The three women dissolved into laughter.

"He's so hot." Ella fanned her face. "You get all the hot guys. It's not fair."

"There's one out there waiting to find you, El," Hannah said. "And whatever man wins your heart will be the luckiest guy in the world."

"I think she's got her eye on one already," Charley said.

"Do tell!" Hannah said.

"I don't," Ella insisted.

"She always says that," Charley said, "but if you ask me, she knows exactly who she wants, but damn if I can get it out of her."

"Shut up, Charley. Why do you always have to be such a pain in the ass?"

"It's part of my charm."

"Is Charley being a pain in the ass again?" Molly asked as she came in carrying more dishes.

"Yes!" Ella said. "Do something about her, would you, Mom?"

"Darling, I've been trying to do something about her for thirty years now."

Charley snorted with laughter at the true statement. "Keep trying."

"I'll never give up," Molly said. "What's she being a pain about now?"

"She's hammering Ella because she thinks Ella has her eye on someone, but being the smart girl that she is, Ella won't tell Charley," Hannah said.

"I wouldn't tell her either, El," Molly said.

Ella sent a smug, satisfied look to Charley.

"Say what you will, my friends, but she's hot for someone, and I'm going to figure out who it is."

"Why don't you spend your time figuring out who Colton's hot for," Ella said. "That'll be a much more satisfying mission."

"I'd like to know that, too," Molly said. "Two weekends in a row he's a no-show for Sunday dinner."

"I'm on that as well," Charley said. "Luckily, I can work multiple missions at the same time."

"Where were Max and Chloe today?" Hannah asked her mom about her youngest brother.

"Poor Chloe has been hit with morning sickness that's more like all-day sickness. Max decided to stay in Burlington with her."

"Ugh, that's gotta suck," Charley said.

"I was so lucky I never had that with any of you, or I would've had a whole lot less kids," Molly said.

"That might've been a good thing," Ella said with a pointed look at Charley.

"You love me," Charley said. "You know you do."

"Stay out of my business, and I'll continue to love you."

Charley pounced. "See! I knew it! She has business!"

"Ugh!" Ella twirled and stomped out of the room.

"Leave her alone, Charley," Molly admonished gently. "You know how private she is."

"What right does she have to be private when the rest of us

are forced to share every detail of our lives with this family?" Charley asked.

Hannah couldn't exactly argue with her rationale, even if she didn't always agree with her tactics.

"Leave her alone," Molly said more sternly. "I mean it. If she's got business, as you put it, she'll share it with us when she's ready to. Hammering at her isn't going to get her to spill it any sooner."

"That's true," Hannah said.

"Now tell me, Hannah," Molly said, "what can we do to help you for next weekend?"

"We're going to need a ton of food." Hannah was never sure what they went through more of during a Sultans weekend—food or beer, so she always had plenty of both on hand.

"*That* we can help with, right Charley?"

"Yeah, sure," Charley said, pouting a bit after failing to break Ella. Hannah knew she'd keep at it until she got the info she wanted. That was Charley.

In the other room, she heard Wade say good-bye to their grandfather. Hannah went into the dining room to stop him before he could leave. She drew her brother into the hallway. "How are things going?"

"I got an e-mail from Mia last night, letting me know she can't meet me anymore." The utter devastation on his face broke her heart.

"Oh no. Did she say why?"

He shook his head. "I'm so afraid he found out about our friendship and now . . . The thought of what she might be going through kills me. I don't know what to do. I feel like I'm losing my mind."

"Please don't do anything crazy, Wade, or put yourself in jeopardy when you have no idea what's really going on there."

"I can't just sit here and do nothing."

"That might be the best way to keep her safe."

"I don't know." He ran his fingers through his hair, which was loose today. "I'm going to take a hike on the mountain and burn off some of this energy."

"That's a good idea. Will you call me if I can do anything or even if you just need to talk?"

"I will." He hugged her. "Thanks, Han."

Shortly after Wade left, Nolan slid an arm around her waist. "Everything okay?"

She nodded even though she was desperately worried about her brother and what he might do to ensure the woman he cared about was safe.

"Wade seemed worked up about something."

"Maybe a little." She glanced up at him. "Are you ready to go?"

"Whenever you are."

As they were saying good-bye and thank you to her parents, she heard her dad say, "Take good care of my little girl."

"I fully intend to," Nolan replied as he shook hands with her dad.

Touched by his love and concern, Hannah hugged her dad, who held on tighter than usual. Her parents had suffered right along with her when she lost Caleb. They'd loved him, and they'd worried endlessly over her. She knew it was a relief to them to see her moving forward with her life and spending time with a man they liked and respected.

"You survived," she said to Nolan when they were back in his truck.

"Just barely," he said with a teasing grin. "Everyone was really nice. No one asked anything inappropriate, which was shocking."

"I didn't get so lucky."

"I knew it! Your sisters were grilling you, right? What did you tell them?"

"Nothing. Much."

"*Hannah . . .*"

"I didn't give them any details."

He busted up laughing. "And yet somehow you gave them the full picture."

"I did no such thing."

"Whatever. I know how you Abbotts roll."

"Does it bother you that everyone knows we've been, well, fooling around?"

"If I had my druthers, no one would know but you and me, but I get that's not the world we live in. There aren't many secrets in Butler or in the Abbott family."

Hannah thought of what Wade was going through with Mia, that Hunter had feelings for Megan, that Ella might be interested in a man none of them knew. "We have our share of secrets."

"Apparently, you and me and what we're up to isn't going to be one of them."

"That one's harder to keep."

"I'm looking forward to when our relationship is no longer in the headlines."

"How long do you think that'll take?"

"A while probably," he said with a sigh. "The people in this town don't fool around when it comes to gossip—and they're all extremely protective of you."

"Good thing I picked the right guy to spend time with. At least they've got nothing bad they can say about you. Everyone loves you."

"I guess we'll find out for sure, won't we?"

They headed around the mountain, past the entrance to the sugaring facility that Colton ran and north to the outer limits of Butler, where Gavin's logging company was headquartered. He lived in a log cabin on the property adjacent to the sawmill he'd built four years ago. Hannah hadn't been up here in a long time, but at first glance she could see the business had grown tremendously.

She felt a surge of pride for what Gavin had accomplished, much of it fueled by relentless grief and the need to pour all that emotion into something productive. Her recently satisfied stomach turned with worry about how this visit might go. The thought of being at odds with Gavin or his parents was unimaginable.

As Nolan parked his truck next to Gavin's, he said, "Relax, honey. It's going to be fine."

Hannah wished she could be so certain. She got out of the truck and wiped her suddenly sweaty palms on her jeans. As they walked to Gavin's front door, she felt Nolan's hand on the small of her back guiding her and took comfort from his solid presence by her side.

She knocked on the door and waited anxiously until Gavin appeared wearing only a pair of faded jeans. As always, the sight of him was a stark reminder of the husband she'd lost, and it took a moment to recover her bearings. "Hey, Gav," she said. "Could we come in for a minute?"

Without a word, he pushed open the screen door to admit them.

Nolan squeezed her shoulder as he followed her inside to Gavin's cozy home, which boasted a big-screen TV set to a Boston Red Sox preseason game.

Gavin went to the fridge, got a beer and cracked it open. "Want one?"

"No, thanks," Hannah said.

"I wouldn't mind a beer," Nolan said.

Gavin gave the one he'd opened to Nolan and got another for himself.

Hannah sat next to Nolan at the bar. Gavin stayed in the kitchen, facing them, drinking his beer and waiting for one of them to say something.

Nerves fluttered in her belly as she tried to think of what to say.

"I heard you came by the garage yesterday," Nolan said.

Hannah was grateful to him for the opening salvo.

"Uh-huh."

"I assume your parents told you Hannah and I are seeing each other."

He kept his expression unreadable when he said, "Right."

Hannah couldn't bear to remain silent any longer. "Gavin—"

"Don't, Hannah. Please don't say anything. Whatever it is, I don't want to hear it." He put down his bottle with a loud thunk. "No, wait. That's not true. I'd like to know why you didn't tell me yourself when I saw you the other day."

Thrown by Gavin's angry outburst, she said, "I should have. I don't know why I didn't. My only excuse is that it's still new, and I wasn't exactly ready to talk about it yet. With anyone."

"You saw fit to tell my parents."

"Because I didn't want them to hear it through the grapevine."

"But it was okay that I did? It was okay that I was at the diner and heard you two had been there and were getting rather cozy? Can you imagine what it was like to hear that from someone I barely know when I had just seen you?"

"I'm sorry," Hannah said softly as tears formed. "I never meant to hurt you."

"We should've told you," Nolan said.

"How long have you been interested in my brother's wife? When he was alive, too?"

"No! God no. You know how I felt about him."

"Yeah, I do, which is why I find this so unbelievable."

"Why, Gavin?" Hannah asked, feeling desperate to make him understand. "Why is it so unbelievable that I would have feelings for an old friend, and he would have them for me?"

"What I find unbelievable is that this only happened recently."

Hannah stared at him, stunned by the implication. "I, um . . . I have to go." Blinded by tears, she got up and rushed out the door.

CHAPTER 21

---◆◀◆▶◆---

*The army chaplain came three days ago. I still
have no words . . .*

—From the diary of Hannah Abbott Guthrie, age
twenty-eight

"Seriously?" Nolan said after Hannah ran out of there. "You're honestly accusing her of fooling around behind Caleb's back?"

"How do I know what to believe?"

"You disappoint me, Gavin. We've been friends a long time, and I know you've been to hell and back. That's the only reason I'm not going to drop you on your ass for saying something like that to her."

"Go ahead and give it your best shot."

Nolan's hands rolled into fists he kept planted at his sides so he wouldn't be tempted to flatten a man he'd always considered a friend. "It's taken her all this time to get to the point where she'd even consider being with someone else. If you've undone all that progress with your thoughtless comments, I'll never forgive you. You owe her an apology, and until she gets it, I have nothing to say to you."

He was almost to the door when Gavin called out his name. His better judgment told him to keep going. Instead he bowed to the bonds of decades-long friendship, turned and raised a brow in inquiry.

"Have you given any thought at all to what he'd say about you banging his wife?"

Infuriated by Gavin's word choice, Nolan fought to keep the rage out of his voice. "Yeah, Gav. I've given it a lot of thought and a few sleepless nights, too. I think about him all the time, and I wish more than I wish for anything in this life that he hadn't died. But he did, and the rest of us are left to do the best we can with the hand we were dealt. I love her, but I never touched her until very recently. Believe what you will, but that's the God's honest truth. And after her faithful devotion to your brother, Hannah deserves a whole lot more than the pile of shit she just got from you."

Fuming and panic-stricken about what must be going through Hannah's mind, Nolan let the screen door slam behind him. He went outside to find her sitting in his truck, staring straight ahead without so much as blinking. Anxious to get her out of there, he got into the truck and left dust in his wake as he floored the accelerator. When they reached the main road, he stopped long enough to reach across Hannah for the seatbelt, which he fastened around her.

That's when he noticed her hands trembling in her lap as unshed tears brightened her eyes.

Motherfucker, he thought, shocked and horrified by Gavin's extremely out-of-character behavior. In his heart, Nolan believed that Gavin knew she'd been faithful to Caleb. His accusations were coming from a place of deep, unrelenting grief, but that didn't give him the right to disrespect Hannah the way he had.

"Talk to me, baby," he said, reaching for her freezing-cold hand. All he could think about was how happy and carefree she'd been for most of the weekend. He'd loved seeing her that way, and the thought of her brother-in-law's bad behavior undoing all that progress infuriated him. "He's just spouting off. He didn't mean that. You know he didn't."

A sob escaped through her tightly clenched lips, and a flood of tears spilled down her face.

Nolan pulled the truck to the side of the road, unclipped both their seatbelts and lifted her into his lap.

She fought him at first, but he kept his arms banded tight around her, giving her no choice but to lean on him as her heartbroken sobs filled the cab of his truck.

"That was a shitty thing for him to say, and he knows it. He's hurting at the thought of you moving on without Caleb, and he has a right to those feelings, but he has no right at all to take it out on you."

"I never looked at another man for the entire twelve years I was with him," she said, hiccupping on her sobs, "or for the seven years since he died. For nineteen years, he was the only one."

"I know, baby. I know, and so does Gavin. If he doesn't already feel like shit for inferring otherwise, he will before long, and you'll hear from him. If I know him at all, and I know him as well as I know anyone, you'll hear from him."

"That he could even *think* that, let alone say it . . ."

"I know." Nolan regretted that he hadn't dropped Gavin on his ass when he had the chance. It was the least of what he deserved.

"I always thought he was one of my closest friends," Hannah said. "We've been through hell together."

Another thought occurred to Nolan that had his mind reeling with implications. "Is there any chance that he might've, you know, held out hope that you might one day be interested in him?"

"*What?* No! God no. There's never been anything like that between us. We were always just friends."

"Maybe as far as you were concerned."

"I can't get my head around that possibility. It's so far outside my comfort zone it's not even conceivable."

"It might explain why he behaved the way he did."

"No," she said, whimpering as new tears wet her face and spilled onto his coat. With only her heartbroken sniffles to break the long silence, she finally raised her head from his chest. "I'd like to go home now, please."

She may as well have erected an invisible, electric fence between them. That's how profoundly he felt the distance creep in, despite the fact she was still sitting on his lap with his arms wrapped around her. He had no choice but to release her when every instinct he had was screaming at him to hold on tighter. Yeah, he really should've punched Gavin Guthrie when he'd had the chance.

Hannah put her seatbelt back on, pulled a tissue from her purse and wiped the tears from her face. She didn't say another word as he drove them to her house. When he carried her bag to the porch, she turned to face him. "Thank you for a wonderful weekend."

"Why do I feel like everything that happened between us this weekend was undone by one insensitive comment?"

Hannah sighed and her chin trembled.

Nolan wanted to go back to Gavin's place and take out all his frustration—and he had a lot of it all of a sudden—on Hannah's brother-in-law.

"I just need some time to think."

"*Why*, Hannah? We both know exactly how this happened." Nolan felt like he was fighting for his very life. "Why would you give him the satisfaction of driving a wedge between us right when things are going so well?"

"If he thinks that, maybe other people do, too."

"*No one* thinks we were together before Caleb died! *Gavin* doesn't think that. He's lashing out because he misses his brother and wants everything the way it used to be. It has nothing at all to do with you—or me."

"I need some time."

"How much time?"

"I don't know."

"Please don't do this."

"I'm sorry." Taking her bag from him, she slipped into the house. The door closed quietly behind her.

Nolan wanted to scream with frustration and fear and love and regret. He never should've let her be part of the conversation with Gavin. If she hadn't been there, she never would've heard his ugly accusation, and Nolan certainly wouldn't have shared that with her. Everything would be as it was this morning when they awoke wrapped up in each other.

If he could go back in time twenty-four hours, he wouldn't have told her Gavin had come by the garage. That was his first huge mistake.

After slamming the driver's side door to the truck, Nolan started the engine and left dust in his wake as he pulled away.

The last place he wanted to go was home where he might encounter his father, who'd surely run through the money Nolan had given him by now.

So he went to the garage and spent the rest of the day catching up on all the paperwork he'd let slide over the last month, desperately trying to think about anything other than the taste of paradise he'd experienced with Hannah and his overwhelming fear that it might be over before it even started. He was paying the bills when Skeeter came into the office.

"What're you doing here, boss man? Thought you was off romancing your lady this weekend."

"We're back now."

Skeeter took a closer look at Nolan, tipping his head and puckering his lips. "You don't look too happy to say you finally got what you been wanting for a long time."

"It's all screwed up." Nolan hadn't planned to say that, but once the words were out, the story of what'd happened up at Gavin's poured out behind it.

"*Damn*," Skeeter said as he took a seat. "He really said that?"

"He really did."

"Doesn't sound like the Gavin Guthrie I've known most of his life."

"That's what I said, too. It's his grief talking. There's no way he thinks she was fooling around with me when Caleb was still alive. He knows better. But there's no telling Hannah. All she heard was the accusation coming from someone she loves, someone she's relied upon greatly over the last seven years." Nolan smacked his open hand on his desk. "The worst part is she was really happy all weekend. We had a great time together. And now we're back to square one, all thanks to Gavin."

"You know . . . I'm just speculating here so bear with me . . . She might've taken a step back anyway, even if Gavin hadn't spouted off."

"What makes you say that?"

"I assume this was the first time she's . . . you know, done what she probably did with you, since Caleb died. Once the reality of that sets in, there's apt to be a bit of a meltdown or whatever women call it when their emotions get the better of 'em."

Nolan hated to admit that Skeeter was actually making some sense, not that he'd ever tell his old friend that.

"You just gotta be patient with her and let her know you're not giving up, no matter what gets thrown in your way. This thing with Gavin . . . it's a setback. It ain't the end of the world."

"If you could've seen her face when his meaning registered with her, you wouldn't be so sure it wasn't the end of the world."

"It's a big thing for her to be moving forward with her life after such a terrible loss. There's apt to be some stopping and starting along the way. You gotta stay calm and roll with it so she knows you're in it for the long haul."

"So what am I supposed to do?"

"Nothing for now. Give her the time she asked for, and be patient with her. It would've been a lot to process without Gavin's unfortunately timed comments."

"Thanks, Skeet."

"Any time," he said with a smile, seeming pleased to know that his words had brought comfort to Nolan.

"What're you doing here anyway?"

"I got a coupla things to finish that didn't get done during the week, and Dude is off at her sister's place today, so I figured I'd work while I had the time. If that's all right with you."

"You getting responsible in your old age?"

"*Shit*, boy . . . Don't get too excited."

Nolan laughed, which thirty minutes ago he wouldn't have thought possible. "At least it isn't religion."

Skeeter let go with a barking laugh. "No prayer of that happening."

"The church is better off without you."

"You know it. Don't sit around here fretting. Go find something productive to do with all that energy you got zipping around inside you."

"Thanks again for covering this weekend."

Skeeter waved off his thanks. "Any time. By the way, Dude said you can have the puppy Wednesday. I figured you'd want to wait until after next weekend's events to bring him home." Nolan had finally told Skeeter about the plans for Homer's funeral.

Nolan wondered if it was still a good idea to get the puppy for Hannah, but he'd deal with that after Homer's funeral. "You figured right. I'll see you in the morning."

"Might be afternoon. I wouldn't want to be too reliable."

Nolan laughed and stepped into the waning afternoon light. He dropped the mail into the outgoing box and walked to his truck. The hell with it, he thought, heading for home despite the expectation that Vernon would show up again soon looking for more money.

He had a ton of wood he could split for next weekend to keep the fire pit going. That was something he could do for Hannah while he waited to hear if all they were going to get was one amazing weekend together.

After Nolan left, Hannah wandered aimlessly through the big house, trying to think about anything other than what Gavin had implied. She knew Nolan was right, and that Gavin's harsh words had come from a place of grief rather than anger. However, that he was hurting over something she had done was impossible for her to handle on top of the other recent changes in her life.

She started a load of laundry and curled up in bed to reread Caleb's journals, flipping through each page slowly so as to absorb every word. Then she took some time to record the latest events in her own journal, something she'd done just about every day of her life since a teacher suggested she keep a journal in sixth grade. The crazy hours she and Nolan had kept during the weekend caught up to her, and she dozed off for a while.

The dream started slowly, wrapping around her subconscious subtly, the same way Nolan had over the last couple of years while she knew he was waiting patiently for her. He wasn't patient in the dream. Rather, he was passionate and loving, his body wrapped around hers from behind as he slid into her with slow, sensual strokes while his hands cupped her breasts and teased her nipples.

Hannah woke up gasping, on the verge of release, an insistent throb between her legs reminding her of the pleasure she'd known in his arms. She wanted to call him and beg him to forgive her for sending him away, but she couldn't get her leaden limbs to move to reach for the phone.

For a long time, she lay there looking up at the ceiling as the throbbing subsided and a new ache took up residence in her chest. He'd waited so long, and she'd turned him away. What if she'd driven him away forever? What if she'd tried his patience one time too many? What if . . .

"This is ridiculous," she muttered as she got up and ran her fingers through her hair to restore some order. Glancing to the other side of the bed, she expected to see Homer there, where he always used to be, and her breath caught in her throat at the reminder that he was gone. "It's all too much."

She went to the bathroom to splash cold water on her face and decided to get going on the cleaning that needed to happen before the Sultan invasion began on Friday. Starting with the attic bedroom, she scrubbed and dusted and vacuumed all ten bedrooms and five bathrooms until they gleamed.

The washer and dryer ran all night with linens and towels that had grown musty after a year in the linen closet. It had been that long since the Sultans last came together, for the sixth anniversary of Caleb's death. The usual Labor Day gathering hadn't happened last year because one of them had gotten married in late August, so everyone had been together then.

Austin and Debra's wedding at Lake Tahoe had been beautiful and poignant and agonizing because Caleb wasn't there to serve as his oldest friend's best man, so Austin's other best friend, Gavin, had done the job both brothers would've done had Caleb been alive.

Gavin . . .

How he could imply that she'd ever been anything other than entirely faithful to his brother remained beyond her ability to comprehend hours later.

She was still grappling with how to handle the rift with Gavin the next day. Fresh off the sleepless night, she was at the grocery store when it opened at seven and arrived home two hours later with everything she needed to make five lasagnas, a huge pot of chili, cornbread, salsa, beef stew and the chicken enchiladas she was famous for among the Sultans. No weekend together was complete without them, or so they always told her.

The doorbell rang at noon as she was putting the third pan of lasagna in the oven to bake. Hannah wiped her hands on her apron and went to answer the door on legs that were starting to tire after the long hours of work.

"Hey, Mom. Come in. I'm not used to you ringing the doorbell."

"I don't want to interrupt anything," Molly said with a wink.

The reminder that there was nothing to interrupt slammed into Hannah's gut, leaving her breathless and exhausted from the effort to outrun the pain. She was almost surprised to discover the pain had sharpened from a dull ache into a lacerating wound while she was busy cooking and cleaning. The frenetic activity hadn't helped at all.

"Hannah? Honey, what is it? What's wrong?" Molly took a closer look at her oldest daughter. "Why do you have dark circles under your eyes that weren't there yesterday?"

Over coffee in the kitchen, Hannah told her mother what'd happened at Gavin's and how she'd reacted to it.

"Oh honey. Why in the world would he say such an awful thing to you?"

"That's the part I don't get. He knows it's not true. Nolan says he's reacting out of grief and doesn't really believe it, but still. He said it, so the thought must've crossed his mind."

"For what it's worth, I think Nolan is right. It was a shock for Gavin to hear you're dating again and seeing someone who has been a close friend to him and his brother since childhood. Because his reaction is so far out of character, we probably need to give him the benefit of the doubt and chalk it up to grief."

"I hate that something I did hurt him."

"That's not what hurt him, Hannah. Caleb's death is what hurt him. It's what continues to hurt him after all this time. You haven't done anything wrong by spending time with Nolan."

"What if other people in town think we were together before Caleb died?"

"No one who knows you even the slightest bit would ever suspect such a thing."

"Gavin did, and he knows me as well as anyone does."

"Gavin wasn't thinking clearly when he said that." She laid her hand over Hannah's, infusing warmth into Hannah's cold hand. "You sent Nolan away because of this?"

"I was reeling. I needed to think, and I couldn't do that with him here."

"And have you done your thinking?"

Hannah nodded.

"And?"

"And I love Nolan. I've loved him for a long time. Whenever one of you would tell me he'd asked for me—which was just about every day for years—I'd get this tingle in my belly at knowing he was thinking of me. I always knew he was waiting for me to be ready, and I thought I was ready."

"You *are* ready, Hannah, or you never could've spent a weekend away with him. Judging from the glow you were wearing when you got home yesterday, it's safe to assume an awful lot transpired between the two of you while you were gone."

"It did."

"Please don't let one person's poor reaction undo all that progress."

"It's not just any person, Mom. It's *Gavin*."

"I know, honey. But even he doesn't have the right to stand between you and the happiness you so richly deserve."

"Before I see Nolan again, I need to be sure I'm ready. I can't keep jerking him around like this. It wouldn't be fair."

"Then take a couple more days, but don't wait too long to make up your mind. He looks at you like a man in love. Your father said that last night, and I had to agree. It's a lovely thing to see after all the time you've spent alone."

"It is a lovely thing," Hannah said softly.

"Then don't let it go, Hannah. Do your thinking and move forward the way you have been, so courageously and with such conviction. Gavin will come to his senses and realize he owes you a huge apology. I'm surprised you haven't already heard from him." Molly took a look around at the mess Hannah had made of the kitchen. "Are you trying to cram a week's worth of work into one day?"

"Maybe," Hannah said with a sheepish grin.

"A little at a time, my love. Let's get this cleaned up before you fall over from exhaustion."

CHAPTER 22

———◆———

People say the stupidest things. "At least you're still young. You can marry again." "Thank goodness you didn't have children." "Time heals all wounds." "Caleb would've wanted you to love again." They mean well, but how do they know that? He never said that to me, so how do they know? I wish now I hadn't been so rigid about waiting for him to grow up before we had children. I didn't know he'd never get the chance to finish growing up. I've learned that Caleb bought extra life insurance when he joined the army, so he left me with more money than I know what to do with. It would've been nice if he'd also left me some indication of how I'm supposed to LIVE without him. The pain is ruthless. I want to go to sleep and never wake up.

—From the diary of Hannah Abbott Guthrie, age twenty-eight

Hannah slept fitfully that night and was up early on Tuesday to prepare for her meeting with Mrs. Hendricks, the owner of the Butler Inn, who'd agreed to mentor her through the opening of the retreat.

She rushed through a shower, dried her hair and got dressed in jeans, boots and a lightweight sweater. After grabbing a travel mug of coffee, she went out the mudroom door and found Gavin leaning against her SUV. The sky above them was dark and stormy looking.

Startled to see him, Hannah nearly dropped the coffee. When she recovered her bearings, she took a closer look and saw that his eyes were red and raw, as if he hadn't slept or had been crying. Either was possible. He also hadn't shaved and his hair was unrulier than usual. As always, she knew a moment of disquiet at his shocking resemblance to her late husband.

"Sorry to scare you. I was working up the nerve to knock on your door."

Hannah knew she should say something, but she couldn't seem to form the words and part of her didn't want to let him off the hook too easily.

"I'm so sorry, Hannah." His eyes filled with tears as he said the words. "I don't know what in the hell possessed me to say that to you the other day when it has never once crossed my mind that you were anything other than faithful to him."

As she blew out the deep breath she'd been holding for two days, she blinked back her own tears.

"I was shocked to hear you're seeing Nolan, and I behaved badly. Will you please forgive me?"

"Yes, of course I forgive you." The alternative was impossible to consider, and his apology had been beyond heartfelt.

The relief on his face was palpable. "On the way over here I was thinking about what I'd do if you couldn't forgive me. I wouldn't have blamed you if you hadn't, but the thought of losing you, too, was . . ." He shook his head and stared at something over her shoulder.

"You hurt me, Gav."

His wince was audible. "I know."

"You hurt Nolan, too."

"I'm going to see him next."

"It took me a really long time to work up the nerve to go out with him. A really long time, and you know what he did for all that time?"

Gavin shook his head.

"He waited." Hannah curled her hands around the warm mug. "I should've told you myself when I saw you last week. I'm sorry I didn't."

"It wouldn't have mattered how I heard. Between that news and losing Homer . . . I was thrown off balance last week. That's my only excuse."

"You think I don't know how precarious the balance can be, Gav? I get it. Trust me, I get it better than anyone, but you and me . . . We've been in this together from day one, and it would break me if I lost you, too."

"You're not going to lose me." He stepped forward and put his arms around her.

Hannah relaxed into his embrace, relieved and thankful for his apology.

"So you and Nolan, huh?"

"If I haven't blown it."

He drew back from her. "What do you mean?"

"After what happened at your place, I sort of took a step back from him so I could have some room to think."

"How about I tell him you're done thinking?"

Hannah smiled and shook her head. "I'll take care of it. Don't worry about it."

"I will worry about it until I know you guys are back on track."

"Someone was bound to say something that would send me reeling, so don't beat yourself up."

"I'm really sorry it was me. You both deserved better from me, and it won't happen again."

"I'm sorry you were blindsided. That won't happen again either."

"Fair enough."

"Could I ask you something so incredibly awkward it doesn't even bear asking, but it occurred to me the other day, and now I can't stop thinking about it."

"After that segue, how could I resist?"

Hannah could barely make herself look at him. "I just, I wondered . . . because of how upset you were about me see-ing Nolan, if perhaps maybe you had held out hope of some sort that you and I—"

He held up his hands. "*Whoa*, Hannah. I might've considered it for about ten minutes after Caleb first died, but I immediately dismissed it as something that could never happen because of how strange it would be for both of us—and I knew that no matter how hard I tried or how much I look like him, I could never fill that void for you. Whoever you chose to date, I think the first time would've thrown me for a loop. In my mind, you'll always belong to him."

"I will *always* belong to him, Gavin. Always. But I may also belong to Nolan, too, and I need you to be okay with that."

"I am. I swear I am."

She eyed him skeptically.

"I'm getting there."

Smiling, she hugged him again. "Thanks for coming and for clearing the air. You're so important to me. Regardless of where I am or who I'm with, I'll always be a Guthrie."

"We wouldn't have it any other way. See you this weekend?"

"I'm counting on you to give Homer a world-class send-off."

"I'll be there."

Hannah watched him go, noting the familiar stride that was just like his brother's. The hunch of his shoulders reminded her of the weeks after Caleb died, when his devastation had been so profound she and others had worried about him looking for a way out of the pain. Sometimes she suspected the only reason he hadn't taken that route was because of what it would've done to his parents.

Gavin drove off in his company truck, and Hannah got in her car and headed to her appointment with Mrs. Hendricks. Afterward, she would stop by Nolan's garage to get her tire pressure checked.

Pleased with her plan, she could only hope he'd be pleased to see her.

Returning from a service call that had required him to change a tire in the pouring rain, Nolan was soaked to the skin, pissed off and sleep deprived when he pulled up to the garage.

He hadn't slept since sometime on Saturday, and his muscles were screaming from the workout he'd put them through splitting wood. While he'd appreciated Gavin's visit earlier and was relieved to hear he'd apologized to Hannah, Nolan still hadn't heard from her and until he did, his entire world was tilted off its axis.

If he'd never experienced the sweet surrender he'd found in her arms over the weekend, he probably could've gone on with his life. But knowing what they could have together and wondering if they'd get the chance to find out had left him edgy and out of sorts.

According to Skeeter, he was cranky as an angry alligator. It was probably an apt analogy, because he felt like he could bite someone's head off if they looked at him the wrong way.

"Um, boss man?"

Nolan never slowed on his path to his office. "Not now, Skeet. I'm wet, cold and in bad need of dry clothes."

"But, Nolan . . ."

"*Not now*, Skeeter."

"Alrighty then. Don't tell me I didn't warn you."

Nolan threw open the office door to find Hannah sitting at his desk, booted feet on the desktop and an issue of *Car and Driver* in her hands. He nearly fainted with the rush of oxygen that flooded his brain at the sight of her.

"Did you know the new Corvette Stingray V-8 coupe has 455 horsepower and 460 pound-feet of torque?"

He leaned against the doorframe, mostly so he would remain standing when the initial blast of adrenaline deserted him. "Do you have any idea what that means?" he asked, amused by the question.

"Not the first clue, but I take it to mean it's fast as hell and turns on a dime."

"Excellent deduction, Einstein. What're you doing here?"

"I needed to get my air pressure checked. My tires were looking a little soft."

"Skeeter could've done that for you."

She looked directly at him. "I don't want Skeeter."

"What do you want?"

"You."

Nolan's heart beat double time. "Are you sure?"

"That was never in doubt, Nolan."

"I take it you saw Gavin this morning?"

"I did. You, too?"

"Yeah. By the time he was finished groveling, I wanted to apologize to him. It's hard to see him still so messed up after all this time. I keep hoping it'll get better for him, but sometimes I wonder if he'll ever be able to move past it."

"He will, eventually. When he's ready." She took a closer look at him. "How'd you get all wet?"

"Road-call tire change in the mud. Long story." He looked behind the door and was disappointed to find the hook where he kept extra clothes empty. Then he remembered taking everything home to wash a week ago. The clothes he'd hoped to change into were home in his dryer. "I'm going to run home to change. Want me to check your tires first?"

"No, but maybe you could take me home with you?"

Nolan wrestled with a hundred different thoughts that raced through his mind at lightning speed. Hannah wanted to go home with him, which meant Hannah wanted to be alone with him. Since he wanted nothing more than to spend more time with her, he wanted to grab her hand and drag her out of there. Then there was the concern that his father might show up. But Vernon would expect to find him at the garage at this time of day, not at home, so it might be safe.

"Let's go."

Her eyes lit up. "Really?"

"Hurry up or I might change my mind." As if he'd ever change his mind where she was concerned.

Her feet dropped to the floor and she was out of the chair in two seconds flat. "Could I keep this?" she asked of the magazine.

"Sure, knock yourself out."

"I want to know more about cars."

"Because you're thinking about a new one?"

"That and because you're interested in them."

Nolan wanted to drag her into his arms and kiss her senseless, but he was wet and dirty and she was pretty and perfect and looking at him as if he'd hung the moon. "Move it," he said in a low growl, as he gave her a swat on the backside to get her going. "Skeeter," he called into the garage. "I'm going to run home to change. Don't tell anyone where I am." Skeeter knew exactly what that meant.

"So by anyone, do you mean—"

"*Anyone.*"

"Got it." Skeeter smiled as he took in the sight of Nolan's hand riding low on Hannah's back. "Take your time. I'll cover for you."

"Shut up, Skeeter."

"I'm available *all* afternoon if need be."

"Shut *up*, Skeeter."

"I'm shutting up, and I'm going back to work. For the afternoon."

Hannah was giggling madly by the time Nolan handed her up into his truck. "Quit laughing. You'll only encourage him."

"He's adorable."

"Oh yeah. Positively adorable the way a skunk in heat is adorable."

That set her off again.

Shaking his head and filled with overwhelming joy to hear her laughing again, he walked around to the driver's side. Before he started the truck, he stared at her for a long, breathless moment.

"What?"

"I missed you. Even though it was only one day, I was going crazy without you."

"Nolan," she said softly as she slid across the bench seat to lay her hand on his face. "I'm so sorry."

"Stop. No apologies for doing what you needed to do."

"Then I won't apologize for doing this either." She drew him into a warm, soft, sweet kiss that would've brought him to his knees had he been standing.

"You never have to apologize for doing that either."

"I missed you, too."

Nolan reached around her to find the center lap belt, which he clipped around her waist to keep her sitting right next to him as he pulled out of the parking lot. He'd never been so sorry that his garage was right across the street from the Abbotts' store. Otherwise, he might've sat right in his parking lot and made out with her until their lips were numb.

As it was, he was already hard as a rock despite wet, cold pants that were becoming tighter by the second. And then her hand landed on his thigh, and the last thing he was thinking about was the cold. "Don't get too close. I'm dirty *and* wet."

"I don't care."

The slap of the windshield wipers kept pace with the gallop of his heart. "I do."

She leaned over to speak directly into his ear. "Have I ever told you how sexy I find men who get dirty from hard work? Huge turn-on."

"Hannah . . ."

She bit his earlobe, and the truck swerved.

"*Hannah!*"

Her soft laughter had him pressing the accelerator much harder than he should have in his haste to get home. The twisting, winding roads that made up the Butler Mountain foothills had never intimidated him until Hannah was next to him, filling his senses with the scent he'd become addicted to. Turning into the dirt road that led to his house, he sped through puddles that splashed mud all over his truck. He'd worry about that some other time.

He braked hard, and the truck fishtailed in the mud. "Come on." Releasing both their seatbelts, he took her hand and all but pulled her from the truck.

The heavens chose that moment to open in a freezing torrent.

Hannah squealed with laughter as they splashed through mud on the way to his front door. "Wait. Stop." She pulled on his hand.

"Are you crazy? We're getting soaked."

"We're already soaked." She slid her arms around his neck and kissed him. "What's a little more soaked?"

"You are crazy."

"Apparently so." The rain came down hard as they stood in his yard, wrapped up in each other, the heat of their kiss warming him from the inside. Only when he felt her shiver in his arms did he break the kiss to lead her inside. They kicked off boots in the mudroom.

"Shower," he said. "Now."

Hannah's lips had a bluish tinge as she nodded in agreement.

"This way."

As he led her through the small house to his bedroom, Nolan said a silent prayer of thanks for the woman he paid to keep the place clean. Every dime he'd paid her for years had led to this moment. The bathroom attached to his bedroom sparkled as he turned on the water and helped her pull the soaking sweater over her head. Steam from the shower soon filled the small room as they tugged at clothes and laughed at the difficulty of removing wet denim.

Nolan followed her into the shower and wrapped his arms around her from behind. "This, right here, has to be what heaven feels like."

Hannah leaned her head back against his shoulder. "Definitely."

They stood under the hot water until Hannah stopped shivering, and then she turned to him, flattening her hands against his chest. "Hi, there."

"Hi, yourself."

"I'm having déjà vu. Seems like we've been here before."

"Two whole days ago, even if it feels like two years have passed since then. We've got a lot of time to make up for." He bent his head to kiss her. "Starting right now."

"Want me to wash your back?" Hannah asked.

"As long as you do the front, too."

She smiled as she held out her hand for the liquid soap he squeezed from a bottle and proceeded to fire every nerve ending in his body with a sensual massage that had the muscles in his legs quivering. And then she slid her soap-slicked hand up and down his rigid shaft, and he gasped from the almost painful pleasure that coursed through his body.

"My turn," he said abruptly.

Her hair hung in wet strands around her face, which was rosy red from the heat of the shower. "No fair! I was just getting to the good stuff."

"More good stuff to come after I get my turn with the soap." The first thing he did after he filled his hands with the liquid was to ensure her breasts were nice and clean. Her shuddering responses had him hurrying as he rinsed them both. Reaching behind her, he shut off the water and then grabbed two towels. "Allow me," he said when she would've taken one of them from him.

He dried her slowly, reverently, tending to every inch of porcelain skin before towel-drying her hair.

She returned the favor and drove him mad with the drag of the cloth over his straining erection.

Nolan took the towel from her and dropped it on the floor as he directed her from the bathroom into the bedroom, where he moved quickly to pull down the navy and cranberry plaid quilt he'd bought at the Abbotts' store.

The matching navy flannel sheets were warm and cozy as he followed her into bed.

"Am I ruining your business with all the distractions lately?"

"I couldn't care less if you are."

"You do too care."

"Right now all I care about is you. In fact, most of the time all I care about is you." He kissed her with all the pent-up passion of the last few difficult days. "I desperately need to be inside you." His hand slid over her belly and down to test her readiness with two fingers.

Hannah arched into him, her legs falling open to welcome him. "I dreamed about this the other night," she whispered in his ear when he'd moved on top of her. "I woke up throbbing and needy."

"You should've called me. I do house calls."

Laughing, she said, "I almost did."

He aligned their bodies and thrust into her tight heat in one long stroke that had them both gasping. "You can call me any time—day or night—and I'll come to you and give you anything you need."

"Anything?" she asked as she wrapped her legs around his hips.

Pushing harder into her, he said, "*Anything.*" He intentionally moved slowly, intending to draw out the pleasure for as long as he could. But she had other ideas, moving her hips, squeezing him from within and running her tongue over the outer shell of his ear.

"Slow down," he whispered desperately.

"Can't."

He pulled back and withdrew completely from her. "Yes, you can."

"Nolan!"

Bending his head, he latched on to her nipple, licking and sucking until it stood up tall and proud and very red from his ministrations. Then he turned his attention to her other breast, drawing a keening sob from her as he worked to regain his own control.

Her fingers dug into his back as she moved under him, trying to get him back where she wanted him, but he refused to be rushed. Skeeter had the garage covered, and they were somewhat slow today anyway because of the lousy weather. There was really no reason at all he couldn't spend the rest of the day in bed with Hannah. The realization calmed him and gave him the patience he needed to kiss his way to her belly, focusing on each hipbone and loving her reactions, which ranged from breathy sighs to moans to begging.

He parted her legs and propped them on his shoulders, her thighs quivering as he pushed them farther apart. Cupping her bottom, he lifted her to his mouth and feasted on her sweetness. She came almost instantly, calling out his name in the throes of intense release. He'd never heard anything he loved more than the sound of his name on her lips at that moment.

"Again," he whispered against her most sensitive flesh.

"I *can't.*"

"Yes, you can." He squeezed her bottom and went back for more, taking her up slowly this time as his cock throbbed under him, wanting in on the party.

Hannah fisted the sheets, her head thrown back as the desire once again peaked in a shuddering, trembling climax that nearly consumed him, too.

He quickly lowered her legs and moved up to enter her, prolonging her release with deep thrusts that finished him off in a tidal wave of pleasure that topped anything he'd ever experienced before, even with her. Their eyes met and held, and he grasped her hands, propping them over her head as he continued to move inside her.

"Let me have my hands," she said.

He released them and wrapped his arms around her, wanting to keep her as close as he could get her.

She curled her arms around his neck, her fingers combing through his hair in soothing strokes.

"I love you, Hannah. I love you more than anything."

"I love you, too."

After hours and hours of uncertainty, Nolan could finally breathe again.

CHAPTER 23

*Thank goodness for Hunter and Will and the rest
of my family, but particularly them. They sleep
here every night, taking turns, so I never have to
be alone. Homer sleeps next to me, whimpering in
his sleep. I think he knows.*

—From the diary of Hannah Abbott Guthrie, age
twenty-eight

Despite her concerns about his business falling apart because of her, Hannah didn't protest when Nolan insisted they spend the rest of the rainy afternoon in bed. They made love again to the sound of raindrops beating against the roof and then fell asleep wrapped up in each other for a couple of hours.

After another shower, Hannah donned one of his flannel shirts and insisted he show her around his small but tidy home. On his desk in the living room, she found a roll of architectural plans and asked him what they were.

"The house I'd like to build on this property. Someday."

"Show me."

He unfurled the plans for the post-and-beam house he'd envisioned.

"It's beautiful," she said of the architect's rendering of the finished product. "When are you going to build it?"

Shrugging, he rolled the plans back into a tight cylinder. "I don't know."

She felt the wall go up around him, the same one he'd erected when she asked about his family. While she desperately wanted to know what he was thinking, she didn't push him, hoping he'd open up to her when he was ready to. Wandering to the window that overlooked the yard, she noticed a huge pile of freshly split firewood. "What's with all the wood?" The burning season was all but over for now.

"Takes a lot of wood to keep your fire pit going for an entire Sultans weekend."

She turned to him. "You did that for me?"

"I had to do something with all my extra energy while I was waiting for you to do your thinking."

"I'm sorry I put you through that."

"I told you not to apologize to me."

"I still feel like I should."

"Well, don't. As great as things are between us, I know we don't live in a bubble, and there will be some bumps as people get used to us together. I just hope you know . . ."

She went to him in the kitchen, where he'd put soup on to warm, and wrapped her arms around his bare torso. "What do you hope I know?"

"That no matter what anyone says or does or thinks, it doesn't have to change things for us. We may not live in a bubble, but perhaps we should build one around ourselves and our relationship so other people's crap can't get to us."

"That's a really good idea," she said, leaving a line of kisses between his shoulder blades as his belly fluttered under her hands.

"Glad you think so, because this weekend is going to be another test. You know that, don't you?"

"Yes," she said with a sigh.

"If you want to play it cool until after it's over, you won't hurt my feelings."

Dropping her hands to his hips, Hannah encouraged him to turn to face her. "I don't want to play it cool. I don't want to hide what we have together from our friends."

"They were Caleb's friends before they were your friends or mine," he reminded her.

"True, but they're ours now, too, and there's never going to be a perfect time to ease them into the idea of me dating again. Or falling in love or anything that doesn't involve Caleb. So there's no time like the present."

"And what if one of them says something like Gavin did?"

"I'll be ready for it this time."

"We'll both be ready for it, and we'll deal with it together."

Hannah nodded in agreement and went up on tiptoes to kiss him.

His arm banded tightly around her as the kiss went from light and sweet to hot and sultry in the span of three seconds. "Food first," Nolan said when he came up for air. "Then more of that."

"You're a spoil sport."

"I'll make it up to you."

After a lunch of delicious vegetable soup and thick turkey sandwiches, he spent the rest of the afternoon making it up to her in every way he could think of. "I hate to say it, but I have to go soon," Nolan said as their bodies cooled and their breathing returned to normal. "My crew chief was able to finagle a couple of hours of practice time on a track in New Hampshire that's more than ninety minutes from here."

"This was a very nice and very decadent day."

"Indeed it was."

"I won't come near you during your workdays anymore. I'd hate to be responsible for running you out of business."

"No chance of that, babe. The business is very flush despite my inattention recently. You can bother me any time your tires need checking."

Hannah giggled with mirth at her flimsy excuse. "I figured that was quicker than an oil change."

He cupped her backside with one big hand and squeezed. "I'll give you a complete lube and filter job any time you need it."

"I might need it tonight after you get back."

"It'll be late."

"I'll wait up."

"Mmm," he said, losing himself in another kiss. "I'll be there as soon as I can."

* * *

They spent that night and every night that week together. After he dropped off the wood for the weekend on Thursday afternoon, he took her with him back to his place to shower and change his clothes after the long workday, and they never made it out of bed again until pounding on the door woke them out of a sound sleep at four in the morning.

"What the heck?" Hannah muttered as she came to.

They'd been up late and had only gone to sleep around two.

Knowing exactly who would be pounding on his door in the middle of the night, Nolan was immediately awake and in motion, pulling on a pair of jeans and zipping them. "Stay here. No matter what you hear, please . . . If you care about me at all, stay here."

As he shut the bedroom door behind him and went to deal with his drunk and belligerent father, Nolan tried not to think about the stricken expression on Hannah's face after he spoke to her so harshly.

"Open the goddamn door, boy. I know you're in there."

Nolan opened the door and gave his father a shove to get him away from the house. He pulled the inside door shut and went out into the chilly night, oblivious to the cold even though he was barefoot and shirtless. "You need to get the hell out of here."

"Not until I get what I came for." Vernon's words were slurred, and he smelled like he'd fallen into a vat of gin.

"I'm all done. You've gotten the last penny you're ever going to get out of me."

"Is your fancy lady putting those ideas in your head?"

"Hardly. You think I'd be foolish enough to tell her about you? If you want to get yourself cleaned up, I'll gladly pay for that, but that's the only thing I'll pay for where you're concerned. I've been paying my whole life, and I'm done."

"You're done when I say so, and not one second before."

"I'm done now. If you think I don't mean it, push me on this and I'll have the cops out here before you know what hit you. You're trespassing on my property and causing a nuisance."

"Listen to you all high and mighty. *Your* property. This was *my* father's place."

"Yeah, and he left it to *me*, not you. So you'd better get your ass out of here or deal with the cops. I'm all through with you and your brand of emotional blackmail."

Vernon seemed to realize all at once that Nolan was dead serious. "You got some nerve talking to me like that, boy."

"You've got some nerve showing up here time and time again and acting like I owe you anything. Now get going or go to jail. Your choice."

"You never talked like this 'til you took up with that fancy Abbott girl."

"She's made me realize I deserve better than what I've gotten from you. Don't you ever get tired of living this way? Why don't you let somebody help you?"

To Nolan's immense dismay, Vernon broke down into deep, gulping sobs. "You don't know how hard it is."

"No, I don't, but I do know if I continue to enable you, you'll never have a good reason to get help. You know where I am and the offer of help has no expiration date. But don't come around here again looking for a handout. I'm tapped out in every possible way." It took everything Nolan had to turn his back on his father and walk up the stairs to the porch.

"Nolan."

He kept his back to his father. "What?"

"She's too good for you."

The barb went straight to the source of all his insecurities where Hannah was concerned. "Yeah, Dad, I know, but for some reason she loves me anyway." He went inside and closed the door, leaning against it for several minutes until the trembling subsided and his heart rate returned to normal.

Having his father show up with Hannah tucked in his bed was his worst nightmare come true. How would he handle the questions she was sure to ask without also sharing the ugly truth about his family? He waited until he was as calm as he could hope to get before returning to the bedroom, shedding his jeans and sliding back into bed with her. The warmth of her body immediately soothed the part of him that had gone cold with fear when he realized who was pounding on his door in the middle of the night.

"Everything okay?" she asked as she snuggled into his embrace.

"Yeah." He waited for her to press him for answers, but she didn't. Thank God she didn't. But as Nolan felt her relax into sleep next to him, he stared at the ceiling for a long time, aware he'd only dodged the bullet for now. It was only a matter of time before he had no choice but to come clean with her. When that happened would she realize his father was right? Was she way too good for the likes of him?

The thought of that filled him with irrational fear. He wasn't his father. He knew that. But he'd spent his whole life being ashamed of where he'd come from and hiding the truth of his family from the friends who'd become his family. A lifelong pattern of denial was a hard habit to break.

Hannah had bared her soul to him. She'd shared the personal letter Caleb had left behind for her and talked of her deepest fears and hopes. How could he give her less than what she'd given him?

The question tortured him through that long night, and by the time the sun rose on Friday, he still had no good answers.

Final preparations for the weekend kept Hannah so busy on Friday she had very little time to think about what had happened the night before at Nolan's. She hadn't been able to hear much from the bedroom where he'd asked her to stay, but she'd heard him arguing with another man.

When he'd returned to bed, she'd hoped he would open up to her, but he hadn't. And she'd forced herself not to push him. She'd let him think she was asleep next to him, but she'd been awake for a long time, aware of his turmoil and wishing she could do something to ease his burden. But until he decided to share it with her, there wasn't much she could do.

The closed-off side of him was a source of concern to her. Every other part of their relationship seemed to work almost effortlessly, but getting him to open up about things he found unpleasant or potentially embarrassing could turn into a big challenge for them.

Hannah didn't want to be in a one-sided relationship, even one that worked as well as theirs did most of the time. If he was unwilling to share all of himself with her, there'd always be a part of him that was off limits to her.

She was still puzzling over the dilemma when the doorbell rang just after two o'clock. Hannah was thrilled to find her grandfather on the front porch, holding an ornately carved wooden box that had been stained and finished with gleaming varnish.

"Oh my goodness," Hannah said as she opened the door to him. "It's incredible, Gramps!"

Elmer had insisted on working with Myles to prepare Homer for burial, to spare her from having to handle that dreaded task. "You think so?"

Fighting tears, Hannah said, "It's beyond anything I could've imagined."

Hobbling on his recently sprained ankle, Elmer carried the box straight through the house to the back deck, where he put it on a table. "It's lined with soft flannel and he's wrapped in his special blanket. It's also completely sealed so it won't attract any unwanted attention from the rest of the animal kingdom."

Hannah hugged her grandfather. "You thought of everything."

He kissed her forehead and returned the hug. "Nothing but the best for our Homer and our Hannah."

"Thank you so much."

"Landon took care of the marker," he said of her younger brother who'd inherited his woodworking skills from Elmer. "He said to tell you he'll bring it with him later."

"You guys are the best."

"You ready for all of this?" he asked, gesturing to the yard that was littered with chairs and coolers and the keg of beer her father had generously donated and had delivered the day before.

"As ready as I ever am. It'll be fun and a bit sad, but mostly fun."

"Any time you feel too sad, you come find me and we'll go for a walk. I've got a whole bunch of new jokes I've been saving up for just such an occasion."

"You got it," Hannah said, charmed by him.

Clearing his throat, he looked down at her, his face unusually serious. "I need to say this because it's been on my mind a lot lately, and I believe in telling people how I feel about them." He took a moment to gather himself. "I'm awfully proud of you, Hannah. Not just for the way you've gotten through the worst thing life could've handed you, but because you keep doing things like this that keep Caleb alive for all of us who loved him, despite how hard it must be on you. I wanted to tell you I admire you more than just about anyone I know."

"Gramps," she whispered, moved by his heartfelt words. "That means the world to me coming from you."

He hugged and kissed her again. "Now enough of the mushy stuff. When does the party start?"

She laughed at his attempt to change the subject. "I expect the invasion to begin around four."

"I'll be back by five."

"It wouldn't be a party without you." She gestured to the gorgeous box that contained their darling Homer. "I can't thank you enough for this."

"It was an honor and a privilege, my love." He kissed her cheek again and was gone before both of them could dissolve into tears.

As Hannah ran her hand over the smooth finish, she noticed the engraved metal plaque her grandfather had affixed to the box.

HOMER GUTHRIE

*A good and faithful companion
who was much loved by his people,
Caleb and Hannah Guthrie,
and everyone who knew him.
May he rest in peace.*

The simple perfection of the words her grandfather had chosen reduced Hannah to tears. Caleb would definitely approve.

Newlyweds Austin and Debra were the first to arrive and greeted her warmly, expressing their sorrow over Homer's death. Both were blond and athletic and well suited to each other. Before their wedding last year, Austin had confided in her how difficult it was to marry someone Caleb had never gotten to meet. Hannah had assured him that Caleb would've loved Debra, who was absolutely perfect for Caleb's oldest friend. The two army brats had met in kindergarten at Fort Stewart and remained close until the day Caleb died.

Austin produced a bottle of Jägermeister from his suitcase and handed it proudly to Hannah, who cringed. Jäger was one of the more foul Sultan traditions. "Awesome," she said dryly.

Debra laughed in solidarity. "I suggested that maybe we've outgrown Jäger, but my thoughts were shot down."

"I imagine they were," Hannah said. "I've been fighting that battle for years to no avail."

"One of these days they have to grow up, don't they?" Debra asked as she followed Hannah to the kitchen with a tray of brownies she'd packed in bubble wrap in her suitcase.

"Never!" Austin said as he brought up the rear.

The others arrived in waves over the next two hours—Turk and his girlfriend, Cicily; Mark and his brother Chris; Ethan; Liam; Josh and his wife, Ava; Jack and his guitar; Dylan and his fiancée, Sophia, who seemed overwhelmed by her first official dose of the rowdy Sultans. They ran the gamut from childhood friends to high school to college to hockey to the army.

They'd met through Caleb and become closer than brothers to each other during years of adventures dreamed up by their fearless leader. They'd continued their traditions in the years since they lost him. And now they came together to say good-bye to Homer and to remember Caleb on the seventh anniversary of his death.

Gavin came in carrying a huge pan of chicken wings that he swore he'd made himself, kissing Hannah's cheek and looking at her for signs of residual damage.

But Hannah felt nothing other than happy to see him— and delighted to razz him about the wings she knew for a fact he'd bought and made to look homemade.

Her family showed up with food and beer and champagne and yet another bottle of Jäger donated by Will. Hannah put him in charge of getting the fire started in the pit.

Nolan was almost the last to arrive, all apologies about an emergency road call just as he was closing down for the weekend.

Since they had the kitchen to themselves for the moment, he gave her a lingering kiss and studied her intently. "How're you holding up?"

"So far so good. It's always great to see everyone." She looked up at him. "I'm going to tell them about us tonight so there's no chance for gossip or speculation. Okay?"

"Whatever you want to do is fine with me."

She curled her hand around his nape and brought him in for another kiss before they went outside to join the party.

As it always did, the Friday night gathering turned into a rager with the booze flowing freely and the food mostly overlooked because everyone was too busy talking and catching up to take time to eat. Before she lost them all to alcohol-induced stupor, Hannah clinked a rock on her beer bottle to quiet the crowd.

They focused their solemn attention on her, as they always did when she requested a moment of their time.

"I want to thank you all for coming on somewhat short notice to honor Homer. As you well know, this is exactly what Caleb would've done if he had outlived his beloved Homie. And I have to thank Nolan for coming up with the idea for an over-the-top Sultans funeral."

A round of cheers followed her statement and everyone raised their bottles in a toast to Nolan, who laughed and shrugged off their praise. He'd stayed close to her side all evening, providing steady support and comfort that Hannah appreciated even though he didn't get close enough to start any tongues wagging. Which had led to the second half of her impromptu speech. She'd given this a lot of thought and had decided to learn from her mistake with Gavin by coming clean about Nolan at the beginning of the weekend.

"The other thing I want to say is I have a bit of news I want to share with you."

Nolan glanced at her, sending a supportive smile.

Hannah reached for his hand, and he offered it willingly, curling his fingers around hers in a move that drew the attention of everyone gathered around the fire pit.

"Nolan and I have been seeing each other lately." She added that last word, *lately*, intentionally, lest there be any doubt about when their relationship actually began. "We're very happy together, and I hope all of you can find it in your hearts to be happy for us. That's all I wanted to say. Carry on."

A murmur of surprise went through the group before Turk, known for his boisterous laugh and irreverent sense of humor, raised his bottle in salute. "To our patron saint, Hannah, who has weathered the storm and kept us around despite our horrendously bad manners, may you know many days of happiness with our brother Nolan. You deserve every good thing that comes your way."

"Hear, hear," Dylan said.

Jack began to strum his guitar to the tune of their theme song, "Sultans of Swing," and soon everyone was singing at the top of their lungs.

"Well," Hannah said to Nolan, leaning in close to him so he could hear her over the din, "that went well."

"I guess we're now officially out of the closet."

"Looks that way. No going back."

"Wouldn't go back for all the tea in China."

She could tell by the way he looked at her that he desperately wanted to kiss her. "Save it for later," she whispered. They'd decided he would spend the weekend at her house, and they were counting on the drunken antics of the others to get away with their plan.

"I've got lots of things saved up for later," he said with a playful waggle of his brows.

Hannah shivered with delight and relief that she'd shared their news with Caleb's closest friends and gotten over that hurdle unscathed, thanks to Turk's kind words of support. She relaxed into her chair, but kept her firm grip on Nolan's hand. For the first time in seven years, she didn't feel like her heart was breaking all over again as she sat in the midst of Caleb's band of brothers.

Rather, she felt a whole new chapter was beginning—one that paid tribute to the past while holding out hope for a future filled with love and joy.

CHAPTER 24

*Caleb's Sultans are coming for the weekend.
Gavin organized the gathering, and he asked if
they could have it here because it's tradition.
How could I say no? I'm looking forward to seeing
everyone, but I can't imagine what it'll be like
without Caleb in the middle of everything. Nolan
came over today with firewood and helped me set
up. He's been such an amazing friend through all
of this—he's always THERE, but he doesn't
overwhelm me the way some people do.
I appreciate him more than he knows.*

—From the diary of Hannah Abbott Guthrie,
age twenty-nine

It was nearly three the next morning before the fire was
doused and all of Hannah's guests were settled. Her family
had gone home for the night, promising to be back for
Homer's official funeral at two the next afternoon. Gavin had
crashed on the sofa in the sitting room, and after she covered
him with a blanket, Hannah led Nolan up the back stairs from
the kitchen to her bedroom on the second floor. He carried a
duffel bag and garment bag hooked over his shoulder.

She expected to encounter someone in the hallway, but no one was around as they entered her room. Hannah closed and locked the door behind them, grateful as always for the bathroom that adjoined her room.

"Finally alone," Nolan said as he tossed his bags into a chair and kissed her with hours of desire pouring forth in an embrace that landed them on her bed in a tangle of limbs. The scent of smoke from the fire pit filled the air around them.

Hannah laughed at his bumbling efforts to free her from her clothes without missing a beat with the kiss.

"Stop laughing and help me."

She only laughed harder at his dismay, but she took off her sweater and wiggled out of her jeans with all due haste.

"Better," he said, stopping her when she would've unhooked her bra. "Let me." His index finger traced a path from her chin to her throat and down to hook his finger over the front clasp of her bra. "All night long, the only thing I could seem to think about was how lucky I was to get to be alone with you later. For a while there, I thought later might never come, but these guys aren't as young as they once were, and thankfully they hit the wall earlier than they used to."

"I've noticed you don't try to keep up with them when it comes to drinking." He'd often been the one helping her to get Caleb to bed after a big night with the Sultans. "Why is that?"

"I don't know. It's never been necessary for me to get totally loaded to have a good time."

"That's certainly music to my ears."

"I'd imagine it would be." Nolan leaned over her and kissed the upper slopes of both breasts. "You were amazing telling the guys about us."

"After what happened with Gavin, I wanted to do a preemptive strike so we could relax and enjoy the weekend."

"You were perfect."

"Did anyone say anything to you about it?"

"Just a few slaps on the back and a couple of innocent questions, nothing disrespectful though. How about you?"

"Same. They were naturally curious, but overall happy for me—and for us."

"I'm very happy for us," he said with a big grin that exposed the adorable dimple in his left cheek.

"I am, too." She thought of the episode the night before and the many questions she longed to ask him.

"What's with the frown? That doesn't look happy to me."

"I am happy. You know I am."

"Except?"

"Let's talk about it another time. After the weekend."

"No, let's talk about it now."

"Please? It can wait. I promise, it's nothing awful." She ran her fingers through his hair and down to curl around his neck. "I'm all talked out after today, and besides, you got me all warmed up when you were pulling at my clothes . . ."

His mouth lifted into a half smile. "Did I?"

"You know you did."

"I can't let all that warmth go to waste."

"You really shouldn't."

With the snap of his fingers, her bra sprung open, and she forgot about everything other than the sweet pleasure she found in his arms.

At promptly two o'clock the next afternoon, the usually rowdy Sultans appeared in suits and ties. They'd showered and shaved and even combed their hair for the occasion. While Hannah was touched by their coordinated effort, it reminded her a little too much of another memorial service, seven years ago when they'd come together to honor Caleb.

As Nolan came downstairs dressed in a navy suit with a light blue shirt and red tie, Hannah's breath caught at how gorgeous he looked. "Clearly you guys have been making plans behind the scenes," she said as she laid her hands over his lapels.

"We wanted to show our respect to Homer—and to you."

"You're all too much," she said, shaking her head in amazement and love for the friends who'd come from near and far for the occasion.

"Are you ready for this?"

"As ready as I'll ever be."

He kissed her cheek and left the scent of his appealing aftershave behind as he took her hand. "Hold on to me. I've got you."

Grateful for his support, Hannah held on tight to his hand as they walked out to join the others. The scattering of chairs from the night before had been organized into rows on the lawn. Homer's casket had been given a place of honor at the front of the assemblage, and the Sultans were welcoming a flood of people from town.

"Oh wow," she whispered as she saw the size of the crowd.

"People wanted to come," Nolan said simply.

On a stool next to where Homer's casket had been laid, Jack strummed out a slow, reverent version of "Ventura Highway," another of Caleb's favorite songs from his time in Southern California. Jack had played the same rendition of the song at Caleb's memorial, so the tune immediately brought tears to Hannah's eyes.

Her parents arrived with her grandfather, followed a short time later by Caleb's parents. All her brothers had worn suits and ties, Hannah realized as they trickled in one by one. Cameron, Ella and Charley had dressed up, too. Becky and Hannah's other Thursday afternoon friends were there, along with Myles Johansen, Mrs. Hendricks, everyone from the store and Hannah's beading friends from the craft guild. People brought chairs and covered dishes they put on a table someone had put by the arbor that led into her backyard.

"Oh my God," Nolan muttered as Skeeter came in with Dude, both of them wearing suits and ties and solemn expressions.

Hannah could feel Nolan trying hard to hold back laughter, and the tension inside her eased when she realized all these people had come mostly for her—and many of them had come for Caleb, too. She had asked Turk to be master of ceremonies, and when the people finally stopped coming, he stood before them, handsome in a dark gray suit and burgundy tie.

"Friends, on behalf of Hannah, I thank you for being here today to celebrate the life of our dear departed Homer Guthrie. For more than sixteen years, Homer was the faithful companion of first Caleb Guthrie, then Caleb and Hannah, and most recently Hannah. I happened to be with Caleb the day he found Homer abandoned by the side of the road. He brought him home, washed days of filth off the poor boy and fed him the first good meal he'd had in a long time. During the course of that first night, Caleb gained a loyal friend who remained by his side for the rest of his life. In typical Caleb style, however, he set out to find the rightful owner, knowing that's what he would want if he'd somehow managed to lose his dog. Little did Caleb know then that Homer had finally found his way home to the place he was always meant to live and the person he was meant to live with.

"Caleb used to say that people are either dog people, or they aren't. 'There's really no gray area' he would say. Caleb was a dog person. More to the point, he was a Homer person. Hannah told me this week that it's given her comfort to think of Homer crossing the rainbow bridge and jumping into Caleb's waiting arms. Ever since she shared that thought with me, it's given me comfort, too. The loss of Homer is the end of an era for all of us who loved him and Caleb. May they live together forever in the kingdom of heaven, where no one ever dies and there's never a shortage of beer or dog biscuits."

Laughter, applause and tears followed Turk's comments.

Hannah gratefully took the handkerchief that Nolan offered and dabbed at her eyes.

"Hannah has asked Gavin to say a few words about Homer," Turk said, "and after that, anyone else who wishes to speak is more than welcome to. Gav?"

Wearing a pinstripe suit with a white dress shirt and a tie that had belonged to Caleb, Gavin made his way to the front of the gathering. He rested a hand on Homer's box before turning to face the audience.

"The news of Homer's passing brought back a lot of memories I'd sooner forget. I'm sure many of you felt the same way. But if there's one thing I've learned over the last seven years, there's no such thing as outrunning grief. It manages to find you no matter where you hide and makes you do stupid things you immediately regret." This was said directly to Hannah and Nolan.

"After Hannah asked me to speak today, I thought a lot about the time I spent with Caleb and Homer. Our duo became a trio after Homer adopted Caleb. Everywhere we went, he came, too. Fishing, skiing, snowboarding, hiking, camping. You name it. Homer did it. We once took him camping, and Caleb got the big idea to leave him in the tent while we went into town to get a pizza. We came back to find our tent running around the campground with Homer still zipped inside. He was not pleased to have been left behind, and he made his point rather convincingly. We never did that again."

Even though the story was legendary, it still resulted in hysterical laughter.

"I'll never forget the first time Caleb took him skiing with us. I'd questioned the wisdom of bringing Homer with us, but Caleb reminded me of how ornery Homer could be when he got left behind. So I relented even though I still wondered how it would work. We got on the lift with Homer sitting between us, and the lift operator says, 'How the hell are you going to get the dog down the mountain?' Caleb says, 'I'm far more worried about getting my brother down the mountain than I am about old Homer here.'"

Everyone cracked up laughing as Gavin was known for his lackluster skiing skills and had taken an endless amount of abuse from Caleb, Hunter and Will, who were outstanding skiers.

"Sure enough, when I finally made it to the bottom of the hill, Caleb and Homer were waiting for me, ready to do the whole thing again, much to my dismay. There was nothing Homer wasn't game for, no adventure Caleb could dream up that Homer couldn't handle. When Caleb traveled or deployed, Homer would sit by the door day after day until his best friend finally came home. After we lost Caleb, Homer mourned right along with us. You'll never convince me he didn't know exactly what'd happened, and he turned his faithful devotion toward Hannah for all his remaining days. Will any of us ever forget the way he'd run to Caleb and leap into his outstretched arms? I know I never will."

Tears flowed freely down Hannah's face as Nolan kept an arm tight around her. She wasn't the only one sniffling over Gavin's touching words. Hannah noticed her sister Ella wiping her tears without ever taking her gaze off Gavin.

"In preparation for today, I poked around a bit on the Internet, looking for something that would adequately portray the bond between Caleb and Homer, and I think this story says it all." Reading from a paper he withdrew from his suit coat pocket, Gavin said, "It's called 'A Man and His Dog' and the author is unknown, but I could picture Caleb and Homer in this story, and I hope you can, too." He relayed the touching story about a man who declined to take his place in heaven because he couldn't bring his dog. Later, he learned the first place was really hell. The real heaven, he discovered, allows pets.

"Thank you all for being here to remember Homer. It means a lot to Hannah and to my parents and me that you still care for Caleb, too. Jack has another song for us, and then you're welcome to share your memories of Homer and Caleb."

As Gavin returned to his seat and received a hug from Ella, who was sitting next to him, Jack strummed the opening notes to "Stand by Me," a perfect song to sum up the relationship between Caleb and Homer.

The funeral turned into an Irish wake of sorts after that, with unlimited whiskey for the numerous toasts and tributes to Homer. Before everyone got too drunk, Nolan suggested they carry Homer to the final resting place he'd prepared in Hannah's garden at the foot of an old oak tree.

Landon produced a beautifully carved cross that had Homer's name on it along with 16 YEARS OF FAITHFUL COMPANIONSHIP.

Hannah hugged her younger brother. "Thanks so much, Landon. It's lovely."

He kissed her cheek. "I'm glad you like it."

They buried Homer and placed the cross to mark his grave, and then the party resumed. Suit jackets and ties came off, shirtsleeves were rolled up, cigars were produced and the beer and liquor flowed freely. Someone started the fire, and no one left until close to sunset, when the locals began filtering out.

In need of a breather, Hannah went into the kitchen to check the enchiladas she'd put in the oven to heat and found Ella up to her elbows in soapsuds, tending to a huge pile of dishes. "You don't need to do that, El."

"Someone's gotta. Why not me?"

"Thank you."

"This was a really nice day. Caleb would've loved it."

"He would've. At times like this I can almost feel him with us."

"Me, too," Ella said.

"Are you crying?"

"Maybe a little. I miss him."

Hannah slipped an arm around her sister's waist and kissed her cheek. "I know." She leaned against Ella's shoulder. "Could I ask you something?"

"Sure."

"The business we talked about at Mom's the other day. Is it Gavin?"

If she hadn't been wrapped around Ella she wouldn't have felt every muscle in her body go tense. "No. Of course not."

"Ella . . ."

"It's nothing, Hannah. Don't go there."

"I saw you watching him when he was speaking. It didn't look like nothing to me."

"Please, Hannah. He barely knows I'm alive. He's a god. What would he want with me? He could have anyone he wanted."

"Are you serious? Do have any idea how gorgeous you are?"

"Don't try to make me feel better. It's never going to happen. I accepted that a long time ago."

Aghast, Hannah raised her head from Ella's shoulder. "How long ago?"

"A long time," Ella said with a resigned sigh.

"How long?"

"Around the time when Caleb died. Gavin was hurting so badly. It was hard to watch. It still is. I realized then I had feelings for him, but that's as far as it's ever gone."

"Why haven't you ever said anything?"

"What was I supposed to say? 'Hannah, I think your brother-in-law is hot, and his pain makes my heart ache?' "

"To start with, yes."

"And then what?"

"And then I tell him my baby sister, who's the sweetest person I know, thinks he's hot and wants to kiss him better."

Ella blanched with horror. "You'd better not. I swear to God . . . Hannah."

"What?"

"Don't do it. I mean it."

"What shouldn't she do?" Nolan asked as he and Gavin came into the kitchen carrying dirty dishes.

"Nothing," Ella said emphatically.

"Whoa," Gavin said. "Looks like we interrupted something good."

"I'll get it out of her," Nolan said, coming at Hannah with a gleam in his eye.

"No, you won't," Ella said, reaching for a dish towel to dry her hands and then fleeing the room.

Hannah moved to go after her, but Gavin stopped her.

"May I?"

Hannah eyed him warily, wondering if perhaps Ella's one-way street might not be so one way after all. "By all means."

"What was that all about?" Nolan asked when they were alone.

"Apparently, my sister has a thing for Gavin and has for a while now."

"Wow. I'm learning all kinds of Abbott secrets hanging out with you."

"I never knew there were so many secrets until lately. Don't say anything, okay?"

"My lips are sealed." He eyed the stairs and then looked back at her. "I'm going up to change into something more comfortable. Want to join me?"

"Is that a come-on line?"

"Take it any way you want to."

"Go, quick before someone comes in."

They scurried up the stairs laughing all the way.

CHAPTER 25

—◄●►—

*Every time I see Nolan, he makes me feel so
special. He's easy to talk to and is always happy
to see me. I find myself putting off buying a new
car because my old SUV requires frequent
maintenance, which gives me an excuse to see
Nolan every now and then. Thank God for such
amazing friends. I never would've survived
without them.*

—From the diary of Hannah Abbott Guthrie, age
thirty-two

Gavin looked for Ella in the sitting room and dining room
before heading outside, where he found her on the porch
swing. She appeared lost in thought as the swing swayed in
the late afternoon breeze.

"You know, my grandfather built that swing for my grandmother when they were newlyweds," Gavin said as he leaned
against the porch railing.

She seemed surprised to see him there. "It's in good shape
if it's been here that long."

"We've taken good care of it over the years. A lot of Guthrie family history has transpired on that swing. Push over,
and I'll tell you all about it."

Ella hesitated before she moved over to make room for him.

"You may not know this," he said when he was seated next to her, "but my grandmother told my grandfather she was pregnant with my dad right here. And when my parents were dating, this was one of their favorite spots."

"This is where Caleb proposed to Hannah."

"Told you—lots of history. Three generations' worth."

"I've always loved it here. It's so peaceful."

"One of my favorite places."

"Your eulogy for Homer was amazing. Very moving and humorous and perfect."

"Thank you," he said, oddly touched by her approval. Her dark hair, so much like Hannah's and Hunter's, fluttered in the breeze.

"Caleb would've loved all this. Everyone coming together on Homer's behalf."

"Yes, he would've. The times with his friends and family around him were always his favorite, even if the occasion was sad."

"I hope you know how much we all miss him. It's nothing like what you've been through, but I think about him all the time. He was like another brother to me, and losing him was the worst thing to ever happen to me." She looked away, seeming embarrassed.

"It means a lot to me and my parents that the people he loved still remember him so fondly."

"Could I ask you something that's none of my business?"

"Sure, why not? We're practically related, right?"

"We're not related," she said forcefully—so forcefully that Gavin wondered what she was really thinking. "But what you said about outrunning the grief . . . Do you ever get any relief from it?"

"Do you know, you're the first person to ever ask me that?"

"I don't mean to pry. It's just that I hate to think of you in that kind of pain all the time."

Had he ever known anyone sweeter than her? Not that he could recall, and the way she looked at him . . . "You're not prying, and it's a great question. I get some relief out of my work. It keeps me so busy I don't have time to think about anything else, and I like it that way. I work twelve or even fifteen hours a day so when I get home I'm too tired to do anything but sleep. That's how I outrun it on many a day."

"Does it work?"

"Sometimes."

"What do you do when it doesn't work?"

"Drink," he said with a lazy grin. "A lot."

Her brows knit adorably, and he just knew she had other questions she was dying to ask.

"Go ahead. I'm an open book."

"Have you ever considered that therapy might be better for you than booze?"

"Sure, I've considered it, but the booze gets the job done. For the most part."

"For the most part. What does that mean?"

"It means," he said with a sigh, "when the booze doesn't work, those are the really bad days."

"How often does that happen?"

"You sure you aren't really a shrink, Ella?"

"I'm sorry. I'm being terribly nosy, but it's just . . . I hate to think of you hurting like that for all this time without let up."

"It's not quite as bad as it used to be. At least I'm no longer convinced it was all a big misunderstanding, and he'll be showing up to say 'psych' any day now."

"How long did you hope for that?"

"Far longer than I should have. At the beginning, I couldn't conceive of a life without him at the center of it, where he'd been my whole life. Sometimes, I still hope I'm going to wake up and find out it was all a bad dream. Like the end of the *Newhart* show. Remember that?"

Ella shook her head. "I remember the show but not how it ended."

"It was one of my mom's favorite shows when we were kids. Bob Newhart played an innkeeper in Vermont with a hot-to-trot wife and a bunch of lunatics around him. The last episode showed him waking up in bed with his wife from the earlier *Bob Newhart Show*, and he told her all about the dream that had been the second show. It was clever."

"That is clever. I love it."

"I want to know how I can manufacture things so the last seven years were nothing more than a bad dream. I'll wake up in bed with a gorgeous woman who will hold me when I cry about the awful dream I had that my brother, my very best friend in the world, died at twenty-eight with his whole freaking life ahead of him."

Ella placed her hand on his arm, the gesture comforting and something more. Something he couldn't quite fathom. "I wish I could make that happen for you. For all of us."

"That'd be nice, right?" He glanced at her, noticing the specs of gold in her dark eyes and the light smattering of freckles on her nose that he'd never seen before. She was really quite lovely. "Did you know Hannah tried to talk him out of going in the army?"

"She did? I never heard that."

"Don't let on that I told you. He told me. I guess they had several big fights over it. She didn't understand why he would turn down a possible career in professional hockey to be gone all the time in the military. He loved the army life when my dad was on active duty. He liked the moving around, making new friends, the whole thing. I never had a doubt which way he would go, but I guess Hannah was blindsided when he chose the army over hockey."

"She never let on that she was upset about it. To us, it seemed like she rolled with it all in typical Hannah fashion."

"I think she'd tell you their senior year of college was one of the more trying periods in their relationship. A lot of decisions to be made. Many late nights. Lots of fights."

"They sure did make it seem easy from the outside looking in."

"It wasn't without its challenges. In case you hadn't noticed, he could be a bit of a handful."

"*Nooo.* I never would've guessed that."

They shared a laugh that ended with him gazing into gold-speckled eyes, noting not for the first time how gorgeous Ella Abbott was. "You're a good listener. Thanks for letting me vent."

She finally withdrew the hand that had been resting so sweetly on his arm. He immediately mourned the loss of her warmth. "Thanks for answering my nosy questions. I hope if the pain ever gets to be too much for you, you'll reach out to someone who cares."

"I will." Gavin kissed her cheek and discovered she smelled

as good as she looked, something light and fruity and femi-
nine. "I'd better get back to the party before Turk and the boys
burn down the house. Are you coming?"

He got up and held out a hand to her.

She looked up at him, and the affection he saw in her gaze
staggered him as she took his proffered hand.

Maybe the next time he couldn't outrun the grief, he'd call
Ella. The idea brought a measure of comfort and peace he
seldom experienced anymore.

"I'm going straight to hell for this," Hannah said, staring up at
the ceiling as Nolan did the same next to her. "I've got a yard
full of guests, and I'm up here messing around with you."

"*Messing around?* I'm hurt." He turned on his side, propping his head on his hand. "*That* was making love."

She smiled up at him. "Yes, it was, but I'm still going to hell."

"I'll see you there." His free hand worked its way under
the sheets to her belly. "Look at it this way, at least all the
parents have left."

"There is that."

"So all that remains are Caleb's drunken buddies and
some of your siblings. We'll never be missed."

"Yes, we will, and the abuse will be substantial."

He pulled her closer to him. "Then we'd better make sure
it was worth it."

"Nolan! No! No more."

His lips and tongue on her neck scrambled her brain and
made her forget all about her guests for another half hour.

After a quick shower, they got dressed in jeans and
sweaters.

"You're a very bad influence on me. I'm a good girl. I don't
do things like this."

He snorted with laughter. "You weren't such a good girl a
little while ago when you were—"

She squished his lips shut with her fingers. "Don't finish
that thought under any circumstances."

He placed his hands on her hips and pulled her into his
embrace. "I can't help that I'm unable to keep my hands
off you."

"Yes, you can help it, and you will help it until tomorrow afternoon when they all go home."

"I won't last that long."

"Fine, then last at least until bedtime."

"I'll do my best."

"You gotta let me go now."

"One more minute." Her hair was soft and fragrant against his face as he exhaled a deep breath full of love and satisfaction. "I love you, Hannah. I love everything about being with you."

"I love you, too. I love laughing with you and teasing you and making love with you."

He let out a groan. "Come on! Don't say that and then hold me at arm's length for hours and hours."

"Bedtime," she said. "And not one minute before."

With tremendous reluctance, he released her. "Even though you're torturing me, after everyone leaves tomorrow, I have a surprise for you."

"What kind of surprise?"

"The kind of surprise where you don't get to know what it is until tomorrow afternoon."

"It's very unfair for you to tell me you have a surprise and then make me wait more than twenty-four hours before I can have it."

He couldn't believe that she sounded genuinely pissed. "I wanted to give you something to look forward to."

She unlocked the bedroom door and opened it. "Well, your plan backfired, and now I'm mad at you. Bedtime is off."

"No way."

"Yes way unless you tell me what the surprise is."

"I'm not telling you."

"Okay then. You know the consequences."

He gave her a playful spank on the bottom as they headed downstairs. "I'll change your mind."

"Change her mind about what?" Colton asked as they landed in the kitchen.

"Trust me when I say you don't want to know," Hannah said.

"Ew. Gross."

"Exactly. Nolan, go outside and check on our guests, will

you? I need to grill my brother about where he's been spending his weekends lately."

"Only if you tell me what he says."

"Well, yeah, of course I will."

Nolan kissed her and headed out to the yard.

"I see you've already got him trained."

"He's coming along quite well," Hannah said with a smile.

"I like you two together. It makes sense in an odd sort of way."

"He's been very good for me and to me, and not just since we started dating."

"I'm so glad to hear that, Hannah. It makes me happy to see you happy."

She rubbed her hand on his bare cheek. "I barely recognize you without the fur. What gives?"

Shrugging, he popped a couple of grapes into his mouth. "Time for a change."

"And all your mysterious getaways? Is that part of the change, too?"

"Perhaps."

"Come on, Colton! Don't be all secretive with me. What gives?"

"I'm not ready to talk about it."

"You won't tell me *anything*? Like how you met her?"

"Through a friend."

"Colton!"

"*Hannah!* You of all people should appreciate the fact that I'm trying to maintain a bit of privacy for as long as I possibly can in this hornet's nest known as our family."

"It's not fair. Everyone knows about me, but you get to maintain your *privacy*?"

"You made the mistake of having an affair with a man who drives around with his name on his truck and parks said truck in front of your house until all hours. I could give you some pointers on how to be a bit more subtle in these matters."

"Give me a break. This is your first 'matter' in who knows how long, and suddenly you're the expert?"

"May I remind you that no one knows who I'm seeing, and everyone knows who you're getting busy with?" he asked with a smug smile.

"No, please don't. Fine, have it your way, but you'd better watch your back, mister. I'm going to be keeping my eye on you."

"Have at it. You don't scare me."

Hannah was still coming up with a retort when Gavin led Ella through the kitchen by the hand. Ella had a dreamy, gobsmacked look on her face that had Hannah grinning widely at her sister.

As she went by, Ella mouthed "Oh my God" to Hannah, and followed Gavin into the backyard.

"Um, excuse me," Colton said. "What was that about?"

"That might've been about someone extremely wonderful getting exactly what she wants. We shall see."

"Ella and *Gavin*? Since when?"

"Since about five minutes ago it seems."

"I need to come down off my mountain more often. I miss out on too much up there."

"Do you ever think about relocating? I mean you could still run the sugaring facility without living up there."

"I think about it once in a while. More often lately."

"Any particular reason?"

"End it, Hannah. You're not going to break me."

"Give me time."

"Oh there you are," Cameron said when she came into the kitchen with Will. "We were just about to go home, but we wanted to see you before we left." She gave Hannah a hug. "The service for Homer was awesome—and the best part is I came away feeling like I know Caleb a little bit now, too."

"Thanks, Cam. I'm so glad you could be here. If you have some time this week, I want to talk to you about an idea I have for the retreat."

"Oh tell me now."

"Because we weren't leaving or anything," Will said, rolling his eyes at Colton.

"Be quiet," Cameron said. "You can wait five more minutes to get me alone."

"What if I can't?" Will asked.

Cameron glared playfully at her boyfriend. "Anyway, Hannah . . ."

"I had this idea for a bracelet for the women who visit the

retreat. War widows receive a gold star pin from Congress in recognition of our loss. There's an entire organization for gold star widows and widowers. I thought it would be nice to take that symbol and incorporate it into a bracelet that is customized for each woman, based on things that remind her of her husband. I could offer themes based on areas of interest such as sports or cars or hunting or whatever they were into. But the gold star would be at the center of each bracelet. What do you think?"

"I love it, but why limit it to the women who come to the retreat? You could offer the custom-made bracelets via the website, too."

"Only if I could donate the proceeds to an organization that supports military widows and widowers."

"Another great idea. Let's get together one day this week to talk about that and next steps for the retreat."

Hannah hugged Cameron again. "Thanks for everything."

"My pleasure. I love the plans you've made for this place. I can't wait to dig in deeper."

"It's a really nice idea, Han," Will said when he kissed her good-bye.

"Thanks. Hey, did you get a new car, Cameron?"

"He talked me into a big ugly SUV," she said with a pout. "I hate it."

"It's safe," Will said.

"It's *ugly*."

"I hope it's not red," Hannah said. "Fred loves red."

"It's black. Fred better not have a thing for black, too."

"I can't wait to see it. I'm sure it's not as ugly as you think it is."

"Anything is ugly after my adorable Mini."

"Which was totally impractical for life in Northern Vermont," Will said.

Colton fist-bumped his brother in agreement.

"I'll remember that you sided with him," Cameron said to Colton.

"Hey, don't suck me into this."

"Too late," Cameron said. "Hannah, thank you for a lovely, memorable day. William, let's go."

"I thought she'd never say that."

Cameron took him by his loosened tie and led him from the kitchen.

"Speaking of well-trained house pets," Colton said.

"He's never been so happy."

"I'm going, too. I need to get back up on the mountain and get some work done."

"Thanks for being here today."

"Wouldn't have missed it."

"When you're ready to talk about your little romance, you know where I am."

"How could I ever forget?" He gave her a one-armed hug and kissed her cheek. "Oh and by the way, I don't think it's going to be a *little* romance. See you later."

He bolted before she could reply to that outrageously suggestive comment.

Hannah tried to picture Colton, the confirmed bachelor and mountain man, in *love*. That'd be something to see—that is if he decided to expose his lady to the Abbott family.

CHAPTER 26

—◄•►—

Caleb has already been gone six years. Some days
it feels like five minutes. Other times it's like
I haven't seen him in forever. I miss him so much.
I miss feeling hopeful. I miss feeling young. I miss
feeling like a woman. I removed my wedding
rings and put them away in a safe place where
they could never be found if the house got broken
into. I like that I'm the only person in the world
who knows where they are. It seemed time to take
them off, but my hand feels naked without them
where they've been for thirteen years.

—From the diary of Hannah Abbott Guthrie, age
thirty-four

Seconds after she closed the door on the last of her guests
on Sunday afternoon, Hannah pounced on Nolan, taking
him by surprise when she jumped on his back and wrapped
her arms and legs around him. He'd been walking through the
yard with a garbage bag, cleaning up the last of the stray cans
and bottles.

"Holy crap, woman! Are you trying to break my back?
What good will I be to you then?"

"I want my surprise."

"What surprise?"

"Nolan . . . If you ever want to have sex with me again, do not mess around right now."

"I'm seeing a whole new side to you, and I'm not sure I like it."

She tightened her arms around his neck.

He made dramatic gagging and choking noises. "Easy, killer. Dismount and let me go make a phone call."

"You better be calling about my surprise."

"What were you like as a kid at Christmas?"

"I always found the presents, unwrapped them and rewrapped them. No one ever knew."

"This is a very worrisome character trait. I may need to reconsider a few things."

"Make the call. Now."

Laughing, he walked away, and Hannah took great pleasure in watching him go. Her house was a mess, her yard was a mess, she had a month's worth of laundry to do, but she didn't care about any of that when there was a surprise to be had.

He came out the back door five minutes later. "Let's go, you nosy wench."

She let out a squeal of excitement, dropped the garbage bag she'd taken from him and ran toward him.

"How about you jump me again, but on the front side this time."

"Let's see how good your surprise is, and I'll take that under consideration."

"Oh I do love you."

"Now take me to my surprise."

"Yes, ma'am. Note to self, never again give her a preview that a surprise is coming."

"You're learning, my friend."

He deposited her into the front seat of his truck with a lingering kiss that she broke away from.

"No stall tactics. I've already had to wait forever."

"One day is not forever."

"It is for me when I know there's a surprise coming. Move it."

"You are too much, you know that?"

"Uh-huh. Now hurry up."

He seemed to take his own sweet time, at least as far as she was concerned, getting into the truck and putting on his seatbelt. By the time he pulled away from the curb, Hannah was practically bouncing in her seat.

"I hope the surprise lives up to the anticipation," he said.

"I do, too."

"Jeez, no pressure much." Nolan drove through town, over the one-lane covered bridge and past her parents' barn on Hells Peak Road.

"How much farther?"

"Not that far, but listen, Hannah . . . I'm starting to worry you might not like this surprise as much as I thought you would. And if you don't want it, it's okay to say so. I promise you won't hurt my feelings if you aren't up for it."

"It's not bungee jumping or mountain zip lining or anything like that, is it?"

"No," he said, laughing. "Nothing like that."

"Caleb learned the hard way that those things don't count as surprises to me. They count as nightmares."

"Good to know."

"So it's something you thought I would want, right?"

"It's something I *hoped* you might want. But like I said, no hard feelings if the timing isn't right."

Hannah thought that over for a moment. "I'm sure if you thought I'd like it, I will. Either way, it's nice to know you were thinking of me."

"Hannah," he said with a laugh, "I think about you *all* the time."

"You do? Really?"

"Yes, really."

She smiled at him, happier in that moment than she'd been in longer than she could remember.

"Do you think about me a little?"

"Occasionally."

His mouth fell open in shock that had her laughing hysterically.

"You're so easy."

"You're going to pay for that later. Ever had your ass spanked?"

Hannah's entire face heated with embarrassment and arousal. "I refuse to dignify that with a response."

"Be as prissy as you want, I saw your face light up with interest. We'll discuss this later."

"No, we won't."

"Yes, we will." Nolan took a hard right off the main road.

"What're we doing at Dude's place?"

"Sit still, and you'll find out."

"I don't want to sit still." She already had her seatbelt off and was straining to see beyond the next bend in the road.

Chuckling at her enthusiasm, Nolan said, "I can't imagine what your children will be like, woman."

She looked over at him, all thoughts of surprises obliterated by his casual mention of her future children. "Children? What children?"

"The ones you're going to have with me." He shifted the truck into park. "Come on and see your surprise."

Still reeling from his pronouncement about the children they were going to have together, Hannah fumbled her way out of the truck and took the hand he held out to her. "You can't just drop a bomb like that and walk away like you never said it."

"Am I walking away? Seems to me I'm getting in deeper by the second." Before she could say a word, he kissed her hard. "Another thing we'll talk about later. Now, I thought you wanted to see your surprise."

"I do." She did, but her senses were still recovering from the wallop of his revealing comment, and it was hard to think about anything other than the prospect of their children—the children she'd long ago accepted that she'd never have.

Hannah took a deep breath, determined to clear her mind and enjoy whatever he'd arranged for her.

Dude came out to greet them both with hugs. Today, she was back in her overalls and straw hat, looking much more like the Dude they all loved than she had yesterday in her suit and tie. Trailing behind her were two dogs, a cat, a rooster, a chicken and a raccoon. They were all extremely obedient as they fell into line behind their leader. "Right this way," Dude said.

"Where are we going?" Hannah asked.

"She's about to pee herself with excitement," Nolan commented dryly, making both women laugh.

"I'm not that bad," Hannah said.

"Yes, you are." This was said with a warm, affectionate smile that softened his entire expression.

The way he looked at her made her feel light-headed and breathless at the same time.

He put his arm around her, seeming to sense that she needed him.

They followed Dude into her decrepit barn to a stall where a mother slept while several puppies frolicked in the hay around her. "Oh," Hannah said. "Oh they're adorable!"

"They're a lot bigger than they were this time last week," Nolan said. "And look at him, still hanging off to the side, watching the chaos rather than jumping into the scrum. He's the one I thought you might like to have, Hannah. He reminds me of you and the way you keep watch over your siblings. You only get involved in the chaos when you absolutely have to."

She looked up at him, wondering if she'd heard him correctly. "You picked him for me?"

"Um, yeah. I know Homer just died, so if you aren't ready for another dog, I totally understand."

"I do, too," Dude said. "I'd even be willing to keep him for you until you're ready."

Hannah's heart beat hard and fast from the rush of emotion that came with the understanding of what he'd done for her. "Could I . . . Could I hold him?"

"Sure, you can." Dude opened the stall door and went to scoop up the solemn boy who sat off by himself, watching them with big, wary eyes. She handed him to Hannah.

"Hi, buddy," Hannah whispered as he snuggled up to her, sniffing madly to make her acquaintance. "You're such a handsome fellow." His face was almost all brown except for the white circle around his left eye. The rest of his body was a hodgepodge of brown, black and white fur. He had short stumpy legs with big round paws—one of them white, one black, one brown and the other white with brown spots. He was, without a doubt, the cutest thing she'd ever seen. "What breed is he?"

"I haven't got the first clue," Dude said.

"Who cares, right? You're your own breed. One of a kind." Hannah looked up at Dude and Nolan, who was watching her warily. "Do I really get to keep him?"

"If you want him, Dude says he's all yours."

"That's right. Nolan put dibs on him last week, and when he told me he was for you, I wholeheartedly agreed that you'd give him a good home."

The puppy got a mouthful of her hair and gave a playful tug.

Hannah gently extracted her hair from his razor-sharp puppy teeth, and he gave her a wet kiss on the cheek. Laughing, she hugged him and glanced at Nolan. "This is the best surprise ever. Thank you so much. Both of you. He's just what I needed."

Nolan seemed to release a deep breath he'd been holding. "What will you name him?"

Hannah held up her new best friend for a closer look at his adorable face. "In my family, it's tradition to stick with a name that works, so what do you think of Homer Junior?"

"I think that's a perfect name for him," Nolan said.

"I agree," Dude said. "It's not too much name for a little guy like him, even if those paws are a sign he's not going to be little for long."

"I think I'm in love," Hannah said, sighing at the sweet kisses little Homer was placing all over her face. Was there anything sweeter than puppy breath?

"Thanks again, Dude," Nolan said, putting an arm around Hannah to lead her from the barn.

"Wait," Hannah said. "He needs to say good-bye to his mom and his family."

"He can come see his mom any time he wants to," Dude assured her, "and his siblings will be close by, too. I don't like to break up families."

"Oh good," Hannah said, putting him down to see his mom.

The puppy went over to nuzzle his mother's face and engaged in a scuffle with the other puppies before he turned and walked back to her, sitting at her feet and looking up at her.

"He's already decided you're his person," Dude said, her eyes sparkling with unshed tears. "I love when that happens."

Hannah bent to pick up the puppy and snuggled him in close, thrilled and honored that he had chosen her.

"He's had his first set of shots, but he'll be needing more soon," Dude said, handing a sheaf of paper to Nolan. "Here're his records."

"I'll take very good care of him, Dude."

"If I had any doubt at all about that, I never would've let you have him."

"Thank you for trusting me with him."

"My pleasure, honey. Anyone who'd throw a funeral like the one you gave Homer deserves this little guy in her life. That was some tribute to Homer Senior."

"We thought his life warranted the proper send-off."

"Indeed it did. You take care now, and bring him to visit any time you'd like."

"We will."

Nolan put his arm around Hannah as they walked to the truck. "The surprise comes with a crate, a bed, toys, food and anything else he needs to get started. So next stop is the pet store."

"Thank you so, so much for him, Nolan. I love him, and I love you."

"I love you, too, and I'm glad you're happy with your surprise." Nolan helped her into the truck and fastened her seatbelt since her hands were full of puppy. Before he withdrew from the cab, he kissed her and laughed when little Homer tried to get in on the action. "I can see I'm going to be competing for your affections with your new friend."

"No competition. As Cameron would say, there's plenty of me to go around." She looked down at the puppy and then at Nolan. "This is what Caleb meant when he said he wanted me to have joy in my life."

Smiling, Nolan ran his index finger over her cheek. "I was really hoping it wasn't too soon after Homer died."

"Dude told me yesterday that the best way to honor Homer's memory is to give another pet a good home. I thought that was lovely. As soon as I got time, I was going to visit the shelter."

"Maybe we can do that to give Homer a pal to play with someday."

Hannah glanced over at him. "You're making a lot of plans, my friend."

"Should I not be?"

"I . . . um, I don't know."

"We're not getting any younger, Hannah. I want a family. I want a wife and kids and a home to call my own. I want all those things with you and Homer Junior. It may be too soon to even have this conversation, but please have no doubts about what I want with you."

Hannah snuggled up to Homer, overwhelmed by Nolan's intense words and the emotion she heard behind them. As much as she wanted all the same things he did, she couldn't help but wonder how any of that would be possible as long as he was keeping critical parts of himself locked behind a wall too high for her to scale.

By nine o'clock Sunday night, Homer Junior had completely taken over Hannah's life, and she loved every minute of it. They played with Homer until he dropped into a lump on the sitting room rug and fell into a deep sleep. Even his little snores were cute.

Nolan was lying on his side with his back to the fire watching her gaze at the puppy.

"I don't even know how to thank you for him," Hannah said, running a hand over the puppy's silky soft back. "He was just what I needed after losing Homer Senior. I think he would approve of me finding a new furry friend to love."

"I know he would, and I'm happy you're happy."

"I'm so happy." She shifted her focus from adorable puppy to sexy man. On her knees, she scooted over to Nolan and stretched out on top of him. His arms came around her and his hand smoothed the hair back from her face. "I never expected to have this again."

"To have what?"

"This. You, me, us, all of it. And it's not just the companionship, as nice as that is. It's the connection, too. Even before we were officially together, I felt that connection. I felt something every time my family told me you'd been asking for me. I felt the connection then and even more so now."

"I feel it, too, babe. Why do you think I waited so long for you?"

Hannah raised her head and brought her lips down on his, giving him the softest sweetest kiss she possibly could.

His hand tightened in her hair, and he hardened against her belly, but neither of them made a move beyond the slick meeting of lips.

The sound of a fist pounding on her door spoiled the moment and woke Homer, who yipped with outrage at the interruption. "Probably one of my stupid brothers," she muttered.

"You get the door," Nolan said. "I'll take Homer."

Hannah reluctantly raised herself off his warm, muscular body. "I was enjoying that."

"More where that came from."

"Don't forget."

"I couldn't if I tried."

Hannah was wearing a broad smile when she opened the door to a man she'd never seen before. He wore a ragged coat, his hair was greasy looking and his face was puffy. A stale aroma surrounded him. "May I help you?"

"I want to see my son."

"I'm sorry, but who is your son?"

"I know he's in there because I saw his truck with his name all over it, so if you would just get him . . ."

"Oh Mr. Roberts. Please come in."

"No, Hannah." Nolan appeared behind her with the puppy asleep in his arms. "Don't let him in."

She hadn't heard that dull, flat tone from him before. "But, Nolan, he's your father."

"Don't let him in." Without looking at her, he handed her the puppy and stepped around her, closing the door behind him as he went outside.

Through the closed door, she heard Nolan angrily ask him what the hell he was thinking showing up at her house.

"You're never home anymore, boy. Where else was I supposed to look for you?"

"I told you I'm all done, and I meant it. You've got no right coming here and sullying her home."

"Listen to you all high and mighty just because you're getting a piece of quality ass."

Hannah winced when she heard thumping and other sounds of struggle.

"Get the fuck out of here before I call the police. You come here again, and I will call."

"You ain't got the balls."

"If it means keeping you away from her, you'll find my balls are big and brass. Now get going, or I'm calling."

"I'll go but this ain't over."

"Yes, it is."

"You're fooling yourself if you think a girl like her is ever going to be satisfied with a grease monkey like you!"

Tears ran unchecked down Hannah's face. When she heard the storm door jolt open, she wiped the tears on Homer's fur. She'd never seen Nolan looking so furious or so wounded. The combination broke her heart, but she knew better than to say anything. It had to come from him.

"I'm sorry about that. He never should've come here, to your home . . ." His voice broke on the last word, and he turned away from her.

Hands on his hips, head down, she watched his shoulders strain under the weight of the burden he carried, and she couldn't bear to see him suffer. Hannah went to him, placed her hand on his back and leaned her head on his shoulder. It felt so insignificant under the circumstances, but she feared he wouldn't accept anything more from her.

"I should go."

"Please don't go. You're not alone anymore, Nolan. Just like what you said to me—you don't have to do this alone."

"I don't want it touching you. You're beautiful and sweet and kind. You have no ability to understand this."

"I *want* to understand. I love you, Nolan. I love all of you. Let me in. Please, let me help."

"Hannah . . ." The single word contained a world of agony.

She took his hand. "Come sit with me."

CHAPTER 27

<hr/>

Myles Johansen has been a godsend as Homer has gotten older and more fragile. He comes to the house to check on Homie at least once a week, and we talk at length about how I'll know the time is right to let Homer go. I don't want to make the decision about me when it should be about him, but it's hard to overlook the fact that when he goes, I'll truly be alone. I'll be all that's left of the little family I once treasured. Myles asked me to have dinner with him, but I'm not ready for that. I know it's been almost seven years, but I suppose when I'm ready I'll know it. At least I hope I will . . .

—From the diary of Hannah Abbott Guthrie, age thirty-five

N olan didn't fight her when she led him to the sofa and tugged him down next to her.

She deposited the sleeping puppy on an oversized pillow and turned to Nolan.

Staring straight into the fire, his face was flat and devoid of emotion.

"You don't have to say a word if you don't want to." She took his hand and curled her fingers around his. "You once told me you'd be satisfied just to hold my hand, and that's how I feel, too." She brought their joined hands to her lips. "This is more than enough for now if it's all you're able to give."

He ran his free hand through his hair over and over again as the silence stretched between them. "I've been ashamed of my family all my life. I don't know how to share that part of me with you, because I've never shared it with anyone."

"You don't need to be ashamed of anything, Nolan. Everyone in this town respects you for the person you are, the friend you are, the businessman you are. Nothing you tell me about your family will change the way I feel about you."

He expelled a harsh laugh. "You say that now."

"I say that unconditionally."

Nolan leaned forward, resting his forehead on his other hand. "He drinks all the time. He always has, but in the last few years, he's been expecting me to pay for his habit. I cut him off recently, and he's not taking it well." He turned his head and looked at her for the first time since his father interrupted their evening. "You know the house plans I showed you?"

Riveted by his words, Hannah nodded.

"I haven't built it because I've been giving him all the money I would've put into the house. Go ahead and say it. I'm an idiot and an enabler and at the very least a huge fool."

"You've been a good son to a man who doesn't deserve you."

"I've never known him to have a job. In my entire life, I've never seen him work. Can you imagine that with a father like yours who goes to work every single day even though he probably doesn't have to anymore?"

"No, I can't, but again, there's no comparison between your father and you, who works six or seven days a week and has for as long as I can remember. You worked after school, weekends, summers."

"Fortunately, I had my grandfather to show me how to be a man, because my own father certainly never did."

"Your grandfather taught you to be one hell of a man, who is well respected and well regarded by everyone in this town.

I remember your grandfather so well. He came to everything at school. Never missed a game or a play or a band concert."

Nolan pressed the heel of his hand to his eyes. "He's the only reason my childhood wasn't a total disaster. He and families like yours that took me in and showed me how it was supposed to be. You have no idea how much the nights I spent at your house meant to me. Your family and Caleb's . . . You all saved me."

Hannah subtly wiped away a tear that escaped despite her best effort to contain it. "Where was your mother?"

"That's another lovely story. Her drug of choice is heroin. Last I heard she was selling herself online to pay for her habit. I haven't seen her in years. Thank goodness." He shook his head. "Earlier today I was caught up in the fantasy about the wife and kids I want to have. Who'd want to marry me and have kids with me knowing what they'd be getting with my shitty genes?"

"I would."

"Don't say that to make me feel better, Hannah. I don't want or need your pity."

"I don't pity you. I love you, and I'll marry you and have your children, and I'd do both those things without hesitation."

"You shouldn't say that without knowing what you're getting into."

"Is there more you haven't told me?"

"That wasn't enough?"

"It was more than enough, but is there anything else?"

"No."

"Then I know what I'm getting into and my answer hasn't changed. If you don't believe me, ask me."

"Ask you what?"

"Ask me to marry you."

"Not like this. Not when I'm all wound up about him coming here."

"You pick the time and the place. You already know what my answer will be."

He extended his arm, and Hannah curled up to him, relieved that he hadn't left, that he'd let her into his private pain. "I'm not going to hold you to that if you change your mind."

"I'm not going to."

"Hannah . . ."

"Nolan."

"*Hannah*."

"*Nolan*."

"What?"

"Can we go back to what we were doing before we were rudely interrupted?"

"What were we doing?" he said with a sweet smile that gave her hope he might believe her when she said she loved him unconditionally. "I don't remember."

Hannah moved slowly and carefully so she wouldn't disturb Homer and straddled Nolan's lap, wrapping her arms around his neck. With her lips hovering a fraction of an inch above his, she said, "It went something like this."

Nolan called a little after two on Friday. "Are you guys ready?"

"I am," Hannah said, "but Homer Junior isn't interested in traveling in his crate."

"It's too far for you to hold him, and besides, if we don't get him used to the crate, he'll be spoiled rotten."

"Um, yeah, about that . . ."

"Hannah . . ."

"I can't stand to listen to him cry! All he does is cry in the crate."

"That's because if he keeps it up long enough, he knows you're going to come rescue him."

"He's just a baby, Nolan. He needs to be with me."

"Are you going to be like this with our babies, too?"

It was the first time all week he'd referred to the conversation they'd had on Sunday night. "Maybe . . ."

"How very lucky they'll be to have you as their mother."

"And you as their father."

"I'll be there to get you and the spoiled brat in a few minutes. Bring the crate even if you have no intention of using it."

"Hear that, Homer? Daddy says we have to bring the crate."

The puppy whimpered pitifully.

"Did you hear that?" she asked Nolan.

"I heard him. Bring the crate."

"Hurry up. We're ready to go."

"Be there in ten."

Hannah's emotions had been all over the place this week, ever since she laid her heart and future on the line to give Nolan what he needed. He'd slept in her bed every night and had made passionate love to her. He'd helped with the puppy and even cleaned up his share of puppy pee.

Despite his close proximity in bed and out, she could tell he was a million miles from her, reliving the encounter with his father and trying to figure out how she could possibly mean what she'd said.

Hannah planned to spend this entire weekend proving to him every way she could that she'd meant it and that she wanted a life with him. She looked forward to learning more about his passion for racing and to meeting his friends on the team.

He came up the stairs fifteen minutes later and came in the front door without knocking, like she'd told him to. "Ready?"

"Yep." Hannah handed him the crate. "All his stuff is inside."

"See, it's good for something."

"Homer says that's all it's good for. Doncha, buddy?"

Homer licked her chin and made her laugh.

"He's got you so wrapped around his paw already. I've lost complete control of this situation."

"Your mistake, my friend," she said over her shoulder as she brushed by him, "was thinking you ever had control in the first place."

"Ain't that the truth?"

Nolan let his eyes drop to the sassy sway of her ass, which was covered in perfectly faded denim. She'd brushed against him and set every nerve ending in his body on fire. That's what she did to him.

He'd thought endlessly about what she'd said to him on Sunday night and had been nearly crippled by the painful yearning to take her at her word before she wised up and changed her mind.

After he checked to make sure the front door was locked, he followed her to the truck and stashed the crate and her duffel bag in the back of his truck. The thought of Hannah as his wife and the mother of his children filled him with a kind of longing he hadn't often experienced.

Though he wouldn't have blamed her if she had, she hadn't run away in disgust when she heard about his degenerate parents or his less-than-stellar bloodline. If anything, she'd done the exact opposite and stunned him with her willingness to overlook all the ugliness in his life. His father was right about one thing, Nolan thought as he buckled his seatbelt. She was far too good for him.

"Just so you aren't disappointed, the place we're staying isn't fancy, but they'll allow Junior in the room."

"I don't care where we stay. As long as my baby Homer can stay with us, I'll be fine."

"You're going to make him into a total mama's boy. You know that, don't you?"

"Of course I do. That's the goal."

Nolan laughed at the face she made at him, as if he'd said the stupidest thing in the history of stupid things. She was so far gone over that little ball of fur it wasn't even funny, but he loved seeing her glowing with excitement and pleasure. At the end of the day, her happiness was the only thing he cared passionately about. And knowing he had made her very happy with the puppy made him happy, too.

During the nearly two-hour ride to New Hampshire, she peppered him with questions about the car he drove, the team, racing, the track, how fast he really went and about the safety measures they employed. She was particularly fixated on that last part, which made him wonder what she was really thinking. Whatever it was, she didn't share it with him.

They arrived in time for pizza with the team. Along with Skeeter, who was their chief body guy, Hannah met Dave, the crew chief, the other mechanic, the pit crew and a couple of younger guys who were introduced as the team "bitches," a term that made both young men laugh and blush.

"We basically run and fetch," the younger of the two, Carl, said.

The pizza was tasty and the beer cold. Homer Junior lay curled up in Hannah's lap, completely out of sight of the restaurant staff, who no doubt would've balked if they'd known he was in their establishment. Even though she was the only woman in the group, Hannah more than held her own with Nolan's friends, teasing and sparring with the guys like she'd known them forever.

"You're a good sport," Deke, one of the pit crew guys, said as the party was breaking up for the night.

"I have seven brothers, Deke," she replied. "There's nothing you can throw at me that I haven't heard before."

"She's a keeper, Nolan," said Deke, who was already more than halfway in love with her.

Nolan put his arm around her. "Believe me, I know."

They headed for the hotel, which was actually more of a motel, with rows of doors facing the parking lot. He wished he'd thought to book something better than the place where they normally stayed when racing at Riverside. Hannah deserved the best of everything.

"Sorry the place is kind of dumpy."

"Is it clean?"

"Yeah."

"That's all that matters. Don't worry about it. Not every weekend can be the Candlewick Inn."

"I wish it could be."

"We're here together, and we have Homer. What else do we need?"

Nolan deposited their bags inside the door. "A Jacuzzi and a fireplace would be nice."

"It's got a bed," Hannah said suggestively. "A really big bed."

"That's about all it has."

"Like I said, what else do we need?"

Her words shot straight to his cock, which hardened against his fly. "I'll take the brat out to pee."

"Don't call him that," Hannah said, sprinkling kisses all over blissful Homer's face.

Nolan had never imagined a scenario in which he'd be jealous of a nine-pound puppy. "Hand him over."

"Go with Daddy and do your business, and then you can sleep right next to me."

"He's sleeping in the crate."

"He's sleeping with me."

Nolan clipped the leash on Homer's tiny collar. "*Crate.*"

"With me or I'm not sleeping with you."

If he didn't think she was so damned adorable, he would've dug into the argument. But he knew a losing battle when he saw one. "Come on, *Homer.* Let's go outside so we can both get some of Mommy's attention."

"Much better," Hannah said with a sweet smile that only made him harder. How did she do that with just the subtle curve of her lips?

Homer took his time sniffing every bush in the parking lot before he finally lifted his leg and peed for what felt like an hour. Thinking about Hannah, waiting for him in bed, intensified the throbbing in Nolan's groin. "Thank you for taking your own sweet time. You know us guys need to stick together, and you're not helping me out by demanding so much of her attention. Don't forget I'm the one who brought her to you. Maybe you could thank me by lightening up on the Velcro baby act, huh?"

Homer looked up at him disdainfully and continued on his beeline back to the room where his faithful Hannah awaited his return. The sad thing was, Nolan felt the same charge of excitement at knowing she was in the room waiting for him.

They went into the room to find every light off except for a faint glow escaping from the bathroom nightlight. There was just enough light for Nolan to see Hannah's dark hair fanned out on the pillow.

Homer whimpered, wanting to be lifted onto the bed with Hannah.

Nolan unclipped the leash and gave him what he wanted.

Tripping over his own big feet, Homer ran across the bed to her, making Hannah giggle when he licked her face. "There's my sweet baby boy."

"The other one is here, too," Nolan said as he unbuttoned his shirt and took it off.

"Daddy is feeling a little jealous, Homie, so how about you go to sleep so I can give him some attention?"

"I can hear you," Nolan muttered as he went into the bathroom.

Hannah's soft laughter and Homer's little yips were comical to listen to as he brushed his teeth.

By the time he emerged from the bathroom and slid into bed, Hannah had settled Homer into a tiny ball on one of the throw pillows.

"It's so cute how he just collapses when he's done," she said.

"You think the way he breathes is cute."

"Well, yeah, that too."

"I think the way you breathe is cute," Nolan said, reaching for her. "Holy shit! Are you totally naked under there?"

"So what if I am?"

"Oh my God. Get over here, will you?"

"Since you asked so nicely." Moving carefully so as not to disturb Homer, she scooted to Nolan's side of the big bed.

"So, he's going to get one half of the bed, and we get the other?"

She curled up to him, her breasts against his side, her arm across his belly and her smooth, silky leg slipping between his. "Do you have a problem with that?"

"No, I'm good."

Hannah's laughter thrilled and aroused him. "Thank you for putting up with me and my Homer obsession."

"It's a mess of my own making."

"True, so you really have no one to blame but yourself."

He tickled her and made her squeal.

"Stop! You'll wake the baby."

"I better find a way to quiet you down then." He gave her a tug and arranged her on top of him, capturing her mouth in a deep, searing kiss that had him desperate and throbbing in two seconds flat. "Most of my team is in love with you after one night," he whispered, sitting up to kiss her neck and throat before shifting his focus to her breasts. Cupping them in his big, work-roughened hands, he stared into her bottomless dark eyes. "Too bad for them you're all mine."

"Yes, Nolan," she whispered, her arms around him. "I'm all yours."

He sucked her sweet nipple into his mouth and pinched the other gently between his fingers at the same time, making her gasp. "Shh. Don't wake your baby."

Her smile lit up her face, and he'd never loved her more. She squiggled around on his lap, making him go blind with lust. "*Hannah* . . ."

With her hand wrapped around his cock, she guided him into her wet heat. "Is this what you want?"

"More than I've ever wanted anything."

She came down on him inch by torturous inch, and it took everything he could muster to keep from losing it the second he was fully seated inside her tight channel.

"Christ, that's hot," he whispered.

"Feels so good." She moved her hips, taking them on a slow ride to paradise.

Nolan cupped the cheeks of her ass and squeezed as he surged into her again and again.

Her breasts rubbed against his chest, the hard points of her nipples arousing him to a fevered level of need that he'd never experienced before.

As she made love to him, he knew without a doubt he was ruined for all other women. She was the only one for him. "Love you, Hannah. Love you so damned much."

"Love you, too. Just as much." This was said in a breathy voice against his ear, which detonated a chain reaction that made his balls ache and his dick even harder as he gripped her ass and pumped into her.

She tripped over the finish line first, crying out as her inner muscles milked an explosive release from him.

Homer yelped out a bark that made them laugh even in the throes of passion.

Breathing hard, Hannah laughed until she cried. "We've scarred him for life."

Nolan kissed away her tears. "He'd better get used to it."

Hannah's head landed on his shoulder, and he tightened his hold on her as he continued to throb inside her.

He reclined against the pillows, bringing her with him and she fell asleep with him still lodged deep inside. He was right where he wanted to be for the rest of his life. Nothing else mattered when she was in his arms—not his deadbeat family or his hardscrabble upbringing. Maybe he wasn't good enough for her, but he'd be damned if he'd ever let her go. Soon enough, he'd make her his forever.

CHAPTER 28

✦

I had the dream again last night. It was the same dream I always have. Caleb was there with Homer, and they were waiting for me. But this time Nolan was there, too. He held out a hand to me. Caleb did the same. I looked at him and at Nolan. Then I took both their hands and let them lead me forward. I'm not sure exactly what I'm supposed to take away from this version of the dream, but apparently I have room enough in my heart for both of them.

—From the diary of Hannah Abbott Guthrie, age thirty-five

The next day was a frenzy of activity that began with a quick breakfast with the team before they headed to the track for a day of time trials and testing of upgrades they'd recently made to the car, thanks to the sponsor money that had rolled in after Nolan led them to five wins last season.

After he got Hannah and Homer—who'd come despite Nolan's suggestion he remain in his crate in the motel room until they broke for lunch—settled in the bleachers, where she could see all the action but remain close to the crew, he donned his protective gear and got down to business. It took a huge effort to focus on what he was doing when he wanted to constantly check to make sure she was still there.

While they ran safety checks and went over track conditions, he couldn't help being distracted knowing she was watching him. It gave him a thrill to know she cared enough to want to be part of this important aspect of his life—and that she'd put aside her fears about him being hurt to come here and see what it was about. He loved her for that as well as so many other things.

"Nolan," Skeeter said under his breath. "Quit staring at your lady and pay attention."

"I'm not staring at her."

"Yes, you are. Now knock it off, and get your head in the game."

They were sharing the track with five other teams who had agreed to participate in a practice race.

Nolan winked at her before he put on his helmet and got into the car. The minute he was strapped in, he pushed every other thought out of his head to concentrate fully on the task at hand. One wrong move behind the wheel could spell disaster for the team, not to mention what it would mean for him. And with Hannah watching, he wanted only to show her the thrill of the chase without any undue drama.

They took a couple of practice laps, each car jockeying for position. As he pressed the accelerator and made a move to pass the car in front of him, a kick of adrenaline shot through him. Only one other thing in this world could fire him up the way racing did, and she was sitting in the stands watching him. Determined to give her a good show, he pressed the pedal to the floor on the straightaway.

Hannah's mouth was dry and her hands were damp as she watched Nolan's white car, with the large number 18 painted in red on the side, dart between the others at what seemed like a thousand miles an hour. He couldn't possibly be going that fast, but what did it matter? At that speed, the slightest miscalculation would result in certain death.

He was going to die. The feeling came over her like a tidal wave, drowning her in unspeakable fear. She couldn't do this again. No way would she survive it a second time.

Homer squirmed in her lap, disturbed by the high-pitched whine of the engines as the cars roared past them. Gas fumes and dust filled the air as the cars briefly disappeared from view as someone waved a green flag. And then, impossibly they were moving even faster than they'd been before.

Nolan shot out to an early lead, his car literally flying around the curves of the oval track and passing her again in a blur of speed and color and exhaust.

Hannah couldn't breathe. Fear riveted her to the aluminum bleacher seat. She wanted out of there, immediately, but that would require moving, which she couldn't seem to do.

He was going to die, and she would see it happen. At least when Caleb died, she hadn't been there to watch it unfold before her.

Her hands were shaking, and only when Homer let out a yelp of discomfort did she realize how tightly she was squeezing him.

Skeeter landed next to her. "Ain't he something? Look at him go! He's a natural." He looked at Hannah and did a double take. "Honey, what's wrong? You're white as a sheet after it's been bleached."

"I, um . . . I . . ." Before she could say the words, the car in front of Nolan's seemed to spin out of control in slow motion, going airborne. A scream got caught in her throat when she watched Nolan dodge around the car before it flipped over twice and landed on its hood in the infield.

A yellow flag was waved as people and rescue vehicles and trucks raced to the hobbled car.

"Please," Hannah whispered. "I need to get out of here."

To his great credit, Skeeter didn't say a word. He simply rose and took her hand and led her out of the bleachers to a side exit she never would've noticed had he not been leading the way. Once they were in the parking lot, he stopped, still holding her hand. "Where do you want to go?"

"Could I please go back to the motel?"

"You don't want to wait for Nolan?"

She shook her head. "Not here. I can't be here."

"Whatever you need, honey. I'll take you back myself. Let me just get my keys and tell the guys where I'm going."

"You don't need to be here?"

He smiled at her. "Nah, they only need me when the car gets smashed up, which hardly ever happens with Nolan at the wheel. He's really good. That's my truck. I'll be right back."

Hannah had seen with her own eyes that Nolan was a really good driver, but the feeling of absolute certainty that had come over her watching him race had left her panic-stricken. Somehow, someway she'd managed to survive losing Caleb. If she knew anything for certain, she knew she'd never survive losing the man she loved again.

While she waited for Skeeter, she put Homer down so he could pee and then picked him up to nuzzle his sweet face. He licked at the tears that flowed freely down her face when she realized the future she'd wanted with Nolan wasn't to be if it meant living with this kind of fear on a regular basis. She'd already done that during Caleb's deployments, and she'd discovered that was no way to live.

Skeeter emerged from yet another door and jogged over to her, unlocking his truck and holding the door for her. "Sorry it isn't cleaner. I wasn't expecting guests."

"It's fine," Hannah said. "I appreciate the ride."

They drove the short distance to the motel in silence that was only broken by an occasional yip from Homer.

As Skeeter pulled up to the door to the room she was sharing with Nolan, he put the truck into park. "It's none of my business, Hannah, so tell me to stuff it if I'm totally out of line here, but that boy . . . He's crazy about you, and if you asked him to give up the racing, he'd do it in a second if it meant he got to keep you."

"I'd never do that, Skeeter. He loves it. I've seen that in the way he talks about it. I could see that in the time I spent with you all last night and today at the track. It's in his blood."

"So are you."

"I appreciate what you're trying to do, but I can't ask him to be anyone other than who he is. He'd hate me for that someday."

"I think you're selling him short and vastly underestimating how far around the bend he is where you're concerned."

"Thanks for the ride, Skeeter. I really appreciate it."

"You got your key?"

Hannah nodded and reached for the door handle. Every step toward the room where they'd known such bliss the night before felt like a thousand-mile march. Once inside, she curled up on the bed with Homer, willing her heart to stop pounding so fast she felt like she might hyperventilate.

No matter how slowly she tried to breathe or how hard she tried to think about something else, her brain was fixated on that moment of certainty that had come over her while she watched him race. Sobs shook her body at the thought of losing him, too, and she cried until there were no tears left.

When she heard Nolan knocking frantically on the door she realized she'd fallen asleep. "Hannah! Open up. I don't have my key."

Homer howled and yipped with outrage.

"Shh. It's okay." She patted him and got up, smoothing her hair as she went to the door and pulled it open.

"Oh God, Hannah." He still wore the jumpsuit that had patches all over it and his hair was wild as if he'd pulled off the helmet and run for her. "You've been crying. I'm so sorry. Skeeter told me you were upset. I'm fine. Look. The car in front of me wrecked, but I'm totally fine."

Even though he was fine—this time—she felt dead inside from the certainty that someday he wouldn't be. "I know. I can see that."

With his hands on her face, he forced her to look up at him. "What are you thinking? Please tell me. Whatever it is, we'll get through it, but I can't do a damned thing if you don't talk to me."

A sob caught in her throat as tears fell from her eyes. As much as she didn't want to, she couldn't help but cry at the thought of losing this wonderful, beautiful man who'd managed to make her fall completely and totally in love with him.

"Don't cry, honey. I can't bear it. I won't race anymore if it upsets you this much."

Hannah shook her head. "No. Don't say that. You love it."

Smiling, he shook his head with disbelief. "I don't love it anywhere near as much as I love you."

"I can't ask you to give up something that's such a big part of your life."

"Hannah . . ." He closed the door that had remained open and took her into his arms. "The only thing I couldn't live without is you. Don't you know that by now? I was perfectly happy as one of the mechanics for the team, and I'll be perfectly happy going back to that role if it means you never again look as wrecked as you do right now."

"I'm a mess. I know."

"Baby, you're as gorgeous as ever, but it's the wrecked look in your eyes that's killing me."

"I had this feeling, this utter certainty that you were going to die out there. It was so real and so profound."

He encouraged her to sit on the bed and knelt in front of her, taking her hands and kissing each one of them. "I'm not going to die, Hannah. I'm going to live to be so old you'll be wishing I was dead just so you can get rid of me."

"Never."

"I'm going to live that long just to prove you wrong, but I won't race anymore."

"But what about the team? They're counting on you—"

He kissed her, keeping his lips pressed against hers until some of the starch left her spine. "Deke is my backup driver. With a little more practice, he'll be every bit as good as I am."

"And you won't hate me someday for forcing you to give up something you loved?"

"You're not forcing me to do anything. You're just giving me a chance to prove there's nothing I wouldn't do if it means making you happy and giving you peace of mind." He kissed away the tears on her cheeks before focusing again on her lips. "I understand where all this is coming from, honey. I get it, and I'm only sorry I didn't anticipate how difficult it would be for you to see me doing something most people consider pretty dangerous."

"Most sane people."

That drew a laugh from him. "Stay there for one minute." Still on his knees, he reached for his duffel bag and pulled it close enough to unzip a side compartment. He withdrew a small black box and turned to her.

"What is that?"

"Hold on a minute."

"I don't want to hold on a minute. I want to know what it is."

Laughing, he leaned his head against her chest and then looked up at her, his heart in his eyes. "I can't believe I'm actually going to take you on for life with your complete and utter inability to deal with surprises." He opened the box and placed it on her knee. "Usually, the question comes first and the ring comes second, but in light of your *issues*, we'll do it your way."

Hannah gasped at the sight of an exquisite diamond in a vintage setting. She looked at the ring and then at him and then at the ring again. "Where did this come from?"

"It was my grandmother's. I've had it for years waiting for the right woman to come along. For a long time now, I've known that the only right one who'd ever come along was you. I had no plans to propose to you in this tacky motel room, but I suppose this won't be the last time things with you don't go according to my plan. Hannah, will you marry me and have a family with me and grow so old with me that you'll get sick of me?"

Once again she couldn't seem to breathe as she looked down at him.

"You promised me I could count on your answer."

"Yes," she said, laughing through her tears. "Yes, I'll marry you." She combed her fingers into his hair and brought order to the strands that were in disarray from his helmet. "I never thought I'd have this again. I'd given up on so many things until you came along and showed me I still have my whole life ahead of me." With her hands on his face, she brought her lips down on his.

"Your love has made me feel like the luckiest guy in the history of the world." He wrapped his arms around her and lifted her off the bed when he stood and came back down on top of her. "Wait! The ring." Lifting himself off her long enough to retrieve the box that had fallen on the floor, he removed the ring and slid it onto her left hand. "There. Now, where were we?"

"I was about to ask you how in the hell we get you out of this thing." She tugged at the jumpsuit impatiently, which made him laugh loud enough to wake Homer, who came to with an indignant howling yip that sounded anything but fierce.

Hannah and Nolan dissolved into laughter, and the over-whelming joy she felt at that moment obliterated the fear from earlier. She'd gotten her second chance, and she planned to enjoy every minute of it.

EPILOGUE

———◆◆———

Engaged . . . again. Nolan promised to live long
enough to drive me crazy as an old man. I look
forward to that and everything else we'll
experience together. On this joyful day I'm also
grateful to Caleb for setting me free to love again.
I'll always love him, too, and I'll never forget the
precious time we had together.

—From the diary of Hannah Abbott Guthrie, age
thirty-five

Lincoln Abbott had just shut off his computer for the day
and was getting up to leave when his father-in-law came
hobbling into the office carrying a bottle of champagne and
wearing a big smile.

The bottle landed on Lincoln's desk with a loud thunk.
"*Engaged*, my friend! How do ya like them apples? One dead
battery and a ring on our girl's finger!"

"Where're your crutches?"

"Oh to hell with them! I'm here to celebrate!"

Ringo and George raised their heads from their beds in the
corner to see what all the noise was about. Seeing Elmer, they
got up to greet one of their favorite friends. As always, he had
biscuits in his pockets for both of them.

Amused by Elmer's effusiveness, Lincoln smiled and shook his head. "I still can't believe it myself. I take it the love-birds have been to see you."

"Indeed they have, and we had one hell of a celebration." Elmer took a seat in front of Lincoln's desk. "I can't tell you what it means to me to see my little girl smiling again from ear to ear. Never thought I'd live to see that."

"I know what you mean. Molly and I were talking about that last night. Were you surprised they got engaged so quickly?"

"A little, but as they said, they want kids, and they're not getting any younger. We both know what it's like to find a perfect fit and not want to wait to get going on a life together."

"Yes, we do." Lincoln had taken one look at Molly Still-man and had known almost immediately that she was going to change all his plans.

Elmer leaned forward to pop the cork on the champagne and poured the fizzing bubbly into two coffee cups on Lincoln's desk. "Hope they're clean."

"Just rinsed them out this afternoon."

Elmer handed one of them to Lincoln. "Two for two," he said, raising his mug.

Lincoln clinked his mug against Elmer's. "We're on a roll."

"Who's next?" Elmer asked as he sat back to enjoy the bubbly.

"I've been thinking about that. We've got quite a list of possibilities to choose from. It's come to my attention that our oh-so-serious and focused Hunter has his eye on Megan from the diner."

Elmer's white brows knit with confusion. "Cranky Megan?"

"The one and only."

"Hmm, not sure I approve of that match. I'll have to take a closer look at her before I decide she's worthy of our Hunter. What else have you got?"

"Max and Chloe could use a little *assistance* in getting their act together before the baby is born."

"Let's get him out of college before we go there."

"Good point. Then there's Ella."

Elmer sat up a bit straighter in his chair. "What about her?"

"Did you see the way she was gazing at Gavin Guthrie at

Homer's funeral? If that's not a girl in a serious crush, then I don't have ten kids."

"Well, well, well . . . That's rather intriguing. Gavin's a fine fellow. Every bit the man his brother was, and I'd love nothing more than to have another Guthrie in the family."

"I'm not sure he's quite *there* yet though. The poor guy has been through hell, and that one will take some finesse. We might want to practice our technique a bit more before we move on to them."

"You make a good point. We've had some significant beginner's luck with Will and Hannah, and we wouldn't want to get too big for our britches or anything."

"God forbid."

Elmer took a sip of his champagne as he appeared to puzzle over their options. "Where does that leave us?"

Lincoln sat back in his big leather chair and rested his feet on the desktop. "Colton."

Obviously intrigued, Elmer said, "Do tell."

"Remember the day Cameron and her friend Lucy pitched the website to us?"

"That was the same day she and Will got back together and ran off into the sunset."

"Right. Molly and I invited Lucy to dinner, and Colton joined us. The two of them hit it right off, and he offered to see her back to the inn after dinner. Far be it from me to interfere with that kind of spark, so naturally we took him up on the offer. Since then, he's shaved off the beard he's had since high school, cut his hair and has dropped his dogs with us for several weekends *away*. He's never said another word about Lucy since that night, but if you do the math—"

"I can't believe you're just telling me this now! We've got work to do! Any friend of Cameron's—"

"—is a friend of ours."

"You said it! So what's our plan?"

Lincoln picked up a flyer from his desktop and handed it to Elmer.

Elmer took the paper and scanned it, his face turning bright red as Lincoln fully expected. "What the hell is this?"

"It's a conference coming up in New York City."

"I can see that. I'm talking about the . . . the . . . *things*."

"They're 'pleasure aids' for people of all ages."

"What in the name of tarnation sakes . . ."

"Don't knock it till you've tried it," Lincoln said with a smug smile.

"You'd better watch yourself, boy. It's not too late for me to come fetch my daughter away from you."

Elmer's flustered reaction got a laugh out of Lincoln. "I think it might actually be ten kids too late for that."

"I ain't too late as long as I'm still drawing a breath." He tossed the paper back on the desk. "What's all that got to do with Colton?"

"I'm going to ask him to attend the conference and help me decide if we should offer the product line in the store."

"You want to bring that . . . *stuff* . . . into *my* store?"

"Don't have an apoplexy over it. That *stuff* sells like gangbusters, and we'd be crazy not to at least look into it."

"I like the idea of sending Colton, but I'm not sold on the product line."

"I'll consider that a half victory."

"You think you're so smart, don't you?"

"Whose idea was it to hire Patrick's daughter to build a website for the store? And look at how that worked out. Have you ever seen Will happier?"

"It was my idea to mess with Hannah's battery," Elmer grumbled.

"We're tied at one a piece. If this works out between Colton and Lucy, that counts in my column because she came through Cameron."

Elmer rolled his eyes at Lincoln's logic. "What makes you think Colton will want to go to a *pleasure aid* conference in New York City? What's that got to do with maple syrup?"

"Not a damned thing. It won't be about the conference, Elmer. If he snaps up the opportunity, we'll have our confirmation that Lucy's the one he's been running off to see every chance he gets."

"You make a good point, even if I can't picture those products in our store."

"Leave that part of it to me."

"Gladly."

"So we've got a plan?"

Elmer raised his mug. "It's a plan. Let's go for three."

Thanks for reading *I Want to Hold Your Hand*! Watch for book three, *I Saw Her Standing There,* Colton and Lucy's story, in November 2014.

I Saw Her Standing There is available now for preorder from all major retailers and at marieforce.com/books/the-green-mountain-series. Turn to page 333 to read chapter 1 of *I Saw Her Standing There*.

Now that you've finished *I Want to Hold Your Hand*, join the Reader Group at facebook.com/groups/IWantToHoldYour Hand to discuss Hannah and Nolan's story. Remember that spoilers are allowed and encouraged in the individual book groups, so don't join until you've read the book. Also join the Green Mountain Reader Group at facebook.com/groups/Green MountainSeries for series news and other updates! No spoilers in the series group please. You can also join my mailing list at marieforce.com to be notified about new books, and feel free to contact me at marie@marieforce.com.

ACKNOWLEDGMENTS

In preparing to write a book about a war widow, I connected with Cait Needham, who lost her husband, Master Sergeant Robb G. Needham, U.S. Army Reserves (Activated), on September 20, 2006 in Baghdad, Iraq. Cait introduced me to Dee Baily, who lost her husband, Army Spec. William L. Bailey, on May 26, 2007 in Iraq, and Army Lt. Col. Rebecca Eggers, who lost her husband, Army Captain Daniel W. Eggers, on May 29, 2004 in Afghanistan. Each of these brave women generously shared intimate details of their loss and the journey of rebuilding their lives. I'm so grateful to them and thankful for their service and the tremendous sacrifices they, their husbands and families made on behalf of our country. Rebecca was also a huge help with the details of Caleb's army career and read the book to make sure I got it right. Thank you, Rebecca!

I read and was incredibly moved by *The Letter: My Journey Through Love, Loss and Life* by Marie Tillman, wife of Army Specialist Pat Tillman, who famously left a lucrative professional football career to become an Army Ranger after 9/11. He was killed in Afghanistan on April 22, 2004 and was posthumously promoted to corporal.

I also recommend *Two Kisses for Maddy: A Memoir of Loss and Love* by Matthew Logelin; *Where You Left Me* by Jennifer Gardner Trulson; *I'll See You Again* by Jackie Hance and Janice Kaplan; and *Boots on the Ground by Dusk: My Tribute to Pat Tillman* by Mary Tillman.

My thanks go to Bob Cupp for his assistance with car-racing details and for providing some real-life fodder for the character of Skeeter.

I'm so fortunate to have an amazing team working with me to help keep things running smoothly at home and at work so I can focus on my books. Thank you to Team HTJB, especially my assistant and right hand, Julie Cupp, as well as Holly Sullivan, Isabel Sullivan, Lisa Cafferty, Nikki Calquhoun and Cheryl Serra.

To the amazing team at Berkley, including my lovely editor, Kate Seaver, as well as Leslie Gelbman, Susan Allison, Erica Martirano, Erin Galloway, Courtney Landi and Katherine Pelz. You all have been so fun to work with as we bring the Abbott family to life.

A very special thank-you to my agent, Kevan Lyon, for all her support and assistance.

To my lovely beta readers Ronlyn Howe, Kara Conrad and Anne Woodall, I appreciate your willingness to make time for me when I need you! You're the best!

As always, a special thanks to my family, Dan, Emily and Jake, and to my dad, who listens to every detail about the business and provides sage wisdom and advice. I wrote this book during a time of tremendous personal change as I saw my oldest off to college and my youngest off to high school. There's a tad bit of grief involved with the end of one era and the beginning of another. Writing Hannah and Nolan's story gave me a productive outlet for all those emotions, and they took me on an amazing journey. Many of you know I was a Navy wife for the first ten years of my married life, and I have huge respect for the sacrifices service members and their spouses make every day.

Big hugs to Brandy and Louie, my fur friends who keep me company while writing, and I know which one of you keeps stealing my stuffed Fred the Moose. Now I just have to catch you in the act!

Finally, my heartfelt gratitude to the readers who've loved my books and embraced my characters. You make every day so much fun, and I appreciate each and every one of you.

xoxo,
Marie

Turn the page for a bonus short story
featuring Nolan and Hannah,

A HARD DAY'S NIGHT

A Green Mountain Series Short Story

CHAPTER 1

———◆►◄◆———

Sitting at her desk in the sunroom she used as a studio, Hannah Abbott Guthrie studied a growing pile of papers and determined her lists were giving birth to baby lists. She'd gone from being somewhat bored and out of sorts a few short weeks ago to knee-deep in wedding plans while also trying to get an ambitious new project off the ground.

It was all too much, and she was beginning to feel a bit ragged around the edges. She reached for the cup of tea that had cooled while she attempted to make order out of the chaos on her desk. Grimacing at the bitter taste of the cold tea, she sighed as she placed the cup back on the saucer.

"I know that sigh," her fiancé, Nolan Roberts, said as he came into the room, bursting with energy that Hannah wished she could bottle. "That's the sigh of someone who needs a break." He plucked the pen out of her hand and gave the same hand a tug. "Come with me."

"Where to?"

"It's a surprise."

"Nolan, you know I don't like surprises."

"I know you don't like too much time to *think about* a

future surprise. This one is immediate, so there's no chance it'll get me into trouble."

Though she so didn't have time for surprises or anything that didn't involve the lists that were multiplying daily, she let him lead her from the sunroom. Realizing something was happening, her puppy, Homer Junior, popped up from his bed next to her desk and followed behind them, yipping with excitement.

Nolan walked through the kitchen to the door that led to the backyard. "Close your eyes."

"I don't want to close my eyes."

"Hannah . . . You'd try the patience of a saint."

"But you love me anyway."

He smiled, put his arms around her and kissed her. "It seems I do. Now close your eyes."

"I don't want to."

"Fine, you give me no choice."

"About what—" The air whooshed out of her lungs as Nolan hoisted her over his shoulder and headed outside. "You can't just pick me up and haul me around like a sack of potatoes!"

"Apparently, I can."

"This is not funny, Nolan! I'm seriously mad with you right now, and it would be just what you deserve if I puke tea and toast all over your back."

"I'll take my chances."

The ground rushed by so quickly Hannah closed her eyes so she wouldn't actually get sick. She was forming an all-new protest when he finally came to a stop down by the trickling stream that served as the property line and put her down abruptly.

She raised her hand to give him a thorough thump to the chest and caught sight of a red-plaid blanket spread out on the grass and what looked like a picnic basket. "What's all this?"

"This, my adorable-but-impossible-to-surprise love, is an afternoon off."

"I don't have time for an afternoon off and neither do you."

With his hands on her shoulders, he compelled her to look at him. "Hannah, you're going a hundred miles an hour, and I don't like those dark circles I'm seeing under your eyes. You're tossing and turning all night. If I had it to do over, I never would've pushed for a wedding this summer."

"So you don't want to marry me after all?" she asked, knowing the question would set him off. She wasn't disappointed.

His eyes flashed with anger and passion and the desire that was ever-present between them. "That is *not* what I said, and you know how much I want to be married to you. Rather than purposely trying to start a fight, why don't you sit your butt down, and eat the lunch I brought you. After that, we're going to nap in the sun."

"*You* might have time for napping in the sun, but I—" Again with the whoosh of air leaving her lungs as he picked her up again and spun her around this time.

"Nolan! *Oh my God!* I'm seriously going to puke!"

Homer Junior went crazy, barking and yipping and snapping at Nolan's legs. Sadly for Nolan, he was wearing shorts in deference to the first truly warm spring day.

"Ugh," he grunted as he swayed precariously, "the little bastard actually *bit* me."

"Good boy, Homer! Bite Daddy again! He's being mean to Mommy!"

"Ow! *Shit!*" Since he was under attack, Nolan had no choice but to put Hannah down.

Once her head stopped spinning, she reached for her baby Homer and gave him a big hug. "You're such a good boy, defending Mommy from the evil Daddy." Homer licked her face in response. "Honestly, Nolan, his heart is beating so hard it's going to burst."

"Can we talk about the fact that I'm bleeding over here?"

"You brought that on yourself." Since it seemed she'd be taking some time off, despite her other plans for the day, Hannah sat on the blanket and snuggled Homer.

"Blood," Nolan said, dabbing at his leg with a bandanna he pulled from his back pocket. "*Actual* blood."

Hannah buried her face in Homer's soft fur, laughing silently at Nolan's indignant tone.

"I know you're laughing at me, Hannah, but don't forget who got you that rotten ball of fur."

"Oh my poor baby. Don't listen to what Daddy says. He doesn't mean it, Homie. You know he secretly loves you even if he's jealous because I love you more than him."

"*Ah-ha!* I knew it!"

"Mind your own business. I'm talking to Homer, not you. We're mad at you."

"This is what I get for trying to give my best girl a relaxing afternoon off," Nolan grumbled.

"It was very nice of you," Hannah said sincerely, realizing the time for joking was over. "And I'm sorry if Homer bit you. Sort of."

"Had to add that last bit, huh?" he said with a laugh as he hooked an arm around her and brought her closer to him.

Homer let out a low growl, which was anything but sinister, and made them both laugh.

"Call off your beast," Nolan said.

"Is there anything in that basket for him?"

"Not that he deserves it, but there might be a rawhide with his name on it."

"Oh Homie, did you hear that? Daddy got you a treat! Now kiss and make up with him." She foisted the puppy into Nolan's lap and dove into the picnic basket, suddenly curious about what else she might find.

The delicious aromas coming from the basket made her mouth water. "What did you get? It smells amazing." Her stomach let out a loud growl that made Homer bark.

"I think Mama is hungry," Nolan said to the puppy, who was kissing his face and apparently trying to repent for his bad behavior. Because Nolan secretly loved Homer as much as she did, he was allowing the puppy to kiss and make up with him.

"Mama is starving." Hannah began unpacking the basket and discovered containers filled with gourmet treats. Reading the labels on each one, she found roasted chicken, marinated artichoke hearts, tomato pasta salad, a wheel of Brie and a French bread baguette. The basket itself was a work of art with linen napkins, silverware and stoneware plates. "This is amazing! Where did you get it?"

"At a place I heard about in St. J."

"You drove all the way to St. Johnsbury to get lunch?"

"Nothing but the best for my girl. There's more. Look under the plates."

Hannah lifted the plates from the basket and found a cold bottle of chardonnay and a box of chocolate-covered strawberries. "Oh I love them!"

"The rawhide is in the side pocket."

Hannah retrieved it, unwrapped it and handed it to Nolan. "It's your gift. You should get the credit for it."

With a grin for her, Nolan took the rawhide, which was shaped like a large pretzel, and held it up for Homer's inspection.

The puppy grabbed hold of it and settled in the grass next to the blanket with his treasure.

"That ought to buy me a few minutes of peace," Nolan said.

"And what will you do with those minutes?"

A sexy smile lit up his handsome face as he held out his arm to her. "Come here, and I'll show you."

Hannah scooted across the blanket and into his loving embrace.

"Much better," he said when he had both arms around her.

"Thanks for this. I wouldn't have said I needed it, but now that I've been cajoled into it, I can see it's exactly what I needed."

"I know, baby." He lay back on the blanket, bringing her with him. "I hate to see you stressed out and overloaded. If you want to push the wedding back a bit—"

"No. Definitely not. I don't want to do that."

"I don't want that either." He turned on his side to face her and propped himself on his upturned hand. "I can't wait until you're my wife."

"I can't wait either." She reached for him and brought him down to her for a kiss that she planned to keep short and sweet. However, he had other ideas.

He coaxed her mouth open and teased her with his tongue, which was all it took to make her wish they were inside, in her bed, where they'd spent every night since their engagement.

"Let's go in," Hannah whispered against his lips. "We can have our picnic in the house."

"We're having it right here." His fingers moved down the

front of her, and that's when she realized he was unbuttoning her shirt.

Hannah covered his hand with hers, halting his progress. "Not here."

"Right here."

"Nolan, we can't! I have neighbors."

"Who can't see anything down here, which is why I chose this spot. We're hidden by the trees."

"And I have a family that's forever breezing in and out of here."

"They've been told to stay away today."

She looked up to find a determined expression on his face. "You told my family to stay away."

"I did." His lips were busy on her neck, making her squirm and wriggle under him. "Is that a deal breaker?"

"Not at all. That might actually entitle you to some special favors."

He raised his head and met her gaze, his eyes heavy with desire. "I love your special favors."

Hannah looped her arms around his neck and lost herself in his kiss, letting the worries and stress fade away. Determined to enjoy the stolen interlude he'd arranged for them, she got busy tugging his T-shirt free of his shorts. When her hand made contact with his flat, muscular belly, he gasped against her lips.

She loved that her touch had such a powerful effect on him, that he always made her feel she was the most important thing in his life. And she had no doubt she always would be, which was one of many reasons she couldn't wait to marry him later in the summer.

He broke the kiss and laid a heated trail from her neck to her chest, releasing the front clasp on her bra. The heat of his mouth and the warmth of the sun on her breasts were a heady combination as he continued to her belly, which growled loudly, making him laugh and Homer bark.

Leaning his forehead against her belly, Nolan said, "Sounds like I need to feed you before I ravish you."

"That might be a good idea." Hannah sat up and began to set her clothes to rights.

"Don't."

"Don't what?"

"Don't cover yourself. I want to see you."

"I can't sit here half-naked." She glanced around to find the trees truly did hide them from the neighbors on either side of her. The next closest neighbor in the back was more than a mile away, on the other side of the stream.

"Yes, you can." He held up a forkful of chicken for her.

She leaned in to take the bite. "Only if you do, too." As the savory flavor exploded on her tongue, she watched him reach for the hem of his T-shirt to pull it up and over his head.

"Better?"

"Much. Let me have some more of that chicken."

"Greedy wench."

She sent him a saucy smile. "I'm doing what I was told and enjoying my picnic. Now hurry up and feed me so we can get back to the ravishing."

CHAPTER 2

———◄•►———

Hearing her provocative words, Nolan's eyes darkened with lust as he broke open the Brie and fed her crackers and soft cheese.

Hannah returned the favor, feeding him the same way he'd fed her. With each bite she held out to him, he managed to nibble on her fingers, too. She wouldn't have thought that could be sexy until Nolan did it. For seven long years, she'd lived without sensuality in her life, and she'd been making up for lost time since she fell in love with him. He'd reminded her that despite the crushing loss of her husband, Caleb, she was still very much alive and very much a woman.

By the time the final chocolate-covered strawberry had been consumed, Hannah was ready to rip his clothes off so she could realize the promise of the sultry looks he'd been directing her way while they ate.

"Do you want—"

She cut off his words with a kiss designed to show him exactly what she wanted. Thankfully, he was more than capable of taking a not-so-subtle hint and wrapped his arms around her. The rough brush of his chest hair against her sensitive nipples sent a bolt of heat straight through her, causing an insistent throb between her legs that required immediate attention.

Hannah slid her hand from his chest to his belly, which quivered in response to her touch. Tugging on the button to his shorts, she unzipped and freed him from his clothes.

"Hannah," he said gruffly. "God, that feels good."

There was something so decadent about lying in the afternoon sunshine in her backyard as they drove each other into a heated frenzy with well-placed kisses and caresses designed to arouse. The sweet fragrance of spring—blooming flowers and freshly cut grass—filled her senses, along with Nolan's now-familiar scent of soap and subtle cologne. Despite the dirty work he did at the garage, he always smelled amazing when he touched her.

She burrowed her nose into the curve of his neck, breathing him in while he unzipped her jeans. Rather than remove her pants, he slid a hand inside and cupped her sex as he took her mouth in another incendiary kiss. Between the strokes of his tongue and the press of his fingers, he brought her to the precipice of release, and he'd barely touched her.

Feeling desperate and needy, she pushed at his shorts, shoving them down over his hips, gasping when he slid two fingers inside her.

"Hannah," he whispered against her ear. "You're always so ready for me." He curled his fingers, seeking the spot deep inside that set her off, stroking and coaxing until she cried out from the overwhelming pleasure that took her away from all her worries and reminded her of why they were moving heaven and earth to be married as soon as possible.

Nolan kept his fingers deep inside her until the last waves of her orgasm had passed, withdrawing only to remove the rest of their clothes. When they both were naked and he was settled on top of her, he gazed down at the face he'd dreamed about for years before he knew the joy of waking to her every day.

"I can't believe we're doing this in broad daylight in the backyard," Hannah said, her face flushed with desire and embarrassment that he adored.

"Believe it." As he brought his lips down on hers, he glanced over to ensure Homer was still happily occupied with the rawhide. Nolan wanted to give Hannah his complete, undivided attention.

"You've turned me into a regular trollop," she said, arching into him as he paid homage to her neck before moving down to focus on her breasts.

Hearing the usually proper and reserved Hannah Abbott Guthrie use the word *trollop* to describe herself had Nolan laughing—hard. "You can be a trollop with me any time you want, babe. In fact, the more often the better." He punctuated his words by drawing her nipple into his mouth and sucking on it as he ran his tongue back and forth over the hardened tip.

The press of her fingers into his back told him she liked what he was doing, so he kept it up until she was squirming beneath him and testing his intention to draw this out as long as possible. By the time this afternoon ended, he wanted her as relaxed as he could get her. With that in mind, he kissed his way down to her belly, taking his own sweet time to ensure that every sensitive area received equal treatment.

He'd never known desire like the kind she inspired in him. He'd never known it was possible to feel so deeply, to want so madly, to need so completely. She occupied about ninety-five percent of his thoughts, making it difficult to concentrate on anything that didn't involve her.

Moving farther down, he used the width of his shoulders to push her legs apart and cupped her bottom. He was addicted to the taste of her, and as her unique flavor exploded on his tongue, he decided she was sweeter than any of the delicacies they'd enjoyed earlier. He'd take her over a chocolate-covered strawberry any day.

She was sensitive and wet from her earlier release, and he stroked her with his fingers before he added his tongue, focusing on her clit.

Hannah grabbed fistfuls of his hair and held on tight as he set out to drive her crazy. Judging from the whimpers and moans that came from deep inside her, he was succeeding. Nothing pleased him more than pleasing and pleasuring her. It hadn't taken long for him to wonder how he'd managed to live for thirty-five years without this kind of desire in his life.

And now that he'd known it with Hannah, no one else could ever do it for him.

She was it. She was everything, and he wanted to make sure she knew that every day.

"Nolan." The way she said his name, breathlessly and pleadingly, only made him harder, if that was possible, but it also made him more determined to take his time. "*Nolan.*"

He turned his face into her thigh, taking a nibble that made her lurch. "I'm busy."

"Come up here."

"Not yet."

"*Nolan.*"

"Not yet."

She flopped onto the blanket, her arms falling over her head in surrender. He wished she could see how incredibly beautiful she looked, spread out before him like the sweetest meal of his life. He took her by surprise when he reached up to cup her breast as he gave her his tongue once again. The combination tripped her orgasm, and her cries nearly took him with her. God, she was so effortlessly sexy, and he loved her with everything he had.

Kissing his way up the front of her, he reveled in her soft, silky skin and the scent he'd know anywhere as hers. "Still with me?" he asked when his lips hovered above hers.

"Barely."

"Is it nap time?"

"Not quite yet." She wrapped her arms around his neck, and her inner thighs hugged his hips. "I'm still a little hungry."

"Is that right?" he asked, endlessly amused by her. He never would've guessed that sweet, quiet Hannah had an inner vixen who loved to tease and torment him. And he adored every bit of it.

"*Mmm.*" This was said against his ear right before she bit down on his earlobe and sent his urgency level straight into the desperation zone.

"What can I get for you, babe? Some more strawberries, perhaps?" He felt her smile curve against his neck.

"I was thinking something more . . . filling." She raised her hips to rub her slick heat against his cock.

Jesus. As much as he enjoyed her playful side, he was

about to lose it all over her if she kept that up. So he took matters in hand—literally—and gave her what they both wanted so badly.

"Yes," she whispered as her lips parted seductively and her eyes closed ever so slowly.

He took advantage of the opportunity to run his tongue over her lips while he pressed deeper into her. Even when he hadn't worked her into an orgasmic frenzy beforehand, she was always ready for him. She'd once told him the sight of him made her ready, and what guy wouldn't fall in love with a woman who said things like that? Her desire for him was one of the many, *many* reasons he was ass-over-teakettle in love with her.

She stroked a hand down his back to grip his backside, keeping him deep inside her and nearly making his head explode from the effort it took to hold back and wait for her. He freaking loved when she grabbed his ass and held on tight while he made love to her. Being with her this way was the closest thing to heaven he'd ever find on earth.

"Baby," he said through gritted teeth. "Gotta move."

"Okay," she said breathlessly as she released him.

Like a horse that had broken free from its restraints, he let go of all thoughts of control or delaying gratification. He wanted everything, and he wanted it right now. It took all the willpower he had to hold off until Hannah got there right ahead of him. Nolan clung to her as he surged into her one last time, the pleasure overwhelming him. When he'd recovered his senses, he glanced at the puppy, who was still happily gnawing on the rawhide. Because he had no immediate plans to let her go or let her get dressed, he grasped a handful of the blanket and pulled it over them in case a member of her family hadn't got the "leave us alone" memo.

Her hand caressing his chest had his immediate attention, as did the soft kisses she placed on his face and lips.

The sun beat warm upon them, but not so warm as to be uncomfortable. Nolan was more relaxed than he could remember being in, well . . . ever. All the burning questions had been answered to his extreme satisfaction. The woman he loved was in his arms, in his bed and in his life forever.

This right here, he thought, *is what paradise must be like.*

* * *

Hannah woke slowly, and for a moment, she couldn't remember why she was in the backyard. Then she realized she was naked and wrapped up in Nolan's tight embrace. The picnic came back to her in a flood of sweet memories that made her smile as she breathed in the masculine scent that had become so familiar to her.

Even Caleb, as crazy and adventurous as he'd been much of the time, had never convinced her to have totally naked sex in the backyard in the middle of the day. That thought nearly made her laugh out loud, but she contained herself so she wouldn't disturb Nolan. He worked incredibly hard and rarely took time off during a workday. Seeing him so relaxed made her happy that he'd talked her into the picnic and the afternoon off. They'd both needed it.

She glanced at the sky to realize the sun had dropped considerably, making her wonder how long they'd been asleep.

Nolan stirred, his eyes opened slowly and his smile unfolded just as slowly. That sexy grin got to her every time.

"Good nap?" Hannah asked, pushing the hair back from his forehead.

"The best nap ever."

"What time is it?"

He raised his arm to consult his watch. "Four thirty."

"We slept for *two hours*?"

"I guess we needed it."

Then she sat up abruptly to check on Homer and found that the rawhide had been abandoned. "Oh my God. Homer! *Homer!*" Hannah's stomach dropped as she stood to grab her shirt. She jammed her legs into her shorts, forgoing underwear in her haste. "*Homer!* Come to Mama!" She scanned the yard, but saw no sign of the puppy.

Her gaze settled on the stream, and her legs nearly buckled from the wave of fear that assailed her. "Oh my God," she whispered.

"He's fine," Nolan said, squeezing her shoulder. "He's probably asleep under a bush, and we just have to find him."

"Please, Nolan. Please. We have to find him."

When he brushed the tears from her cheeks, she discovered she was crying. "I'll find him. Keep calling him. Your voice is the one he wants to hear." He looked her dead in the eye. "I *will* find him, okay?"

Thankful for his reassurances, she nodded, even as her heart pounded and her mind raced with all the possible awful places her darling Homer could be.

Nolan headed for the water as she continued to call Homer's name. She looked under every bush, under the outdoor furniture that had recently been uncovered for the funeral of Caleb's dog, Homer Senior. On her belly, she crawled under the latticework that surrounded the stairs to a dank space under the house. "Homer! Come here, buddy. Come see Mama."

She blinked back new tears when her queries were met with silence. The only thing she needed to be happy right then was the sound of Homer's little yips. But all she could hear was Nolan's deep voice calling Homer's name over and over again along with the splashing of water as he ran along the stream.

Nolan came back into the yard a few minutes later with his cell phone pressed against his ear. "Just come as soon as you can, and bring anyone who's free."

Hearing him call for help sent Hannah's spirits plummeting.

"Hunter is coming, and he's bringing Will and your dad." Nolan never stopped moving as he spoke, heading for the gate, which was latched but high enough off the ground for an industrious puppy to squiggle underneath.

"How could we have let this happen?" Hannah said between sobs. "He's only a baby. We should've been watching him."

"We fell asleep, Hannah, and he was happily occupied. We didn't do anything wrong."

"There're so many things that could've happened to him. He could've drowned or run into the street or—"

"Hannah." He gripped her arms, forcing her to look at him. "Don't go there. He probably caught a sniff of something and followed his nose and got lost. Happens all the time. I want to go look for him, but I can't leave you when you're so upset."

She made an effort to pull herself together, because she

wanted him looking for Homer and not comforting her. "I'm okay."

"Stay back here. I'm going around front. Give me a shout if you find him."

"You, too."

"I will, honey." He kissed her forehead and took off through the gate, calling for Homer as he went.

Though she was all but certain Homer wasn't anywhere in the backyard, she still looked again under every bush, making a wide circle of the big yard. She stopped at the site of Homer Senior's grave and looked down at the wooden cross her brother Landon had carved with Homer's name. "Please, Homie," she whispered. "Help us find baby Homer."

If there was anything Homer Senior or Caleb could do from their lofty post in heaven, Hannah had no doubt they'd come through for her. The thought of them watching over her—and Homer Junior—brought comfort as she went around to the front of the house where Nolan was consulting with her twin, Hunter, as well as her brother Will and her dad, who came over to hug her.

"We're going to find that naughty little bugger," her dad assured her, kissing her forehead. "Try not to worry."

"It's hard not to. He's so little." Her voice caught on a sob. "It's all my fault. I fell asleep, and I wasn't watching him."

"Honey, don't do that. You take beautiful care of that little guy, and everyone knows it. He'll be back looking for you in no time at all. He couldn't have gone far."

"We were asleep for two hours."

Hearing that, her dad took a deep breath and let it out. "We'll find him, honey."

Over the next three hours, every member of Hannah's family came to aid in the search. Nolan's friend Skeeter came as did his lady friend, Gertrude "Dude" Danforth, who'd given Homer Junior to Hannah.

"I'm so sorry, Dude." Hannah's eyes were red and raw from an endless stream of tears. "I love him so much. I'd never let anything happen to him."

Dude, a massive woman who was known for being somewhat stoic and standoffish, surprised the heck out of Hannah by wrapping her in a tight hug. "I know you love him. And this stuff happens with pets. They wander off, and we search until we find them."

"But what if—"

"No what-ifs," Dude insisted. "We're going to find him and bring him home to you."

Hannah held on tight to Dude's certainty. She didn't want to think about the possibility that they might never find her baby Homer.

CHAPTER 3

————◆————

Nolan was like a man possessed by the devil as he searched for the little bundle of fur that Hannah loved more than she loved him. He couldn't believe that Homer had actually wandered away from Hannah. He called the puppy the "Velcro baby" because he was always attached to Hannah, to the point that Nolan had actually been jealous of a twelve-pound fur-ball on more than one occasion.

Now he'd give everything he had, everything he'd ever have, to be able to put that little fur-ball back in Hannah's arms, where he belonged. He couldn't imagine how she'd ever survive losing Homer after giving her heart to him so completely right after Homer Senior died. After losing Caleb and then Homer Senior, she'd already been through enough, damn it.

After Nolan had put out the call for help, Skeeter had arrived with every high-powered flashlight they had at the garage. His friend had even thought to bring extra batteries, a detail for which Nolan was extremely grateful.

Nolan beat through the weeds and bushes in a vacant lot at the end of Hannah's street, calling for Homer until his voice was hoarse and his throat was sore.

"Anything?" Hunter asked as he joined Nolan in the field.

"No." Nolan's anxiety level had hit the red zone about an hour ago and was venturing into dangerous territory as night fell over Butler. "We've got to find him, Hunter. She can't go through this after everything else. It'll break her. Especially because of what we were doing when he disappeared."

Hunter rolled his eyes. "Spare me the details, please."

"I'm not trying to be funny." Nolan felt like his entire life and his every chance at happiness was on the line here. He knew Hannah, and if they didn't find Homer, she'd never forgive herself for being so lax when she should've been watching the puppy. Nolan was far more concerned that she'd never forgive him for so thoroughly distracting her.

That last thought sent a laser of panic searing through him, leaving him breathless with fear.

"Nolan." Hunter's hand on his shoulder snapped him out of the panicked state he'd fallen into. "Are you okay?"

"I will be when we find him. Until then, not so good."

"Let's keep looking. He's got to be around here somewhere. He'd never leave Hannah."

"That's what I keep thinking, too, so where the hell is he?" He rubbed at the end-of-the-day stubble on his jaw as he thought it through. "Let's go back to the beginning and fan out from the yard again. That dog doesn't leave her side. He wouldn't just wander off if it meant leaving Hannah."

"I'm with you, brother," Hunter said. "Let's go."

As they tramped through the field and back to Hannah's yard, Nolan could hear Hannah's brothers, sisters, parents and grandfather calling for Homer as flashlight beams shone all over the street and nearby yards. After the Abbotts descended en masse, neighbors had come out to see what all the commotion was about and had joined in the search. Everyone loved Hannah. No one wanted to see her sad or upset again, least of all Nolan.

"This is all my fucking fault," he muttered to Hunter.

"How is it your fucking fault?"

"She's been so wound up about everything—the wedding, the inn for war widows, her work. It's a lot, and I wanted to give her a break."

"So you took her on a romantic picnic in her own yard, and the two of you fell asleep. And yes, I'm intentionally skipping over other obvious details in the interest of keeping my head from exploding. How is that your fucking fault when you tried to do something nice for her?"

"If we can't find him, she'll always remember how we managed to lose him and that'll always be tied to me kidnapping her and convincing her to laze the afternoon away when she should've been working and watching him."

"As much as I'd love to argue that point, knowing how Hannah thinks, I really can't," Hunter said with a sigh.

"She felt awful about leaving Homer Senior for the day when she came back to find him so bad off. She'll never forgive herself—or me—if we don't find Junior."

Hunter pushed open the gate to Hannah's backyard and held it for Nolan who went in ahead of him. "So you were on the blanket when you woke up and saw he was gone?" Hunter asked.

Nolan zeroed in on the rawhide that had been abandoned and was filled with sadness at the thought of never seeing Homer's cute little multicolored face again. He was a mutt in every sense of the word, but he was their mutt, and they loved him. "Yeah."

Hunter moved the picnic basket and lifted the blanket to shake it out.

The two men froze when they heard a faint sound.

"What was that?" Nolan asked.

"I don't know, but I heard it, too."

They stood perfectly still, hoping to hear it again.

Another whimper was followed by a soft mewl.

"Where's that coming from?" Nolan asked frantically.

"It's close."

"We've looked everywhere! Where could he be that we haven't looked? Homer! Come here, boy. Come see Daddy." He'd mocked Hannah's insistence on calling him Daddy when she talked about him to Homer. Now he'd give anything for their little boy to come back to him.

A small, frightened squeak had both men zeroing in on the picnic basket.

"You've got to be fucking kidding me," Nolan said as they dove on the basket, opened the heavy flaps and found Homer buried under heavy stone plates, cloth napkins and silverware. The strong scent of puppy pee hit Nolan square in the nose. Moving carefully, he extracted the tiny body from under the plates and was rewarded with weaker-than-usual licks and nips to his face.

"Thank God," he whispered. Tears filled his eyes at the oh-so-welcome sight of the puppy. He ran a gentle hand over every inch of Homer's body, flinching as Homer cried out in pain when Nolan touched a lump on his head.

"What's wrong?" Hunter asked.

"He's got a knot on his head. I bet he nosed his way into the basket, got conked on the head by one of the plates or the lid and was knocked out. That's why he couldn't hear us calling him."

"Unbelievable," Hunter said. "Let's get him back to Hannah."

Nolan was already walking toward the gate with Homer squiggling in his arms. "You scared the hell out of us, little buddy."

Homer seemed as relieved to have been found as Nolan was to have found him. That relief compounded when he saw Hannah standing in the street with her sisters Ella and Charley, and Will's girlfriend, Cameron. The other women were comforting Hannah, who was inconsolable.

"Anything?" Cam asked when she saw them approach.

Nolan would never forget the look on Hannah's face when he held out the squirming bundle and placed him in Hannah's arms.

"Oh thank God! Oh Homie!" Tears poured down her face as she hugged and kissed the poor little guy to within an inch of his life. The puppy let out a pained squeal when she connected with the knot on the back of his head. "What happened?"

Nolan explained his theory to the stunned group of women.

"So the lid or a plate fell on him and knocked him out?" Charley asked.

"We'd tossed everything back in there sort of willy-nilly after we ate," Nolan said. "I don't know how he managed to do it or how we managed to sleep through it, but I think he must've been knocked out. Otherwise, he would've heard us calling for him and barked."

"If he was knocked out, we need to call Myles," Hannah said, referring to the town veterinarian.

"I'll call him," Hunter said, "and I'll let everyone else know we found him. Take him inside, Han."

"Thank you all so much," Hannah said tearfully to her siblings. "Thank you."

"Nolan found him," Hunter said.

Nolan sent a small, grateful smile to his longtime friend and future brother-in-law. "Doesn't matter who found him. All that matters is that he's safe and back where he belongs."

Hannah surprised him when she went up on tiptoes— while still holding on tight to Homer—and kissed him in front of her brother, sisters and friend. "It matters who found him. Thank you so much."

"Anything for you, babe," he whispered gruffly, overwhelmed with love for her as well as relief and gratitude that their frantic search had resulted in a happy ending.

Hannah insisted on ordering pizza for all the people who'd helped them look for Homer, which is how she ended up with a crowd in her kitchen, living room and dining room.

Myles had come right over to give Homer a quick check and had determined that other than the lump on his head, he was perfectly fine. He'd refused payment, so Hannah insisted he stay for pizza and a beer.

Homer basked in attention from the entire Abbott family and most of Hannah's neighbors as he was passed from hand to hand so everyone could give him a kiss and tell him how happy they were to have him home safe.

All the time, however, the puppy's eyes were trained on Hannah, making sure she was close by. His devotion filled her with an unreasonable amount of love. She knew her affection for him was over the top, but she refused to apologize for loving with her whole heart.

Speaking of her whole heart . . . Nolan came into the room, looking pale and exhausted. He'd had very little to say after he found Homer, but she could see his relief was every bit as profound as hers. She knew he loved Homer almost as much as she did, not that he'd ever admit it. No, it was much more amusing to both of them when he poked fun at her crazy love for Homer.

Hannah held Nolan's gaze as he crossed the room to her. He put an arm around her and kissed her temple. "Did you eat something, babe?"

"Not yet. My stomach is too wound up to eat." She glanced up at him. "Did you?"

"Not yet. Same problem."

She put her arm around his waist and leaned her head against his chest. No words were necessary in that moment. Rather, she chose to hold on to him, fortified by today's reminder that things can change without warning, and it was important to hold on with all your might to what mattered most.

The house cleared out a short time later, and Nolan went around locking all the doors before they walked upstairs together. Homer was asleep in Hannah's arms, done in by his big day. She laid him on the pillow he'd claimed as his own on the far left side of their bed.

Nolan had insisted he could have one side or the other, but not the middle. He didn't want anything—especially an overly faithful bundle of fur—standing between him and Hannah when they were in bed. She'd acquiesced to her fiancé's wishes and now she happily slept between her two best guys, most of the time wrapped up in Nolan's arms while Homer slept pressed up against her back. She wouldn't have it any other way.

As she changed into a nightgown and brushed her teeth, she realized how drained she was from the emotional ride she'd been on for hours. It had been a truly awful feeling to not know where Homer was, and she hoped she never felt anything remotely like that again.

She was already in bed when Nolan joined her. Rather than turn toward her the way he always did, he stared up at the ceiling seeming lost in thoughts he was keeping to himself.

Hannah rested her hand on his belly, and he covered her hand with his, but he kept his gaze fixed on the ceiling. "Are you okay?" she asked him.

"Yeah."

"Nolan . . . talk to me. What're you thinking?"

"I'm so damned sorry this happened. It's all my fault."

Touched by the genuine regret she heard in his voice and saw on his face, she propped herself up on her elbow. "No, it isn't. Homer is my dog. I should've been watching him."

"He's *our* dog, babe. We both should've been watching him."

Hearing him admit that Homer was his, too, brought new tears to her eyes.

"Oh God, please don't cry. I seriously can't bear to see you cry anymore today."

"Okay, then don't look." She nuzzled into the space between his neck and shoulder and felt his arms come around her, holding her tight against him.

"I can feel those tears."

She smiled and kissed his neck, adding a dab of tongue. "It's not tears you feel."

His low chuckle filled her with hope that by this time tomorrow, they'd be back to normal and over the shock and fear that had gripped them for hours today.

"Are we going to be awful parents if we can't keep track of a puppy?" she asked, voicing one of the fears that had overtaken her during the hours in which Homer was missing.

"We're going to be great parents—even more so after today when we got a huge wake-up call about what happens when you don't pay close enough attention. Our kids will be extremely well supervised."

"I suppose you're right."

"You're going to be an awesome mother, Hannah. Every kid should be so lucky to have someone like you for a mom. I can't wait to see that."

"You're going to make me cry again."

"In that case, you're going to be a horrible, awful, terrible mother, and I feel sorry for my poor, pathetic future children."

She laughed through her tears and then turned his face into her kiss. "Before the big scare, this was a truly lovely day. Thanks for all you did to make it happen."

"I'm sorry it went bad on us."

"Can we do it again sometime, without the high drama?"

"Sure. Any time you want. Just let me know."

"I think I'd rather let you surprise me."

His eyes widened. "I thought you didn't like surprises."

"I'm starting to realize your surprises are the best ever, so I'll take my chances."

"I love you, Hannah. I'm so glad you got your baby back."

"I love you, too. You're my hero in every possible way."

Hearing that, his dark eyes went soft with love as he kissed her.

Hannah fell asleep in his arms with Homer pressed against her back and everything once again right in her world.

C olton Abbott had never considered himself a particularly private person—that is until he had something big to hide from his loving but overly involved family. His six brothers, three sisters, two parents and one grandfather were *dying* to know how he was spending his weekends lately, and Colton was *loving* that they had no idea. Not the first clue.

A smile split his face as he drove across Northern Vermont, from his home in the Northeast Kingdom town of Butler to Burlington, where his family owned a lake house and where his "secret" girlfriend would be meeting him in a couple of hours. He wanted to get there early and hit the store for supplies so they could relax and enjoy every minute of their time together.

Colton had big plans for this weekend, the sixth one he'd spent completely alone with her. During that time, they'd talked about every subject known to mankind, they'd kissed a lot, fooled around quite a bit and last weekend, they'd even gone so far as to take each other all the way to blissful fulfillment. But they'd yet to have sex.

He intended to fix that this weekend before he lost his mind from wanting more of her. He'd tried to respect her wishes to "take things slow" so they didn't "get in over their heads" when they lived so far from each other and had so little time to spend together. Of course he'd heard people say for years that long-distance relationships sucked, but until he'd experienced the suckage personally, he'd had no idea just how totally the situation sucked.

It got worse with every weekend they spent together when he was left wanting more and having to wait a full week before he could see her again. They'd been lucky so far. Other than the weekend he'd stayed home for the funeral of his sister Hannah's dog Homer, they'd had six straight weekends with no other commitments to get in the way of their plans, but he knew reality would interfere eventually. They both had busy lives and families and other obligations that would mess with the idyllic routine they'd slipped into over the last month and a half.

They'd met halfway the other times, and this would be the first time since they met that she'd come to Vermont. Since he wasn't quite ready to expose her to the austere life he led on his mountain, he'd asked his dad for the keys to the lake house.

And what an odd conversation that had been . . . With time to think about it during the two-hour ride across the state, Colton had the uncomfortable suspicion that the one person he wasn't fooling with his secret romance was his dear old dad.

Colton had planned his attack stealthily, coming down off the mountain on a rare Thursday to see his dad at the office. Waiting until most of his siblings had left for lunch—except for Hunter, who never seemed to leave the office for any reason except a fire alarm—Colton had sat in his truck and watched his dad step out of the diner and head back across the street to the office above the family-owned Green Mountain Country Store in "downtown" Butler, if you could call Main Street a downtown.

Colton had emerged from his truck and followed Lincoln up the back stairs that led to the offices where he and five of Colton's siblings ran the store. Colton kept his head down as he walked past Hunter's office and knocked on his dad's door.

"Hey," Lincoln said with obvious pleasure. His father was always happy to see him, which was one of the many things in life Colton could count on. "This is a nice surprise. Come in."

Colton shook his father's outstretched hand and took a seat in one of his visitor chairs.

"To what do I owe the honor of a rare midweek visit from the mountain man?"

"I needed a couple of things in town, so I figured I'd stop by."

"Everything okay up the hill?"

"It's all good. Quiet and relaxing this time of year, as always." Colton thought of early summer as the calm that followed the storm of boiling season, during which he produced more than five thousand gallons of the maple syrup that was sold in the store. After eleven years of running the family's sugaring facility, his life had fallen into a predictable pattern governed by twenty-five thousand syrup-producing trees.

"I'm glad you stopped by. I was going to come up to see you today or tomorrow."

"How come?"

Lincoln rooted around on his desk, looking for something in the piles of paper and file folders. "Ah, here it is." He pulled out a light blue page and handed it over to Colton.

As he scanned the announcement of a trade show in New York City, he skimmed the details until he realized what he was reading. "What the hell, Dad? *Pleasure aids and sensual devices?* What's that got to do with me?" He nearly had a heart attack at the thought of his father thinking he needed such things to move the relationship his father wasn't supposed to know about forward.

"I'm considering the line for the store, and I'm looking for someone to send to the show. Since this is your off-season, I thought you might be able to make the trip for us."

While trying to wrap his mind around the idea of "pleasure aids and sensual devices" on sale at their homespun country store, he tried to keep his expression neutral. Though he was slightly appalled at the reason for the mission, the location interested him very much.

In the interest of keeping his big secret a secret, he kept his reaction casual and uninterested. "What do the others have to say about that product line?"

"I haven't exactly mentioned it to them yet. I figured I'd let you check it out first and see what you think before I bring it to them."

"Why me?"

"Why not you? Everyone else is up to their eyeballs in work and life stuff, so it seemed to make sense to ask you now that your busy season is over for the time being." Lincoln shrugged. "But if you're not up for going—"

"Never said that." He'd be a fool to pass up a chance to spend a whole week with her. "I'll do it, but with the caveat that I think this product line has no business in our store."

"So noted."

"And I think you're in for yet another battle royal with your kids over it."

"I live for a good row with my kids," Lincoln said with a grin that made his blue eyes twinkle with mirth.

"Don't I know it," Colton muttered. The latest row had involved the website designer Lincoln had hired behind the backs of his children, who'd made it clear they had no interest in taking their store online. Then Cameron Murphy had come to town and won the hearts of the entire Abbott family, especially Colton's older brother Will, who was now madly in love and living with Cam as she designed the website for the store. Lincoln Abbott had a way of getting what he wanted, and Colton and his siblings had learned to be wary of their father's motivations.

In this case, however, Colton couldn't care less about his father's motivations. Not when he was looking at a full week with his lady.

"Talk to Hunter about getting you registered," Lincoln said, clearly pleased with Colton's capitulation.

"I will." Colton folded the flyer into a square, with the images on the inside, and stashed it in his pocket. "Since you now owe me a favor, I was wondering if I could use the lake house this weekend." When his father gave him an oddly intuitive look, Colton added, "I feel like doing some fishing."

Lincoln didn't move or respond for a long, uncomfortable moment.

Colton had begun to sweat under the steely stare his father directed his way.

"Of course, son," Lincoln finally said, withdrawing a set

of keys from his top desk drawer and handing them over. "You remember the code right?"

Since the code was his parents' wedding anniversary and had been for as long as they'd owned the house, Colton nodded and stood. "Thanks."

"Have a good time."

"I will."

"Are you taking the dogs with you?"

"I thought I would if that's okay."

As Lincoln Abbott was the biggest "dog person" Colton had ever known, he wasn't surprised when his dad said, "Of course it is."

Now as Colton drove to the lake with his dogs, Elmer and Sarah, asleep in the backseat, he pondered the odd look his father had given him when he asked to use the lake house and wondered what it had meant. He thought about the bizarre conversation with his older brother Hunter, who'd questioned what in the hell their father wanted with pleasure aids and sensual devices in the store, before he begrudgingly registered Colton for the trade show that would take place in New York in two weeks.

Colton had merely shrugged and refused to engage in the war of words that would no doubt take place between his father, the CEO, and his brother, the CFO. Let them duke it out. No way was Colton going to get in the middle of their dispute when he'd been handed a free pass to a week in New York.

He couldn't wait to tell her the good news.

An hour later, he pulled up to the lake house that was one of his favorite places in the world. Made of timber and beam and glass and stone, the house sat on the shores of Lake Champlain, right outside of Burlington. His parents had gotten a sweet deal on it about ten years ago when it was sold at auction after the previous owner defaulted on the mortgage. The Abbotts had enjoyed many a good time there in the ensuing years.

In fact, his older sister Hannah would marry her fiancé, Nolan, at the lake house later in a few weeks.

The house was stuffy and hot from being closed up, so he walked straight through the massive living room to open the sliding door to let in the breeze coming from the lake. He never tired of that view of the lake with the mountains in the distance. Late on this Friday afternoon, a handful of jet- and water-skiers were enjoying the warm sunshine and the all-too-short Vermont summer.

Relieved to be out of the truck after the long ride, Elmer and Sarah ran straight down to the private stretch of beach, where they frolicked in the water.

Colton smiled with pleasure and relief at being here, at having pulled off another escape from Butler and the Abbott family clutches, and at knowing he had four full days to spend at his favorite place with the woman who was quickly becoming his favorite person.

Three hours later, Colton had been to the grocery and liquor stores to stock up on necessary supplies, and he was beginning to worry.

While he waited, he made dinner—pasta with grilled vegetables, salad and bread, which was now keeping warm on the stove while he paced from one end of the big house to the other, filled with nervous energy.

When he got tired of pacing, he flopped onto the big sectional sofa that faced the two-story stone fireplace.

Sarah came over to give him a lick, which he rewarded with a pat to her soft blonde head.

"Thanks, girl. I know she'll be here soon, and you and your brother are going to love her." If anyone knew how often he talked to his dogs, he'd be committed. But they were his only companions on the mountain, and he kept up a running dialogue with them during the long days and nights he spent completely alone with them.

For most of his adult life, he'd lived by himself on that mountain, happily content with his no-frills lifestyle. He was the only person he knew who lived without running water, electricity, TV, an Internet connection or any of the modern conveniences most people took for granted.

He'd lived that way since he was seventeen, fresh out of high school and anxious to take over the sugaring facility that had been in their family since his grandparents—the original

Sarah and Elmer—had bought the place as newlyweds. His mother had hated the idea of him living up there alone when he was so young, but his dad had encouraged her to let him be, and he'd been there ever since.

Rather than pine for what he didn't have, Colton had preferred to focus on what he did have—a beautiful home in the midst of the majestic Green Mountains, two dogs whose devotion to him was boundless, a job he loved and was good at, a family he adored close enough to see at least once a week and a life that made sense to him.

Until lately.

For the first time in the eleven years he'd spent on the mountains, what he *didn't* have had begun to bother him. For one thing, he wished he had a phone so he could talk to her every day. For another, a computer with an Internet connection would come in handy as he navigated a long-distance relationship.

He was twenty-six years old and forced to use his parents' phone to call her because he didn't own one of his own. That was one thing he planned to do something about soon. His mountain was one of the few places around Butler that had reliable cell service, thanks to its clear proximity to the cell towers near St. Johnsbury.

But the rest of it, the electricity, the running water, the Internet connection . . . Those were things he needed to think about. He'd yet to bring her to his home on the mountain, mostly because he was afraid of what she might think of it. She was used to the city, where she had everything she wanted or needed at her fingertips.

What did he have to offer someone who was accustomed to so much more when he didn't even have electricity or running water? What modern woman would find his lifestyle attractive? And was he willing to change everything about who and what he was for a woman he'd known for only a couple of months?

Unfortunately, he had no good answers to any of these questions, and the more time he spent with her, the more muddled his thinking became on all of them.

And then there was the fact that she was happy in her life, settled in her work and home, living close to her own family and not at all interested in uprooting her existence. He knew this because she'd told him so. But knowing that hadn't kept him from seeing her almost every weekend for the last six weeks. It hadn't kept him from wanting more of her every time he had to leave her. It hadn't kept him from lying awake at night and wondering what she was doing and if she missed him between visits the way he missed her.

What if she didn't? What if she never gave him a thought from one weekend to the next? He had no way to know if she did or not because he didn't talk to her very often between visits. That had to change, and getting a cell phone would be the first thing he did after this weekend.

Maybe by then he'd have a better idea of how she really felt about him and what'd been happening between them. He had this niggling fear that for her it was just a fun interlude with someone different from the guys she normally dated, while for him it became something more involved every time he was with her.

He was determined to get some answers this weekend, to figure out what this was and where it was going. Then the doorbell rang and every thought that wasn't about her finally arriving fled from his brain as he sprinted for the door.

Yeah, he had it bad, and he had a feeling it was about to get a whole lot worse.

Penguin Group (USA) LLC is proud to mark its
5th anniversary in the fight against breast cancer
by encouraging our readers
to "Read Pink®."

read pink®

Penguin Group (USA) LLC is proud to join the fight against breast cancer

In support of **Breast Cancer Awareness** month, we are
proud to offer six of our bestselling mass-market titles by
some of our most beloved female authors.
Participating authors are Catherine Anderson, Marie Force,
Janet Chapman, Lisa Gardner, Jayne Ann Krentz, and Nora Roberts. These special
editions feature **Read Pink** seals on their covers conveying our support of this
cause and urging our readers to become actively involved in supporting
The Breast Cancer Research Foundation.

Penguin Group (USA) LLC is proud to present a $25,000 donation
(regardless of book sales) to the following nonprofit organization in support of its
extraordinary progress in breast cancer research:

The Breast Cancer Research Foundation®

Join us in the fight against this deadly disease by making your own donation to this organization today.

How to support breast cancer research:

To make a tax-deductible donation online to **The Breast Cancer Research Foundation**
you can visit: bcrfcure.org

You can also call their toll-free number, 1-866-FIND-A-CURE (346-3228), anytime between 9 A.M. and
5 P.M. EST, Monday through Friday. To donate by check or a U.S. money order, make payable and mail to:

The Breast Cancer Research Foundation, 60 East 56th Street, 8th floor, New York, NY 10022

About The Breast Cancer Research Foundation®
bcrfcure.org

The Breast Cancer Research Foundation (BCRF) advances the world's most promising research to eradicate breast cancer in our lifetime. Founded by Evelyn H. Lauder in 1993, BCRF has raised more than $500 million to fuel discoveries in tumor biology, genetics, prevention, treatment, survivorship and metastasis. This year, we invested $45 million in the work of more than 200 researchers at leading medical institutions across six continents. By spending 91 cents of every dollar on research and public awareness, BCRF remains one of the nation's most fiscally responsible charities. We are the only breast cancer organization with an "A+" from CharityWatch, and have been awarded a 4-star rating from Charity Navigator 12 times since 2002. Join us at **bcrfcure.org**.

If you would like to learn more about **Read Pink**,
visit www.penguin.com/readpink.
Read Pink® today and help save lives!

Read Pink is a registered trademark and service mark of Penguin Group (USA) LLC.

LOVE
ROMANCE
NOVELS?

For news on all your favorite romance authors, sneak peeks into the newest releases, book giveaways, and much more—

"Like" Love Always on Facebook!

 LoveAlwaysBooks